A Taste of Fame

A Taste of Fame

A Novel

Linda Evans Shepherd
and Eva Marie Everson

a division of Baker Publishing Group
Grand Rapids, Michigan

Published by Revell
a division of Baker Publishing Group
P.O. Box 6287, Grand Rapids, MI 49516-6287
www.revellbooks.com

Printed in the United States of America

Library of Congress Cataloging-in-Publication Data
Shepherd, Linda E., 1957–
    A taste of fame : a novel / Linda Evans Shepherd and Eva Marie Everson.
       p.   cm. — (The potluck catering club ; #2)
    ISBN 978-0-8007-3209-7 (pbk.)
    1. Caterers and catering—Fiction. 2. Reality television programs—Fiction. 3. Women—Societies and clubs—Fiction. 4. Women cooks—Fiction. 5. Female friendship—Fiction. I. Everson, Eva Marie. II. Title.
PS3619.H456T37 2009
813'.6—dc22   2009023305

This book is a work of fiction. Names, characters, places, and incidents are the product of the authors' imagination or are used fictitiously. Any resemblance to actual events, locales, or persons, living or dead, is coincidental.

Contents

1. *Lisa Leann*—Hot News 7

2. *Vonnie*—TV Dinner 11

3. *Donna*—Catered Comedy 20

4. *Evangeline*—Party Plans 30

5. *Lizzie*—Taste of Fame 39

6. *Vonnie*—Animal Crackers 48

7. *Goldie*—Warming Worry 58

8. *Donna*—High-Altitude Cooks 67

9. *Evangeline*—Happy Trail Mix 77

10. *Lisa Leann*—Subway Sandwich 89

11. *Donna*—Back at the Ranch 99

12. *Evangeline*—Mixed Up in Manhattan 109

13. *Goldie*—Home Cooking 120

14. *Lisa Leann*—Taste of New York 126

15. *Evangeline*—Chinese Jam 138

16. *Lizzie*—Seasoned Traveler   149

17. *Donna*—Tea Time   156

18. *Vonnie*—Anniversary Dinner   167

19. *Lisa Leann*—Stewed Pair   177

20. *Lizzie*—Consuming Couple   189

21. *Goldie*—Fishy Business   195

22. *Evangeline*—Chilling Note   205

23. *Lizzie*—Tasting Trouble   214

24. *Lisa Leann*—Marriage Melts   220

25. *Donna*—Cajun Cooking   225

26. *Vonnie*—Knock-Out Punch   232

27. *Goldie*—Going Bananas   240

28. *Lizzie*—Heart Beats   250

29. *Donna*—Locked in a Low Boil   256

30. *Lisa Leann*—Half-Baked Accusations   264

31. *Lizzie*—Soup Kitchen   273

32. *Evangeline*—Bubbling Betrayal   283

33. *Vonnie*—Team Brunch   293

34. *Donna*—Taste of Deception   299

35. *Lisa Leann*—Instant Prayer   307

36. *Donna*—Final Feast   312

The Potluck Catering Club Recipes   319

Meet the Women of the Potluck Catering Club   363

1

Hot News

"Excuse me?"

Kat Sebastian's voice crackled through the phone line from her New York City studio. "Team Potluck will be featured tomorrow evening on our new reality show, *The Great Party Showdown*. It was a last-minute decision."

I stood up and squealed into the phone as if I were a June bug who'd landed on a robin's wing. "You're kidding me!"

"I never kid. It's too late to back out. We have your signature, and it is binding."

My head spun and I aimed my derriere for the nearest office chair and sat. "Wait a minute, wait. I'm not sure the girls even remember signing your release, and now you're saying we have to fly to New York? When? Tonight?"

Kat's voice was clipped. "No, no. We're airing an edited version of the submission tape your son shot of your team catering the Byrd-Dolton wedding. Then it will be up to America to decide if your team will continue in the competition."

I ran my free hand through my hair, disregarding the havoc to my appearance. "Meaning?"

"If you make it through this round, a film crew from Stirring Productions will be in Summit View, Colorado, next week to tape your catering company in the next challenge. I'm faxing you the information you'll need, including all the stats on the accommodations and the grand prize. That's a carrot that should refresh your team's memory."

My fax machine started to purr as Kat said, "Call me if you have any more questions."

I opened my mouth, but before I could find my voice, the dial tone hummed in my ear. I hung up and walked to my fax machine, which was perched on a nearby marble-topped table. I caught the first of several pages gliding toward me. I stared at the document. Kat was right, it all looked legal. Though "binding" was how she'd put it. I closed my eyes.

Who would have thought my son's class project would lead to this?

During his spring break from college, Nelson had flown up from Austin, presumably for a bit of skiing. But instead of hitting the slopes, he'd joined my girlfriends and me and filmed our little Potluck Catering Company working the wedding of Becky Byrd and Allen Dolton, a young couple from church. At the time, Nelson had told us the footage was for a class project in his advanced marketing class at the University of Texas. Then he revealed he was also sending his tape to a TV reality show looking for contestants. Sure, we'd all signed off on the paperwork he'd handed out, but we were only playing along because he seemed so excited. No one wanted to squash his dreams. Besides, we figured reality would do that for us.

The fact was, reality had just given me a wake-up call. How would I ever tell the girls we were about to be on national TV?

I stopped to rub the beginnings of a headache in the center of my forehead. The real question was, how would I tell my husband? Henry would never go along with this.

I walked down the spiral staircase of my wedding boutique to my dessert bar by my front register and poured myself a cup of coffee. I took a sip then walked to the front window to watch the cars drive down Main Street. It was a beautiful July afternoon. The edges of the blue sky were embroidered with the silhouettes of jagged peaks that surrounded our mountain valley. Across the street I could see Clay Whitefield's jeep parked in front of the Higher Grounds Café. As usual, Clay, our local reporter, was there looking for a story. But despite the fact that we're practically colleagues, with the local paper carrying my advice column and all, I wasn't about to give Clay the scoop, at least not yet.

I took another sip of my coffee and drifted back to my worries. My biggest problem was Henry. Things had been tense between us, and we'd made zero progress in our weekly counseling sessions with Pastor Kevin. News like this could . . . well . . . I shuddered.

I turned and walked through the shop's plush sitting room to the kitchen in the back. I pushed open the swinging door and rinsed out my china cup in the stainless steel sink.

After I placed it in the drying rack, I looked at my gold Chico's watch and saw it was already past five.

A few minutes later, I pushed the accelerator of my Lincoln Continental a few miles over the speed limit, keeping a sharp lookout for Deputy Donna and her speeding tickets. It was dangerous to speed when she was on duty, but I had a lot to do if I was going to prepare for an emergency meeting of our Potluck Catering Company. I felt my forehead knit. Who should I call first? Evangeline Benson Vesey?

I shook a "no" to myself. Poor Evie. She still saw herself as president of what was left of the old prayer club. Never mind that once I'd arrived to town, the club had morphed into a catering company. Sure, we still had our famous potluck meetings, complete with prayer and gossip. I mean, that was a bonus. Plus, it was always a treat to see the dishes my friends cooked up. Which reminded me, I'd have to remember to pull one of my emergency leek quiches out of the deep freeze.

I was afraid that, as good as it was, my quiche wouldn't be enough to buffer news like this. This was enough to put the team into a full-blown panic. Sure, they'd been supportive of me during my recent marriage crisis, but just how far would their sympathies go?

I turned into the driveway of our luxury retirement condo overlooking Golden Lake. Sure enough, Henry's truck was missing from the garage, which meant he was off fishing in the Blue River. I'd have to deal with him later. I checked my Crock-Pot steaming with a summer squash soup, added a dash of pepper, then hurried to the phone next to the kitchen table. I hesitated, then picked up the handset to dial Vonnie, knowing full well that my news would soon change our lives, for better or for worse.

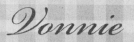

2

TV Dinner

I'd been taking a little nap in my favorite recliner with my dog Chucky, a king kong bichon, when the phone rang.

I reached for the portable handset I kept within arm's length and said, "Hello?"

A Texas-accented voice rang out, "Thank goodness I caught you!"

I kicked the chair out of its reclining position and sat upright, shooing Chucky to the floor. His little white face peered up at me and his brown eyes filled with reproach. "Lisa Leann? You sound like you're in a panic. Is everything all right?"

"I'm calling an emergency meeting of the Potluck Catering Club, tomorrow night at six."

I slowly stood, stretching the kinks out of my back. "Oh dear. Is this about Henry? He hasn't left you, has he?"

"No . . . Well, not yet."

"That doesn't sound good." I walked from my darkened living room to where rainbows of light glinted through my baby doll sun catchers in my window above my kitchen sink. I held the phone between my ear and shoulder and poured water into my teakettle. I was so looking forward to a quiet cup of tea, a luxury I'd only recently been able to enjoy since Mother moved back home with Dad to their condo in the neighboring town of Frisco. Thank goodness that ankle of hers had finally healed.

"Is there anything you need me to do?" I asked.

"Well, I need a favor. Could we have the meeting at your house?"

I set the kettle on the stove and turned the heat on high, sighing as I thought of the chore of tidying up and dusting around my ever-expanding doll collection, which lined the shelves of my living room and filled every cranny of my home. "Why here?"

"Well, you and Fred just got one of those new flat screen TVs, right?"

"Yes, but . . ."

"And you're on satellite?"

"Yes . . ."

"Do you think Fred will mind if we girls watch a show together at seven?"

"Luckily, it's Fred's bowling night, but why can't we watch the show at your place?"

Lisa Leann sighed loudly. "That would never do. Henry. You know?"

I didn't know, but I pretended I did. "Oh, right. Okay."

"And, ah, one more thing. How about if you were to make your famous Mississippi mud cake?"

"All right."

Before the kettle could whistle, Lisa Leann said, "See you tomorrow," and with that she was gone.

Later that evening, my balding Fred and I were sitting in our matching blue recliners, watching Fred's favorite monster truck show. When I stood to take our dinner plates back to the kitchen, a commercial came on about a new reality show called *Great*

Party Showdown something or other. A sexy female voice said, "Ten catering teams from around the country compete to take home our extreme award, a million dollars and a catering kitchen makeover."

Fred's voice rose an octave. "Isn't that you and the girls?"

I turned just in time to see a clip of what looked like Donna Vesey and me giggling as we iced a giant cake. I blinked, but the TV image changed to a group of men dressed in baseball uniforms, singing as they stirred a huge pot of chili.

My heart pounded, but I shook my head. "How could that be?"

Fred laughed. "I think you'd know if you were going to be on a reality TV show. Right?"

I nodded, feeling too nervous to mention that the woman who looked like me had been wearing my favorite butterfly monogrammed sweatshirt.

I'd fretted about it for an hour and probably should have called Lisa Leann, but the idea seemed so far-fetched I made myself believe it was all a coincidence. Just because those gals looked and dressed like us did not mean they were us.

I chuckled to myself the next morning as I attacked the dust bunnies that sometimes hide in the corners of my hearth behind my vintage Raggedy Ann and her china doll friends. I couldn't help but imagine the girls and me on a TV reality program. The idea was simply outrageous.

But as I thought about the clip of the two women icing that cake, I suddenly remembered Lisa Leann's son Nelson taping us girls catering Becky and Allen's wedding last March. Oh, dear. I switched on the television, hoping to catch the commercial again. But every time I heard it start to play, I was either out of the room or saw a clip different from the one that aired the night before.

I would have called Evie to tell her of my concerns, but I remembered this was Vernon's day off. I hated to disturb the newlyweds with my silly fears.

Just before six, David, my handsome biological son, dropped by to take Fred to the bowling alley. It was so good to see the two of them together—a young man who'd never had a dad, and Fred, who'd never had a son. But now they both had me in common, and that seemed to make us family. It had been rocky when my husband first discovered that I, his wife of over three decades, had been a widow before I'd married him, much less had a son who'd been given up for adoption. But my reunion with my son had been a happy one, and now God was answering my prayers as I watched the growing friendship between the two men in my life.

As Chucky danced around us, I once again noticed how much David looked like his father, Private Joseph Jewell, who was killed in Vietnam. David gave me a squeeze. "Donna told me the girls are heading your way tonight."

I smiled at the thought that our club's youngest member, Donna Vesey, was getting closer to David. I wasn't sure if they were going out, but I hoped so. Donna was like a daughter to me, and to think of her and David making a match? Well, the idea warmed my heart.

"What did Donna say?" I asked.

"Only that Lisa Leann was absolutely frantic. What's up?"

"I wish I knew."

As soon as the boys drove out of sight, Lisa Leann's Lincoln Continental pulled up in front of the house. I'd just had time to put Chucky on the back porch before running to hold the door for her, allowing the cool of the summer evening to freshen my home. I glanced at the sky, which was just beginning to turn a golden teal as the setting sun started its descent.

Lisa Leann, a petite redhead in her late forties, was dressed in a gorgeous button-down teal sweater over a lacy T-shirt and designer jeans. She rushed through the expanding shadows, up my front steps, and into my living room. I took her warm quiche, buffered between pink pot-holders, to my kitchen table before returning to see her tug off her sweater.

She opened the front closet door and reached for a coat hanger. "Is there anything I can do to help?"

"Why don't you pour the tea in the glasses?"

She disappeared as the front door swung open again. "Lizzie!" I said.

My librarian friend bent down to give me a hug, then pulled off her black windbreaker, revealing a crisp red shirt that brightened her usual pale complexion. Her blue eyes sparked beneath a splash of salt and pepper bangs. "How are Michelle and Adam?" I asked.

"Still on their honeymoon. Do you know what this crisis is all about?" she asked.

"I'd hate to speculate," I said as she handed me her salad.

Lisa Leann called from the kitchen, "Lizzie, how's that little bride?"

"Michelle? I got a text message this morning that said, and I quote, 'Love Adam and Niagara Falls.'"

"Young love." I sighed, thinking how beautiful Lizzie's daughter had been on her wedding day last week.

I put Lizzie's salad on the table, then ducked back to the front door just in time to greet Goldie, a good-looking strawberry blonde in her late forties. She looked so polished in her matching camel-colored top and business jacket. "You look like you came straight from work," I said.

"I did." She walked toward the kitchen with a package of rolls. "Is the oven warm? It'll just take a second to heat these."

"Sure, let me."

After slipping the rolls into my oven, I looked out the kitchen window to see a red pickup pull up in the driveway. Wasn't that Donna with Wade and little Pete? I walked to the front door and watched Donna scamper up the front steps. She was looking good these days, since her dreadful, cropped hairdo had finally grown into flattering blonde curls.

Donna was a tiny, feisty thing, and her too-short hair had been her way of looking tough in her role as a sheriff's deputy. But even that bad haircut hadn't been able to hide her natural beauty. In fact, Donna, much to her chagrin, was the dream girl of most of the single men in these parts. Now that she was finally starting to recover from some difficult losses, she'd even ventured into the dating game.

I gave Donna a hug and watched Wade's truck disappear down the street. "Wade dropped you off?" I asked nonchalantly.

"Yeah, he's been over at my house with his cousin Pete. Pete had to interview someone in law enforcement for a class project. He's in summer school, you know."

"It wasn't a date?" I asked.

"I don't date twelve-year-olds," she said with a laugh.

"But Wade's not twelve," I teased.

"No, he's not. We go out sometimes, though I do have a date with David this Friday."

"Really?" I winced as I realized my enthusiasm showed. I had to be careful. Though Donna was like my own daughter, I couldn't interfere. She had to make up her own mind when it came to matters of her heart.

Donna smiled and handed me a jar of cinnamon-flavored applesauce as she pulled off her leather jacket to reveal that she was wearing her standard black jeans with matching tee. She was looking . . . what did the young people say? Hot.

"How are you going to get home?"

"I'll catch a ride with Lizzie," she said.

Lisa Leann swooped up the jar of applesauce and was busying herself in the kitchen, putting the contents into a bowl, when the door blew open once again. I ran back to see Mrs. Evangeline Vesey holding her "in a pinch" rice dish. "Sorry I'm late," she huffed. "Had to make Vernon's dinner."

Donna looked surprised. "My dad can cook."

"If you like grilled cheese every night," Evie said with a hint of a smile. "Good thing I'm finally there to change all that."

Donna pasted on a hard smile. These two had their troubles, but Donna had the good sense to play nice with her new stepmom.

Evie followed me to the girls, who were already gathering around the table. Goldie was just pulling her rolls out from the oven and placing them into my linen-covered basket.

"Lisa Leann, what's the big emergency?" Evie said as she sat at the table.

"Let's pray first," Lisa Leann said. We all settled down, and Lisa Leann bowed her head. "Lord, have mercy on us," she said.

So help me, I peeked and caught Evie's startled expression. She raised her eyebrows at me as if to ask, *Do you know what this is about*? I shook my head and closed my eyes again.

Lisa Leann continued. "Please, Lord, please!"

After the "Amen," there was a long silence as the girls stared at Lisa Leann, one of the strongest women we'd ever known. But there she sat, pale and shaken. "What is it?" Lizzie cried. "Is Henry leaving you?"

Lisa Leann shook her head. "No, no. Let's eat and then I'll explain in a moment."

Since I was sitting next to Lisa Leann, I leaned in and whispered, "This doesn't have anything to do with a TV reality show, does it?"

Lisa Leann sputtered a cough and grabbed her napkin to cover her face. "You'll know soon enough," she said.

Donna, who was sitting to my left, asked me in a low voice, "What did you say to her?"

I hesitated. "I think I'd better let her explain."

Forty minutes later, I'd poured the flavored coffee while Evie and Lisa Leann moved my oak kitchen chairs to the living room for our business meeting. Once we'd settled in, Lizzie and Goldie served everyone a plate with a generous slice of Mississippi mud cake, while Donna and I followed with steaming mugs of coffee.

Lisa Leann stood unsteadily before us, looking like someone had wiped all the blush off her cheeks. She put on a brave face. "Girls, I have good news."

Evie stuck her fork in her cake and piped, "I thought this was some sort of emergency?"

"It all depends on the perspective you choose to take," Lisa Leann said. "I like to think of this as a chance for us to raise a million dollars for the building fund at church."

I plopped my coffee so hard onto the coffee table it sloshed on my napkin. "This is about that reality show. What's it called?"

"*The Great Party Showdown*," Lisa Leann said. She reached under her chair and pulled out her briefcase, then pulled out a batch of packets, which she passed around the table.

Evie was already balking. "A reality show? You've got to be kidding. You'd never catch me on something like that."

Lisa Leann walked over to the TV and flipped on the switch. "I hate to hear you say that, Evie, because tonight you're a star!"

Evie's jaw dropped. "What?"

A preview for the show popped onto the screen, and sure enough, there was Evie's face, smudged with a bit of flour as she pounded a huge ball of dough in my bridal shop kitchen. That same sexy voice I'd heard earlier said, "How will the Colorado church ladies of Team Potluck fare in their battle against the Wild Cajun Cooks of Baton Rouge?"

A team of men dressed in long white aprons sporting the name "Wild Cajun Cooks" appeared on the screen. One fellow, whose white chef's hat read "Bubba," looked like he'd had a few too many. Bubba sipped a beer before pouring the remains into a bubbling pot, then whooped for the camera. The voice continued as pictures of the other teams flashed on the screen. "Or our other competitors? Stay tuned for an all-out food war on *The Great Party Showdown*, coming up next."

Lizzie asked, "Wasn't that clip from Allen and Becky's wedding?"

Lisa Leann nodded as Donna rose to her feet, her hand on her hip, like she was reaching for her gun. "What's the meaning of this? We didn't sign up for any reality show."

"Calm down, everyone," Lisa Leann said. "I can explain."

"Well, you'd better," Evie said.

"Remember when my son Nelson was here with his fancy video camera? It was state of the art, just like the kind they sometimes use on TV reality shows. His dad and I had bought it for him on eBay to use for a marketing class at U Texas."

"But how did his footage get on that program?" Evie asked. She leaned back in her chair as she knitted her brows into one long line of worry.

"Evie, I'm getting to that. Like he said, Nelson sent the footage to this reality show as part of his assignment. You might recall we each signed off on it. Though I don't think any of us thought something like this could actually happen."

Ever the legal secretary, Goldie recovered her voice to ask, "But I didn't sign my permission."

Lisa Leann pulled out a packet of papers from her briefcase and held it up. "Actually, I have a copy of it. Don't you remember signing the waiver and other paperwork for Nelson?"

Goldie reached for the papers. "Well, yes, but . . . it was part of his class assignment." She studied her signature. "I guess I didn't read the fine print."

Lisa Leann shrugged. "None of us did."

Just then, the commercials ended and the musical intro for the show started as all eyes fixed on the television.

I felt my stomach do a flip-flop.

What had Lisa Leann gotten us into this time?

3

Catered Comedy

As we finished the vanilla lattes Vonnie had made from my special homemade mix, Gianne Gillian looked into the camera, her blue eyes twinkling. "America, I hope you've come hungry," she said. "Our ten catering teams from around the country are about to whip up a party, and you're invited. Find out which team can outcook, outcater, and outparty the other teams. America, it's up to you to say which teams stay in the competition. What's at stake? For starters, our winning team receives a cool million dollars plus a one-hundred-thousand-dollar kitchen makeover by Fridgnetic."

The girls and I exchanged glances. "Think church building program," Lisa Leann said in a stage whisper, to which Vonnie added, "Here's to a new youth wing."

Gianne continued. "But first, America, let's meet *The Great Party Showdown* judges. First up, meet Teresa Juliette, star of her own cooking show, *Teresa Sizzles*. Welcome to the show, Teresa."

Amid thunderous applause, a plump African-American woman

glimmered in a sparkling chef's hat that topped off a matching white coat dress. She waved a white sequined spatula at the crowd. "Thank you, it's good to be here."

"Teresa, can you tell us the role of the judges on the show?"

"We can't vote off the contestants," Teresa said. "We're only here to offer America our expert opinions."

"Very good," Gianne said. She stepped over to a small man with beady blue eyes. "Next, meet Brant Richards, our British import, and famous chef and party planner in his own right. Brant has been quoted as saying, 'Nothing of good taste and nothing that tastes good comes from America.'"

The crowd booed, and Brant held up his hands as if to greet cheers. With his British flair, he said, "Mine is a discriminating palate."

Gianne asked, "Do you expect to see a team you'll approve of?"

"If you put it that way, no."

Gianne stepped to the right. "Well, then, America, meet Isabelle Salazar, a popular Brazilian party planner and caterer."

A spicy young woman in a black cocktail dress jumped to her feet and vibrated like an excited puppy as she let out her trademark "*Muito bom*, baby!"

The crowd went wild with applause, and Gianne stepped back into the shot. "My goodness, Isabelle, you seem excited to be here."

"Food and parties are my life," Isabelle shouted into the camera, waving her hands above her head.

"I wonder what she's on?" I asked as the girls twittered.

"Who knows," Evangeline answered.

"Personally? I'd like to administer a breathalyzer."

Lisa Leann winked at me. "Well, if we make it through the next couple of rounds, maybe you'll get your chance."

"Does that mean we might actually go to Hollywood?" Vonnie asked.

Lisa Leann shook her head. "Nope, this show is broadcast live from New York City."

Goldie gasped. "New York City?"

Lisa Leann shrugged. "It wouldn't be for a couple of weeks." She shushed us as the camera panned back to Gianne for a close-up. "Coming up, can the ladies of Team Potluck really stir it up? Stay tuned."

When the commercials started, Vonnie said, "Oh dear, I'm so nervous I'm shaking."

Evangeline, who was sitting in Fred's recliner, reached for her hand and gave it a little squeeze, then shot a stern look at Lisa Leann. "Vonnie, I know just how you feel," she said.

Lisa Leann's cell phone blasted Sandi Patty singing "Majesty," and she answered. "Hello? Nelson? Yes, sweetheart, we're all watching. What's that? A warning?" She was silent for a moment, then said, "Okay, thanks for letting me know. Oh, did you talk to your dad? Oh, okay. Talk to you after the show."

She hung up. I turned to her. "Warning?"

"Nelson wanted me to know that he may be providing some of the commentary introducing our team members. He hopes no one gets too upset."

"How bad can it be?" I asked. "Nelson lives in Austin. He barely knows us."

"That's not true, Donna," Evangeline said. "He was here over spring break helping with the wedding. Besides, he knows whatever his mother told him."

We all turned and stared at Lisa Leann. "Listen, I don't know what he said on camera, but he just used the word *embellished*. He said he's sorry, he never thought the footage would go to air. He was just trying to be funny and get a good grade."

Vonnie asked, "But he was behind the camera, so how could he film himself?"

"His tripod," Lisa Leann answered before turning back to stare at another TV commercial for insurance.

I decided to get comfortable, so I stretched out on the floor with my hands cupping my head, looking up at the screen as the theme music of the show started to play. Gianne said, "Meet Team Potluck from the Colorado high country." Nelson's face appeared on the screen. He was a fresh-faced college kid, handsome with his green eyes and blond hair. He was wearing a waiter's uniform, and the wedding reception was in full swing behind him. "I'm not really part of Team Potluck. I'm just helping out," he said. Suddenly a wide shot of several of us Potluckers appeared as we scrambled in studio-enhanced fast motion to set up the buffet while music from the Keystone Cops played in the background. A breeze had picked up, so when the footage slowed back to normal, there I was under the table, taping the edges of the tablecloth down with duct tape. I looked at the camera and smiled. "This ought to hold her," I said. The camera cut back to Nelson. "That's Deputy Donna. She's the hottest chick on the team, and the word on the street is she knows a lot about duct tape and has used it to subdue a few criminals."

I sat up. "What?"

The camera cut back to Wade helping me carry the wedding cake to one of the tables. Honestly, he looked like Brad Pitt in a waiter's uniform. The voiceover continued. "Wade is one of the deputy's boyfriends." Wade put a dot of icing on my nose, and I playfully hit him with a fist.

I groaned.

Another clip showed me carrying the punch bowl with Vonnie's son David, who happens to be an Enrique Iglesias look-alike. Nelson said, "But then again, there's David."

More footage showed David whispering something in my ear, and I laughed. Nelson piped up, "So as we can see, though the woman carries a gun, it certainly doesn't scare off the guys around here. Though rumor is she's had to use that gun more than once."

I flopped back on the floor and stared up at Vonnie's ceiling. "No, no, no, this isn't happening."

Vonnie leaned down from her recliner and patted my shoulder. "It could have been worse, dear," she said, as if that were any consolation.

Just then the camera focused briefly on Becky dressed in a flowing white gown as she clutched a bouquet of silk wildflowers and headed down the aisle to meet her groom, who was dressed in a black tux. The next shot was of Vonnie, who was grinning from ear to ear as she straightened the gold table runner down the buffet table. She was a cute, plump grandma, her round cheeks pink beneath her white hair, which fluffed in curls around her face. Nelson said, "Meet Vonnie Sunshine—she's the happy pill of Team Potluck."

Vonnie put her hand to her mouth. "Oh, dear!"

The next few shots of Vonnie showed her in a hugging frenzy—hugging Donna, then David, then Lisa Leann, then Evie, Wade, the bride, the groom, Lizzie, and even Nelson, who crossed his eyes then winked.

Nelson's face came back on the screen. "It's said they didn't have to use sugar in the wedding cake." The wedding cake, perched on a linen-covered table with the gorgeous Colorado Rockies in the background, appeared on the screen. "Vonnie only had to put her finger in the batter to sweeten it." The last frame was of Vonnie's face in full grin, with the special effect of sparkles bouncing off her pearly whites as chimes played.

Vonnie closed her eyes to block out the image as the camera panned to Lisa Leann. Nelson said, "This is the little lady known as Lisa Leann, and I can only say nice things about her because she's my mom and, well, she's the brains of this outfit." The camera showed Lisa Leann hugging Nelson, and he leaned down and kissed the top of her red hair.

"So moving on, let's talk about Dizzy Lizzy." One shot after the other showed Lizzy turning and pointing as she helped direct traffic. Nelson said, "The only reason this ol' gal's dizzy is because the other team members rely on her so much."

Nelson continued, "Next up, meet our golden girl, Goldie the Goalie." One clip after the other showed Goldie tossing items to team members: a rolled-up pink apron, a roll of paper towels, a fat candle still packaged in cellophane, even a camera.

Goldie shrieked. "Do I really do that?"

We all turned to her and replied as one, "Yes."

"That's what I get for marrying a high school coach," she muttered.

Then the camera focused on Evie, whom I noticed was beginning to glow from a light perspiration. "Next, meet the woman some folks call Evil Evie," Nelson said. The camera zoomed in to show Evie frowning, then panned back to show her hands on her hips. "But I say she's really not all that bad, just occasionally grumpy. So judges, be warned."

Evie squealed. "How could Nelson say such a thing? Everyone knows I'm as sweet as pie."

I shot her a look and nodded. I kept quiet so I wouldn't sound insincere. Vonnie Sunshine patted her leg. "Of course you are."

Now the camera panned to show all our wonderful dishes displayed in their full glory while we, the smiling ladies of the club, minus Lizzie, stood by ready to serve. There was a succulent roast beef royally displayed, baby carrots in a light yellow sauce, fresh homemade rolls, gravy, fruit salad, and so much more.

Lisa Leann narrated the menu while a smiling Nelson helped by lifting lids, then tasting each dish on a china plate.

His face filled the screen. "Really, this is delicious." The camera zoomed even closer, and he whispered, "Mom paid me to say that."

The screen faded to black, and I was surprised that our three-and-a-half minutes of fame was already over. It was amazing the producers were able to show so much in such short, zippy clips. Gianne appeared with Teresa Juliette, who held her glittering spatula as if it were a scepter. Gianne asked, "What do you think of Team Potluck, Teresa?"

25

"I wish I could wave a wand and make that team more organized. Those women are a mess."

Brant Richards smirked. "It was sheer chaos. And what were they thinking serving the rolls next to the gravy? A good caterer would never do that. But then, these women aren't good caterers. They're amateurs. Even the bride and groom were amateur."

Lisa Leann gasped. "I hope Becky and Allen aren't watching."

We watched Teresa playfully whack Brant on the head with her spatula. "Don't be such an idiot, honey. I'm glad they're not like you. Why, you're already on wife number four. This bride and groom were so sweet, this was no doubt their first wedding."

Gianne said to Brant, "Doesn't it bother you to give this kind of critique to Team Potluck when you know that Deputy Donna carries a gun and Evil Evie can be grumpy?"

"Hmph, this team will never make it through this round. I have nothing to fear from that girly deputy or the so-called Evil Evie."

My cheeks burned, and I flopped onto my back. "Ugh." Then I turned over and perched on my elbows to see Isabelle Salazar stand and gyrate like she was shot by a jolt of electricity. "Muito bom, baby!" she called. "I love the Colorado cheesecake."

"I didn't see any cheesecake," Gianne said.

"I'm talking about those spicy waiters, Wade and David. Vote this team through so we can have another serving. Muito bom, baby!"

Gianne laughed. "America, you've heard from our judges. We'll be right back after the break."

A Toyota commercial appeared, and one after another our cell phones rang, making the room sound like the warm-up for an orchestra as each phone played a different tune. First Nelson called Lisa Leann. I could hear her say, "It wasn't that bad. No. I think the girls liked it. Really."

I rolled my eyes and then listened in on a cell conversation between Evangeline and my dad. Evangeline was saying, "So you saw it? No, I didn't know we were going to be on. I'm appalled, I tell you, appalled. Did you hear what he called me? Evil Evie!"

Goldie was saying, "Jack, I just can't understand how this could happen either."

A call came in on my cell from our Clay Whitefield. "Donna, why didn't you tell me you and the girls were going to be on that catering show?"

"I didn't know it myself."

"Well, I want an exclusive."

"Gotta go. Wade's trying to ring through." I hung up with Clay and turned my attention to Wade. "Hey," I said.

"Why didn't you warn me about the reality show?"

"Sorry, but I had no idea about it."

Wade laughed. "Well, I guess I don't mind being called a cheese-cake on national TV.

"Oh, so you think it's funny now?"

"I do. Would you care for a slice?"

"Ha! I don't think so. Look, the show's starting again. I gotta go."

As soon as the theme music started, our voices fell silent and we watched the packages the network had put together for the nine other teams. The teams included the Wild Cajun Cooks from Baton Rouge and the Boston Bean Team, which featured men in funny paper hats. Then there was Team Tex Mex from San Antonio. The caterers were made up of cappuccino-skinned beauties twirling in yellow skirts as they served up some great-looking Mexican dishes. I was a bit confused by the Moon Beam Team of Sedona. They all wore crystal necklaces and served tofu dishes on clear platters, which they referred to as vortexes. Do people really eat that stuff?

Then of course there was the New York favorite, Team Batter Up, an all-guy team from New York City and dressed in baseball uniforms. Another team that presented well was the Comfort Cooking

Team from Savannah, Georgia, a group of June Cleaver look-alikes who served heaps of fried chicken and mashed potatoes along with some beautiful pecan pies. Then there was a bunch of college guys who looked like fraternity boys and did a lot of cooking with beer and French fries. They called themselves Team Gators and were from somewhere in Florida. Also included was Team Hollywood, a bunch of beauties dressed like starlets. They served elegant but strange and tiny appetizers. Mysteriously, they were the only group that got high marks from Brant. And last but not least was Team Café Mocha, a group of housewives who specialized in soups, coffee, and coffee-flavored desserts.

The hour passed quickly, and in the final moments, Gianne showed each team's highlights with individualized phone numbers so the viewers could vote. "America, voting will be open for the next hour. Tune in next week to see which eight teams remain in the competition. If your favorite team is chosen, we're flying to location to tape the results of their next great party challenge on their own home turf. Tune in for the results. Good night, America, and bon appétit."

I began to rapidly dial one of the numbers on the screen while Evie tried to stop me. "Honestly, Donna, you don't want us to make next week's show, do you?"

"No way," I said. "I'm calling to support Team Batter Up."

"Hold it, everyone," Lisa Leann said. "And hold your phone calls. I have more news."

"Now what?" Evie asked.

"Did you hear what Gianne said? If we make it through this round, we'll have a film crew from Stirring Productions in town on Thursday, that's in two days. Kat, the producer, is going to call me here, in an hour, to tell us if we made the cut and to tell us what the showdown challenge will be."

"Oh, dear," Vonnie said. "Do you think we'll make it through this round?"

"Maybe. And girls, remember, if we win this thing, Team Potluck can sponsor the church building fund. Let's do this for a good cause. Agreed?"

The girls mumbled an agreement while Goldie said, "Well, Lisa Leann, I'm for supporting the church. Who knows? Maybe something good will come from this fiasco."

Lisa Leann nodded. "That's the spirit!"

Evie snorted, but before she could comment, I asked, "What now?"

Lisa Leann replied, "Now we wait for the phone to ring."

4

Party Plans

It had been a full sixteen hours since my premiere on *The Great Party Showdown*, and I still could not get over Lisa Leann's . . . what's the word I want to use here . . . *bravado* at entering our small but successful company as contestants. Who does she think she is, anyway? The president?

Okay. She is the president. The president of the catering company, but not the Potluck Club itself. That puppy belongs to me. Well, the club doesn't belong to me, but the presidency does. After all, I'm the one who—years ago—came up with the idea for the prayer group. A tiny little fact everyone seems to be forgetting, which I brought up to my husband Vernon on Wednesday.

He stuck his fork into some scalloped potatoes piled alongside the tuna salad sandwich on his plate. "Not that you've had a prayer meeting in a while," he said, then quickly shot the fork of potatoes into his mouth.

I froze in my seat at the kitchen table across from him, my tuna sandwich halfway to my gaping mouth. Returning the sandwich to one of my everyday plates, I said, "Well, of course we haven't. What with Lisa Leann starting this catering business, keeping us busier than fans on a hot July afternoon, and Michelle's wedding not two weeks ago and Goldie's daughter having her baby and the big Summit View Fourth of July bash we worked ourselves silly at. Who has time to meet and pray?"

Vernon took a long sip of iced tea before answering. "I just think you've let the core of your group get away from you." Vernon's baby blues widened, and he scratched his neck at the spot just under his full head of gray hair. "I've never been much of one for talking about my faith to the masses—you know that—but you women met every month no matter what for years. I can't imagine anything getting between you and prayer."

I had to ponder that for a minute. We had let things come between us and our prayer group, and I, for one, thought it was time to get some things back on track.

"I know what you're thinking," Vernon said with a wink.

"You do no such thing."

"Yes, I do," he said, popping the last of his sandwich into his mouth.

"Okay, smarty. What?" I mocked him by popping the last of my sandwich into my mouth as well, then got up from the table and headed over to the coffeemaker to make a fresh pot. Hopefully the caffeine would get me through the rest of the day.

"You're thinking it's time to get the girls back on the straight and narrow."

Okay, so he can read my mind . . .

"But," he added with flourish, "now you've got the added problem of a new venture. You're going to be a movie star."

I turned from the counter where I'd scooped just the right number of spoonfuls of aromatic grounds into the filter and slapped the top of the coffeemaker shut before pressing the "on" button. "I am not going to be a movie star." Then I grinned at him. "I'm going to be a television celebrity."

It was true. I—we—were going to be featured on *The Great Party Showdown* the following Tuesday. The call had come in about an hour and a half after the show ended. Lisa Leann was sitting on the sofa, her cell phone in her hand. Fred and David, who'd come in from bowling, sat next to her and talked about their game. The rest of us sat in stunned silence and waited.

Occasionally one of us would speak. Vonnie said, "If we win, I don't know how I'll tell Mother I'm going to New York City. She's never liked me leaving the state of Colorado much . . . not since . . . I was younger."

I knew what Vonnie was referencing, of course. Her college-years marriage to David's biological father and subsequent life in Los Angeles.

Lizzie said, "At least I don't have to be back at school until some time in August." Lizzie is the high school media center specialist. In our day, we called them librarians, but I suppose that's not fancy enough anymore.

Goldie was, out of all of us, in the biggest pickle. "Oh, Evangeline," she said, leaning over and whispering in my ear. "I just took off time from work for the Fourth of July events and Michelle's wedding. Seems to me all I've done since I started working at Chris Lowe's law firm is ask for time off. What will I do if we get voted clear through to New York?"

"What do you mean, Goldie Dippel? What will any of us do but go along with this harebrained idea of Lisa Leann's. How in the world that woman has managed to get us into so many fixes . . ."

I could say more on the topic of Lisa Leann Lambert's "fixes." Why, she hadn't been in Summit View even a year, and so far she'd managed to turn our lives into one wild ride. But, I have to be honest here. She's growing on me, and I'm finding myself as intrigued with her antics as Vivian Vance was of that other redhead, Lucille Ball.

When Lisa Leann's cell phone finally—and I do mean finally—rang, she threw it up in the air as though tossing a hot potato, then caught it and stared at the glowing screen. "It's Kat Sebastian," she squealed.

"Well, for crying out loud, Lisa Leann," I said, sliding to the edge of my seat on the sofa, "answer it. And don't make a ninny of yourself." *And be sure to tell her my name is* not *Evil Evie, while you're at it.*

Lisa Leann took a deep breath, then exhaled out her nose. She flipped open the phone and chirped, "Lisa Leann Lambert."

Not a soul in the room moved. Heaven help us, I'm not sure we even breathed, for that matter.

"Yes, hello Kat . . . yes, we did . . . yes, we are . . . yes . . . no, I don't think so . . . yes, yes! Oh, really? . . . We did? . . . We will? . . . Oh, my goodness, yes . . . okay . . . I understand . . . got it. Yes, talk to you tomorrow then. Good-bye." She slapped the phone shut.

Donna frowned. "I take it we made it to the next level."

Lisa Leann stood, threw out her arms, and said, "Ms. Donna Vesey! Come on down! You're the next contestant . . ."

From that moment on, nothing has been the same. The phone calls poured in, including requests for interviews from Denver radio and television stations and the *Denver Post*. Of course, our very own Summit View ace reporter, Clay Whitefield, made it over to Vonnie's house before any of us even had a chance to come back to earth. I suppose he wanted to make sure he was the first to know if we'd made it to the next level, but Kat had informed Lisa Leann—and she us—that we were not to say a single word and contracts were to be faxed the following day.

Of course, Clay wasn't the only one dashing to Vonnie's doorstep. Neighbors and friends and church members came, but Fred and David stood on the front porch and made apologies, saying we were unable to come to the door and they needed to go home and leave us to our business. On the other side of the door, we were gaga with plans and ideas for the following week's show. We were, as Fred later said to Vonnie, fluttering like hens in a coop with one rooster.

Well, Lisa Leann has had us hopping. We had less than twenty-four hours, she told us—if we count that we can't work while we're asleep—before the film crew was to arrive. According to Lisa Leann, we'd been given a few guidelines, a budget of two thousand dollars, and the orders to throw a themed party. "And what great plan do you have for us now, Lisa Leann?" Donna asked. "What will we do to win the hearts of America for our next catering caper?"

"I think," she said, pointing a finger in the air, "we should throw a surprise birthday party for . . . girls, any of you having a birthday?" She looked from one to the other of us.

We all shook our heads.

She turned to Fred and David, but they both claimed they wouldn't be getting older any time soon.

Then she looked at Vonnie. "I know. We'll have a surprise birthday party for your mother."

"My mother?" Vonnie pressed her palm against her chest. "My mother's birthday isn't for another two months." She blinked. "And why my mother?"

"Because," I said, "she's available."

"Well . . . yes, but . . ."

"Perfect," Lisa Leann said, as though that settled it. "So, she'll have it a little early. She won't mind; I'm just sure of it. Call her and tell her whatever you need to tell her to get her to the church. She'll have a birthday bash she'll not soon forget and she'll love you for it." Lisa Leann paused momentarily. "Or at the very least, she'll love me for it." She turned slightly, then swung around again to face us, her little soldiers. "Okay, girls. Tomorrow morning. Zero-eight-hundred hours. Be at the bridal boutique, and we'll start to plan."

We left Vonnie's in a flurry. The July air was crisp and inviting as we each slipped into our own vehicles, anxious to get home to our respective families.

My family is my husband of nearly seven months, Sheriff Vernon Vesey, who I'd secretly loved since I was twelve years old. I would have married him a long time ago had it not been for Donna's mother, Doreen, who we now call Dee Dee. Doreen had been one of my best friends, but with her wanton ways she managed to slip Vernon from my naïve prepubescent fingers. They dated off and on through school until they married, leaving me loveless and forlorn.

Naturally the marriage didn't last; not with Doreen's—Dee Dee's—insatiable appetite for men. She left Vernon and four-year-old Donna and ran off with our church's choir director. They lived in California until she ran off with someone else and then someone else, and on and on it went. Then, last year, she returned home, so to speak. Between her and Lisa Leann, Summit View has become a little Peyton Place.

But even with her arrival and the disruptions it caused, Vernon and I managed to finally find true love in each other's arms and, as the end result, matching wedding rings on our left third fingers. At nearly sixty years of age, we now were as complete as could be, except that neither of us had ever starred in our own reality show.

As soon as I finished rinsing off the lunch dishes and slipping them into the dishwasher, I dashed to the bathroom, where I brushed my teeth, ran a comb through my short, wavy hair, then added a slick touch of gloss to my bottom lip. I rubbed my lips together, spreading the sheen, then frowned. I'd never worn lip gloss until Lisa Leann had come into my life and insisted it would give me "color." Now I vainly wore it every day. I told my friends— the Potluck girls—that it was because Vernon seemed to like it so much. He said it gave me—and I quote—a "sexy edge."

Men.

But the truth is, I wear it now because I like it. I like the way it brings out the natural pink to my cheeks and helps me to feel more feminine. Not that I'd ever tell Lisa Leann or anyone else, for that matter.

With a cup of coffee to go in hand, I dashed out the front door a few minutes later. I gave a quick wave to my husband, who'd already stretched out on the sofa for an afternoon nap. Vernon knows I prefer that if he is going to do this, he does it on the den sofa or—better still—in our bed. But with bare minutes to spare before I was due back at the boutique for more cooking and planning, I didn't have a second to nag. I called a heartfelt good-bye and then scampered to my awaiting car parked in the driveway.

I arrived back at work with no time to spare. I ran in via the front door, through the front rooms and into the back, where we did the majority of our catering. Lisa Leann glanced down at her watch as though in scolding, to which I replied, "What? I'm not late." I reached for my apron and, tying it around my narrow waist, said, "Where's Donna?"

"Donna," Lisa Leann answered, "has run down to Denver. We've found a Hollywood memorabilia shop, and they have exactly what I'm looking for."

Lisa Leann had decided that because Vonnie's mother had been born in 1930—during the golden era of Hollywood—we should go with one of 1930's most beloved films, *Animal Crackers*. Lizzie had been on the phone all morning calling a select group of townspeople to tell them about the party, of its hush-hush nature, and that they had less than twenty-four hours to find a Marx Brothers costume (if they were male) and a lacy black dress, long strand pearls, and feathered hat (if they were female).

Lisa Leann wanted the feel of the party room to be that of Mrs. Rittenhouse's gala, an important setting in the plot of the movie. Vonnie and Goldie had been shopping at some of our downtown stores earlier but, before lunch, had moved on to Silverthorne's outlets. Goldie had called in at one point that morning to inform us that her husband Jack, also our high school's coach, had contacted the drama instructor, who had contacted several students on the drama team, and that they were now preparing to perform several of the more memorable lines and scenes from the movie.

"Like what?" Donna had asked.

I looked at Lisa Leann and she at me. In an unusual moment of unity we simultaneously and with dramatic flare said, "Last night I shot an elephant in my pajamas. How he got in my pajamas, I don't know." We pretended to waggle cigars near our grinning faces, then doubled over in laughter.

Ah, to be older . . .

I dragged myself home near midnight. Everything was ready. Remarkable but true. The social hall of our quaint church was decorated to the nines, looking more like Mrs. Rittenhouse's parlor than Mrs. Rittenhouse's parlor ever did. In the kitchen adjacent to the hall, the food was in the refrigerator or in sealed containers, and our workstations were well prepared for the next day. Back at the boutique's kitchen, every inch of stainless steel shone under newly applied polish, and the countertops were wiped down spotless. There was nothing left to do but pray.

But pray for what, I wondered. To win? To go to the next level on *The Great Party Showdown*? Or to lose and go back to life as usual—crazy as it had become—here in Summit View?

As I eased myself between the sheets of our bed, Vernon stirred and rolled over. In the moonlight sneaking between the blinds at the windows, I spied the brilliance of his eyes peering toward me. "Hi," he said.

"Hello to you too."

"Got it all done?"

I nodded, adjusting the covers as though to end the conversation. I needed to get some rest, I thought, as though all the sleep the night could afford would make up for how hard I'd worked—we'd worked—that day.

"You think you've done a good enough job to win?"

I sighed. "Oh, Vernon. I don't know if I want to be made a fool in front of the whole world by losing or to win and have to continue the competition in New York. What in the world was that woman thinking?" I didn't need to define who "that woman" was.

Vernon chuckled, and I turned on my side, exposing my back to him. He placed a hand on my hip and sighed deeply. "Get some sleep," he said, patting me. "Tomorrow we'll just have to wait and see what God allows now that you've done all you can do."

From the back of my mind came the rush of an old saying, one taken from Ecclesiastes and Isaiah: eat, drink, and be merry . . .

And in the quiet I whispered its end: "For tomorrow we die."

5

Taste of Fame

The smell of coffee traveling from our kitchen, tiptoeing up the middle-to-top staircase of our split-level home, and sneaking around our bedroom door finally made its way to our bed and into my nostrils. I inhaled deeply, smiling. Then I frowned. What day was it?

Oh, Lord, I prayed. *Not Thursday already.*

I peered at the clock on my bedside table. It glowed red at me, telling me it was but a few minutes after seven. A groan emitted from deep within. Why couldn't I have slept later?

Typically I was up with Samuel, my husband, even before the sun rose. Together we would make coffee, then go to the patio, where we would sip from steaming mugs in silence until the sun rose and we were forced to get up and do our individual "thing." During the summer months, my "thing" is to hang out at home, read, work in my garden, and—occasionally—go to work with the catering company. Samuel's is to get ready, then head out to the Gold Rush Bank, where he is VP.

39

But today . . .

You know, Lord. You know I didn't make it home until after midnight. And you know that—tired as I was—I found I couldn't sleep. And you know, Lord . . . you know how long it took me to finally get to sleep.

Three and a half months ago, I'd have reached for a bottle in an effort to ease the tension from my aching muscles and to help my troubled mind release all rambling thoughts. Now I praise God daily for the night Donna Vesey pulled over my speeding car and realized I was driving intoxicated. It was what I needed to stop depending on alcohol and start depending on God's holy and supportive Spirit.

I stretched as I continued my inner prayer. *Thank you, Lord. Thank you for this day. Thank you for the tiny little bit of sleep I was able to get last night. And thank you for a husband who quietly prepared coffee this morning and who miraculously didn't wake me when he got up.*

I sat up, slid my feet into well-worn bedroom slippers, and then padded down the stairs and into the kitchen, where Samuel stood before the coffeepot, pouring himself what I was sure to be a second cup. He looked over his shoulder, and his lips parted in a smile, gorgeous slicing into handsome.

"Well, good morning, Mary Sunshine," he said. "I tried not to wake you."

I sidled up to him for a kiss, then reached into an overhead cabinet for a mug. "You didn't," I confessed. "But the smell of this coffee did."

Samuel chuckled deep within his throat. "What time'd you get home last night?"

"After midnight." I poured coffee into my mug and inhaled deeply.

"You girls ready?"

"As ready as we'll ever be." I began preparing my coffee as I like it. "To be honest with you, Lisa Leann's idea of using the Hollywood 1930s theme of *Animal Crackers* has me a bit worried."

"How so?"

I shot him a quick look, then took a sip of coffee. "I've heard of *Animal Crackers*, of course. You can't work in the media center and have a decent background in Hollywood cinema if you haven't heard of it."

"You do love those old classics."

I grinned at him. "That's why I love you, Samuel Prattle."

"Touché."

I sighed. "It's just, I thought the theme of . . . I don't know . . . *Little House on the Prairie* might be a good idea. But Lisa Leann wouldn't hear anything of it." I turned and rested my hip against the counter, then took a sip of coffee.

Samuel, in like manner, rested his backside against the opposite counter. Crossing one arm against his middle, he brought his coffee mug up to his pursed lips, then blew. "Why not? Too backwoodsy?"

"*Passé*, I believe, was the word she used. 'We don't want people thinking we're still living back in the days of cowboys and Indians, do we?'" I chuckled lightly. "No, Lisa Leann," I said, as though she were present, "we want them to think we live in a time where fashionable women wore berets and chinchilla."

Samuel chuckled at my terse humor. "This isn't like you, Liz."

I shook my head. "I know. And maybe I should have said something, but I didn't. Let Lisa Leann have her fun. No one is going to get the connection between *Animal Crackers* and Vonnie's mother's date of birth, we'll lose the round, and life in Summit View will return to normal."

Samuel discreetly cleared his throat. "Allow me to play the devil's advocate for a minute; what do you think will happen if you win?"

"I'll eat crow."

"I bet I know what will happen," he said, then took a sip. He swallowed hard, commented, "That's still hot." Then added, "You'll go to New York."

I thought about that for a moment. "Do you know how many years it's been since I've been to New York?"

"Quite a few." His eyes twinkled.

"More than a few. I believe we called it our honeymoon."

Samuel chuckled again. "That was fun, wasn't it?"

I reached across our narrow kitchen and playfully slapped his arm. "Samuel Prattle."

He rubbed the spot where I'd slapped him as though I'd severely wounded him. "Ow. Well, it was fun. The theater . . . the sightseeing . . . the dining . . ."

"The shopping . . ." I countered.

"Ah, yes. I bought you a beautiful little trinket at Tiffany's, if I remember."

I touched the hollow of my throat with my fingertips and said, "I'll have to remember to wear that if we go to New York. Maybe it'll bring us good luck if I wear it." My special wedding gift from Samuel had been an Elsa Peretti necklace. "Like you," Samuel had said as he presented it to me in Tiffany's classic blue box tied off with white ribbon. "Dainty and beautiful."

I shook my head. "Not that I believe in luck, mind you. You know that."

"I know that."

"I'm praying that God's will be done. However his will lands, I'll accept it."

Samuel took a step toward the kitchen door leading to the upstairs staircase. "I've got to get moving here," he said. "God's will for me is to get to work on time, I'm afraid."

"I love you," I called after his retreating form.

"And I love you."

An hour later I was sitting on a family room sofa in an empty house that was beginning to feel too large. With last month's wedding of our youngest daughter, our children—all four of them—were now grown and gone. We were officially empty-nesters, and I was working hard to stay out of my children's business. Especially that of Michelle, our youngest. Not only has she been deaf since birth—tying us to each other with tighter apron strings than normal—but she was the baby and she'd lived with us the longest. I felt, often, she depended on me more than the others.

But she was proving me wrong.

I let out a sigh. I missed her. Not that she wasn't just a phone call or a short drive away. But, I missed having her here in our house, running in and out, signing excitedly about this and that. Her quirky mannerisms. Her little girl giggle.

I was about to pick up the phone to give her a call when it rang. I jumped, startled, then smiled, thinking it was Michelle being telepathic (not that I believe in that). Calling me because I'd been thinking of her.

"Hello?" I said, ready to hear the TDD operator announce that Michelle was on the line. Instead, I got Evangeline Vesey's voice.

"Lizzie? Good morning. I didn't call too early, did I?"

"No . . ."

"Are you okay?"

"Yes, of course. I thought you were going to be Michelle."

"Oh. Well, I'm not."

"I know."

"The reason I'm calling is that I think we should meet earlier than originally planned. I think our Potluck Club should gather for its original intent. To pray together. The good Lord knows we need it now more than ever."

I nodded once for good measure. "Indeed we do, Evangeline. I can't help but say I've been thinking the same thing. Good for you for taking the initiative. What time did you have in mind?"

"Lisa Leann wanted us to meet at the boutique at 3:00 because of that interview we're supposed to give to some Colorado-based women's magazine—"

"*Women of Colorado*," I informed her, as though she needed reminding. Evangeline knew exactly who we were being interviewed by; she just didn't want to admit Lisa Leann had bought us some exposure with her tactics. "I'm not sure if they're an online publication or print."

"Whatever. So, I say a good half hour before that. Thirty minutes should give us plenty of time to stand before the Almighty and make our petitions known."

I pressed my lips together to keep from bursting into laughter. Evangeline has such a way of expressing her spirituality and understanding of theological issues. "I think you're right," I said. "I'll see you then."

I left my house with enough time to swing by the full-care facility now housing my mom, who suffers from Alzheimer's. Though she recognizes me as her mother rather than her daughter and is getting the best of care without me, I still feel it is my duty to check in on her as often as possible. Sometimes I help give her a bath, sometimes I help feed her, and sometimes I just sit and stare at the television with her. There have been days when we've talked a while, but in the end I am left feeling drained and depressed. These are the times I wish we'd said nothing at all.

I arrived at the facility to find the nursing and other medical staff gathered around the front station, gabbing like teenagers on the Monday after prom weekend. Seeing me enter, they all turned and headed toward me like a tsunami approaching a sleeping harbor town. I held up my hands in defense, worried that my mom had done something awful like running naked through the hallways.

They spoke at once:

"Mrs. Prattle, tell us everything!"

There's really nothing to tell at this point.

"Is Gianne as eccentric in real life as she appears on television?"

I wouldn't know. I haven't met her. Yet.

"Do you think you'll make it all the way to the finals?"

Only the good Lord knows.

"Donna Vesey told me there's going to be all kinds of security tonight at the church. How will Mrs. Westbrook ever get her mother to the party?" This from the charge nurse, Janie Pearson, who was on our exclusive invitation list.

Indeed. How will she?

"I'm just here to check on Mom," I said. My hands were still raised as though I were a bank clerk being held at gunpoint.

Janie stepped up then and raised her voice an octave. "Okay, boys and girls! That's enough! Back to work now."

Janie looked at me, large brown eyes batting long dark lashes. Janie was young—probably in her early thirties—and a little thing, but she was like a small keg of dynamite when it came to running her shift and its staff. "Sorry, Mrs. Prattle. Even I got caught up in the mayhem."

I nodded. "That's okay. How is Mom today?" We began walking toward my mother's room.

"She's doing just fine. Of course, in her condition, she could be in dire circumstances and not know it. She just seems happy to be here and happy to be alive."

"That's good," I said. "So, you'll be coming tonight?"

"Oh yes. Luckily for me I have a dress for the occasion. Last year we had a 1920s swing dance for our seniors. and I dressed the part of a perfect hostess."

I smiled. "I'm sure you'll be adorable. Fortunately the caterers wear the pink tux suits and our pink aprons Lisa Leann designed." I winced at the thought just as we stopped in front of Mom's room door, which was closed.

"Well, I think it's all going to be fun."

"I'm just not sure anyone is really going to get the theme. How many people have ever heard of *Animal Crackers*?"

"I have. My roommate in college was a film major."

Ah, my point exactly. "But if she weren't?"

Janie shrugged. "I can't really say, now can I? Anyway, who cares? It's a party, it'll get Marty and me out of the house for an evening, and you'll have lots of good food. Like I said, it'll be fun."

"I'll take your word for it." I turned toward the door, then back to Janie. "Oh, and speaking of food, be sure to sample the honey-and soy-glazed salmon." I winked at her. "I remember how much you love seafood, and this is especially delicious."

"I'll do that," Janie said, beaming. "I'll leave you to your mom, now. Stay as long as you'd like."

I glanced down at my watch. "I have to be at the church in a half hour, so I won't stay long."

"This early?" Janie asked, cocking one hip and crossing her arms.

"Yes. We have an interview with Women of Colorado at 3:30, and then the film crew arrives at 4:00. But the six of us are going to gather at 3:00 for prayer time."

Janie patted me on the shoulder. "Yes, ma'am," she said. "Don't forget to pray before this madness begins."

Madness was right. When I arrived at the church there was already a team of county and local law enforcement ready to direct traffic and keep the uninvited away. I frowned at the thought. I hated that Lisa Leann had given me a list of "only socially accept-able" people to invite. At the same time, I understood that some people would see this as their chance at stardom and hurt our chances of winning or simply disrupt the show entirely. I spied the cars of my fellow potluckers—including Lisa Leann's Lincoln that I assumed hadn't been parked long, seeing as she'd made a quick trip to the airport to get Nelson, and no doubt his camera, earlier in the day.

I parked next to Donna's Bronco and then slipped out of the car and began walking toward the social hall doors and the gathering of law enforcement. Standing in the middle of the uniformed finest was Sheriff Vernon Vesey, ready to take command. I waved to him and he waved back to me as I neared the building. I had my change of clothes on a coat hanger hooked to my index finger. It swung from side to side, almost joyous at having arrived for the evening's festivities, which were to begin at 7:00.

"Lizzie," Vernon said. "It's okay," he called out to the others. "She's one of the caterers."

"Your wife is here, I see," I said to him.

He grinned. "And ready to take control of her prayer group."

I nodded. "Well, that's how we got started," I said. "I'm just not sure whether to pray to win or pray to lose."

He laughed. "Evie feels the same way, I think. Pray God's will, I told her. A loss still gets you plenty of local exposure, but a win will give you national and international exposure."

"True." I pointed to a cargo van with rental car plates on the back. "Film crew?"

Vernon nodded. "Evangeline said if there was one thing you girls could be thankful for it's that the first show doesn't show the frantic mess of the preparation."

"Not this show, anyway. If we make it to New York, the whole world will see we're not totally sure of what we're doing." I gave a mock laugh.

"You know what you're doing," he said with a chuckle. "And if you don't, Lisa Leann will show you how to fake it till you make it, as they say."

I wrapped my arm around his beefy shoulder and squeezed. "Ah, Vernon. You always know just what to say to make me smile."

I entered the social hall then, ready to pray . . . ready to prepare . . . ready to serve God on national television if he so willed. Come what may, the Potluck Catering Club had a new purpose. And, maybe, so did this aging empty-nester.

6

Animal Crackers

The cameraman had followed my every move since barging in on our group's afternoon prayer time. Now, sitting across from me in the passenger's seat of my Ford Taurus, he said, "Relax, Mrs. Westbrook. Just pretend I'm not here."

I squeezed the steering wheel. "That's easy for you to say; your side of the camera doesn't show on national TV."

Mike Romano, one of the three cameramen who'd flown in to film our catered event, laughed. "You're doing just fine," he said as we pulled in front of my parents' modest condo nestled in a small grove of aspen. Mike, dressed in jeans and a black T-shirt with the words "The Great Party Showdown" emblazoned across his chest, got out of the car. He filmed me as I climbed the steep front steps to ring the bell. A moment later, Mother peeked out of her door and scowled. She was dressed in her favorite black pantsuit, topped with a floral shirt-jacket. "What's all this?"

"The camera crew got here early," I said. "They've been following us around all day, creating something they call 'a package.' I thought you were going to wear that dress we talked about."

Mother didn't budge from her spot halfway behind her door. "This *is* the Colorado high country, you know. I don't do dresses." She stared at Mike. "So, what's a package?"

I answered, "You know, a little personal interest clip, the back-story behind Team Potluck."

Mother stuck out her head a little further into the late sunlight. "Oh, so they want me to tell America what kind of daughter you are?"

"Ah . . . I guess."

Mother stepped outside and stared into the camera. "Let's just say, Vonnie's the kind of daughter who would embarrass her dear mother on television by dragging her to a piano recital. I could be here, at home, watching my own television, you know." Mother faced me and frowned. "Now that I've seen this camera, I'm tempted to stay put. What do I care about piano recitals? Mrs. Hempshaw's students are dreadful. Everyone in town knows this except the parents who pay her their good, hard-earned money."

I took Mother by the arm and began to guide her down the front steps while I lied my head off. "Mother, we've been through all this. This TV challenge came at the last minute, and Mrs. Hempshaw's piano recital was the only thing happening in town this week."

When we reached the bottom of the stairs, Mother pulled her arm from mine and placed her hand on her hip. "Fine, but you don't need me. You've already got your father helping in the kitchen. Why can't you keep me out of this?"

I held up my hands in exasperation, then snuck a look at the camera, hoping for sympathy. However, staring into the camera's unblinking lens only quickened my sense of stage fright. I turned back to Mother and said, "Don't make me spoil the surprise."

Mother tilted her chin defiantly. "What surprise would that be?"

So help me, I made my lie even bigger. "It's David. He's been learning to play the piano. He wanted to dedicate his piece to you tonight."

"Why didn't you just say so," Mother said, turning toward my car. "If this is about David, well, that's different."

I smiled at my deception. To think I'd been able to use David as a lure. I never would have thought such a thing possible, considering Mother had been the one responsible for his adoption to that Hollywood actress. Now, only a few months after Mother had met him for the first time, David had somehow managed to wrap her around his little finger. It was a grand moment, but I couldn't help but feel guilty. Here I was, lying to my mother on the way to church.

Soon enough, we pulled up in front of Grace Church. "Are we the last to arrive?" Mother asked, looking at the cars that filled the parking lot.

"Looks like we're running a tad late," I said. I sighed with a blend of pleasure and relief as David stepped out the front door of the church and rushed to open Mother's side of the car. He looked so handsome in his black tux with a pink bowtie and cummerbund that matched Team Potluck's aprons. Lisa Leann had insisted the guys wear all pink, but pink tuxes weren't available, even in Denver. Personally, I thought it was a lucky break. Besides, Wade, our mountain cowboy, claimed he'd walk away before he wore a pink tux on TV.

Mother latched on to David's arm, never dreaming our scheme was launched. "David, I hear you're playing the piano tonight."

David shot me a perplexed look while Mother said, "Don't be upset that I know. I can't tell you how proud I am."

I stepped out of the car and followed the pair into the foyer of the activity center, praying Mother would keep her cool. Another cameraman appeared as we walked inside. Lisa Leann, who was playing the role of *Animal Crackers*'s Mrs. Rittenhouse, seemed to materialize out of thin air. She was draped in a coral chiffon, floor-length dress that looked as if it could have come straight from the 1930s. Her red hair was styled with ripples and sparkling clips, which made her look like Mrs. Rittenhouse herself. She said, "Why, Mrs. Swenson, don't you look lovely."

My mother gave her the once over. "And just what are you supposed to be?"

"I'm playing hostess to the tea party tonight, after the recital," she said, going along with our rehearsed ruse. "But dear, I have a favor to ask you."

My mother wrinkled her forehead, her suspicion aroused. "What kind of favor?"

Lisa Leann pointed to the closed doors that led to the activity center, then to an African-styled litter, a small couch-in-a-box on poles surrounded by scarlet curtains.

"For the sake of our theme tonight, we're asking all the ladies to enter the room by way of our litter."

Mother stared at the fake tiger fur and plush pillows.

"You want to carry me in—inside a box—on those flimsy sticks?"

"Certainly," Lisa Leann purred. "It's quite safe. All the women have done it."

"Well, not me," Mother said. "I won't have any part of that."

I could have told Lisa Leann this was going to happen. Just as I resigned myself to walk Mother through the doors, David said, "Grandma, what if I was one of the guys who carried you inside? Would you trust me enough to do that for me?" He took her by the hand and smiled, then slowly tugged her to the awaiting litter. "Go ahead, Grandma. Climb in. Please?"

So help me if Mother didn't do as he instructed—a miracle if I ever saw one.

Suddenly, our team of tux-clad waiters, including Fred, Vernon, and Wade, joined David and lifted the poles onto their shoulders. The box, which hung by four stout ropes, gently swayed between them. "Forward march!" David said as Mother shrieked.

A young man's voice floated toward us. "And now, our guest of honor, Mrs. Inga Swenson."

The doors to the activity center opened as if by magic. Mother made her grand entrance. Just behind her, Donna and Evie carried a large birthday cake covered in lit sparklers.

"Oh my," she said as she gazed upon what only could have been Mrs. Rittenhouse's parlor. Our guests stood and applauded. Our women guests were smart in black dresses draped with long ropes of plastic pearls. The men looked elegant in their suits.

The room was ablaze with lights and the greenery we'd rented from a nursery in Denver. Hefty, hand-sketched windows of paper and foil were carefully stuck to the walls, mimicking their movie counterparts. A large, roughed-out painting of an Englishman on a white horse hung between two curtains just behind the head of our table. The painting was a contribution from the local high school art teacher, who'd done a great job making it look like the canvas that hung at the heart of *Animal Crackers*'s plot.

Five teen boys, dressed to look like butlers, greeted my mother. Their young voices sang a silly ditty from the movie and ended with a rousing chorus of, "Let's give her what she deserves, what she deserves!"

Our porters carefully settled the litter on the ground, and with the help of David, my mother climbed out. "What's all this?" she hooted, much to the delight of the crowd.

Nelson, Lisa Leann's son, stood before her, dressed like Groucho Marx. He wore round, wire-framed eyeglasses and sported heavy, black brows that were glued above his green eyes. His look was completed by a thick but very fake mustache. He's blond hair was dyed black and parted down the middle. He waggled a cigar between his fingers and said to the crowd, "Thank you for this magnificent washout, I mean turnout." Then to Mother, he said, "Do you mind if I don't smoke?"

I held my breath, wondering if she would catch the spirit of the fun from this icon she would certainly recognize. She smiled and said, "Of course not."

Nelson pointed to Donna and Evie holding the birthday cake. "Good, it looks like your cake is *already* smoking."

"Surprise!" the guests shouted in unison.

"What's all this?" Mother asked again as I rushed to her side and kissed her on the cheek. "Happy birthday, Mother."

She scowled. "It's not my birthday. You shouldn't rush me to get any older than I already am. My birthday's not for two more months."

Lisa Leann joined us in the spotlight and said, "Two months? That's close enough for reality TV," while the crowd tittered with laughter.

"Groucho" turned to Mother and, in a flirty Groucho sort of way, said, "You've got beauty, charm, and money! You have got money, haven't you? Because if you haven't, we can quit right now."

Bless her if she didn't laugh.

As our porters carried the litter back into the foyer, Lizzie swooped in and led Mother to the head of our lovely table. It was really a string of long tables pushed together, then covered with white linen. Its long center line blossomed with a lovely arrangement of mirrors, plastic pearls, greenery, and china.

Nelson turned to his mother and, in his best Groucho voice, said, "Why, you are one of the most beautiful women I've ever seen, and that's not saying much for you."

The teen playing the head butler cleared his throat. "Announcing our celebrity judge, Mr. Brant Richards!"

The party guests gasped, then stood and cheered as the judge who'd been chosen to observe our event made his entrance inside the litter. As Brant climbed out, Groucho wiggled his eyebrows and said, "Welcome! You must stay. Too bad you must be going."

The two men shook hands, then Groucho said, "I'd buy you a parachute if I thought it wouldn't open."

There was more laughter as Goldie directed Brant to a seat next to the guest of honor. A mistake if I ever saw one.

The butler clicked his heels together and announced, "Our next honored guest has arrived! Introducing Miss Gianne Gillian, the esteemed host of *The Great Party Showdown*." Gianne, dressed in a glittering gold dress, leaned out from behind the crimson curtain of the litter and waved at a room full of adoring fans.

So help me, Nelson swooned then recovered in time to help her stand. He waggled his cigar. "Ever since I met you, I swept you off your feet."

The audience applauded as Lizzie led Gianne to a seat next to Brant. Nelson turned to his mother, who said, "This leaves me speechless."

He replied with his Groucho flair, "Well, see that you stay that way."

The head butler proclaimed, "Announcing the professor."

The double doors swung open once again, and just like the movie, out came our own version of Harpo Marx, the silent, maniacal Marx brother. I squinted. *Is that Dad?*

Sure enough, there was my dad wearing a trench coat, a blond wig, and a stovepipe hat. When the butler reached for his coat, Dad revealed a peek at his undershirt and boxers. The crowd went wild, and Mother reddened. Seemingly unconcerned with the lecture he was sure to get, Harpo tooted his rubber-bulbed horn and slipped back into his trench coat before hurrying to sit in the only open chair next to Mother.

Mike Romano zoomed in for a close-up of my parents, capturing whatever pointed thing she was saying about Dad appearing in public in his underwear.

Soon, the girls and I, along with Wade and David, whisked out a crisp salad with raspberry dressing, honey- and soy-glazed salmon, hot rolls, twice-baked potatoes, and green beans with almond slivers, while our cheerful guests dined. Personally, I kept an eye on Brant.

Who knew what he might say to my mother, or what she might say to him in return. So far so good, but I wouldn't relax until this affair was over. The way I saw it, either Mother or Brant could erupt at any given moment. I didn't know the man, of course, but from what I'd seen of him, he was as grumpy as our guest of honor.

Before we served the cake, the kids from the drama class performed a skit. One of the boys, dressed like Chico Marx, sat down at the baby grand piano we'd rented. Our Chico wore an elfin-pointed hat over a black curly wig. His velveteen jacket was open over a striped button-down shirt and tie. Honestly, the kid, who was one of Mrs. Hempshaw's best piano students, played pretty well, though he seemed to have a little trouble ending his piece.

Nelson, still in his Groucho persona, strode to the piano. Chico looked up and said, "I can't think of the finish!"

Nelson replied, "That's funny, I can't think of anything else."

Just then, David, on his way to the kitchen, tried to brisk by Nelson. Nelson, wagging his eyebrows and cigar, reached for David's arm and spun him around. Nelson said, as if in deepest confidence, "I'm sick of these conventional marriages, aren't you? One woman and one man was good enough for your grandmother, but who wants to marry your grandmother? Nobody, not even your grandfather."

I was just serving Brant his piece of our banana cream birthday cake with fluffy cream cheese filling when he snorted his first laugh of the evening at the classic Groucho line.

My mother pounced on him. "Surely you're not laughing at me?"

"Why wouldn't I?" Brant coolly replied. "You're one of the funniest hicks this town has to offer."

Mother pushed her chair back and stood. "Well, I never," she said.

My dad leaned toward her. "Calm down, Inga," he said. "Let's not do anything rash."

"Yes," Brant said, balancing a big bite of cake on his fork. "Dearie, be a good little woman and mind your husband."

Two cameras zoomed in as Brant leaned in to take his first bite of heaven. Before he could taste the creamy delight, Mother whacked him in the back of his head with her black clutch, smashing the cake on his fork into his nose.

"Serves you right," Mother said. With that, she sat down again, looking a bit proud of herself. The partygoers froze with their forks in midair, unsure how to react.

Brant took his linen napkin and wiped the cake off the end of his nose. He turned to my mother. "I guess this is the kind of thing I can expect so far from civilization," he said.

Mother put her hands on her hips. "If you don't behave, young man, I'll treat you to a second helping of what you just got."

While Brant sulked, Mother began to actually enjoy herself. But the climax came when Brant stood up to give a toast, not knowing the "champagne" was actually sparkling apple juice we'd used to be in compliance with the church activity center rules. He said, "Here's to the worst meal and company I've had in eons" and tipped his glass back to inhale its contents.

He spewed the juice as soon as his senses alerted him to the fact he hadn't actually imbibed. When he grabbed his napkin and tried to wipe down his tux, he streaked it with icing.

Mother absolutely cackled and she stood and patted his arm. "What's the matter, dearie? Are clean air and clean living a bit much for you?"

Brant took another sip of his juice and smacked his lips as he lifted his glass high. "Here's to getting out of Dodge," he said.

Nelson swept in and in classic Groucho told Brant, "Don't look now, but there's one too many in this room, and I think it's you," as our guests tittered in laughter.

Brant shot back in perfect Groucho, "There's one thing I always wanted to do before I quit . . . retire! Good night, everyone." He sat his unfinished drink on the table, and while the room applauded his celebrity, he made his exit.

Later, when cleanup began, Mother held court in the foyer with a few of the well-wishers who remained while I grabbed a broom. Evie stopped to give my shoulders a squeeze. "When are you going to learn how to rein in that mother of yours?" she teased.

I blew a puff of air that made my bangs dance above my forehead, then with a Groucho flair, I picked up a carrot stick from a nearby tray of unused hors d'oeuvres and wiggled it like a cigar. "I had a perfectly wonderful evening, but this wasn't it."

Evie laughed. "That Brant Richards is a card, isn't he?" As I nodded, to my delight, Evie reached for her own carrot and said, "He may look like an idiot and talk like an idiot, but don't let that fool you. He really is an idiot."

Laughing, we realized too late that our little scene had been filmed by Mike, who was also the acting onsite producer. We both glared at him until he shrugged. "Sorry, ladies, just doing my job."

As soon as Mike turned away, Evie giggled. "Good news, Vonnie. It looks like we won't be going to New York after all."

"Wouldn't that be a relief," I said. "Million dollars or not."

Goldie

7

Warming Worry

Since the filming of the show the previous Thursday evening, my job as legal secretary and receptionist for Chris Lowe had been more about answering my own phone calls than his. So far, he'd been kind about it. Including, I might add, that when the whole crazy thing started, I'd brought him a copy of the contract I'd signed with Nelson and he'd graciously gone over every jot and tittle.

"Yep," he'd said, eyes twinkling behind reading glasses. "You're locked in like a kid under curfew."

I'd frowned for effect. "Chris . . . as long as we're here in Summit View, there should be no problem, but I don't know what I'd do about this office if we go to New York and—"

Chris raised his hand to stop me. "Think nothing of it. Jenna is home from college right now. I'm sure she'll be happy to relieve you for a few days."

Jenna, Chris's daughter, taught me everything she knew about this job before leaving for college just a few semesters previous. Since then—and since the death of my father in the spring of this year—I'd taken a few online courses, broadening my mind and my skills, wanting to be the best for Chris. He'd offered me a job back when I had no skills to speak of. He repeatedly told me he hadn't regretted it, and I felt confident in those words. Still, I wasn't sure I was ready to give up the comfort zone of my office for the glamour of New York City.

Lately the office had been about anything *but* the law practice. Family from out of town—mostly my Georgia relatives—called during work hours because "Six o'clock is suppertime, and anything after that and we're in bed." They didn't want to disturb me, they said, during "family time." Funny, they didn't mind disturbing me at work.

Add to them the reporters who called. Even *People* magazine's editors called—but mostly . . .

My office phone rang, startling me. "Good morning," I said, glancing at the digital clock nearby for clarity as to the hour. Yes, it was still morning: 11:30 to be exact. "Chris Lowe's office," I finished.

"Mom?"

"Olivia?"

"What are you doing?"

I sat straight in my chair. "Why, is something wrong? Something with the baby?" My daughter had given birth two months previous to an adorable baby girl, rounding out her little family to four. "Big Brother Brook," as her oldest had come to be known, had taken the disappointment at not having another boy to play with in stride and had come to practically worship the cherub Olivia and her husband Tony named Ena, an old Celtic name I'd found in a book of unusual baby names. It still floored me that my typically stubborn, do-it-myself-thank-you-very-much daughter took my suggestion and ran with it.

"Ena is fine. Brook is fine too, before you ask. Listen, Tony took the day off from work today and—"

"Why? Is Tony sick?"

"Mom! What is this, twenty questions? Actually, we're getting TiVo installed today, so Tony's hanging around until the technician comes and, while he's waiting, keeping busy doing some jobs on my honey-do list."

I smiled. Tony was a fine husband. The finest. I was so proud my daughter had found such a man and married him. "So why are you calling, then?"

"Actually, Tony suggested you and I go out to lunch today. You don't have plans, do you?"

I rolled my eyes. If I knew Olivia—and I do—she was up to something. My daughter, as much as I love her, works hard to make sure I'm on the straight and narrow at all times. Last year, when her father and I separated for a few months, she'd kindly opened her home to me. But when I'd gotten a job and then my own apartment, she frowned in disapproval. When a man—a friend of Chris's—showed interest in me, she'd nearly gone into cardiac arrest.

My daughter is more the morality police with me than I ever was with her. *Ever.*

Not that I ever had to be. Nor did she; not really.

"No, I don't have plans. I take my lunch at noon." I glanced at the clock again.

"Okay. Want to meet at Higher Grounds Café?"

I nodded. "I'll see you at five after."

"Good. See ya then."

I started to hang up, then brought the phone back to my mouth. "And Olivia?"

"Yeah?"

"You're buying."

Before I left for lunch I received a phone call from Lisa Leann—the winner of Most Calls to Goldie. This was our second of the day. "Goldie, what time will you be at the church? I'm asking because

I think the girls should arrive early. Way early. Much earlier than everyone else."

"Whoa, Lisa Leann," I said, laughing. "Take a breath."

"I'm here now," she said.

"You're where now?"

"At the church. Keep up, girlfriend."

"Why are you at the church?"

"Because the big screen TV has been delivered, and I want to make certain the chairs are set up the way I envision them."

The big screen TV. Hmmm. This whole thing was beyond anything I'd ever seen or heard of. With the whole town behind us, hoping for a win after tonight's show, the board of deacons at Grace Church had voted to rent the biggest big screen TV and bring cable into the social hall, thereby allowing all of Summit View to watch the show together. The very same room where we'd served up Mrs. Rittenhouse's party would be the setting for watching Team Potluck, along with three other catering companies from across the country, vie for the million dollar prize, as the other four teams still in the competition would compete the following week.

A familiar fluttering returned to the pit of my stomach. I'd felt it the first time immediately after Lisa Leann told us about the show, the evening we were at Vonnie's house. It had hardly left me since. *Oh Lord, oh Lord, oh Lord,* I prayed. *I've never been to New York. I'm not cut out for New York. Tall buildings . . . subways . . . pickpockets. Please don't make me go. Pleeeaaassssseeeee don't make me go.*

I sounded like Jonah sailing away from Nineveh.

"Goldie, are you listening to me?" Lisa Leann's voice brought me back to reality.

"I'm listening." I looked at the desk clock. It was noon. "Lisa Leann, I have to meet Olivia at Higher Grounds in five minutes so I have to go. But . . . what time do you want me there?"

"The show starts at 8:00. People will start coming in at 7:00 to eat. Oh, and again, don't worry about the fact that you've not been at the shop helping cook this morning. Donna couldn't make it either. But the rest of us were there and we'll have plenty for the town to eat."

"That's nice of you. Lisa Leann, I have to—"

"Go. I know. Arrive by 6:30. Did I say that already? That will give us time to make sure everything is set and ready to go. Food wise, anyway." She coughed out a laugh. "I'm as nervous as a cat! You?"

I stood, pulled open the bottom left-hand drawer where I kept my purse, and yanked it out. "Like nobody's business. And I'm late. See you tonight."

Donna was coming out of Higher Grounds as I was stepping up to the front door. "Hey, Goldie," she said. She flashed her cell phone, still clutched in her right hand, as though she were showing her badge. "I just got off the phone with Lisa Leann. She said you were headed this way."

I smiled at the pixie deputy I'd grown to love like my own over the years. She and Olivia had been school chums. They'd gone from Brownies to Juniors and finally Cadets in Girl Scouts. They'd been in youth group at church together. I fleetingly thought of Olivia, already seated in a booth beyond the glass front windows of the café, and her settled life versus Donna's with her dangerous job, late-night hours, and the men who wondered which of them might finally win her heart. Why didn't she just pick someone and get married?

"Hey, Donna. I'm meeting Olivia."

Donna shut the door as she stepped onto the sidewalk, thereby blocking my entry. "Yeah. I just spoke with her. So, Goldie, what time'll you be at the church?"

"Lisa Leann said 6:30."

"Yeah, that's what she told me too. Anyway . . . thing is, Goldie . . ." Donna shifted her weight until she stood with her feet about twelve inches apart. "What I'm wondering is . . . what chance do you think we have here? Of winning, I mean."

I glanced toward the window, then back at Donna. "I don't

know, Donna. I don't know much about the other contestants. Do you?"

"I did some research on the Internet. There's some pretty good teams out there, and they've been geared up to win for quite a while. Lisa Leann sort of sprung this on us, you know?"

"I'm sure they'll all beat us, then. All we need is for three of the other teams to get more votes than us tonight, and if that happens, we'll never have to board that plane to JFK." I pointed to the door. "I really have to get inside," I said.

Donna looked behind her, then back to me. "Oh! Yeah, Olivia is waiting for you. Sorry. I guess I'm just a little stressed about all this." She smiled broadly. "And you know me, Goldie. I don't stress easily."

That much was true. If Donna was stressed, the rest of us were doomed. I gave her shoulder a quick pat, then said, "You'll be fine. We all will. This time tomorrow all this will be a memory, and then life will go back to normal in Summit View." I sighed in anticipation at the thought. "Now, I've really got to get inside."

We said our good-byes, and I hurried through the door and to the table where Olivia waited none too patiently. A moment later we gave the waitress two orders for captain's stew with a side order of cornbread, which we'd split. The waitress said, "Be right back with your drinks," and left, leaving the two of us alone in a roomful of people. I smiled at my beautiful child as I unfolded my napkin and placed it in my lap. "Lunch without the babies," I said. "What will we do?"

Olivia returned the smile. "I know. I was thrilled when Tony made the offer. How often do we get to do this?"

"Not often enough."

"Ena slept through the night last night," she said. "First time."

"Oh?" *Small talk*, I thought. *She's as good at it as her father.* "What time did you put her down?"

"About eleven. She didn't utter a sound until six this morning."

The waitress returned with our drinks, and I took a hurried sip of my water. It barely made it down my dry throat. "Seven hours. You were never so good for me."

Olivia smiled again, then leaned over, pressing her forearms against the table. "Mom."

"What, Olivia? Go ahead and say or ask whatever it is you're going to say or ask. Because I know you didn't ask me to lunch to tell me about Ena sleeping all night. You could have done that on the phone."

My daughter looked down, then raised her green eyes to me. I was caught, as always, by the adorable swirl of red curls that begins in a cowlick at the crown of her head and ends in a sweep near the top of her forehead, kissing the tips of her ears. "You know me so well."

"I do indeed."

She squared her shoulders. My, my, my, but wasn't this going to be a good one. "Mom, can you explain to me exactly what is going to happen if you win tonight? I mean, will you actually go to New York City? And then what? Will you be running around the city with cameras following you everywhere? I'm just trying to get a grip on this."

I scooted my chair up a notch and discreetly cleared my throat. "Here's what I know," I began, then paused when the waitress returned with our order and placed it before us. We said a quick blessing, and I nodded for Olivia to start eating while I explained. "There are eight teams left in the competition," I said. I picked up my spoon and pushed the thick stew around the bowl. "Four of us will be seen tonight—you're coming to the church, aren't you?"

Olivia nodded; her mouth was full of food.

"The three teams who get voted through tonight will have next week off as four other teams compete. The winners from that show and the winners from our show will then compete in New York City." I shoved meat and vegetables into my mouth.

Olivia took a sip of her "un-diet cola," as she called it. Tall and slender, Olivia has never had to worry about her weight, even when pregnant, so no diet anything for her. I was grateful she'd not had to watch every calorie like her mother. "And what do you think your chances are tonight? Of placing in the top three?"

I put another bite of the stew in my mouth, shaking my head as I swallowed. "Slim and none. Donna was just telling me outside that the other teams have been gearing up for this for some time, and of course we haven't." I sipped at my drink, then added, "And I hear the other teams are strong too, and since the celebrity judge hated us, I'm sure we'll slip into last place and be eliminated."

Olivia visibly relaxed. "Good." Her eyes widened. "Sorry, Mom, but I have to tell you, I've been worried."

"About what? About your old lady actually winning something?" I frowned at her. "That's not very nice, Olivia."

"Oh no, no, no. Not about your winning. About you winning and leaving Dad here. Alone."

I felt the hair on my head bristle on my scalp. Did Olivia know something about her father I didn't? Since we'd ended our separation and returned to our marriage and to counseling, I'd not had any reason to be suspicious of Jack having another affair. Another in a long line of affairs, to be more precise. "Are you trying to tell me something, Olivia? Because if you are, just come out and say it. Do you know something I should know?"

It took a moment for understanding to register on my daughter's face. When it did, she reddened. "Mom, no. No, nothing like that, I promise. I just . . . I'm worried about Dad."

"In what way?"

She shrugged, dipping her head to the right and setting her spoon on the table next to the bowl of stew. "He hasn't looked well lately. He's out of breath when we talk on the phone, and when I see him I think he looks pale. Tony says I have too much Southern in me and I should quit worrying, that Dad is fine. But . . ."

I had to giggle at her "Southern" comment. Yes, we Southerners had pretty much cornered the market on worry. It's a way of life with us. "Tony is right," I told her. "Not to worry. Dad is fine. He had a physical last month after the school year ended, and the doctor proclaimed him a fine specimen for his age."

Olivia's eyes misted with tears. I reached across the table and clasped her hand. "Honey, what is it?" I asked her.

"I don't know, Mom. It's just that . . . with you losing *your* father a few months ago, I haven't been able to help but think what it would be like to lose Dad. In spite of the things he's done, I love him so much." Her voice cracked.

I patted her hand and gave her my best Mother-knows-best smile. "Not to worry, Livvy. Dad's fine, I'm fine, and we're fine." I sat back in my chair. "Now, let's talk about how we're going to celebrate Team Potluck's loss tonight. Just you and me. What's say we hit the outlet malls this weekend for a new outfit? My treat."

8

High-Altitude Cooks

A line of parked cars flowed out of the lot and down both sides of the street outside Grace Church. I pulled behind David's black Mazda 3 and got out. As I started past his car, his door popped open and he stepped out into the summer evening still dressed in his paramedic uniform. "Long time no see," he teased, as we'd both just come from working an accident.

"How's old man Carpenter?" I asked as he fell into step with me.

"He definitely had a heart attack behind the wheel. He was stable when Randall and I wheeled him into the ER."

"Good. It could have been a lot worse, especially if that railing hadn't held."

We hurried through the church parking lot, squinting against the glare of two hundred setting suns reflecting on the windshields surrounding us. "I'll drop by the hospital later to check in on him," I said.

David gave me one of his famous smiles. "Mind if I go with you?"

I smiled back. "Why not?"

"How late are we?" David asked as we ducked into the church.

I checked my watch and tugged on his arm. "Not a minute to spare, come on."

We pushed through the double doors of the activity center. Heads turned to stare as light applause broke out. I was glad the lights were too dim for the crowd to see the flame of celebrity burning my cheeks.

Abruptly, the crowd turned to gawk at the huge flat-screen TV, which was surrounded by greenery and speakers. Wade caught my eye as he stood and waved. "Over here!"

David and I hurried over and squeezed down the aisle to where Wade and his twelve-year-old cousin, Pete, were sitting. As I made my way to the saved seats, I could see most of Team Potluck sitting in the front row. It was too late to join them; Pastor Kevin Moore was already climbing the platform steps to stand next to the wide screen. He was dressed in jeans and a pink tee with the words "Go Team Potluck" printed in large letters. (The T-shirt was, no doubt, a gift from Lisa Leann.)

Microphone in hand, he said, "Friends and neighbors, we're glad you could join our family at Grace in supporting our very own Team Potluck. Most of you know Team Potluck is trying to raise money to help our church. This couldn't have come at a better time. This may, in fact, be God's provision for keeping our land and building from bankruptcy and becoming a new condo development."

So help me if my jaw didn't drop. I had no idea we were playing to meet a *real* need. Not that a youth wing wasn't a real need, but this bankruptcy thing put an entirely different spin on this contest.

More applause broke out as an electric guitar wailed the theme music for *The Great Party Showdown* through the TV's surround sound speakers. The show was starting! Pastor Kevin said, "I'd wish

Team Potluck good luck, if I believed in luck. Instead, I'll wish them God's favor. Say a little prayer, everyone, then pull out your cell phones and call in your votes at the end of the show."

My fellow Potluckers, all in matching pink tees, stood, then turned and waved at the crowd as the room filled with thunderous applause. I kept my seat as Wade leaned over and whispered into my ear, "Nervous?"

I nodded as I tugged off my coat. Pete peered around Wade and waved. "Hi, Donna."

I was struck by the twinkle in his blue eyes. I was proud of how well he'd done since I'd helped remove him and his siblings from the home of his abusive dad and still-missing mama. I'd been able to observe Pete's progress whenever I stopped by Wade's trailer for a bowl of his chili. Much to my delight, Pete had gone from an insecure kid who'd relied on the art of shoplifting to feed his siblings, to a young man with a future that would not likely include prison time. Wade was clearly doing a great job with the boy.

Wade patted my hand. "This torture will be over in an hour, then maybe we can all get back to our ordinary lives. Don't you hope?"

I grinned. "Well, yeah, at least that's what I was praying before I heard about the church's debt."

Wade hesitated. "Wanna grab a shake at Higher Grounds with me and Pete after the program?"

David leaned into our conversation. "Sorry, but Donna and I have a date to run back to the hospital to check on an accident victim."

I gave David a sideways glance. "Come to think of it, I might have to put both offers on hold. I'm going to be stuck here, waiting for the producer to call Lisa Leann with the results."

Wade nodded. "Then Pete and I will bring the shakes and wait with you."

"Pick up one for me too," David whispered just as Gianne Gillian appeared on the screen. She was glowing in a ruby red sequined cocktail dress with a plunging neckline. With pure enthusiasm, she said, "After last week, gone but not forgotten are the two teams that placed last in America's vote. Good-bye to Moon Beam Team from Sedona, Arizona." The studio audience clapped as a clip of a group of ladies wearing dangling crystal earrings and serving strange tofu dishes appeared on the screen. "Also gone is the all-American Team Gators from Gainesville, Florida." The clapping resumed during a clip of a team of tipsy college boys making a big vat of French fries and shoveling them into a large paper-towel-lined aluminum pan.

Gianne flashed back onto the screen. "Tonight, while four of the eight remaining teams take the week off, we've flown our film crew and a celebrity judge to party on location with our four featured teams, starting with Team Batter Up from New York City." Appearing on the screen were five men dressed in NY Yankee baseball uniforms, serving gourmet hot dogs to a black-tie crowd that included *The Great Party Showdown* judge Isabelle Salazar as well as their special guest, "the Donald." Trump took a bite of his hot dog and pointed at one of the members of Team Batter Up before announcing, "You're hired!"

Gianne continued with her voiceover. "Team Tex Mex of San Antonio, Texas." The set pulsated with salsa music as six beauties twirled their long yellow skirts. They smiled while they served plates of enchiladas and black beans to happy, toe-tapping Texans while celebrity judge Teresa Juliette sipped from what looked like a Texas-sized glass of iced tea.

"Team Café Mocha from Seattle, Washington." Six women dressed in mocha brown uniforms topped with creamy white aprons grinned as they held up steaming hot coffees topped with a scoop of chocolate ice cream. The camera zoomed in to reveal young business professionals at a sit-down dinner of soups and grilled chicken salad. Observing the party was our judge, Brant

Richards, with another one of his sour looks plastered across his face. Man, he got around last week.

Gianne said, "Last but not least is Team Potluck of Summit View, Colorado." The gathered crowd cheered and the TV scene changed to show Nelson wiggling his press-on brows as he sampled our twice-baked potatoes. He said in his best Groucho, "I'm not crazy about reality, but it's still the only place to get a decent meal."

As Nelson hammed for the camera, our elegant guests dined in the background while our team scurried to serve them.

The camera recaptured Gianne's sparkling beauty. "America, which of these four teams will you ban from our Great Party Showdown's food fight? Stay tuned to vote at the end of this show."

In the minutes that followed, the show zipped by. I have to say I was impressed with the other teams and their "packages" featuring various team members. I was especially awed by Calista Cruz, a raven-haired beauty from Team Tex Mex. She was a single mom bent on bettering life for herself and her young sons. She and her team were planning to use some of the prize money to help a local women's shelter. Then there was Team Café Mocha. Those women hoped to use the million dollar grand prize to give their children "the educations they deserve." Team Batter Up wanted to study cooking in Paris and around the world. I had to laugh as I whispered to David, "Do chefs in Paris teach the fine art of cooking gourmet hot dogs?"

His shoulder leaned into mine. "Well, if that's all Team Batter Up can cook—they're probably ready to learn something new."

After each team's clip played, the celebrity judges talked about their experience with the team then gave that experience a one to five star rating. Team Batter Up and Team Tex Mex did pretty well, getting four stars each. Though Brant gave Team Café Mocha only two stars. But each time the judges rated the contestants, Gianne reminded the viewers, "Our judges don't get the final say—you do, America; but only if you vote."

My nerves were splitting by the time Team Potluck appeared on the last segment of the show. I sat back, trying not to hold my breath as I watched our team share a prayer together, followed by Vonnie coaxing her mother into her car, then seeing our dinner guests stand on their feet to welcome Mrs. Swenson, our birthday girl.

The church activities center reverberated with laughter as the crowd watched Mrs. Swenson's shocked face when we yelled, "Surprise!"

More laughter followed Nelson's Groucho shenanigans, especially when it came to his interaction with the celebrity judge, Brant Richards.

Then, the camera focused on me, busy waiting tables until Nelson/Groucho appeared on the screen as I worked in the background. Nelson wagged his cigar between his fingers. "It appears our deputy has a dilemma." He stared into the camera and raised his brows. "Who are you going to believe? Me or your own eyes?"

The cameras zoomed in on me getting an extra friendly hug from waiter Wade. That shot was followed by a close-up of Wade saying, "Sure, I'm sweet on Donna, mainly because we have history. We were childhood sweethearts, until . . ." His voice faded without completing his thought as the camera panned back, revealing a lovely Gianne holding a microphone close to her full, pouty lips. "Ohhhhh . . . poor baby. Why aren't you two together now?"

Wade looked like a sheepish Matthew McConaughey. "It's complicated. But I'm working on it."

The room filled with hoots and shouts of "Go Wade!" while I slid down my chair. Wade leaned to whisper in my ear. "Sorry, Donna, Gianne promised me my comments were off the record." But before I could scold him, the camera panned back to Gianne, who was saying, "But the word is, Wade isn't the only eligible bachelor vying for the deputy's affection." I put my hands over my face and watched the screen through spread fingers as the camera caught David giving me a look of pure adoration.

I was stunned.

Before I could react, the theme song from *Hollywood Nightly* blared, and I felt David slide down his chair too. "They wouldn't," he said under his breath.

Hollywood Nightly host Kendra Goodall replaced Gianne's face. "This just in, rumor is Hollywood's most eligible bachelor, the adopted son of Harmony Harris, American's musical sweetheart of the fifties, is making an appearance as a waiter on *The Great Party Showdown*, the summer season's top reality show." The screen filled with a moving image of David wearing his black tux and pink bowtie waiting tables at our *Animal Crackers* birthday party.

"As a child, Harris became a media darling because he was the subject of much speculation as to his true parentage. It had been presumed he was the son of Harmony and one of her leading men, until last year when it was learned he was actually the biological son of nurse Vonnie Westbrook and her late husband, Joseph Ray Jewell, a medic killed in Vietnam.

"Though Harris is now living in Colorado, he's still considered to be one of the most eligible bachelors in Hollywood, as he was the sole heir to Harmony's estate. Even so, it's rumored he traded Hollywood fame and fortune for his birth mother and an ambulance." The screen showed David giving Vonnie a kiss on the cheek, then switched to David lifting an accident victim on a gurney into his awaiting ambulance as the voiceover continued, "And the love of his life."

The camera pulled back from the accident scene to reveal me, dressed in my sheriff's uniform, holding hands with the accident victim while David gave me a look of affection. *Wait! Wasn't that Mr. Carpenter from this afternoon?*

I shook my head. *Hollywood Nightly* hadn't wasted any time getting a crew to town to film David's business. How had they escaped my notice? Unless they'd gotten the footage from the *Denver News* team stationed here to report from the high country.

"The paparazzi are without conscience," David muttered in response to my gasp.

Gianne's face replaced Kendra's. Gianne looked into the camera and batted her baby blue eyes. "Hey, David, if things don't work out with the deputy . . ." She stretched out her pinkie and thumb and held it to her ear like a phone receiver before mouthing the words, "Call me."

You could hear a few uncomfortable giggles from the crowd as a voice rang out, "Donna, who ya gonna pick?"

I sank lower in my seat. Was that Dwayne, the cook from Higher Grounds Café? I frowned. *No doubt.*

"Not you, Dwayne, that's for certain," a voice that sounded like reporter Clay Whitefield's replied from somewhere nearby.

The crowd's laughter faded as the screen suddenly portrayed several scenes from our surprise birthday party—including a close-up of Vonnie's mother swatting our celebrity judge, Brant Richards, in the head with her purse. Next, as the crowd howled, we saw a close-up of Brant with cake smashed up his nose.

But just as our segment was closing, a close-up of me filled the screen. Gianne was asking, "So how badly do you want to win this thing?"

"Well, if we weren't playing for a good cause, I'd turn to the camera and say—don't vote for Team Potluck."

I could hear Lisa Leann choke as the sound effect of crickets played through the speakers. But the moment quickly passed, and soon Brant was in front of a live studio audience, bashing our team. "In my professional opinion, Team Potluck of Hickville, Colorado, deserves zero stars, but as a courtesy—I'm *giving* them one."

The next thing I knew, Gianne was explaining that the phone lines were now open for voting. Around me I could see members of the crowd pull out their cell phones as the dialing began in earnest.

While the crowd dialed, Lisa Leann took the mic to thank our friends while Wade and Pete slipped out to pick up the milk shakes. As the crowd began to dwindle, David and I quietly discussed his appearance on the show. "I just feel bad," I said. "The show used your celebrity just to get more publicity."

"I feel bad for you too." David shrugged. "You were singled out because of me."

I smirked. "Yeah, come to think of it."

"I can't say I'm surprised. I should never have signed my real name on those contracts."

I felt my brows arch as I leaned forward. "Stop. You didn't sign a contract too, did you?"

"Yeah, Nelson asked me, and I have to admit, I signed it without reading the fine print."

"Wait! That means if the team wins, you could get sent to New York with me and the girls."

David nodded and folded his arms across his chest. "Well, maybe I'd like to go. Maybe I'd like to keep an eye on you."

Wade, who had walked up behind us, suddenly cleared his throat. We turned to see him, decked in his jeans, denim jacket, and cowboy boots, holding a drink carrier full of shakes. "Well, Donna. I have a confession to make too." Wade sat down with Pete, then handed us our frosty, hand-blended drinks. He took a deep breath. "I've signed one of Nelson's contracts myself."

"You didn't! The girls and I never realized . . ."

"Don't worry," Wade said. "If the show asks me, I'd love to go to New York City." He glanced at David. "In fact, I wouldn't dream of letting you go without me."

"But what about Pete?"

Pete answered for himself. "I'll get to stay with Aunt Katherine. It'll be cool to be with my little brothers and sister for a few weeks."

Wade grinned. "See, no worries. If we get voted through, it's all arranged."

But I was worried. For starters, I couldn't afford to take so much time off from work. Sure, I could handle a week or two, but according to the show's schedule, I could get stuck in New York for up to four weeks with two lovesick men.

Both were important to me, but this was too much pressure. My own heart was just healing from the wounds of my past. I was beginning to understand God's love for me in a way that had started to help me forgive myself. I didn't think I was near ready to have my love life analyzed on national TV.

I sighed. What I'd really like to do was to dig a snow cave up on St. Mary's Glacier and hide out for a couple of years with my Bible. Then, maybe, I'd be ready for this challenge.

My cell rang and I picked up, expecting to hear my dad chime in his opinion on the night's program. "Hello?"

When I heard only silence, I checked the caller ID. It read "Private."

Probably a reporter with a bad connection, I mused. I clicked out of the call. Lisa Leann caught my eye. "Stay close, Donna, I think we'll hear from New York in the next few minutes."

An hour and a half later, the producer called with the news. Lisa Leann grabbed her phone on the first ring, then held the mic so we could hear her side of the conversation. "Kat? Is that you? How did the vote go?"

Seconds later Lisa Leann squealed, "We got the top vote? You're kidding!"

Our friends applauded while I tried not to groan out loud. Lisa Leann continued. "Right. Yes, ma'am, Team Potluck is headed to New York City! I'm looking forward to getting your fax with the details. . . . Ah, what do you mean, there are a few surprises?"

9

Happy Trail Mix

Lisa Leann made the executive decision that she and one other potlucker should go to New York City by the week's end. "We need to see the lay of the land," she said to the group as we gathered in the boutique on Wednesday afternoon. "Has anyone spent significant time in the Big Apple?" She crooked the index and middle fingers of both hands for emphasis around "Big Apple." She stood near the picture window overlooking Main Street and a glorious Summit View summer afternoon. Looking past her, I caught glimpses of passersby on the sidewalk. Even the summer tourists were enthralled by what was happening here; they stopped to gawk at the boutique, their expressions wide-eyed, their fingers pointing. Fortunately for us, Lisa Leann was unaware of the adulation from beyond the panes of glass behind her.

We all shook our heads. Lizzie raised her hand from her place next to Goldie on the settee. "Samuel and I honeymooned there." Her fingers dropped to lightly touch a delicate gold necklace. "But that was a lot of years ago," she concluded.

Goldie leaned over to look at the necklace. "That's lovely," she said. "Did you get it there?" When Lizzie nodded, Goldie straightened and looked at Lisa Leann. "I can't go early," she said. "I've already asked for time off, and Chris has agreed to bring Jenna in for a week while he looks for help from a temp service. But there's no way I'm asking for more time."

"Count me out," Donna said. She and I sat side by side in matching velvet Queen Anne chairs with a rosewood marble-top table between us. "Dad is nearly frantic, what with having to rearrange the work schedule and handing overtime to some of the other deputies. The county is not too keen on paying overtime, let me tell you."

I inched a finger up in the air. "I can vouch for that," I said.

Lisa Leann attempted to open her mouth, but Vonnie spoke before she could get a word out. "Do you have someone in mind, Lisa Leann? To go with you?"

Lisa Leann's shoulders relaxed. "I do, thank you very much, Vonnie." She turned her baby blues toward me. "I think Evangeline and I should go. We'll get familiar with the city, find out where the best suppliers are—"

"Me?" I said just as Donna piped in, "Can't you just do that on the Internet?"

Lisa Leann shook her head. "Not adequately," she said. "Ladies, this is too important to cut any corners. We're doing this for the church, let's not forget."

"Me?" I repeated. "Why me? What did I do?"

"Yes, you, Evangeline Vesey, and stop acting like it's a root canal. Besides, I've already spoken to Vernon about it, and he approves of your going. I told him all the reasons why you should be there with me, and he agreed wholeheartedly. Now, if everyone will hush and let me talk, I'll explain a little more . . ."

"You said yes?" I said to my husband later that evening. "Why would you do that without asking me first?" We were in our bedroom, my suitcase spread wide on top of the bed. I was already packing—me on one side of the bed, Vernon watching from the other—though our flight was not until Friday. Very early Friday morning, to be exact. Lisa Leann had made the reservations before I'd left the boutique, choosing a nonstop flight that would get us there around 2:30 in the afternoon, what with the time difference.

"I could see her point in your going with her." Vernon shrugged then crossed his arms across his chest.

"Which was?"

"Well, she certainly can't go alone, for one. And, as she put it, you are practical and level-headed and can help find some of the best supply deals in the city, which the show will judge you on, in part."

I turned from the bed toward my dresser and opened my unmentionables drawer. I pulled several pair of precisely folded panties from the stack next to the neatly folded bras, then placed them in the suitcase. "I wonder if any of the other winning teams will think like Lisa Leann and arrive early too." My shoulders sank. "But what gets me is this will be six days more away from you."

Vernon chuckled as I gave him my best pout. He came from around the bed then and wrapped me in his arms and kissed my cheek. "Ah, Evie-girl," he said. "Don't you worry. I'll fly out for next week's show."

I looked at him sideways. "You will? You promise?"

"Did you really think I'd miss my best girl's New York City television debut? Fred and Jack and I have already talked about it."

"What about Samuel?" I turned slightly to look at him face to face.

"Samuel too." Then Vernon shook his head. "Not sure about Henry Lambert, though."

I raised a brow. "Something is not altogether right in the Lambert household, I'm afraid."

"Something you don't know about?" Vernon asked me.

Know? "Is there something I *should* know about?" I mean, other than Lisa Leann's old affair . . .

But Vernon looked stupefied. "What?"

I frowned. "Vernon Vesey, do you know something within the Lambert household I don't know about?"

Vernon laughed. "That'll be the day. What I was intimating—and apparently not too well—was that if you don't know, then no one but Lisa Leann and Henry know." He waved a hand at me. "Never mind; just go back to your packing. Your luggage is blocking my side of the bed."

Friday, at a little after 4:30 in the morning, Lisa Leann and I met at the Delta ticket counter at Denver's international airport. Lisa Leann had already printed our boarding passes online but managed to get them exchanged for front row seats she said would give us more room to stretch our legs during the long flight. We rolled our luggage to the friendly folks at the TSA baggage check, then proceeded toward the train. Minutes later we were walking down Concourse C, each with a cup of Starbuck's coffee, and toward Gate 48, which was, naturally, the very last gate on the right. While my shoulder nearly broke under the weight of my purse (filled with a couple of books to read, a pad of paper for jotting down notes as thoughts and ideas came to mind, and the new digital camera Vernon gave me the night before), Lisa Leann pulled a spiffy pink and white polka dot carry-on case behind her. It was one third of a matching set, the rest having been checked into baggage. I glanced down at it several times before stating the obvious. "Lisa Leann, that suitcase is 'you' to a T."

Lisa Leann grinned at me. "I bought it online," she said. "Tuesday night, as soon as I got home. Overstock.com. Had them overnight it."

"I suppose you just couldn't help yourself," I said.

"Nope," she answered. "Sure couldn't."

"So what do you have in there? A change of clothes? Books? Spy equipment?"

"Ha-ha. Yes to the clothes and the books. And my laptop and some trail mix I made last night just for us in case we get hungry."

I was already hungry. "Will they serve us a meal, do you think?"

"Only if we were flying first class. And we are not flying first class." She winked at me. "Not yet, anyway."

We boarded the plane a few minutes after six and got settled in our coach seats. Lisa Leann insisted on sitting by the window, which was fine with me. At fifty-eight years of age, I knew I would need to sprint to the lavatory more than once in the four hours it would take to get to JFK airport, so I happily took the aisle seat.

Lisa Leann tucked her carry-on behind her legs, wiggled around a bit, then fastened her seat belt. Knowing she'd flown a lot more than I, I followed her lead and placed my purse behind my legs as well. It was then the flight attendant stepped over and said, "Oh, ladies, we'll have to put your bags overhead as this is bulkhead seating. Once we're safely in the air, you can retrieve them if you need to."

"But, this is my laptop," Lisa Leann said. "I was going to do a little work during the flight."

The flight attendant—an attractive woman named Sunny—smiled pleasantly, then repeated herself as though she were speaking to a kindergartener. "Yes, ma'am, I understand. But until we are safely in the air . . ."

I reached behind my knees and pulled out my oversized purse. "Here you go," I said. I am nothing if not agreeable.

Lisa Leann sighed deeply but finally handed over the luggage, to which Sunny said, "Oh, how adorable! I love this." Then she paused, so help me if she didn't, pointed to Lisa Leann, and said, "Oh! Aren't you . . ." Then to me and said, "And aren't you . . ."

Lisa Leann cut in. "If you are wondering if we are on *The Great*

Party Showdown, why yes, we are. I'm Lisa Leann Lambert and this is Evangeline Vesey."

"Evil Evie?"

I frowned. "Never mind that." I jutted my thumb toward Lisa Leann. "That was her son's doing and has nothing to do with the real me."

From that moment on, the world was our oyster. After everyone had boarded but before the door was shut, Sunny approached us, leaned over, and whispered, "Ladies, we have two available seats in first class if you'd like to move. Compliments of the airline."

Personally, I felt a little self-conscious about it, but Lisa Leann scrambled out of her seat so fast she nearly knocked herself out on the overhead luggage bin. Once the plane was airborne and heading east, requests for our autographs came from fellow passengers. The entire first hour was spent signing "Mrs. Evangeline Vesey" (me) and "Loads of Love, Lisa Leann Lambert!" (not me). After we'd been served our in-flight meal, we watched about an hour of television, each with our own personal screen and headset. All I could think was, *Now, if this isn't the life! Wait till I tell Vonnie.*

As we neared New York, Lisa Leann turned to me. "We need to talk finances. A cab from the airport to our hotel is about fifty dollars without the tip."

"Fifty dollars! Good land of the living, Lisa Leann. I wasn't counting on that."

"Shhh, Evangeline. Keep your voice down. People don't expect television stars to poor-mouth."

I shifted in my seat so I could face her better. "Lisa Leann, we aren't stars, exactly. The studio allowed us a certain amount of spending money for our tickets, but your insistence that we come early cost us twice that amount. We're not made of money, you know."

Lisa Leann shushed me again, then looked around at our fellow first class travelers and smiled. "I know that. But some of this is a tax write-off for the company. Not that we have any extra to spend right now. So if you will just listen—"

"And just where is this hotel you've booked us in? Is it the same one the show is putting us up in? Because I know that one has to cost an arm and a leg." I sighed. "Why did I agree to this? Our catering club will be flat broke in no time."

"Oh, stop with the melodrama and acting like a CPA. To answer your question, no, not the one the show is putting us up in. You're right; that one is very expensive. So I booked us in a hotel in SoHo."

"What-ho?"

"SoHo. Don't you know anything about New York City, Evangeline?"

I frowned at her. "Enlighten me, Lisa Leann."

"SoHo means South of Houston," she answered, accentuating the "how" in Houston. "Not *hew*-ston, like we say it in Texas. It's a neighbourhood near Little Italy and Chinatown. Very artsy. Good restaurants and some fun shopping." She leaned in. "Tell me, Evie, what do you know about Canal Street?"

"Is that in New York City too?"

Lisa Leann threw back her head and laughed. "Oh, Evangeline. You are such a stitch. Of course it's in the City. Specifically it's in Chinatown . . . or at least I think it is. Anyway, they have *knockoffs* for sale right there on the streets and—"

"Knock outs?"

Lisa Leann rolled her eyes. "Don't you know anything, Evangeline? Knock*offs*. Purses, scarves, sunglasses . . ." I suppose my face registered that I still wasn't up to the times, because she rolled her eyes and added, "They look like the expensive designer goods, but they aren't. I can't wait to go check them out, and with SoHo being so close by, I thought it would be the perfect place for us to stay. So I booked us a room there."

"I thought we were going to New York early so we could check out suppliers."

"We are, we are." She patted my hand as though I were a child. "But there's nothing saying we can't get a little New York City cultural experience under our belts in the meantime, now is there? Oh, yeah . . . I got us tickets for the Empire State Building. Ordered those online too. I figured you and I could pay for that as it wouldn't be fair to the others even if we are scouting for them. By the way, you owe me forty-one dollars."

I crossed my arms and my legs at the same time. "Let me ask you a question. You've been online for hours, haven't you, mapping out this whole adventure."

Lisa Leann grinned like the proverbial Cheshire cat from *Alice's Adventures in Wonderland*. "You are going to be *so* glad you came with me."

"Mmm-hmm. Back to the cab. Is there no other way to get to this hotel?"

It was then Sunny happened to walk by. "Excuse me," Lisa Leann said. "Sunny, can you tell us . . . do you go to New York City a lot?"

"I have an apartment there," she said.

"Well, then . . . can you tell us how we can get to the Sohotel in SoHo without taking a cab?"

Sunny looked at us for a moment as though we'd lost our minds, then said, "Well, there's the subway."

Lisa Leann reached for her purse nestled under the seat in front of her. Settling it into her lap, she began to dig around until she brought out a folded piece of paper. She made a production of flattening out the creases, then said, "I have the directions if we are arriving by subway here on our reservations." She pointed to a section of about a dozen lines.

Sunny took the paper from her, read it over, then handed it back. "The studio is putting you up in SoHo? I'm surprised you aren't in Midtown, closer to the studios."

"We're staying at the Hilton after next Wednesday, but Evie and I wanted to come in early . . . to get a feel for the city."

Sunny beamed. "Oh, you'll love New York. There's no place on earth like it, especially at Christmas. The stores go all out decorating their windows, and there's a kind of magic in the air." She sighed. "I just love New York in the wintertime."

"And what about the summertime?" I asked. "After all, it is summer . . . and we're nearly there." I pointed toward the window.

"Oh, it can get pretty hot when the heat gets trapped between the buildings, but it's still the best city in the world. You'll have a wonderful time." She started to step away, then turned back. "By the way, yes. Those directions will get you to SoHo. While you're there, be sure to check out Canal Street in Chinatown."

Lisa Leann poked my arm. "See! I told you."

I looked at Sunny as I rubbed my new owie. "Is the subway safe?"

"Oh, sure." She giggled lightly. "Keep a watch out for butterflies." Then she waved her hand around as though dismissing her words. "Whenever I take the subway I always think of that precious scene in *You've Got Mail—*"

"My favorite movie!" Lisa Leann said.

"Definitely one of mine too. Anyway, Meg Ryan is in the subway . . . remember? And she sees a butterfly?"

Lisa Leann pointed at Sunny. "It got on at 42nd and off at 59th, where I assume it was going to Bloomingdales to buy a hat . . ."

"Which will turn out to be a mistake . . ." Sunny continued until Lisa Leann joined her with "As almost all hats are!"

I thought I might have possibly landed in some wacky *You've Got Mail* fan club. I looked from Sunny to Lisa Leann and back to Sunny and said, "I take it that's a line from the movie?"

Sunny nodded. "Hey, if you're looking for party themes, what about using themes around some of the movies set in New York City, you know . . . for the different catering shows you'll be doing."

Lisa Leann popped up. "Like?"

"*An Affair to Remember . . . You've Got Mail . . . Breakfast at Tiffany's . . .*"

Lisa Leann grabbed my hand. "Evangeline, did you hear that? Sunny just gave us an excellent idea. Let's plot it out tonight when we get to the hotel. What do you think?"

"I think we have to get to the hotel." I pointed to the reservation papers still in her hand. "Are you sure you know where you're going?"

"Oh, it's easy," Sunny said. "Just follow those directions. You'll be acting like New Yorkers in no time!"

Before we could become real "New Yorkers" we had to get our luggage. We dragged our suitcases from the dark and cramped area known as Baggage Claim and into the stifling heat beyond sliding glass doors. Dodging cars and cabs—none of which we'd be taking—we headed across several lanes of traffic to an elevator that took us downstairs to the JFK AirTrain. For several minutes we walked around, reading signs and looking like two middle-aged women from Summit View, Colorado, who were completely lost in Manhattan. Finally an attractive Asian woman took pity on us and asked, "Where are you going?"

"SoHo," I answered.

"Then you want to go toward Howard Beach," she said.

A train was approaching. "Is that the train?" Lisa Leann asked.

She nodded. "Yes."

"Are you sure?" I asked.

She smiled. "Yes. Do you have subway directions to your hotel?"

Lisa Leann waved them in her hand. "Right here."

"You'll be fine," she said.

The train arrived, and we slipped into its coolness. I dragged my luggage and myself as close to the back of the train as I could, what with about a million people being in there, then grabbed hold of a metal pole and turned just in time to see Lisa Leann and all three pieces of her pink and white polka-dotted luggage stumble through the doors. With all her luggage and the heeled designer (no doubt) sandals, she barely made it in time before the doors closed behind her with a *whoosh*. She looked back at me, somewhat frantic. I pressed my lips together to keep from laughing. Served her right. It was just like Lisa Leann to pack everything including the kitchen sink.

The train's doors closed, and the train sped toward Manhattan.

At Howard Beach we got out and followed the crowd down an open aisle and toward a flight of steps. I turned to Lisa Leann, who was behind me. "Where is the elevator?"

She looked left to right. "I don't see one."

"Well, Lisa Leann, how am I going to get this luggage up these steps?" As we stood gawking at each other, the crowd behind us parted upon reaching us, wrapped around us, and then ascended the stairs.

"You? I've got a lot more luggage than you do."

I looked down. Lisa Leann had placed her carry-on on top of one of the two larger pieces. Her shoulder strap purse had been looped over her head, I suppose to prevent theft. Taking her cue, I did the same with mine. "Okay, we can do this," I said with a sigh. "Let's go."

At the top of the stairs we entered an open, glassed-in room with turnstiles and vending machines. There we were met by a Hispanic woman, short and round, who said, "Where do you need to go?" One look at us, I suppose, and she knew we were clueless.

"SoHo," I said, trying to sound as though I'd been saying it my whole entire life.

"Come with me," she said, and we followed. She took us to the vending machines, which turned out to be for purchasing MetroCards rather than sodas and snacks. "You'll need to first buy a ticket to get into the system," she said, pointing to the appropriate buttons. "That's five dollars. Then you will need to buy a ticket for the rest of your stay. How long will you be here?"

"A few days," Lisa Leann chimed in. Then she looked at me and said, "After next Wednesday it'll be cabs and limos."

Sounded good in theory. But today was Friday and we were about to enter the subway system in Manhattan with trembling knees and, wouldn't you know, butterflies.

10

Subway Sandwich

When the silver A-train pulled into the Howard Beach subway station, I was ready to roll. To keep my hands free, I'd looped my purse around my neck and stacked my smaller suitcase on top of its larger matching bag. I didn't have a way to latch them together, so I'd pulled up the expanding handle on the lower case and somehow managed to loop my hand through the handles of both suitcases. Slowly, to keep things from falling down around me, I pushed my tower of baggage forward as I pulled my smaller carry-on behind me. I called over my shoulder, "Hurry, Evie, before the doors close. I'd hate to lose you; you don't even know where we're going."

"If you weren't such a wide load, I'd already be on the train," Evie shot back.

"I am having a bit of a struggle," I admitted.

Evie barely managed her baggage through the doors before they closed. "And I'm not?"

We snagged one of the hard orange benches and settled our bags before us as the train lurched forward. I took a moment to size up the people around us. Honestly, they looked like ordinary, everyday people with books and newspapers. The only thing unusual about them was they all seemed on the younger side of forty, making us the "elders" in the car.

A few riders stood holding on to the occasional silver pole that speared the center aisle. These commuters stared absently at the advertisement posters above our heads or out the windows at the high wooden walls that flanked either side of the track. As we clackety-clacked toward Brooklyn, Evie leaned into me. "So far so good," she said under her breath as if to congratulate us for a job well done. "But you need to stop staring at everyone, Lisa Leann. It makes you look like a tourist."

"I am a tourist."

"Trust me, you don't want anyone to notice."

"Don't you think our luggage gives us away?"

"Not necessarily," Evie said, slightly indignant. "Just don't make eye contact, and whatever you do, don't blurt out any of your Texas witticisms."

I nudged Evie with my elbow. "Now I might not be the brightest crayon in the box, but I do know how to act in public."

Evie nudged me right back. "See, that's what I'm talking about. You're going to blow our cover."

"So?"

"So, don't you know that the subways are full of pickpockets and people who molest tourists?"

"Who told you that?"

"Vernon. He gave me the lowdown with instructions."

"Instructions? Like what?"

"Don't leave your purse open. Don't let anyone carry your suitcase; you'll never see it again. Don't show off your diamonds." She held her hand out to reveal she'd twisted the diamond in her wedding set so as to hide the glitter inside her palm. "Don't gawk with your mouth open, especially under a skyscraper, or you might have to swallow pigeon droppings."

"Heavens!"

"Don't talk to strangers, and whatever you do, don't tell them where you're from. But in your case, your accent will do that for you, so just keep your mouth shut, okay?"

"You're kidding me, right? And how did Vernon get to be such an expert on New York?"

Evie grabbed my hand. "I'm not kidding. Vernon's been to law enforcement conferences here. So, let's just play it safe, at least till we get to the hotel and put our luggage away."

I nodded, still feeling a bit heated from Evie's "keep your mouth shut" remark. I swallowed and said, "You're as jumpy as spit on a hot skillet. Trust me, we'll be unpacking in our SoHo hotel room then dining in Little Italy before you can snap your fingers."

"Shhh. Keep your voice down."

"What did I do now?"

Evie sighed deeply. "Never mind. Just tell me, what's our next stop?"

I reached into my unzipped purse and checked my notes. "We're going to the Broadway station, where we'll catch the J-train."

Our train finally clattered out of the walled-in track and onto the streets of Brooklyn. Evie and I sat in silence, watching the buildings increase in height. After what seemed like hours, our train finally rocked over the East River, where the Manhattan skyscrapers seemed to loom right out of the water's gray ripples.

Evie leaned in. "What a view!"

"Hotter than a two dollar bill!" I blurted.

"Don't *do* that!" Evie whispered.

"What?"

She interrupted her scolding with, "Is that the Brooklyn Bridge?"

I gazed at the long span of steel, wire, and concrete and said, "Yep. It's a beaut, isn't it?"

"You're talking Texan on purpose."

I laughed. "Sorry, Evie, I'm only doing what comes natural."

We sat in silence, admiring the view as we crossed the river before our now-elevated track cut between the tall buildings, then slowed down for yet another stop. "Is this where we get off?" Evie asked.

"Not yet, though we're close."

A sudden high-pitched squeal interrupted us as a Middle Eastern voice squawked from the public address system somewhere above our heads. Honestly, his voice was so heavily accented and muffled I could only make out about half of what he said between the static. "End of the line . . . *buzzzzztt* . . . Get off now . . . *scrichhhhhffft.*"

Evie looked startled. "Are we supposed to get off here?"

"I think so. He said something about repairs and the next track."

"So what do we do?"

"Follow the crowd," I said as our traveling companions exited the train.

We pulled our luggage out the door and were hit with a blast of summer slow-broil. But more stifling than the heat was the narrow metal stairway that loomed over us.

I gasped. "Where's the elevator?" I stared down a policeman who I hoped would provide an answer. Instead, he turned and looked away, telling me with his body language that he would not soon be helping me get my luggage up the stairs.

Evie slowly shook her head. "I don't think there is an elevator." She began to bump her large suitcase up the stairs. "Come on."

I took a step up, then carefully lifted my stacked cases and placed them one step above me while I pulled my carry-on up the next step beneath me. It was slow going, and by the time I'd made it up six of the twenty or so steps, Evie was at the top. She called down to me. "I'd help you, but I can't leave my suitcase."

"I can do it," I said, not really believing my words. The steps were just too narrow to properly balance between my teetering

92

loads. In a flash, I saw what would happen. My carry-on bag, with my computer inside, would slip from my grasp and crash to the bottom of the stairs. Then, I would tumble down behind it, with the rest of my luggage hurling down to crush me. My feet rocked unsteadily as I swayed between my bags.

A mob of people were clambering up the steps around me, and I couldn't get my bearings. Suddenly a young man's heavily accented voice surprised me. "I'll take this up for you, okay?"

I turned to look into the dark eyes and olive complexion of a Hispanic teenager, who grabbed my carry-on. My breath caught in my throat; I didn't have time to think. I said, "Okay," then winced inwardly. *Good-bye, computer.*

As I managed my remaining bags up the stairs, I was surprised to enter a brightly lit station painted in sunshine yellow. Its walls were covered with lovely mosaics that I would have loved to admire if my heart hadn't been pounding so hard. But even more surprising than finding sudden beauty was to see the teenager who had carried my suitcase up the stairs still waiting for me. "Thank you!" I gushed.

His dark eyes glittered. "No problem. Do you need help going back down?"

"Back down?"

He pointed to another narrow flight.

I looked at Evie, who was already accepting help from yet another teenage boy. "Thank you, dear," she said as he carried her large bag down the steps. My new young friend picked up my suitcase and followed them. When I arrived at the bottom of the stairs, Evie opened her wallet. "Can I give you a tip?" she asked the young man who had helped her.

"No, no. You don't need to do that," my helper said. He then turned to the other teen. "Man, why you take this lady's money like that?"

"I told her no, man!"

Evie spoke up. "Take it. Please."

I smiled. "Tell your mothers you are exceptional young men and they should be proud."

The young men smiled back, then darted up the stairs, pocketing their pay.

The crowd at the platform grew, and soon we lost sight of our guardian angels. There were so many young people surrounding us, I wasn't sure how we were going to fit, plus our luggage, onto the next train. Furthermore, I wasn't sure how I was going to continue to pull my luggage through the belly of New York City. *Do you know how, Lord?* I silently asked. *I'm exhausted and now I'm afraid of what's next.*

Our train soon roared into the station. When the doors opened, I tried to follow the crowd inside, but the wheels of my carry-on fell into the space between the train and the platform. The crowd behind me grew restless as I blocked the entrance. I jerked my luggage, but instead of breaking free, my suitcase caught on the corner of the sliding metal door. *Ugh.*

"Move it, lady; we're all trying to get in," an angry voice called out. With a mighty pull, I broke free from my trap, then scurried (as best I could) across the aisle and fell into the seat next to Evie. I noted the wild look in her eyes as a teenage girl began to mock someone nearby. I was too traumatized to pay attention as to who was being tormented until the girl punched my arm. "I *said*: are you fools going to Chicago?"

Suddenly my mouth went dry. "No," I replied meekly as one of my hot flashes, or perhaps fear, exploded through my body. "We just got off the plane from Denver."

The girl narrowed her eyes and placed fists on her ample hips that stretched out her white tee, which she wore over a pair of jeans. "What's wrong with you?"

I fanned myself and managed to stammer, "It's hotter than a burning stump in here."

"Say what?"

Evie looked away, obviously trying to appear as though she didn't know me. The girl's eyes flashed with recognition. She smiled. "Hey, aren't you one of those cooks on that TV show?"

My head bobbed, and the words flew out of my mouth. "Yes! That's why we're here. We're trying to get to our hotel."

"Why didn't you say so?" the teen asked. "Where you staying?"

"SoHotel," I said. A quick look at Evie and I saw her face go white as a sheet from my mama's laundry. "Then you don't want to miss your next stop. Bowery is coming up next."

I thanked the young lady as the clacking stopped and the doors slid open. Evie and I rose, and the crowd magically parted as we pulled our luggage out of the train and into the scantily occupied station.

We headed for yet another flight of narrow stairs as Evie asked me, "Why did you have to go and tell our business?"

"Just practicing a little Southern hospitality, that's all."

Evie snorted one of her "humphs" and started to pull her luggage up the long flight of stairs while I stared after her. A question began to sear my brain: why had I packed my favorite pots and pans? They had pots and pans in New York, after all. At least that's what Henry had said the one day he'd even spoken to me.

Evie called over her shoulder, "Can you make it?"

I shook my head no but said, "I'll try."

"Take your time."

I lifted my stacked cases to teeter on the step above me, and started what was becoming a familiar but dangerous dance; one step, plop, plop; another step, plop, plop; another step . . . This climb, like my failing marriage, would never work. I was going to fall flat onto my kisser. And by the time I got back home, the kisser I left behind might have flown the coop, maybe even for good. I mean, I needed to get away from all the stress of our marriage, but I didn't want to return to abandonment.

Help, Lord, I prayed for the millionth time that day, that week.

I stopped to steady myself. Evie was now at the top of the stairs, and I cried, "Now, why didn't we take a cab?"

"To save fifty bucks," she called back.

I swayed between my luggage, still only a third of the way to the top. "Didn't we realize our lives were worth more than fifty bucks?"

"We do now," Evie called back.

Suddenly a man dressed as though he was about to go cycling ran up the stairs. "Can I help you?" he asked. "Yes," I said, suddenly too tired to care if he stole my computer, my pots and pans, and even my underthings. What I really wanted was to still be alive when I reached the top of the stairs.

The man swooped in on my carry-on and ran up the flight. To my surprise, he plopped my suitcase at Evie's feet. "Thank you!" we called after him.

When I managed the rest of the stairs, I told Evie, "I always heard New Yorkers were rude, but they seem to know a thing or two about Southern hospitality."

"So it seems," Evie said with a tired smile.

I looked around at the concrete jungle that now surrounded us and felt dismayed. "I sure hope this is a safe neighborhood."

"Are we almost there?"

"Let me check." I opened my purse, which still hung around my neck, and pulled out my notes. "It's only a few more blocks."

"Blocks?"

I breathed in the heat that had already dampened my body with sweat. "'Fraid so. This way." We turned to cross Kenmare Street.

"What street are we looking for?" Evie finally asked.

"Broome Street."

"We've got to be getting close. Right?"

"You'd think."

Evie stopped and watched a Chinese man sweep the sidewalk

in front of his vegetable stand, then walked over to him and said, "Excuse me. Where is Broome Street?"

The man smacked his broom on the sidewalk and pointed up. I saw the street sign. "Here," I said. "He means we're here."

We hurried our luggage across the street, taking in the bakeries, sushi shops, as well as the aroma of garbage that came from the cans and black garbage bags that lined the street.

"Is it far still?"

"Just a couple of blocks."

"I'm so tired I can hardly pull this bag."

"Me too."

"Just promise me that the hotel will have an elevator. Okay?"

"Of course it will. There are laws."

"Then your promise gives me the strength to go on," Evie said with a soft laugh.

After four blocks we stopped in front of a fire station. "I think we missed it," I said. "Let's turn around."

About a block later, there it was: the SoHotel. A glass door led to a narrow staircase filled with golden light that spilled onto the concrete sidewalk. The staircase was in the middle of a darkened lamp store. The scaffolding that laced itself above the entrance had somehow hidden the signage from us on our first pass.

We crossed the street, and Evie squealed. "Lisa Leann Lambert, you promised me, no stairs!"

But before she could say more, the bellman swept down and lifted away our burdens. With rubber for legs, we climbed upward, massaging our aching arms, which must have stretched out a good two inches along our journey. Soon we had our plastic card keys from the front desk, and the next thing we knew, we were painfully climbing up three more flights to our room.

I sat on the floor outside our door while Evie fumbled with the lock. When she finally got the door open, I stood and looked inside. The room was cute and clean but tiny. "This room is only temporary," I said as Evie placed her luggage against the wall, blocking the only route to the bathroom. I set my carry-on on the quilted bed and squeezed in the rest of my bags next to the TV.

Evie flopped on the bed beside my suitcase. "I'd go to sleep now if I weren't so hungry."

"Let's get cleaned up and hit Little Italy. My sister told me there's a restaurant on Mulberry called Il Cortile that has the best Italian food in the world. She said to try the *petto di pollo con asparagi e mozzarella* and at least one of their cappuccinos."

Evie sat up. "Oh, does that sound good. But before we go, there's something we need to do."

"What's that?" I asked.

"Let's get on our knees and thank the good Lord for getting us and our luggage safely here tonight."

"Listen, I'd kiss the floor if I could get to it. But yes, let's pray."

We bowed our heads and thanked the Lord for safe passage.

11

Back at the Ranch

The phone on my nightstand vibrated again. I tried to ignore it, but I opened one eye to check the green letters of my digital clock. *It's six p.m. already?*

I reached for my phone, snapped it open, and held it to my ear. "Hello?"

Except for a bit of muffled breathing, all I heard was a seething silence.

"Hello?" I asked as I climbed out of bed. I cracked opened my heavy drapes to let a dust-speckled beam of sun stream into my bedroom. The call ended, and I checked the caller ID: "Private."

I clicked the phone shut as I considered who could be responsible for all these hang-ups I'd received lately, a sort of red flag for someone working in law enforcement. Harassing phone calls are considered a threat, but since I toted a gun, I felt more annoyed than concerned. Though, the caller seemed to be someone who knew my routine well enough to phone whenever I was trying to sleep between my double shifts. I'd been working around the clock so Dad could get caught up on his paperwork, since he was the one who'd have to cover most of my shifts once I left for New York.

I rubbed the sleep from my eyes as my brain slowly played detective. I didn't think the caller could be my stepmother, Evie. She and Lisa Leann had arrived in New York by now, and they'd certainly be too busy to call and harass me, unless of course they'd wanted to talk but had fallen victim to a bad connection. But as these silent calls had continued for the past couple of weeks, I knew they weren't to blame. Besides, Evie was off my suspect list simply because we'd been getting along pretty well since she'd made peace with my mother.

Speaking of whom, I didn't suspect Dee Dee McGurk either, especially since I'd stopped to give her a ride home from her shift at the tavern the night before. She'd been in a chatty mood, excited about my appearance on *The Great Party Showdown*. So my third guess held the most promise. Maybe this phone prankster was my long-lost sister, Velvet James. Since she'd arrived in town, it seemed we'd never had a moment to get to know each another. The only thing I really knew about her was she'd tried to steal away any man she thought might be attracted to me. And since she'd been jilted by most of her recent obsessions, I'd say the girl had more than enough motive.

Half an hour later, fresh from the shower and dressed in my deputy uniform, I still puzzled over my mystery as I headed to the market to pick up a bag of tortilla chips and a couple of ingredients for my Tex-Ranch dip. I planned to bring my dip to the Potluck Club meeting at Vonnie's house at seven, then leave before my shift started at nine.

When I pulled in to Gold Rush Market, my phone rang again. I checked the caller ID. "Hey, Wade. You didn't try to call me earlier, did you?"

His laugh was low. "Must have been your other boyfriend."

"Ha-ha," I said, allowing my voice a touch of sarcasm. "What's up?"

"Heard you and the ladies were meeting tonight."

"That we are."

"Then I'm planning to crash your little party. David too."

The double doors of the market swooshed open, washing me in refrigerated air. I ignored the tingling chill and grabbed a blue plastic shopping basket and headed for the snack aisle.

"Get serious. Our meetings are for club members only."

"According to that contract I signed, I am a member. Kat Sebastian called and said I'm on the same plane for New York as you."

I dropped the large bag of chips I'd grabbed off the shelf, then stooped to retrieve it. "Then it's finally official."

"'Fraid so. David and I need some answers."

"Like?"

"What's Team Potluck's financial arrangement? I mean, I'm having to take off work and still somehow manage to pay my bills."

"I hear you, Wade," I said as I rounded the corner. I jerked to a stop, almost plowing down Wade's mom, Faye, who appeared to be studying a display of Diet Pepsi. She was dressed in her plump-girl jeans and a pink tee. Her graying curls did nothing to soften her deepening scowl. "Donna, are you talking to my son?"

When I nodded, she put one hand on her hip. "No wonder he doesn't answer, and here I am having an emergency."

"Wade, I'll have to call you back." I closed the phone and put it in my pocket. Despite my differences with Mrs. Gage, I felt myself kick into deputy mode. "Is everything all right?"

Faye pointed toward the street where her car was parked. "Engine trouble again."

I pointed to my basket of goods. "Let me pay for my items and I'll take a look."

Mrs. Gage pulled her cell phone out of her large tan purse. "This is a job for Wade, not you."

I held up my hands as if she had a gun trained on me. "Only trying to help."

101

Faye paused in mid-dial and looked up at me. "Help yourself, you mean."

I shifted my weight. "Excuse me?"

"I hear you're dragging my son to New York with you."

"I don't think I'd explain the situation quite like that."

"Then how would you explain it?" Her voice rose an octave. "You just can't leave my son alone, can you?"

The nearby faces of the market's patrons began to swivel toward us as she continued. "I guess ruining the best years of Wade's life hasn't been enough for you."

I stepped back, surprised at her public assault. I tried to hush her by lowering my voice, hoping she'd follow suit. "You can't blame me for that."

Faye only got louder. "Wade never would have started drinking if you hadn't spun his head."

"Wade's drinking broke my heart as much as anyone. Thank God, he's sober now."

"And I plan to keep it that way," Faye said. She finished dialing Wade's number, then held her phone to her ear. "Now, if you'll excuse me, I'm talking to my son."

She turned and walked away, cooing, "Wade dear, I've been trying to reach you . . . Yes, car trouble again. I'm at the market. Can you come?"

At the checkout stand, I reached for my wallet to pull out my Visa when Peggy Sue, the cashier, asked, "That was quite the scene. You okay?"

I shrugged. "Guess so."

"That Faye's a witch." Peggy Sue folded her arms across her gold-enrod yellow smock with the words "Gold Rush" written in black thread across the front. She said under her breath, "Don't let her get to you."

"I won't give her another thought," I lied.

Later, when I was standing in Vonnie's kitchen, I stirred my

Tex-Ranch dip in one of Vonnie's large ceramic bowls and mentally rehashed my encounter with Mrs. Gage. Vonnie, who was busy pouring freshly brewed tea into blue-tinted glasses, noticed my foul mood. "Is everything okay, dear?" she asked.

"Fine," I said, hoping I could avoid any additional questions. I love Vonnie. She's more like a real mom than anyone else. Still, I wasn't too anxious to discuss my love life with her, especially as I sensed she was rooting for me to fall for David. Falling for David was actually something of a temptation, especially now that I'd gotten to spend more time with him, since we dated a bit and so often covered the same accidents. But the fact that David was a guy I more than admired was beside the point. What my so-called love life didn't need was additional pressure from Vonnie.

Vonnie handed me two glasses of tea. "Set these on the coffee table. We'll talk later, okay?"

I nodded, though I didn't intend to follow through.

Just as the girls and I got settled in the chairs Vonnie and I had already arranged around the coffee table, David walked through the front door. He too was dressed ready for work and managed to snag a seat to my right.

His grin was broad as I announced, "Welcome to one of our newest members."

Vonnie, dressed in jeans and her favorite red blouse, grinned like the proud mother she was. "Yes, son, welcome to the club."

"Glad to be included." He reached for one of the preset plates topped with chips, dip, and Lizzie's tuna sandwiches on rye.

The phone in my pocket chirped, and I pulled it out to read the text message that had just come through. "It's from Lisa Leann," I said.

"What's the news?" Lizzie asked, her blue eyes peering over a set of reading glasses she'd slipped on as she held her handwritten agenda.

I read the text message aloud. "We're safe in NYC. About to go to dinner. More later."

"Safe?" Vonnie asked, her eyes wide with alarm. "Oh dear, safe from what?"

"Just a figure of speech, most likely," Lizzie said as Wade opened the front door and slipped into the party. He quietly sat down across from me. Lizzie added, "Text the girls that we have a couple of new members."

I obeyed. *David, Wade now on our team. Will join us in NY.*

The phone chirped again, and I read her reply. *Nelson too. Txt us report of meeting.*

Later, Goldie led us in a long prayer for help in the competition and for God's favor and grace in our homes and at our places of employment while we were absent. After the amens, we chatted as we sipped tea and balanced our plates in our laps. Wade, dressed in a black tee, jeans, and his famous cowboy boots, sat his plate aside then leaned his elbows back on his chair and stretched out his long legs while he posed a question. "I don't mean to be a killjoy, but how much is this little trip going to cost?" He shot a look at David. "Some of us aren't independently wealthy."

Lizzie, who looked sharp in her navy top over a pair of indigo jeans, seemed to be the go-to Potlucker in Evie and Lisa Leann's absence. She said, "Fortunately, the reality show will pay our way plus our expenses. But they're not paying for our time, except for a small stipend, which we'll have to share."

Wade swiped at a strand of blond hair that hid his blue eyes. "Meaning?"

I piped up, "Meaning we really need to win this thing."

"Hear, hear," the members of our club sang as everyone lifted their tea glasses into the air.

Wade raised his glass halfway but didn't smile. Lizzie asked, "Do you have any other questions?"

He nodded. "Since David and I weren't privy to your financial arrangements, if you do win, how are you planning to split the proceeds?"

There was silence as the girls and I looked at one another. Lizzie said, "We're playing to help pay off the church mortgage and—"

"To build a youth wing," Vonnie added.

"We're not playing for personal gain," Lizzie said. "However, you boys weren't in on our initial decisions, and we'll have to work out some sort of agreement."

David said, "Don't worry about me."

"Well, helping out our church sounds like a good cause," Wade said. "I'm happy to volunteer my time, at least as much as I can afford. But as an independent contractor, if I don't work, I don't eat."

The girls nodded, and Lizzie said, "I'm sure we can come up with something by way of compensation."

David asked, "How long do you think we'll be out there, a week?"

"If we keep advancing in the competition, it could be up to four weeks," Lizzie said.

Wade whistled. "That long?"

Everyone shifted uncomfortably.

"I feel your pain," Goldie said. She was wearing a lightweight peach blazer with matching pants. Now I'm no fashion expert, like Lisa Leann. Still, I couldn't help but notice how much the color of Goldie's outfit complimented her strawberry blonde hair. "I don't know what Chris will do without me in the office. It's our busy time."

With Goldie's words, everyone fell silent, lost in their own dilemmas. We picked at what was left of the food on our plates until Lizzie changed the subject. "Vonnie, Goldie, are your hubbies still planning on joining us?"

"Fred is," Vonnie said.

Lizzie nodded. "We, the actual contestants, will be staying at the Hilton, two to a room. But our husbands will have to fly in and stay at their own expense."

Goldie's eyes seemed to plead. "Can't they stay with us?"

Lizzie ran a hand through her salt and pepper hair then shook her head. "Not according to Kat."

Goldie added, "But they can room together, right?"

Lizzie nodded again. "As long as they make arrangements on their own. Oh, and Samuel's coming and so's Vernon."

"What about Lisa Leann's Henry?" Vonnie asked.

"She hasn't said."

Wade spoke up again. "You know, my mom is thinking she might like to join us in New York."

Because of Faye's reputation for trouble, I wasn't the only one who turned to Wade and stared. It was Lizzie who spoke first. "Your mother wants to join us?"

"At least that's what she said when I was helping her get her car started a few minutes ago."

"What sort of car trouble did she have?" I asked.

Wade chuckled. "Somehow, that distributor cap in her old Chrysler keeps falling off. Luckily I've always found it beneath her car."

That's hardly an accident, I fumed as I felt a scowl tempt my forehead. I made no comment as Wade continued. "Anyway, Mom happened to mention how excited she is about me being on the show, and how much she thinks of you all."

I managed to freeze my eyebrows, which now wanted to skid out of control. "No kidding."

Wade actually grinned. "Right, and, well, since you all know my mom and since everyone seems to get along, can I tell her it's okay if she decides to come?"

The girls and I had no choice. We nodded our assent, and the discussion continued just as if Wade hadn't dropped a bombshell.

Somehow, despite my new worries about Mrs. Gage, I man-aged to learn the producer would expedite our tickets to arrive on Monday and we would all fly out early Tuesday morning, arriving just in time to make a live appearance on the show that evening. Though, apparently we wouldn't actually be competing, as this was our week off. According to Lizzie—who said this was according to Lisa Leann—the reason we had to be in the studio was so we would be in place when the top six teams started work on the first of their New York City parties. As we were already in the top six, since being in the winner's circle last week, we had to be on-site so we could get our marching orders the following morning.

After polishing off a slice of Vonnie's apple pie a la mode, I stood to leave. "Gotta run, everyone. My shift starts at nine."

Before David could respond, Wade stood. "Think I'll walk the deputy to her Bronco."

David nodded, a bit smug. "Go ahead, Donna, I'll catch up with you later tonight."

As we stepped onto Vonnie's front porch, I was captivated by the evening sky. It rimmed the last rays of golden light around the edges of the mountains while a full moon glowed in the deepen-ing turquoise.

A breeze played with my curls, which were still too short to pull into a ponytail. Wade followed me to my Bronco, and I turned and leaned into it. "Wade, I can hardly believe your mom wants to join us."

He stood close enough to kiss me, but didn't. "I know. I'm almost as surprised as you."

"But why would you even want her there?"

He smiled down at me in a way that made my heart flutter. "For us."

Before I could respond, he continued. "I know my mother has stood between us, Donna, because of the past. But it's time for a fresh start. I'm ready to show her we belong together."

I clicked my electronic key to unlock the door to my truck. "I'm not sure we have anything to prove, Wade, and—"

He leaned down to give me a gentle kiss. I was so surprised I briefly kissed him back.

His eyes filled with tenderness. "We'll get through this."

"But . . ."

He leaned in to kiss me again, but I managed to slide into my truck, feeling too many emotions to understand them. "We'll talk later," I said, starting the motor. "I'm late."

His smile was wistful. "Then that makes two of us."

A few minutes later, I passed Lisa Leann's darkened condo and realized Henry must either be out or already in bed. But before I could formulate a better theory, my cell phone rang. I checked the caller ID which once again read "Private."

I picked up and listened to the familiar silence before clicking out of the call without speaking.

I bit my lower lip. I suddenly had yet another person to add to my list of crank-call suspects. But unfortunately, this one couldn't scare me more than if she were determined to cut out my heart with a butcher knife.

I shuddered. Faye Gage had me in a tizzy. Me, a law enforcement professional, felled by the fear of rejection. Honestly, I had no more idea how to handle Mrs. Gage than how to fly. But then, I had more to worry about than Mrs. Gage. I had to guard my heart, at least until I could decipher how I really felt about the men in my life. That meant I had to pledge no more kisses until I had a theory I could live with.

12

Mixed Up in Manhattan

I have to admit, Lisa Leann and I soaked up the New York lifestyle like sponges on wet stainless steel countertops. As soon as we'd gotten our bearings, unpacked, and touched base with our loved ones back home, we headed back down the narrow hall and stairway and then swept into the lobby and to the night manager—a lovely young woman of Hispanic descent—on the other side of a high L-shaped counter. Behind her were tiny cubicles, one stacked on top of another, filled with old-fashioned room keys and slender white envelopes.

"Look," I said, pointing rudely. "I think people actually live here!"

The night manager smiled warmly. "The SoHotel is the oldest hotel in New York City. We have rooms for those who live in the city and those who are visitors like yourselves."

"I read that," Lisa Leann said with a nod. "I read that before we came here on the Internet." She shook her head. "What I mean to say is, I read that on the Internet before we came here. We didn't come here on the Internet."

"No, we came here on the subway," I reminded her.

The night manager's eyes widened. "You came here, to the hotel, on the subway? With luggage?" She looked from one of us to the other. "From where? From one of the airports?"

I nodded while Lisa Leann groaned. "Well, heck," I said. "We're real New Yorkers now."

Rose—the night manager—giggled a bit, then said, "Ladies, how can I help you this evening?"

Lisa Leann turned to me. "You know, everyone says New Yorkers aren't friendly. But so far, everyone has been so nice."

I pointed to Rose. "She wants to know how she can help us, Lisa Leann."

"I'm just saying—"

I looked at Rose. "We want to go to Il Cortile on Mulberry. It's a restaurant."

"Yes, I know." She pointed toward the stairs leading back down to the street. "You can literally walk it. Out the front door, take a left, two streets over, take a left. It'll be on your right. Easy as anything."

The night air was warm and the sun had disappeared behind the buildings, but the light around SoHo and leading into Little Italy was silver and magical. I could see, even here in lower Manhattan, why New York City was easy to fall in love with. I took in deep breaths and sighed. I was happy. At nearly sixty years of age, I'd had the first completely spontaneous day in my life, coming to New York City, riding a subway, and now walking in unknown territory to get to a restaurant.

By the time we got back to the hotel and into our room, our tummies were full of some of the best food I'd ever eaten. Lisa Leann had managed to talk the chef into allowing her to check out his kitchen, so she was satisfied in more ways than one. "I now want a warm shower and to fall into bed," she said as we entered the room.

Fine by me; I was ready to call home and let Vernon know how I'd survived my first evening in the Big Apple.

"What's Lisa Leann doing now?" Vernon asked after I'd filled him in on what had transpired since our last conversation.

"She's in the shower," I told him. "And Vernon . . . she and Henry . . . there was a lot of tension in their earlier phone call. I mean . . . I'm not gossiping or anything, but. . . ."

"All right, then," Vernon said. "On to the next topic."

I rolled my eyes. "I get your point. Okay. As soon as Lisa Leann gets out of the shower, it'll be my turn, so I'll say good night now."

"Good night, Evie-girl," he said. "I'll hold your pillow close and pretend I'm snuggling with you."

I felt heat spring to my cheeks. "Vernon Vesey, you say the sweetest things."

When Lisa Leann exited the bath, declaring the showerhead to be in working order and the spray of the water to be just perfect, I was sitting in the middle of the bed, returning a text message to Donna.

I CAN UNDRSTND CONCERN RE: MONEY, I texted. *NOT SURE HOW LNG UR DAD WILL BE ABLE 2 CME.*

"What are you doing?" Lisa Leann asked.

I pressed "send" and looked up, ignoring her question for one of my own. "Lisa Leann, what in the world are you wearing?"

"Pajamas, silly."

"I know they are pajamas, but where did you get them?"

"A place called the Cat's Pajamas. It's on the Internet."

I leaned in for a better look. The pajamas were two-piece poplin. Pink, of course, printed with frosted cakes and other delectable edibles in a variety of yummy colors. "You do beat all for staying within theme," I said to her. "And here I just brought a plain old cotton gown."

She pointed to my phone. "Is that text from one of the girls?"

"Donna. She sent me a text about the meeting tonight." Lisa Leann shot me a look of concern, one that read, *Why are they texting you and not me*? I quickly added, "No need to worry your little red head. Everything is apparently just fine."

Lisa Leann folded up her travel clothes she'd brought with her from the bathroom as she said, "Don't you just love texting? You don't have to talk if you don't want to. You can get right to the point and stay on the point." She shook her head as though in wonder of it all.

I stood from the soft mattress. "Are you through in there? I'm ready to wash this day from my body and go to bed."

"You betcha. It's late, and a good night's sleep is in order. First thing tomorrow, we hit the Empire State Building."

I shook my head as I closed the bathroom door. "I sure hope it sees you coming and moves out of the way," I mumbled as quietly as I knew how.

"I heard that," she called from the other side of the door.

The following morning, after a breakfast of Lisa Leann's home-made protein bars, I stood on one side of the rumpled bed, re-arranging the items in my purse, while Lisa Leann stood on the other doing the same. "Should we leave some of our money in here?" she asked.

I looked around the tiny room. "It might be a good idea to not carry all our cash on us. Where would you suggest we hide it, though?"

Lisa Leann pointed down. "I always put it between the mattresses."

"Are you out of your mind?"

"No, seriously . . . Henry and I put it between the mattresses, and then we make the bed. They'll never think to look there. Believe me, Evangeline. I've done quite a bit of traveling in my day."

I handed her a stack of bills, then pulled the MetroCards from my wallet. One, I remembered, was just to get into the system and was now void. The other would get us through until we were carted around by the studio's limo. I waved the first one at Lisa Leann. "Be sure to ditch the first card we got," I said. "It's no longer any good."

Lisa Leann was busy stuffing money between the mattresses. She looked up briefly, said, "Oh, yeah . . . good idea," then went back to her task.

Ten minutes later—and with our bed neatly made—we were out of the tiny room and on our way to exploring what New York City had to offer. We stopped at the front desk and asked the day manager about the subway to the Empire State Building.

"Right on Bowery, left on Grand," he said. "You'll see the subway. Take the D train."

We headed out, heads held high, shoulders back, and strutted our stuff like we'd been walking the streets of SoHo our whole lives. This morning, without the weight of luggage and hunger, I was able to take in more of the sights and sounds of the city. The crowds were thick and the traffic buzzed, echoing between old cast-iron buildings that apparently served as both commercial and residential. As I made some attempt to count the number of cars and cabs lining the street, Lisa Leann rambled on about the history of SoHo. I craned my neck and looked up to the clear blue sky. The sun was already warming the city and raising the aromas from the local cafés and the strange blended smells of herbs, fruits, and vegetables from a few storefronts. I grinned in delight at it all, the colors, the people, the scents. The flow of the crowd, stopping in unison at cross streets, looking forward at the "wait" sign on the other side, then harmoniously starting up again when the "wait" turned to "walk."

But when it seemed we'd gone over too many cross-streets, I stopped.

Lisa Leann took another two or three steps before she turned. "What's wrong?"

I pointed to an upcoming intersection. A major intersection. "That's . . . what?" I squinted to read the sign. "Canal?" I looked at Lisa Leann, who was glaring straight ahead, a sudden glint in her eye.

"Ooooh. Do you know what Canal Street is?"

"Well, I know what it's not. It's not Grand and it's not the subway."

Lisa Leann waved her hand in a "come here, come here" motion.

I took the few steps toward her; she linked her arm through mine. "Canal Street, dear Evangeline, is in Chinatown. Look," she said, pointing to the buildings. "Look at all the Chinese writing and the reds and golds. This is where all the knockoff purses are. Don't you remember me telling you this?"

"Oh yes. Yes, yes. Purses, watches, scarves . . ."

Lisa Leann swung us around so we were facing the direction from which we'd come and began pulling me with her as she walked. "Well, I'm about as excited as a Texan can get, let me tell you. We are staying no more than three blocks from Canal Street, Evie. The place to see and be seen." She patted my arm. "Tomorrow, you and I are going purse shopping, girlfriend. Prada, Kate Spade, Gucci . . ."

I clutched the strap of the simple black no-name purse that was draped over my body. "Why would I want to buy something I don't need? Foolish waste of money. If we're going to spend money on something, let's spend it on food. I'm ready for some real breakfast; nothing against your protein bars."

We crossed Hester Street and kept walking.

"Don't be silly, Evangeline. The whole point of being here early is to soak up the culture."

"Food can be a cultural experience. Think about last night . . . that pasta stuff was pretty good." I nodded once for effect. "Besides, I thought the whole point of being here was to find the best shops for our next challenge."

114

"That too." She pointed straight ahead. "There it is. There's Grand Street."

We took a right. I kept my eyes open for the Metro sign—a large M. Spotting it, I pointed. "There's the subway."

Lisa Leann and I—still hooked together at the bend in the arms—left one side of Grand for the other. We were met by a barrage of outdoor Asian markets boasting food products, the likes of which I'd never seen.

"Would you look at this?" Lisa Leann asked as we passed them. "Now this is something we need to learn more about." She raised her left arm—the one not linked to mine—and said, "Oh, Evie. All the ways of life one can find here! This is just fabulous!"

I glanced around as we moved forward, then ducked my chin. "You know, for someone who I told less than twenty-four hours ago not to act like a tourist, you sure are acting like a tourist."

She grinned at me. "I cannot help myself."

We made it to the subway. I reached into the pocket of my cotton slacks and pulled out the MetroCard. Clutching it in my right hand, I said, "Do you have your card?"

"In my purse."

"You should probably get it out now."

We'd made it to the subway stairs. I read the letters painted overhead and said, "This is the right place." I pulled my arm from Lisa Leann's then stepped in front of her, grasping the sticky metal rail and slipping in with the crowd, all of whom seemed to know exactly where they were going.

I felt rather than saw Lisa Leann close behind me. We sank into the underworld of New York, the sounds of the city fading as the roar of trains and human voices increased. I cut my eyes to the graffiti on the walls, daring to read a word here and a phrase there. According to the scribble: Chantal is not a very nice girl and we should all give world peace a chance.

We came to the turnstile. I glanced back at Lisa Leann, who was right behind me, face turned into her purse, hands digging for her MetroCard. Heaven help me . . . that woman . . .

The crowd wouldn't allow me to do anything but keep moving. I scanned my card then pushed through the metal rod of the turnstile. Whipped to the right by other subway travelers, I immediately descended another flight of stairs leading to the overcrowded platform with its trains and their tracks.

"Lisa Leann," I called out, as if anyone, let alone she, could hear me above the cacophony.

The appropriate train—D—was right in front of me. I took a step toward it, then two back. I couldn't see Lisa Leann anywhere. I scanned the heads of the crowd surrounding me, but not a single one was a fiery red Texan's. "Lisa Leann," I called out again.

The train doors closed, and the train sped northward into the dark tunnel without me. The crowd had thinned out considerably, and I searched the sea of it again. Thinking I saw Lisa Leann walking the length of the platform, I hurried toward her. But when the figure turned, I saw it was not Lisa Leann at all.

Wonderful.

I looked toward the stairway now filled with a new flock of passengers descending the steps, searching for any signs of my now-lost friend. Or maybe I was lost. Maybe she'd gotten on the train that had pulled away. Another train slid into place, opened its doors, and regurgitated those who wished to get off on Grand. Those who had just come down the steps stepped into the train, taking their place. Again the doors coughed and sighed closed, then the train sped away.

I pressed my back against the cold tile wall as I pulled my cell phone from my purse to call Lisa Leann's. The call wouldn't go through. Another group of people poured down the stairs, and another train slid into place. "This is like a cattle call," I muttered.

Logic told me Lisa Leann had gotten on the first train and I might as well get on this one. I shuffled in, edged my way to the right, and sat on hard benches shoulder to shoulder with strangers. The train doors closed, the train jerked into action, and we zoomed onward.

What seemed like two seconds later—with not one person saying a word to another—the squelching of the announcer informed those interested that we were approaching Broadway and Lafayette. The train stopped, the doors yanked open, people got off, more people got on, and away we went again. It dawned on me then that I had no idea where I was going. Of course, I knew where I *wanted* to go . . . only I wasn't sure how to get there. I was pretty sure Lisa Leann knew, but as spontaneous as she is, that was only a guess.

There was only one thing to do. So far, everyone in the city had been more than kind . . . just like Summit View folks. So, I plastered a smile on my face and turned to the woman sitting next to me. She had a "been there/done that" look across her face, so I assumed she was a local. "What station should I get off at if I want to go to the Empire State Building?" I asked.

The woman smiled, just as I'd hoped she would. "Thirty-fourth."

I returned the smile, then dialed Lisa Leann's cell number again, this time opting to send a text message. *GET OFF AT 34th*, I typed with the pads of my thumbs.

I was getting pretty good at this texting thing.

I kept my phone clutched in my hand and shook my head. Lisa Leann could already be at 34th. She could already be at the Empire State Building. That woman could be anywhere by now. Macy's, Saks Fifth Avenue, or Tiffany's. She could be having her picture made at Rockefeller Center or could even be in the back of Donald Trump's limousine, gliding toward Trump Towers.

The train screeched to another stop. "Washington Square," the announcer said, her voice sounding as though she were pressing her lips into a microphone. The train continued on then, rocking me gently in my seat as fluorescent lights from the subway walls blinked in and out, in and out as we passed. The ride up Manhattan's subway system was dreamlike, and being separated from Lisa Leann was—for the briefest of moments—forgotten. After all, we were grown women with cell phones and texting talents. Somehow—in this city of eight million people—I was certain I'd find her.

We stopped twice more before I heard "Thirty-fourth." I stood, adjusted my purse strap, and then plowed ahead with the rest of those who were leaving the train. For a brief instant I felt as though I were a part of something so much bigger than myself. I pretended I was truly a New Yorker, exiting the silver subway train, passing by the steel support beams running up from the platform. Each one was graced with "34th St." painted in white letters on black squares as though to make certain travelers knew where they were, and yet no one seemed to give them anything more than a passing glance. I was just like all the others ascending the wide steps, heading up to the streets of Manhattan for work or . . .

Shopping.

I cut my eyes to the right, seeing that the subway deposits its passengers on 34th Street at the Manhattan Mall. One step over and I could be in what those who love to shop might call "heaven." But a shopaholic in need of a fix I was not. I took the few steps to the left, out through a glass door, and found myself in another world altogether.

The sights and sounds of Midtown were amazing. I had, quite frankly, never seen anything like it. A river of bumper to bumper yellow cabs seemed to float before me, driving east to west, west to east. Horns honked. People shouted. Music blared. Buildings— some old, some shiny new—stretched outward and upward. The air was both still and blasting with energy.

I took in the faces of the people, none of them a familiar redhead. Everyone seemed so determined. Some heading in one direction, others marching in another, each one keeping pace with the flow of human traffic. Some crossed the street at what seemed to be a three-way intersection. A reading of a sign and I realized I was near Broadway.

I followed the pedestrians with my eyes and watched as folks entered and exited a Dunkin' Donuts across the street. In spite of the rising heat of morning, I needed a cup of hot coffee and a pastry of some sort. I was practically starving.

I looked down at my hand, my phone still held tightly by my fingers, and frowned. First things first, I told myself. Before I fed my hunger, I supposed I really needed to locate Lisa Leann. She was probably frantic by now, trying to find me.

Goldie

13

Home Cooking

Typically, Saturday mornings are for sleeping in. After a long week of work for both Jack and me and five days of getting up early—six, if you count Sundays—this is our morning to laze around in bed. We usually wake up at around 9:30 or 10:00. While Jack slips out the front door to get the morning paper, I start the coffee and warm up a couple of homemade Danish I picked up the evening before at Higher Grounds. Within a matter of minutes, we're back in the bed, backs propped against fluffy pillows, legs stretched under the covers, a plate of sweet bread between us, a cup of coffee on each bedside table, and a section of the paper apiece folded out before us.

But not this particular Saturday. No-sirree-bob, as my grandmother used to say. This particular Saturday I had to get up early and make hay while the sun shone. I had to get my house in order, making sure all the laundry was done by the end of the weekend. I had to shop for traveling clothes and incidentals. I had to pack. I had to go to the grocery store, then come home and prepare meals for Jack for when I was in New York. I also wanted to spend some time with Brook and Ena before the girls and I left on Tuesday.

Good land of the living, how was I going to get it all done?

I had the clock's alarm set for 6:00, but I woke a little after 5:30. It was early, I was tired, I had another thirty minutes I could afford, but then I argued with myself that a half hour saved was a half hour earned.

I sat up and slipped from under the sheet, knees popping and muscles stiff. I groaned, and Jack echoed my sentiment. "Shh," I said, more to him than me. "Go back to sleep."

"What time is it?" he asked.

"Entirely too early," I said, wrapping my robe around myself. "Just go back to sleep."

I stepped into the kitchen and started the coffee, then went out the front door to gather the paper. I placed it on the kitchen table, then went and found my Bible and a small spiral notebook I'd been keeping lately to record the various verses of Scripture that spoke to me. When I had time for such luxury of extensive study. Those days were gone.

Before—when I'd been a homemaker only and not a legal secretary—I'd get Jack out the door for work and then spend great chunks of time in the Word. But since I'd gone to work outside the home, well . . . I was grateful for getting to church on Sundays and the Potluck club prayer meetings.

Not that I hadn't been praying . . . or reading the Bible, for that matter. I just couldn't afford to take as much time as I had before. It was like I'd said to Lizzie just a few days earlier: "Lizzie," I'd said, "I'm telling you right now, when I turned twenty-one my mama said the days would just begin to roll one into the other, and I have to admit, she was right. Seems to me the last twenty-seven years have flown by."

"Just wait till you add another ten years to that," Lizzie had said.

To which I replied, "I know . . . I know. Seems, though, that I wake up and it's Tuesday and when I go to bed it's Thursday."

Lizzie had chuckled, but I knew she knew exactly what I meant.

So today I was bound, bent, and determined to get some Bible reading done. And, I decided, my Bible would go with me to New York. I would begin every day with Scripture reading and prayer. Every day. No matter what.

I opened my Bible, allowing it to fall where it may. I'm not one of those women who says a prayer and then opens her Bible and points to a verse in hopes that God will speak. I typically follow some semblance of order, some book, some outline. But today, with so little time, I just let it open, and I did the pointing game.

When I moved my finger, I read aloud: "Where can I go from your Spirit? Where can I flee from your presence? If I go up to the heavens, you are there; if I make my bed in the depths, you are there. If I rise on the wings of the dawn, if I settle on the far side of the sea, even there your hand will guide me, your right hand will hold me fast." I took a deep breath and exhaled. "Psalm 139:7–9." Another breath, another sigh. "Oh, goodness," I said. It sounded too much like a horoscope for a woman leaving on a jet for New York City than a passage of Scripture.

The coffeepot coughed and sputtered. I left the Bible on the table and began making myself some coffee. *Okay, Lord . . . I prayed that we wouldn't have to go to New York, but you have obviously chosen to answer that prayer in your own way. Now you give me this little tidbit of wisdom. What are you saying to your daughter?*

I took a sip of the hot brew, then went back to the table. I pulled a pen from the coils of the notebook where I'd tucked it days before, flipped open the notebook to the first blank page, and scribbled the verse, underlining a few of the words. Words like *heavens* and *depths* and *sea*. But when I reread the words "your right hand will hold me fast," I drew a circle around it then dropped my pen and prayed.

When I drove my car out of the driveway and onto the street I fleetingly glanced at my watch to check the time. It was 8:00 our time, 10:00 in New York. I wondered what Evangeline and Lisa Leann were already up to. What sights they'd seen. Had they slept well the night before? I thought about calling one or the other, then decided against it, opting instead for calling Lizzie.

"Good morning, Liz," I said when she answered.

"You're up and at 'em early," she said, sounding a bit groggy.

"Did I wake you?" I asked.

"Oh no. I've been up a few minutes. I just haven't said much yet."

I laughed. "I have a mountain of things to accomplish today. Otherwise, I won't be on that plane come Tuesday."

"I know what you mean. I was just sitting here writing out a to-do list."

"A written list. Now, there's a thought. I just keep it all in my head." I smiled. "Which explains all the gray that's been popping up lately."

Lizzie was quick to reply. "Don't even talk to me about gray." She paused, then added, "So, what's up? Besides us . . ."

"Just wondering if you'd heard from Lisa Leann or Evangeline." By now I was pulling my car into the grocery store's parking lot. I slipped the gearshift into park and then stepped out of the car, never missing a beat of the conversation. The summer's warm air hit me squarely in the face, and a hot flash rose from my toes, electrified my face, and spilled my makeup down my chin. So much for the efforts I'd made to look nice.

"No. You?" Lizzie asked me.

"No." I reached into my purse and pulled out a tissue, then blotted my face. "Wonder if Donna has." I pulled my collection of recyclable grocery bags from the backseat, then closed both doors.

"You'd have to ask her."

I jerked a cart from the outside corral and began pushing it toward the store's entrance. "Well, I'll let you go, Liz. I'm at the grocery store now, and I was thinking about our girls."

Lizzie chuckled again. "Can you just imagine Evangeline in New York City all by herself?"

I grinned at the thought. "Well," I said, "she does have Lisa Leann."

"I just hope Lisa Leann doesn't leave her behind in some pink dust."

I couldn't help myself; I had to laugh.

I returned home about an hour later, juggling several bags of groceries in my arms. Jack was reclining in the family room, watching ESPN. I stuck my head in the door and said, "Hey. A little help, please?"

Jack kicked the footrest of the recliner back into place, then bounded up and toward me. "How much more you got in the car?"

"A good load. One more trip ought to do it."

He stepped past me and out the door, kissing my cheek on the way. Less than a minute later, he returned and placed the sacks on the kitchen counter as I continued to pull groceries out of those I'd brought in. "Anything good to eat in here?" he asked.

"Typical question from a man." I looked at him. Looking into one of the green sacks, he reminded me of a little boy peering into his Christmas stocking. "Would you get out of that?" I asked.

He looked up at me then, a pained look etching itself across his face.

"Jack? Jack, what is it?"

He pressed his fist to his chest and pounded a couple of times. "Nothing. Just a little indigestion."

"From what?" I asked as I stepped over to him and placed my hand on his thick arm.

"Coffee, I think. Lately coffee has been giving me indigestion."

I tipped my head. "I didn't know that."

He shook his head a bit, then smiled at me. It was a weak smile, but a smile nonetheless. "Not all the time. Not even often. Just a few times lately."

I looked him in the eyes for any signs of lying. When a woman has lived with an adulterous husband for the majority of her marriage, she learns how to read the man's eyes. From what I could see, Jack was playing it straight with me. "Okay," I said. "But you'll talk to the team doctor about this, okay?"

He stepped back. "About what? Indigestion? Goldie, we're getting older. We just can't eat or drink the kinds of things we always could."

I pulled a few groceries from a sack and set about putting them away. "I won't argue that," I said. "Still . . ." I turned to look at him. "For my own peace of mind." I thought of Olivia and of our conversation at the café in which she expressed her worry over her father's health. "And Olivia's. Just talk to him."

Jack winked. "You're just trying to get out of the trip to New York."

I hadn't thought of that, to be honest. "Do you want me to stay?" I asked.

I was genuinely concerned, but my question only added to Jack's mirth. He burst out laughing. "Oh, Goldie," he said between breaths, hand pressing on his chest. "You do beat all."

14

Taste of New York

Evie and I entered the red brick subway station and walked down a flight of stairs. We melted into the crowd that flowed toward the station's entrance. I opened my big, red Brighton purse and thrust my hand straight to the bottom to fish out my wallet. Evie had been quicker on the draw. With her MetroCard in hand, she followed the crowd, ready to swipe her card and press through the turnstile. I grabbed my wallet and opened my coin compartment and pulled out my MetroCard, just in the nick of time. Just ahead of me, Evie, as slick as greased soap, swiped her card and pushed her body through the rotating metal arms. Next in line, I swiped my card and pushed.

The turnstile pushed back.

I swiped my card and pushed again.

Is it locked?

Like in that old credit card commercial that showed a customer holding up a line of fast-paced shoppers because she tried to pay

126

with cash, the rhythm of the travelers ground to a halt. My neck prickled as I felt the breath of the man behind me. "You're holding up the line, lady. Step aside."

Without turning to look at my critic, I watched Evie disappear down the stairway. I raised my card and called, "Evie, wait!"

She was apparently so caught in the hustle of the crowd she couldn't hear me. I desperately tried to swipe my card again and pushed against the metal arms that should have twirled me through.

But, again, nothing happened.

Feeling as confused as a cow on Astroturf, I stepped aside and stared as the crowd continued their subway dance without me. Each traveler swiping his or her card before waltzing through the ever-turning bars that for whatever reason had barred me. A sense of alarm jangled down my spine. I had to act fast or Evie might take off without me.

I ran to a small glassed-in booth that housed a tiny lady in a blue work shirt over a pair of dark pants. Her jet-black hair was obviously dyed to cover her gray. But the severity of her dye job only served to deepen her frown lines, which appeared to have hardened her face. I pushed a five dollar bill through the open lip of the booth and pleaded, "I need a new card. Mine doesn't work."

The woman shook her head. Her scowl deepened as she avoided eye contact.

"Can you help me?" I shouted, wondering if the glass in the booth was too thick for a real conversation.

The attendant pointed at the subway card vending machines behind her, then helped another woman who pushed in a five dollar bill through the slot. I blinked as the woman promptly received a MetroCard in exchange.

I rethrust my money through the slot. But the attendant thrust it back and pointed at the vending machine again. For whatever reason, that little gal had chosen not to help me. But why? Was it because I was frantic enough to be rude? Feeling punished, I hurried to the card vending machines and fished out my credit card, then swiped it. A message appeared on the machine's display that read "Cannot process."

What in the world? I ran to the next machine, carefully swiping the card in accordance to the illustration on the machine. "Cannot process," the screen said, repeating the previous message. Maybe my credit card company was smart enough to know I'd purchased a one month pass the day before. *Okay, I'll use cash.*

I tucked my five dollar bill into the "cash" slot, but before I could blink, the machine spit the bill back at me. What was this, an episode of *Candid Camera*? I looked around, realizing not only was no one watching me, no one even cared to notice that I was in a dill pickle. This wasn't *Candid Camera*, it was the *Twilight Zone*, I realized. Even the automated machines were giving me the business.

My pink sleeveless tee in a high-fashioned knit suddenly felt damp as I flashed hotter than the blue blazes. At this rate, how was I ever going to get through all the plans and meetings I'd scheduled?

I ran back to the lady in the booth and thrust my five dollar bill at her again and called out, "Machines won't work."

She merely pointed back at the machines. I shrugged to illustrate my plight and shook my head, wondering if she could understand English. I slowed my speech and shouted through the circle of slots in the glass wall that separated us. "I tried. They won't work."

The woman pointed to a gate next to the turnstile, and when I reached it, an electrical sound whirled and I pushed it open. "Thanks," I cried as I waved back. The woman continued to scowl as I ran down the now empty staircase and onto the train platform. There was not a soul in sight as the last couple of trains must have just whisked the crowd away. But where was Evie?

My eyes started to burn as the empty track before me blurred. *Stop that,* I silently chided myself. After all, I was a grown woman, and though I'd just lost my dear friend in the bowels of New York City, it wasn't like she'd deserted me on purpose. And, it wasn't like I'd have to call her new husband and tell him that his wife was missing. I mean, surely she'd find her way to the bottom of the Empire State Building without me. Right?

I pulled the strap of my red purse higher onto my shoulder as I stared at the double yellow lines that stood between myself and the empty track, feeling more alone than I'd ever felt before. As a new crowd began to form around me, I tried to stop my emotional roller coaster, which seemed to be fueled by my fear of abandonment. After all, I was alone in my marriage, and now I was alone in the NYC subway.

When my train finally pulled into the station, I allowed the exiting passengers to swirl around me before I walked inside. As the benches were already occupied, I grabbed one of the center poles and braced myself so I wouldn't fall when the train jerked forward.

As the train started to accelerate, I stared down at my boots just in time to see a woman's hand jut into my open bag. Was this stranger on a fishing expedition for my wallet? I jerked my purse away from her and zipped it shut before looking up to see a well-dressed young woman who diverted her eyes. With her light gray suit and neatly cropped brown hair, she looked like a business professional on her way to work. I broke the unspoken rule of subway silence and said, "Honey, where I come from, women don't paw through each other's purses. It's not polite."

Without speaking, the woman pretended I didn't exist and turned to face the other direction. I tried to make eye contact with the others near us, but they all looked away as if they hadn't seen or heard a thing.

I hooked my elbow around the metal pole and wrapped both arms around my purse as I stared out the window. The dark walls of the tunnel flashed a deep brown as we passed an occasional light.

I tried not to blink so I wouldn't spill the tears that were gathering in my eyes. If I wasn't careful, my mounting stress would soon wash my makeup right down my cheeks. I took a deep breath and tried to focus on the one who always calms my fears. After all, I wasn't alone. I knew Jesus was right there with me. As I thought about his presence, my anxiety melted and his peace calmed my spirit. As my personal darkness lifted, I stood a little straighter.

One of my favorite Scripture passages, from Psalm 51, flowed into my thoughts like a gentle voice: "Create in me a pure heart, O God, and renew a steadfast spirit within me. Do not cast me from your presence or take your Holy Spirit from me. Restore to me the joy of your salvation and grant me a willing spirit, to sustain me."

The words helped me to square my shoulders before I bowed my head to present the Lord with a prayer. *Jesus, thank you for giving me a renewed heart and a steadfast spirit. Thank you for being here now. You alone restore my joy—not my husband, this catering contest, or even my work. My joy comes from you. Lord, you're invited to come with me as my guest today. And, Lord, help me to find Evie. Soon.*

After my prayer, it was as if, like the movie *The Wizard of Oz*, my world changed from black and white to living color. A subway station rocketed past, and I watched a cluster of brightly clad people stare back at us. I turned and looked at the would-be pickpocket. She glanced at me, her face tight with shame. Poor thing. She thought she'd find a bit of happiness in a stranger's wallet. But all she'd done was embarrass herself. Still, her would-be thievery hadn't stolen my joy. It couldn't. I had put my trust not in my wallet, my marriage, or even my friends. I had put my trust in God.

At the 34th Street station, I stepped over the double yellow line onto a path of beige tiles that spread between a series of red columns. I walked to the green metal stairway and soon stepped into the sunlight that filtered between the towering buildings. Instantly,

I was inside a cantata of street noises, punctuated with car engines, horns, and streams of chattering tourists. As I walked past a tour bus trying to merge into a parade of yellow taxis, I unzipped my purse and reached for my cell phone. But before I could dial, Sandi Patty began to sing "Majesty" on my ring tone. I checked the ID and squealed. "Evangline Vesey," I sang into the receiver.

"Where have you been?" she demanded. "Why did you leave me?"

"You left me, friend."

"That's impossible. You hopped a train without me."

"I had a little trouble at the station with my card. It took me a while to get here. In fact, I've just arrived at the 34th Street station."

"What?"

"Never mind," I said. "Where are you now?

"I'm at the Dunkin' Donuts at Herald Square. Across from Macy's."

"I'm practically there now," I crowed as I rounded the corner. As I did, I spied Evie sitting at a booth in the window. The frown she was wearing disappeared into a smile, and before I could wave she ran out the door and gave me a hug.

"I missed you," she said.

"And I you, girlfriend. You're a sight for sore eyes. Powdered sugar crumbs and all."

"What was the deal with your MetroCard?"

"I have no idea."

She put her hands on her hips. "You did use the second card we bought yesterday, right? The first card that let us into the subway system has already expired."

I opened my wallet and looked. Sure enough, there were two cards tucked inside.

"Oh dear, I must have picked up the wrong one," I said as I spied a nearby trash receptacle.

"And here I thought you were the most organized woman I'd ever met."

I dropped the expired card in the trash. "Maybe we need each other more than we realized," I said as I motioned her to follow me.

We walked down the sidewalk on 34th Street as Evie chuckled. "That could be." After a couple of blocks, she looked around. "So, where is this Empire State Building that we're heading for?"

As we were almost to 5th Street, I pointed up. "Look."

Together we stared, not even trying to hide the fact we were tourists. Our mouths gaped open, our eyes grew as large as the donuts Evie had apparently eaten without me.

Evie managed to whisper, "Oh, my."

"And to think," I said, "the Empire State Building, at 102 stories tall, was only 8 floors shorter than the World Trade Center."

"Can you imagine what it would be like if this building were to fall straight down right here and now?"

I shook my head, dumbstruck at the idea of the destruction that had occurred in lower Manhattan that tragic September day in 2001.

Breaking the moment, I fished in my purse and then pulled the two tickets for our Empire State Building tour and held them up. "Time to take our tour."

"Put those away till we get there," Evie said as we scurried down the street toward the entrance to the United States's second tallest building. "You've had enough bad luck for one day."

I nodded and tried not to grin. Because the truth was, Evie didn't know the half of it.

Soon, we were standing on the glowing marble floors in the Empire State Building's lobby, staring up at a large bronze relief sculpture of the building as two American flags saluted from each side of the tall room. Once we passed through the maze of velvet ropes, we boarded an elevator for a short ride before transferring to an express elevator that took us to the 86th floor. From there we were able to make our way to the observatory, a concrete, fenced-in, balcony-like platform just beneath the famous Empire State Building spire. We walked to the edge, then stared between the hurricane fence that surrounded the wrought-iron grill work and looked down upon the island of Manhattan. *Wow.*

Our eyes lifted to gaze beyond the blues and browns of the East River then the Hudson. From our perch, we could see into the surrounding states of Pennsylvania, New Jersey, Connecticut, and even Massachusetts. *What a view.*

We spent about forty minutes circling the ledge and snapping photos of the incredible cityscape below. "Look, there's Times Square," I said, pointing to a cluster of miniature buildings and streets.

"Did you see where the Twin Towers stood?" Evie asked, pointing south.

"Where?"

She led me to look toward lower Manhattan, and we stared in silence at a space void of its former splendor.

Finally, I checked my watch. "We'd probably better get going if we're going to hit Macy's. We have an appointment in an hour and a half, you know."

"We do? With whom?"

"I found out which prop rental house our studio uses."

"Prop rental? What's that?"

"It's everything you could imagine, and it's all for rent. I've snagged a tour so we can preselect some linens and china, floral arrangements, and backgrounds for the parties we have to throw."

Evie put the lens cover on her camera, which still hung around her neck, and we headed back toward the elevators. "Can we do that? I mean, can we shop ahead for the contest?"

"Sure," I said. "We're only window shopping anyway. Though, we are building our New York Rolodex. Besides, we can't cheat, since we don't even know what our party themes will be. So why not play around with a few theme ideas and preselect some table décor to go with them on the off chance we *can* use them. We'll photograph our ideas and jot down some notes. Then, when and if the time comes, all we'll have to do is pick up the phone to order what we need."

"I have to hand it to you, Lisa Leann. You can't get through a subway turnstile, but when it comes to catering, you've got what it takes."

Soon we were back on the busy sidewalks and on our way to the world's largest store. Macy's turned out to be delightful. My only complaint was that Evie kept wandering off. That probably wouldn't have bothered me if I weren't still feeling a little anxious from our previous separation.

As it turned out, Evie, who claimed not to be a shopper, would become so absorbed in whatever she was examining that I think a herd of elephants could have danced next to her for all she'd notice. She got lost twice, once in the ladies sportswear department and then again in the lingerie department. I have to admit that every time she failed to answer me when I called her name, it gave my heart a bit of a patter.

"Didn't you hear me?" I'd ask.

She'd look surprised. "Sorry, I was in my own little world."

This was a side to Evie I hadn't seen before. *No wonder she'd left me on the subway.*

All too soon, Evie and I had to agree that an hour was certainly not enough time to enjoy Macy's and its ten floors of merchandise. But even though our time was limited, we made use of our credit cards, leaving with shopping bags full of items. For me, I'd found the perfect soufflé pan, a couple of bracelets, and a nice pink jacket with a matching chiffon skirt covered in pink roses with lime green leaves. Evie bought some practical underwear as well as a sexy red nightgown. "This is as much for Vernon as it is for me," she said with a giggle.

I rolled my eyes. "I don't need to know the details."

"If we continue to be roomies when the girls come, maybe we can trade off when our husbands visit. You can spend a night with Henry and I'll take Vernon. Henry is planning to come, right?"

I shrugged. "I don't know. He's pretty upset that I went to New York without his blessing."

"You did?" Evie asked.

I swallowed, then nodded.

"Do you want to talk about it?"

I shook my head. "I don't think I can. Not right now, anyway."

Silently we walked outside the store and onto the sidewalk. As if to cheer me up, Evie stopped and splurged on two paper bags full of a street vender's roasted and glazed almonds. We began to munch the warm, sweet nuts as we hailed a cab. Soon my spirits lifted as we watched a small portion of New York speed by.

Fifteen minutes later, Evie and I walked through the revolving doors of a swanky black marble building checkered in glass windows. Once inside, we took the elevator up to the 25th floor. As we walked down the green-carpeted hall toward the prop rental studio, I explained, "Besides table decorations, this store has a pretty large supply of props, many of which were used in some of the movies shot here. We'll make note of some of those too."

"This will be fun," Evie admitted.

We were met by a Mr. Kenny Mitch, a slight man in his early thirties. He was more cultured and less manly than the fellows back home, and he was very enthusiastic about his work. He rose from a large oak desk almost camouflaged in ivy as we entered his suite. "Team Potluck! Ladies, I recognize you from the show! Come, let me show you the linens."

Following him, we entered a room filled with miniature table settings of extraordinary linens and china. My heart just melted with the beauty around us. "Evie, look!"

Evie slowly did a 360. "I am looking."

"Let's spread out and select some ideas for themed parties."

"Like what?" Evie asked.

"You think 'birthdays' and 'weddings,' and I'll think 'glamour' and 'movie themes.'" I pulled a couple of pens and yellow pads from my purse. "If you see something you like or get any other ideas, make a note, then photograph it."

Soon we were matching laces, china, floral arrangements, linens, and chiffons to spectacular place settings. I created one gorgeous look after the other, notating and photographing every detail. Occasionally, Evie would call out "Oh, my" when she found something particularly beautiful.

"Lisa Leann, look," she said as I turned to see a table graced with a lavender chiffon with silver polka dots topper over a purple linen tablecloth. The setting included china that looked like pale lavender presents tied with silver bows. The table was topped off with purple linen napkins and a glorious silver tea service and beautiful arrangements of silk lilacs and rosebuds. "Add a tea party category to your list," I said, running back to layer a table with gold lamé and bronze chiffon. I topped it with elegant crystal goblets and golden china plates that gleamed like mirrors. *Lovely!*

Hours later, as we were leaving with our ideas, Mr. Mitch handed us a thick catalogue.

"What's this?" I asked.

"It's our new catalogue of props back at our warehouse. I thought you might want to study up for some possible backdrops."

I cracked it open to see whole safari, jungle, shipboard, and throne room sets.

"Wow," I said. "Evie and I will be sure to study this."

Mr. Mitch handed us yet another catalogue. "You may also want to check out our costumes as well."

I nodded in happy agreement. "You're the best," I said as his blue eyes twinkled.

"Just doing my job," he replied.

Later, as Evie and I walked down the sidewalk, our arms stretched as we carried our growing supply of sacks and loot, Evie asked, "What more are we going to do to get prepared for the show?"

"I'm planning to take us to Manganaros, a famous Italian market, to sample their prosciutto and fresh canapés. We're also going to visit the fresh food vendors of Chinatown so we can locate some herbs, seafood, and fruits. I mean, we've got to have a few secret ingredients for our dishes, you know."

"Uh-huh. So where to next?"

"Oh!" I grinned. "That's a surprise, and it's my treat. Just follow me."

15

Chinese Jam

When it comes to surprises from Lisa Leann, what might happen next is anyone's guess.

By this time in our day we'd grown fairly adept at riding the subway, and—I might add—without getting separated. I was completely amazed at how one could zip from one end of Manhattan to the other and then back again in no time at all.

At some point in my respite from tourism and as I waited on Lisa Leann to purchase a hot pretzel from a sidewalk vendor, I called Vonnie to share the day's adventures. I was standing with my back against a building and my feet tucked close so as not to become roadkill by the pedestrians.

"You got lost?" Vonnie cried when I told her of the early morning separation.

"Not lost exactly, Vonnie—"

"Oh, if Fred hears this he'll never let me leave Summit View . . ."

"Then don't tell him."

"Have you told Vernon?"

"I haven't spoken to Vernon today, so no."

"Oh, good. Then don't."

I squared my shoulders against the cool stone of the building behind me and arched my spine. "Well, Vonnie . . . I dunno . . ."

"Listen, Evangeline. I've been married way longer than you. Do not tell Vernon. Has Lisa Leann told Henry?"

I frowned as I glanced across the street to where the petite firecracker was squirting mustard on her pretzel. "No, and I doubt she will." I hoped Vonnie caught the tension in my voice. If she did, I could tell her what Lisa Leann had told me about Henry. If she didn't . . . well, I'd have no excuse. It would be too close to gossip. This was really a fine line.

"Good. Keep it that way. Tell me about New York City."

I rattled on as fast as I could about what we'd managed to do in one short day. "Wait till you see this place, Vonnie. I know you lived in Los Angeles for a while, but believe me, this is a world unto itself. I've never seen anything like it. The Empire State Building . . . and Macy's . . . and seeing the city from high above and from underneath." I took a deep breath and sighed. Lisa Leann was now scooting up the crosswalk and heading my way. "Hey, I gotta go. Lisa Leann has her pretzel now, and she's taking me somewhere, but she won't tell me where."

"I worry about you two there alone in that city."

"We're fine."

"You weren't fine this morning."

"Well, if you don't want me to tell Vernon and you don't want Lisa Leann to tell Henry, then let's the two of us not talk about it either."

"Oh, how I dread this trip."

"I know how you feel. I felt the same. But tell the girls it's fabulous!"

Lisa Leann made it back to me then and said, "Is that Vernon?"

I shook my head. "Vonnie." Then to Vonnie: "Okay, Lisa Leann is treating me to something and she won't tell me what, so I have to go now."

"My, my. Hasn't this trip just made you two the best of friends?"

I cut my eyes to Lisa Leann, who was wolfing down her pretzel, savoring each mouthful by closing her eyes and seeming to sigh into it. With her eyes closed, I rolled mine. "Don't get carried away, Von. See you in a few days."

I disconnected the call just as Lisa Leann's eyes flew open. "Carried away by what? Is she overpacking? Did you tell her about the subway?"

"Yes and she said not to tell Vernon or Henry." I furrowed my brow. "You've got mustard on the corner of your mouth."

Lisa Leann's tongue did a quick dart from side to side, and then she said, "Why shouldn't we tell them? Because they'll be upset that we didn't spend the money?"

"What money?"

"The money for the cab."

"What cab?"

Lisa Leann shook her head. "The cab we should have taken instead of the subway."

"Lisa Leann Lambert, you did *not* say one word this morning about taking a cab. You said we'd take the subway. And do not shake your head at me like I'm stupid."

This time she crinkled her nose. "I have no idea what you are talking about, Evangeline, but I'll tell you this: we've got to learn to communicate better or we'll be in a mess come time to do the show." She pointed northward. "This way to my surprise."

We started walking. "All I'm saying is, why didn't you say something this morning about taking a cab?"

"Because this morning I wanted to take the subway. If we couldn't afford a cab yesterday from the airport to the—*oh*! You're talking about . . ." Lisa Leann began laughing. She stopped in midstream of the sidewalk in shoulder to shoulder human traffic and just cracked up laughing.

I stopped too, but I wasn't laughing. "I'm glad you think this is funny."

When she finally wheezed the laughing to its end she said, "You were talking about this morning on the subway and I was talking about yesterday on the subway."

"And you think that deserves this much laughter?"

She looped her arm in mine. "Come on, Evie. Do you know what the Broadhurst Theatre is?"

"No, but I'm sure you'll tell me."

"You're straight shootin' I will. It's nearly one hundred years old and it's a legitimate Broadway theater. Helen Hayes has played there and Vincent Price and Rosalind Russell and . . . oh-oh! William Shatner. You know, the man who played on that outer space TV show."

"*Star Trek*?"

"Yes, him. And . . . let me think . . . Marlo Thomas made her Broadway debut there and Joel Grey has performed there and Christopher Reeve before he was Superman and oh, yeah . . . Jane Seymour was in a play there that was performed over a thousand times and—"

"So we're going there, I take it?"

Lisa Leann nearly burst apart she was so excited. "Yes!" Her arm squeezed mine.

"Are any of those actors going to be there? Personally, I wouldn't mind seeing Jane Seymour. I've always liked her."

"Well, no . . . but I'll give you a hint as to what we're going to see. It's the longest running musical in history—"

"*The Sound of Music*!"

I felt Lisa Leann sigh deeply. "No . . . not *The Sound of Music*."

"I love that movie."

"Guess again."

We rounded a corner about that time, and I came to an abrupt stop. "Good heavens, where are we?"

"This, dear Evie, is Times Square, and all these signs are called JumboTrons. We've been near it off and on all day, and believe me, it was a real effort not to drag you here earlier."

I allowed myself a moment to catch my breath. I'd seen it on television, of course. I'd even managed to stay up a time or two for Dick Clark's New Year's Rockin' Eve, but I'd never experienced a sight such as this in person. Not since . . . well, since earlier that morning atop the Empire State Building. "Oh, Lisa Leann. Have you ever seen so many lights? And in so many colors? Even with it being just dusk, it's amazing."

"Wait till you see it tonight when it's completely pitch black dark."

"Is this where you're taking me?"

Lisa Leann pulled me forward. "No, but it's close. We're going to 44th Street. Come on. We're going to see *Les Misérables*."

Well. Even *I* had heard of *that*. Dear me, wouldn't Lizzie be jealous when I told her where Lisa Leann had taken me?

Sunday morning came too soon. After our adventure at the Broadhurst Theatre, Lisa Leann and I moseyed on back to Times Square, where I treated her to dinner at a restaurant called Cosi, where we feasted on the most delicious Moroccan lentil soup I've ever tasted. Actually, the only Moroccan lentil soup I've ever tasted. New York was filled with cultural experiences, including Cosi's famous flatbread. I'd never had any of that, either.

When it came time to return to SoHo, I told my traveling companion, "I'm not taking the subway this late at night. Let's grab a cab."

What I thought would be easy enough turned out to be nearly a nightmare. Cabs zipped up and down Times Square as though on a mission. Finally, after long minutes of no luck, some nice policeman said, "Head up to 9th Avenue. They're easier to catch there."

Well, maybe it was easier for him, but let me tell you this: no cab on 9th Avenue wanted to take two middle-aged women to SoHo. Why, I couldn't imagine until Lisa Leann said, "I think the fare won't be good for them. It's such a long way down there and then chances are they won't have a fare back."

"Then look pitiful and beg," I said. "There are homeless people starting to bunk down for the night around here, and I'm getting a little scared. What if someone tries to attack us?"

Lisa Leann patted me on the arm. "Don't be scared, Evie. I'm here. I won't let anyone hurt us."

I frowned down at her petite stature. "And what will you do, pray tell? Kick them in the knee?"

"Of course not. But I'll tell you what we both can do. We can do what I did this morning on the subway when you took off without me."

"I did not—"

"Never mind. Let's pray."

And so we did. We prayed right there in the middle of a sidewalk on 9th Avenue in New York City. And, minutes later, we were zooming toward SoHo in the backseat of a black Lincoln Town Car.

"God sure answered us in style," I told Lisa Leann later after we'd nicely tipped the cab driver.

"God's got class, I always say."

We hurried up to our room and repeated our performance from the night before. While Lisa Leann showered, I called Vernon. While I showered, Lisa Leann called Henry. At least I assume she did. I hope she did.

Sunday morning we woke a little later than usual, and still it felt too early. My feet ached from all the walking of the day before. "We're not spring chickens anymore, Lisa Leann," I said to her as we locked our hotel room door and slipped down the narrow hallway and toward the stairs leading to the first floor.

"I'm feeling you, sister."

"Feeling me? I beg your pardon."

"It's what all the kids are saying these days. To 'feel' someone is to understand where they're coming from."

"Oh."

"Lizzie taught me that."

We stepped into the lobby about that time, drawn into its antiquity by the aroma of fresh-brewed coffee. Several of the hotel guests were standing before the table, where it was being self-served, all of them in their pajamas. I was both curious and appalled.

In silence, Lisa Leann and I prepared a cup to go and then skipped down the stairs and out the glass doors and onto the sidewalk, where we turned left. "I read about a little café just down the street," Lisa Leann said. "It was in some of that hotel literature in our room."

I nodded in answer.

Peripherally I saw Lisa Leann turn her head toward me. "What's wrong?"

"Lisa Leann, since when do decent people wear their pajamas into a hotel lobby?"

Lisa Leann waved her hand at me, then took a sip of her coffee before saying, "Oh, I know. It's amazing, isn't it? It's like all of a sudden pajamas are a fashion statement."

"Well, I think it's just awful."

Lisa Leann giggled but said nothing more about it.

After a breakfast of fried eggs, bacon, and toast and after I begged God not to let my arteries harden on the spot, we walked through Little Italy, toward Chinatown. Little by little the landscape changed. Signs printed in bold reds and bright yellows surrounded us as street vendors hawked their goods. The population grew thick until we were shoulder to shoulder with other pedestrians. I felt like the old sardine in the can cliché.

"I've never seen so many people," I said. "And on a Sunday morning when they all ought to be in church. Like us."

"But we're not in church," Lisa Leann said with a wink. She then slipped her arm into mine in the manner she seemed to have favored of late and said, "Did you know there are somewhere between 70 and 150,000 residents in Chinatown?"

"Lisa Leann, what did you do before we left Summit View? Read everything you could get your hands on about New York City? It's like you're a walking encyclopedia since we got here."

Lisa Leann pinked. "Well, it kept my mind occupied and away from the home situation."

This time I squeezed her arm. "I'm sorry," I said quietly. "About you and Henry."

We rounded a corner—Canal Street. Lisa Leann slipped her arm out of mine and, due to the immense crowd, stepped in front of me. I placed my hands on her shoulders so we wouldn't get separated, and for a few moments, we waddled instead of walked. From my vantage point the walking population of Chinatown, at this moment, looked more like penguins heading for water than shoppers heading for the next cheap purchase. As we chugged along, Lisa Leann slipped to my right. This time it was I who slipped my arm into the loop of hers.

We continued west on Canal Street, each step making me more and more aware of the whereabouts of my shoulder strap purse. I clutched it in front of me as though holding onto a life preserver in the middle of the Hudson. Lisa Leann stopped along the way, halting me with her. She purchased a knockoff Rolex watch for Henry, a knockoff Louis Vuitton for Nelson. I couldn't help but notice Nelson's watch cost twice what Henry's cost.

We both purchased silk wraps, one for each of us and then one for each of the girls, including Mandy, Lisa Leann's daughter. We giggled as we chose the appropriate color and style for each of them. Lizzie, I knew, would be impressed with the "Burberry" I'd selected for her.

We continued on. I spotted a short Chinese woman standing on the corner of some cross street and Canal. As we neared her, she spoke to Lisa Leann, who immediately slipped her arm out of mine. The lady—extending her palm and a small piece of paper within her palm—nodded at Lisa Leann, spoke again (though I couldn't hear a word of it over the sound of the city), and then turned and walked north.

Lisa Leann followed behind her. I stood without moving. What in the world was that little redhead up to now?

Lisa Leann turned toward me. "Come on!" she called with a wave of her hand.

By now the Chinese woman was a good half block ahead of Lisa Leann and Lisa Leann was a quarter block from me. Dutifully, I followed, never once reaching Lisa Leann, who kept a fairly good pace behind the Chinese lady.

"Where are we going?" I called, but Lisa Leann didn't hear. Either that or she just wasn't responding.

"Hello?" I called again. I caught sight of a small-framed Chinese man leaning against a building. He wore khaki pants that seemed a half size too big and a black leather belt squeezed around his waist. His shirt was cotton plaid. One sandaled foot was perched against the wall behind him, and a cigarette dangled from the fingertips of his right hand.

"Lady, be quiet," he said. "No yelling. No yelling."

What? In the din of this city's streets, *I* am not supposed to yell?

I gave him my best "who do you think you are" look, to which he replied, "Shhh. Be quiet."

I turned my face from him and toward the back of Lisa Leann's head just in time to see the Asian lady opening a glass door near the corner of the next cross street. Next to the door was another

Chinese man, dressed much like my adversary now a few yards away, who nodded at her and her at him. He held the door open as she disappeared into the recesses of the building, and Lisa Leann followed behind her.

Lisa Leann, I might add, who never once looked back to make sure I was all right.

When I reached the man next to the door, I mumbled, "I'm with the redhead."

He opened the door as though I'd not said a word to him, and I stepped over its threshold. I was now in a semi-dark, long and narrow hallway. Lisa Leann was at the end of it, turned toward the light from the street. She was grinning like the proverbial cat that swallowed the canary. "Lisa Leann, what are we doing here?"

"Shhh," she said.

"Why does everyone keep shushing me?"

"Shhh," she said again, then stepped through a doorway to the right.

I shut up and followed, finding myself in another hallway, this one shorter but just as dark. Several steps and to the left and we were in a small room with a narrow door. This room was brightly lit, and empty other than Lisa Leann and the Asian woman who apparently had decided to wait for us. "In here," she said, pointing to another door.

I felt like a mouse in search of cheese strategically hidden at the end of a maze.

We stepped through the door and into an L-shaped room, its walls covered in purses, the air permeating with the odor of new leather. There were three Chinese people sitting on chairs on the short side of the room. Two of them—women—were ripping plastic from purses. Between them was a large box filled with plastic-covered merchandise. The third—a man—sat with a calculator and a money bag in his lap. He sat closest to the door.

Lisa Leann had slipped over to the long side of the room. Her neck was craned and her eyes danced like a kid's at Christmas. I grabbed her arm and yanked. "Lisa Leann," I hissed. "Where are we?"

"Bootleg," she whispered back.

The lady we'd followed stepped over to us. "Coach, Burberry, Kate Spade, Prada, Coco Chanel . . ." she recited as she pointed. "Good stuff. Good stuff." Then she stepped over to the man with the calculator, who smiled at her and began speaking to her in their native language.

"Is this legal?" I whispered to Lisa Leann just as another group of women entered the "shop."

"Not for them," she said.

"And for us?"

"Well, it's not *illegal*."

Ah, another fine line. "So then why are we here?"

Lisa Leann turned and placed her hands on her hips. "Because, Evangeline. This is part of the New York City experience. And . . . look around you. Is this not fun? Think of it as research and development for our time on the show."

I sighed. "Yes, Lisa Leann. As much fun as a prison sentence to Sing Sing." Being a loyal viewer of *Law and Order* was finally coming in handy.

Lisa Leann waved a hand at me. "Oh, posh. Now, come on. Let's shop to our little hearts' content!" She pointed to an oversized red leather bag. "I wonder how much that is? Excuse me," she said to our "leader in crime," "how much is this adorable bag?"

"Seventy-five but, for you, sixty."

I couldn't help myself. "Sixty dollars plus five to ten with New York's finest," I mumbled behind her ear.

"Lighten up, Evie," she hissed back.

Heaven help me. A half hour later I was one of them. One of the Canal Street Savvy. I now own a Prada purse, a Prada wallet, and some "smokin'" (at least according to Lisa Leann) oversized Coco Chanel sunglasses.

Lizzie

16

Seasoned Traveler

I had a laundry list of things that needed to be accomplished before I could even think about leaving Summit View, the least of which was to pack. I'd spent the better part of the weekend food shopping and then cooking and freezing dinners like chicken potpie for Samuel. "Enough to hold you over a few days," I said. "Or until our daughters or our daughters-in-law ask you over."

"Or I arrive in New York myself."

I rolled my eyes. "*If* we survive long enough on the show. Don't start thinking in terms of what you'll pack. I really don't think this is going very far."

I took time to go by Summit Center, where my mother is now residing under full-time care. A few months ago her Alzheimer's became such that my brother and I were forced to make better arrangements for her. Until then, she'd spent several months living at the Good Shepherd Assisted Living facility. When Mom fell, broke an arm, and cracked two ribs, it became alarmingly evident she could no longer take care of herself. I was relieved of a good deal of stress knowing someone was caring for her 24/7, but I still managed to go by to see her at least three times a week.

Not once had she recognized me as her daughter. A few times she'd called me Karen, a name I could not place to anyone in her lifetime. My brother stated he'd never heard the name either. At least, not spoken by Mom.

On the Saturday before our departure to New York she once again called me Karen.

"Mom, I'm Lizzie," I said to her. She was sitting in the sunroom down the hall from her tiny room, where a bed, dresser, reclining chair, and television set made up her "home." In the sunroom on that bright July afternoon, she watched television with some of the other residents, though her eyes remained blank and unregistering. Nothing was getting through to her brain at all, it seemed.

I sat down next to her and took her hand in mine. "Hey, Mom." I forced myself to sound cheery and optimistic.

She looked at me then back to the television. "Hello, Karen."

"Lizzie, Mom. I'm Lizzie." I don't know why I bothered, really.

She looked back at me, blinked several times, then again turned her eyes to the television.

"Are you enjoying the show?" I asked her.

She remained mute.

I took a deep breath. "Speaking of television, did you know I'm going to be on television? I am. It's a show called *The Great Party Showdown* and I'll be . . . well . . . catering. Cooking, if you can imagine. On national TV. International, actually. I guess." I took another deep breath and exhaled, then turned my attention to the television and, holding my mother's frail and wrinkled hand, watched a half hour of a movie I could barely see through my veil of tears.

My daughter Michelle and her husband Adam hosted a family cookout on Saturday evening. Sunday was, of course, church, and though I could have easily talked myself out of going (I still had not packed nor had I really bought anything to wear), I went. Our pastor, Kevin Moore, called the club up to the altar—sans Evangeline and Lisa Leann—as well as Wade and David. He prayed for us, for our families back home, and that we would be a witness for Jesus while cooking our way into the hearts of America.

On the way home I said to Samuel, "Now I'm so glad I went."

"You still have to pack," he reminded me.

"I will," I said. "Later."

Monday morning I went to the Outlets at Silverthorne, where I purchased several pantsuits and two dresses, one that was glittery on the outside and soft on the inside. I bought some sleepwear and lingerie and travel-size toiletries. As a last-minute decision I stopped at A Cut Above Beauty Salon and Day Spa, where I was treated to a trim, a brow waxing, a facial, manicure, pedicure, and a natural beauty makeover.

By the time I got home Monday evening, I was nearly too tired to finish packing, but I had little choice. I was leaving too early the next morning to put the final touches off another minute.

We met at the Frontier ticket counter, some of us more exuberant than others. All the local television stations had camera crews and reporters ready to film. We were asked for statements and, of course, we gave them.

"Where is Lisa Leann Lambert?" a news reporter from *Denver News 4* asked, stretching her neck to look among the faces of the catering club and our family members.

"She and my wife, Evangeline Vesey, have already left for the city," Vernon answered. Vernon had insisted upon accompanying his daughter to the airport, and I was glad he had. His years handling various newsworthy stories from Summit View on television had made him comfortable with both camera and microphone.

"Sheriff Vesey," the reporter continued, "what do you think your wife and daughter and the rest of the club's chances are for winning the big prize?"

Vernon blushed appropriately. "Well, we're hoping for the best, but more than that, we're trusting God to allow only what he wills."

Score one for Vernon, I thought, beaming.

"Will you be joining Mrs. Vesey soon?" she asked.

"Yes, I hope to."

"And what about Mr. Lambert?" another reporter asked. I turned to see a man holding a microphone with KDVR in bold red letters around it. He was tall and powerfully built, his dark skin a comfortable contrast to the red baseball KDVR-31 cap he wore low over his head.

"No," Vernon said with a wink, "I don't expect he'll be joining my wife."

Everyone laughed, and then Vernon added, "But I suppose you are asking if he'll be joining his wife. Ah—Mr. Lambert had some pressing business this morning or I'm sure he would be here now." He smiled. "Their son, however, will be meeting the rest of the gang in New York later this afternoon."

Another two points for Vernon.

Another female reporter, this one from KUSA-9 News, turned her attentions to David, who stood as close to one side of Donna as Wade was on the other. "Mr. Harris, do you feel as though you are about to get on the bicycle you fell off?"

David's eyes darkened. "Excuse me?"

The reporter flashed a smile and batted her long, feathery lashes. "What I mean to say is, the cameras, the lights, the action. This should feel like second nature to you."

David nodded politely. "I see what you mean. Ah . . . no. It was my mother"—David shot a quick glance over to Vonnie, his birth mother—"Harmony Harris, who was most comfortable on the seat of *that* bicycle. I always just went along for the ride."

Wade shifted. "Well, if we're going to make our plane . . ."

We all turned then, saying our good-byes to the cameras and

reporters with their fat microphones—not to mention the small gathered crowd—and shuffled toward the concourse, where a tube-like carriage for our adventure would soon whisk us through the friendly skies and toward the Big Apple.

As soon as our plane touched down at Newark's airport I pulled my phone from my purse and dialed Samuel's cell number. He answered on the first ring.

"The eagle has landed," I said with a tease.

"How was your flight?"

"Uneventful from where I'm sitting. Of course, what do I know? I slept with my head wedged between the seat and the window most of the way."

"Sounds comfy."

"Ha."

"Call me when you get to the hotel."

"I will. I love you," I reminded him.

"I love you."

Vonnie's luggage was the last to come out onto the conveyor in baggage claim, so while she waited in a panic, the rest of us took nearby seats and tried not to look too anxious. David called the show's producer—take-charge kind of guy that he is—and asked about the limousine that was scheduled to pick us up. "Oh, I see . . ." I heard him say. "That's right . . . I see . . . yes, if you will, please let him know we'll be another few minutes. One of the club members has not gotten her luggage as of yet . . . yes . . . yes . . . thank you."

He flipped his phone shut with a flourish and then stepped over to Vonnie and placed his hand lightly on her shoulder. *Mother and son*, I thought. What a blessing Vonnie had him here with her today.

A half hour later we were all piled in the back of a stretch limo and sipping on colas. Our driver, a middle-aged man of Middle Eastern heritage, drove the car easily into the Lincoln Tunnel and then out to the other side. Manhattan, in all its glory, spanned the horizon as far as we could see. Not a one of us held back. We oooh'd and ahh'd and asked, "What's that?" in rapid succession. Our driver kept the dividing window down and happily answered all our questions as he drove down streets and up streets, finally gliding to a stop in front of the New York Hilton on the Avenue of the Americas.

With the exception of David, we all did a poor job of hiding our amazement at the beauty and wonder of this hotel. The lobby was opulent and bright, perfectly decorated with seasonal flowers and brightly lit fichus trees set high in planters dripping with ivy.

We were escorted to the registration desk, where we were told that Evie and Lisa Leann had already checked in for the day and that we would be picked up by limousine at 6:00 and taken to the studio. We were then divided into groups: David and Wade would share a suite with Nelson, who had yet to arrive; Vonnie and Donna were set to room together, leaving Goldie and me to room together. Goldie and I exchanged grins like schoolgirls on an overnight field trip.

"Well, hello, roomie," she said as she stepped over to where I was standing.

Minutes later we were given our keys and then escorted to our rooms.

I nearly inhaled my tongue when the bellhop swung our door open wide and allowed us entry.

"Would you look at this?" Goldie said.

As the bellhop heaved our luggage off the rack and into the closet of the room he said, "First time to New York?"

"For me, yes," Goldie admitted.

"I came here years ago," I said. I then looked at Goldie. "But I can tell you we didn't stay in a place as nice as this."

The afternoon sun spilled through a wide window sheathed in white drapery sheers, bringing light to a room accented in bold gold, maroon, green, and white. The two beds were decked with thick mattresses, and I imagined myself leaping to get into bed at night. There were six pillows resting against the cherry headboard of both beds and a neck roll pillow that matched the thick comforter.

Next to the window, swathed in accent drapes, was a comfy chair and next to it a round table topped with a basket filled with fruit, chocolates, nuts, and bottles of water.

"Look at this," I said to Goldie, pointing, then turned to find her peering into the bathroom.

"Crabtree and Evelyn bath products, Liz! I love that stuff."

The bellhop gave his speech about the bed and bath collection being of the exclusive Hilton Serenity Collection, that he hoped we enjoyed our stay, and—*wink-wink*—he hoped we won the grand prize on *The Great Party Showdown*. I felt myself blush, said, "Thank you," then slipped a tip into his gloved hand.

When the door closed behind him, I turned to Goldie and she to me. Then we smiled. Then we grinned. Then we grabbed hands and jumped up and down, whooping and hollering.

Giggling, we fell onto one of the beds then sobered. I stole a quick glance at my watch. "How much time do we have before they pick us up?" Then, answering my own question, said, "Two hours."

"I get the bathroom first," Goldie said, springing from the bed and bounding over to where her luggage was standing near the wall.

I propped myself up on my elbows. "Just think, Goldie. In two or so hours, we'll be sitting near the first row in *The Great Party Showdown* audience."

Goldie pressed her hand against her stomach. "Woo! Butter-flies." She took a deep breath, then exhaled. "I can do all things through Christ who strengthens me," she said, then repeated it as she stepped into the bathroom.

I looked after her and said, "Amen."

Donna

17

Tea Time

What had I been thinking when I'd agreed to work till two a.m.?

By the time I got home and finished packing everything I thought I'd need into a giant duffel bag, it was time to squeeze into Vonnie's Taurus and speed down I-70 toward DIA.

You'd think my companions, Vonnie, Fred, and David, would have had enough compassion to let me grab a couple of winks, but between their excited chatter, all I could do was dream of a nap on the plane. But fat chance for that, since my seat assignment was smack between David and Wade. *Nice going, Lisa Leann. I owe you one*, I thought, knowing she'd helped Kat with the seat assignments.

With these two lovesick guys patting my arms and exclaiming, "Oh Donna, this" and "Hey Donna, that," I finally snapped. "Guys, we've got at least a whole week to visit, can't you just let me catch up on my beauty sleep for an hour or two?"

"Sorry, Donna," Wade said.

David countered, "She asked us to be quiet."

I responded by squeezing my eyes shut and counting to ten as their bickering continued.

Finally, I traded seats with Vonnie. "Sorry, guys, it's been fun, but I'm going to have to take a break," I said as I crossed the aisle. But to my chagrin, I discovered Vonnie had been busy blabbing our business to her seatmate, a gentleman in his seventies. This kind-looking chap was just too curious to leave me alone.

"So, you're that deputy on *The Great Party Showdown*, I hear."

"Mmmhmm," I said, shutting my eyes, unhappy to discover that my blatant attempts to lose consciousness did nothing to dissuade this man from conversation. He continued to pepper me with questions about the reality program and my personal life until we finally parted at baggage claim in the JFK airport. "Good luck," he called as he picked up his brown, battered suitcase and headed out the door to the stand of taxis.

I waved back, still feeling as grumpy as ever, though I managed to behave.

But now, even after a power nap at the hotel, I was still in a state of grump. And how could I not be, with Vonnie humming "Jesus Loves Me" the entire time she settled into our room, opening and closing suitcases, drawers, and the closet, and even steam ironing her clothes? When I yanked off the covers, she asked, "Was I disturbing you, dear?"

I tried to lie, but my voice showed my stress. "Of course not."

"Sorry, dear," she said as she patted my shoulder.

Moments later, I ducked into the elegant bathroom to grab a quick shower before I stepped into a pair of black slacks topped by an oversize tee that Lisa Leann had designed and ordered through an Internet site. The words "Go Team Potluck" blared in large, hot pink letters across my chest.

Wade, of course, had balked about wearing anything with a hint of pink, but Lisa Leann had been firm. "It shows everyone you're on our side," she said. "You are, are you not?"

157

A few minutes after I dressed and towel-dried my hair, a stretch limo whisked me and the entire team through the streets bordered with storefronts and sidewalks teeming with people, to the GE building at Rockefeller Center.

"How was your flight?" Lizzie asked Nelson, who was dressed in our team shirt and sitting next to his proud mom.

"Delayed," he said as we sped through Manhattan. "I only just made it to the hotel a few minutes ago."

Lisa Leann beamed. "Just in time for this next phase of our adventure. You ready?"

Nelson nodded, his green eyes flashing. "You better believe it."

I only wished I could share his enthusiasm, but the truth was I hated being on TV just as much as I hated missing so much work. I had bills to pay, and rent. If I missed just one payment, that would be enough for old man Burnett to force me out of my mountain bungalow. He'd been itching to do that anyway, knowing he could get a lot more rent out of a new tenant.

I took a deep breath and tried to relax and enjoy the view. With any luck, this trip was only a free vacation, not a trip to the poor house. I'd be back on the job a week from tomorrow, and the public's memory of this episode would have already started to fade.

Right, Lord?

Once our limo arrived at Rockefeller Center, we walked past the plaza fountain and its golden statue of a boy grasping fire. "What's that supposed to be?" I asked.

David said, "That's Prometheus. He's from Greek mythology."

"What's his story?"

Our college student Nelson beat David to the answer. "He was said to be a Titan. He stole fire from the gods for mankind."

"Oh, dear," Vonnie said, "do New Yorkers really believe that?"

Lizzie, ever the librarian, shook her head. "No, Von. It's just a symbol of acquiring technology."

With Prometheus behind us, we stepped into the welcoming

lobby of the seventy-story GE building. A young woman dressed in a tailored tan pantsuit said, "Welcome, Team Potluck, to *The Great Party Showdown*. My name is Amy Snyder, and I'm Kat's assistant."

She turned on her heels and led us past the lobby's candy shop and three high definition screens, all showing *The Great Party Showdown* highlights. She then led us to the elevator bank and said, "We don't have a second to waste. I'm taking you to hair and makeup so we can get an interview of you to roll in tonight's live program."

An elevator ride later, I was walking into a room filled with mirrors and makeup artists. As several members of our team met the artist who would be working with them, I was greeted by a young woman with black dreadlocks and flashing brown eyes. She was wearing indigo jeans and a white T-shirt that exclaimed *The Great Party Showdown* in bold, orange letters. She said, "My name is Sasha, I'm here to make you beautiful."

"I'm Donna. Can't you just leave me to look like my crabby old self?"

Sasha laughed. "Rough day?" Before I could respond, she pulled a large jar of orange and brown powder twirled with red hot candies from a shelf above her station. "Here, let me make you a cup of my tea I use to relax my guests."

"Sounds good," I said, watching as she put a couple of heaping teaspoons into a Styrofoam cup before adding hot water from a steaming thermos. She handed me the cup, and I took a sip.

"Why don't you sit tight while I work on your friend here," she said, beckoning Nelson to her chair.

"Don't I get some tea too?" he asked.

Sasha laughed. "You, my friend, don't look like you need to chill."

A few minutes later, a styled, pancaked, and powdered Nelson was sent to the green room, and I sat in Sasha's chair. She fingered my curls then pulled out a headband for me to wear while she applied a heavy coat of makeup, concentrating on eliminating the dark circles under my eyes. I didn't protest until she began to tweeze my stray brows.

"Ouch!"

"Trust me, Donna. It's just that I'm going for an overall look of vitality," she said. I quieted and let her have her way until she pulled out a small plastic container of false eyelashes.

"You've got to be kidding," I said as she began to apply glue to a fine line of disembodied lashes.

She turned me so that I couldn't see the mirror and began to apply the synthetic lashes to my eyelids. "If you don't like them, we can always take them off before the glue dries."

She finished her sticky job then fluffed out my curls. When she turned me back to the mirror, I stared at a stranger.

"Is that me?"

"Sure is. Now why don't you head for the green room on the seventeenth floor? You'll see it off to the right when you get off the elevator."

When I entered the room, I was met with applause as I was the last Potlucker through the door. "You win the title of best makeover," Lisa Leann crowed while David and Wade stared, slack jawed. Wade stood. "Donna, you're . . ."

"Beautiful," David said, finishing his sentence and standing next to him.

"Thanks," I said as I sat on the old tan couch next to Vonnie. She patted my knee. Luckily, I had on such a thick layer of paint no one could even tell I was blushing. But before the makeup could melt off my burning cheeks, we were greeted by Kat Sebastian, the producer. She wasn't at all what I'd imagined.

She was about six feet tall, skinny as a stick, and dressed in black, a color that contrasted with her pale skin. She had piercing brown eyes that she hid behind a pair of black plastic spectacles, and a pierced eyebrow that sported a small gold hoop. Her dark hair was swept into a rather chic ponytail that hung at the nape of her neck. But the thing that got me was she was probably all of twenty-seven.

"Glad to see you all made it." She glanced at the clipboard she was carrying. "I've come to take you to our studio, down on 8 H. I'm going to get you miked so you can make some quick comments for tonight's program."

"You don't mean we're going to be on the *Saturday Night Live* set?" Nelson asked, his eyes wide.

"That's the one," Kat said. "Now, if you'll follow me."

Once our little group gathered inside the studio, we walked into a large pit, which was filled with cameras, light poles, and folding chairs. We looked at the elevated stage in front of us, which sported the judges' desks and chairs and a couple of JumboTrons. Flanking either side of the stage were smaller sets with easy access to the pit.

Wade tapped me on the shoulder and pointed up. I turned around to see that the pit we were in was surrounded by elevated seating that looked large enough to hold a small army. "Wow," I whispered.

Kat said, "You and the other teams will be seated here in the pit tonight, but for now, I want you to follow me to the stage we've set up for your spot, which we'll roll into tonight's show. One of our interns will get you miked up so we can start."

The next thing we knew, Team Potluck stood under the glare of light while Kat's voice floated down to us. "We'll start in just a minute as soon as Gianne comes out of wardrobe. By the way, love the shirts. Go Team Potluck."

"Yeah, 'Go Team Potluck' as in *go home*," I responded.

"What was that, Donna?"

I squinted my eyes into the blinding light. "Nothing," I said. "Just feeling a little homesick."

"It's too soon to feel homesick," Kat said, "and with the numbers you've helped bring in, it looks to me you could be in town a while."

Nelson's voice was filled with hope. "We've got numbers?"

"The show pulled in an audience of thirty million last week."

"Dear me!" Vonnie stammered.

Soon, Gianne Gillian, in a glittering black gown cut down to her navel, came rushing down to our set. She had a handheld microphone and was fidgeting with a device in her ear, presumably to hear private instructions from Kat.

Gianne made quick work of our interview, which was full of smiles and polite answers. She seemed to focus a lot on the male members of our team.

She said to Wade, "Welcome to New York. Are you homesick yet?"

Wade put his hand on my shoulder. "Not as long as I'm surrounded by the people I love."

Gianne turned to David. "I hope you'll soon discover that New York has a lot to offer."

What, was she batting her eyes at him?

David grinned. "I've always loved New York." He reached for Vonnie and gave her a hug as he placed his hand on my other shoulder. "But Colorado's my home now."

As soon as we were done, Amy led us to the craft table for a bite to eat while Gianne continued a bit of solo banter on the stage we left behind.

All too soon, we were seated in the pit with the other six teams still in the competition when the theme music blared and the live audience cheered. My heart began to pound with the realization that we were about to go live before thirty million souls.

After the rock music theme played, the cameras panned the cheering audience and contestants before focusing on Gianne in a close-up. "America, last week you voted three teams through to next week's round of our top six. That means another unlucky team will not be joining us tonight. Sad to say," our hostess continued, "but Team Café Mocha has been eliminated from the competition." The JumboTrons showed a clip of Team Café Mocha from Seattle zapping whipped cream on top of steaming mugs of coffee. The crowd gave them a sympathy clap.

"But good news; we've got the three teams that have already qualified for next week's competition and they are in the house. First, let's say hello to Team Potluck!"

The lights came up and the camera panned to show our team sitting in the audience. When we realized we were on camera, we smiled and waved to the cheering crowd.

"Next, let me welcome Team Tex Mex from San Antonio, Texas."

The crowd cheered again as the Texans stood and swished their bright yellow skirts.

"And last but not least is Team Batter Up from New York City."

The all-male catering team, dressed like the New York Yankees, stood and gave the victory sign while the crowd went wild.

"I guess we know who the hometown favorite is," Gianne said as the applause died.

Soon, Gianne was introducing the four teams competing tonight, showing previews of their catered events. "Tonight, America, we'll see Team Hollywood, the Boston Bean Team, Comfort Cooking, and the Wild Cajun Cooks, all catering their own events back home on location with one of our celebrity judges observing. Only three of these four teams will join us in the next level of competition."

Lisa Leann whispered loud enough for our row to hear, "We're safe, at least till next Tuesday's vote."

Soon we were watching the first produced catering package, which showed Team Hollywood catering a ten-year-old girl's birthday party. This bevy of wannabe starlets dressed like Jeannie from the old sixties sitcom *I Dream of Jeannie*. They made their young guests sit on large pillows while they belly-danced tiny éclairs, bite-size pizzas, and what looked to be Cheez Whiz on top of crackers around the room. The peppy Isabelle Salazar was their guest judge and she made a show of clapping and snacking. It looked like a lot of fun till a bit of secret footage showed frozen pastry éclair and pizza boxes in a trash can.

After the clip, Gianne turned to the panel of celebrity chef judges. "Teresa Juliette, we'll start with you. What do you think of Team Hollywood's event?"

Teresa, wearing her white chef dress, waved her sparkling spatula and said, "These cooks seem to think the four food groups are fast, frozen, instant, and chocolate. And what were they thinking about those costumes at a child's birthday party? I'll give them an F for not only having bad taste but for not knowing how to cook."

Our old friend Brant Richards countered, "Who cares? Beautiful girls don't need to cook. Their beauty makes everything more appetizing whether it really is or not. My recommendation, America, is to vote this team through."

Isabelle Salazar, our Brazilian judge, had been wearing a black cape. She stood and flung it off her shoulders to reveal a hot pink genie costume of her own. The live audience went wild as she began to gyrate behind the judging table as the theme music from *Jeannie* played. She shouted, "I'm with Brant. Let them dance!"

When we went to break, Lisa Leann said, "I thought this was a catering program, not *Dancing with the Stars.*"

Goldie leaned over and whispered into my ear, "What next?"

We found out when the music cued again. Lisa Leann's face appeared on the JumboTron as her *Dancing with the Stars* comment aired for the world to hear. The crowd roared, but Lisa Leann slid down her chair until she realized she was live on camera. She sat up and waved and said, "Honest to Betsy, if you TV folks are going to sneak around and record everything I say, then expect to hear the truth, and as Jesus said, 'The truth will set you free.'"

The crowd hooted and clapped with glee.

Next, the Boston Bean Team package began to air. This all-men's team once again wore their sailor hats made of newspapers while they dished up fresh lobster, boiled red potatoes, and, of course, Boston baked beans to serve their local Rotary Club. Judge Brant Richards had been on hand as their on-site judge, but he looked as bored as he was when we'd hosted him in Colorado.

When Gianne asked him what he thought of the experience, he said, "Sorry to say that though the food was good, the theme was boring."

"What theme?" Judge Teresa asked as she waved her "wand." "As far as I could tell, the only theme was lobsters and paper hats. Team Boston Bean, America wants you to get creative. If you stay in this competition, next week you're going to have to demonstrate your party theme with your food and décor."

Judge Isabelle, who had re-draped herself into her cape, said, "I agree!"

The final two teams of the night did a little better. The Comfort Cooking gals of Savannah, Georgia, hosted a Chamber of Commerce black-tie event based on an "Oscar Awards Night" theme, with a local comic emceeing the Savannah Woman of the Year Awards. It was hardly a surprise when the gals from Comfort Cooking, all dressed in black cocktail dresses and pearls, got an award for Outstanding Savannah Women. The party was topped off with large helpings of chicken and dumplings, corn bread, black-eyed peas, corn on the cob dripping with butter, and pecan pie with homemade vanilla ice cream.

Later, the Wild Cajun Cooks of Baton Rouge, who seemed a bit tipsy on camera, served up fried gator balls, boudin sausage, and plates of jambalaya, much to the delight of the on-site judge, Teresa Juliette, who seemed to enjoy dancing to the Cajun band. One close-up had her shouting, "Fabulous!" as she popped a sausage into her mouth. The camera panned back as she jigged to a couple of blazing fiddles from the band.

Both teams got rave reviews from the judges. "My only criticism of the Wild Cajun Cooks is they put too much sauce in their sauce, if you know what I mean," Teresa Juliette said.

"It's impossible to put too much sauce in a dish," Brant countered.

The camera panned to where the Wild Cooks, a group of large, sweaty men, were seated. They laughed as though this was all rip-roaring funny. But I was really too tired to see the humor.

Near the end of the show, Gianne called the night's four competing teams up front and center. "Need I remind you, America, that it's your vote that will decide the fate of these four teams. You decide which of these three will join the three teams who have already secured their place in our top six."

The highlights clips of the four teams played as Gianne called their names. "Who will be eliminated? Will it be Team Hollywood, the Boston Bean Team, the Comfort Cooking Team, or the Wild Canjun Cooks?"

She rattled off instructions on how to vote by phone as well as each team's number and said, "America, only you can say who will be joining our other contestants for next week's show."

The curtains parted, revealing the rest of the teams, including ours, the winners from the previous week. As we waved, a clip appeared on the JumboTron. I looked up to see Gianne say, "So, Donna, I love your shirt. 'Go Team Potluck.'"

Wait, Gianne never said that to me!

My face appeared on the screen as I seemed to reply, "Yeah, 'Go Team Potluck' as in *go home*."

Could they do that—splice comments together like that?

Gianne went live in front of the camera that panned back to our team, focusing on Wade and David. Gianne said, "Is our deputy from Colorado already partied out, or is she trying to keep those Colorado mountain men all to herself? You decide, America. Next week is a show I guarantee you won't want to miss. Until next time, *ciao!*"

18

Anniversary Dinner

I was thankful when the studio lights blinked off, knowing that the eye of the camera was finally asleep. I stood and stretched, trying to get the kinks out of my back. I turned to David, who had been sitting between Donna and me, and asked, "What now?"

My handsome son said, "I don't think we'll have enough time to grab a sandwich. I'm wondering if the craft table is still open."

Wade, who of course was on the other side of Donna, said, "Mike the cameraman told me pizzas would be delivered backstage after the broadcast."

I smiled with relief. "That's good news, dear."

When the delivery company set out the pizza pies on the long tables backstage, I happened to be standing next to one of the Wild Cajun Cooks, Bubba. At least that's what was printed on his green baseball cap. I'd guessed he traded in his chef's hat for the cap as soon as the show went off the air.

At thirtysomething, Bubba had black, wavy hair and intense brown eyes. His chin sported a tuft of a goatee, which was shaved to look like an inverted triangle. He had a slight beer belly that pouched under a white undershirt that was flanked by an open, red plaid shirt. As I'd never met anyone who called themselves a Cajun, I was eager to make his acquaintance. I extended my hand. "My name is Vonnie from Team Potluck. You're Bubba?"

He gave my hand a squeeze. "Bonjour, Beb, yes, I am the man you speak of."

"It's Vonnie, not Beb."

Bubba let out a belly laugh. "I call all good-lookin' women 'beb,' including my grandmother. It's a Cajun thing."

I laughed too. "Like a term of endearment?"

"Just like dat."

"Your team looked good tonight, especially your jambalaya," I said as I let my pepperoni pizza cool on its paper plate.

"You want my recipe, it's yours," he said. "I'll write it up for you tonight."

"Why, thank you. And while we're chatting, I'm wondering if you have an opinion. Which team do you think will be eliminated tonight?"

"Ha! Which mean, I dunno. Though I guarantee it won't be the Wild Cajun Cooks."

"Or Team Potluck," I said with a polite laugh. "We're not on the chopping block tonight."

"Good! I had wanted to meet the deputy beb. I think we could make some spice."

I stammered. "Oh? Well, I'm sure she's here somewhere."

David must have sensed trouble and walked over. "Mom, can I get you anything?"

"Maybe a Sprite," I said.

"You are one of the deputy's beaus?" Bubba asked.

"Well, we are dating, yes," David said.

"Mind if I give you a little Cajun competition?"

"Well, she'd be the one to tell you no."

He laughed again. "Not many women do dat. Where she gone?"

So help me if David didn't look nervous. "She and Wade are making a phone call."

Bubba interrupted. "You let your woman alone with that *canaille* cowboy?"

"Pardon me if my French is a little rusty, but even if Wade is sneaky, as you suggest, I'm certain Donna will be okay," David answered.

To my surprise, Bubba blurted, "The web say those two have a past."

My mouth fell open. "By 'web' you mean the Internet?"

Bubba nodded.

"How could you have read about Donna on the Internet?"

He smiled at me kindly. "Excuse moi, the bayou has WiFi."

I felt my face burn. "Of course, I didn't mean . . ."

"Cher, the message boards say David is your bebe but was brought up by a Hollywood actress. How come?"

I felt a chill. "That's really none of your business."

His tone was warm and sympathetic. "Cher, now you a star. Everybody know your business."

I brought my free hand to my throat. "What else did you read about me and my team on the Internet?"

"Enough dirt to make mud pies. If'n I was you, I'd get a blog so you can, as they say, spin your own truth."

I blinked and turned to David. "What's a blog?"

"I'll explain later," he said as Bubba's team motioned for him to return to their group. After Bubba said his adieus, David and I grabbed our cans of pop and retreated to a quiet spot in the auditorium seating (away from prying contestants and cameras), where I tried to finish my pizza. "What's this about Donna making phone calls with Wade?"

"She may have some sort of lead on the whereabouts of Pete's mother."

I felt shocked. "Thelma's been gone nearly six months. Does Wade think she's in New York?"

"Possibly. At least, one of his aunts thinks so, so he asked Donna to check the lead."

"So Wade and Donna are playing detective?"

"Looks like it."

I hesitated, then dared to ask him what was really on my mind. "David, what I'd like to know is, are you and Donna still dating? Or is she with Wade?"

"I think we're an item, though with Donna, it's hard to tell. Since this reality show started, we've been too busy to spend much time with each other. Though we usually catch up for dinner when we pull the same shift, which is more often than not."

"Donna's been spending a lot of time with Wade," I whispered. "Supposedly to check in on Pete."

"I know. I see her Bronco over at the trailer park."

"Aren't you concerned?"

"Well, yes, but I think that if I make a big deal about it, it will cause it to turn into one. I feel it's Pete *with* Wade that gets Donna's attention. If Donna finds Pete's mom, then I don't think she'd have any more reason to keep seeing Wade."

I nodded. "That could be, but Bubba is right when he says she and Wade share a past—"

Before I could say more, Kat's voice floated around us. "Everyone, please turn off your cell phones. Tonight's contestants, I need to see you on the stage, pronto. All other contestants return to your assigned seats in the pit. We're about to make an important announcement as soon as our doors are locked and secured."

A few moments later, I was sitting in my place beside Team Potluck while four very nervous teams stood with Gianne Gillian on the stage before us. A spotlight hit Gianne as the theme music blared the show's intro. Gianne was holding a folded card in her hand as she said into the camera, "America, I have the results of the votes."

The JumboTrons panned the anxious faces of the teams, many of whom held hands or huddled together in nervous clusters. Gianne opened the envelope and stared. After what seemed like a full minute, she looked up and said, "The team that will be going home . . . will be . . . announced tomorrow morning in *The Great Party Showdown*'s all-new extreme kitchen."

The theme music played again as the cameras panned the shocked faces of the contestants. Some simply blinked into the bright lights while others punched each other in the ribs with their elbows and grinned.

Gianne continued, "Contestants, tomorrow morning, a limo will pick up your teams at eight sharp to take you to the elimination reveal and to see your extreme kitchens as well as your catering assignments. Until tomorrow, good night, everyone."

To say I was happy to return to our hotel room was an understatement. But my happiness faded when Donna scrubbed her makeup off and changed out of her "Go Team Potluck" tee into one of her black T-shirts under a light denim jacket.

"Going somewhere?" I asked, already in my pink nighty and matching bunny slippers.

She nodded. "Yeah, Wade and I are grabbing a taxi to follow up on a lead we got concerning his cousin's missing wife."

"I'm not sure Pete's mom wants to be found."

"That's what I want to find out. Is she safe? Or, do I need to go back to Summit View and look for a body?"

"Oh, dear. What sort of lead do you have?"

"We hear she might be a waitress at one of the local all-night cafés. We're going over to snoop around."

"Be careful, okay?"

"Don't worry, Vonnie. It's only 10:30 and I hope to be back before midnight. Maybe I'll have some good news."

"Oh, I hope you do."

Whether Donna was back before midnight, I can't say, but when our alarm went off at six a.m., I was happy to see her tucked into her bed.

"Good morning, dear. Rise and shine. The team is meeting in the hotel coffee shop in half an hour."

When Donna simply turned and pulled her pillow over her head and groaned, I decided I'd get up and hit the shower so she could sleep a few minutes longer. But after my shower, no matter how much bumping and banging I did, Donna didn't budge from her nest of tangled covers.

Half an hour later, as I opened our door to leave for the coffee shop, I called over my shoulder, "Donna, we're leaving for the studio in an hour. Do you want me to tell the team you need to rest a few more minutes?"

"Would you?" she croaked.

"Want me to pick up anything for breakfast?"

Donna sat up in bed and rubbed her eyes. "Bagel and cream cheese, and coffee, black."

When I saw she was getting up, I hesitated. "Did you find out anything last night about Pete's mom?"

She shook her head. "Maybe a lead. I'll tell you about it when you get back."

But in all the morning's rush, she never got a chance to tell me what she'd found out, or how long she'd been out with Wade. And I knew better than to talk to her about it in the limo. That thing was probably riddled with microphones and hidden cameras. Plus, now that I knew something called message boards was spreading dirt about our team, I vowed to be careful about what I said to whom.

When we entered the GE building, Amy was waiting for us in the lobby again. We followed her up the elevator to *The Great Party Showdown* kitchen on the thirtieth floor. Some of the other teams, along with Mike Romano and his camera crew, were already in position to capture our reaction to our state of the art kitchenettes.

All I can say is our little station was a caterer's dream come true. When Lisa Leann opened the stainless steel refrigerator, she found it stocked with every item one could imagine. I opened the large stainless steel pantry and was amazed to see its shelves completely lined with every manner of baking pans, flour, sugar, and everything we had in our catering kitchen at Lisa Leann's wedding boutique back in Colorado.

After each team had been filmed oohing and aahing over the kitchen sets, Amy had the cast of caterers stand in two different groups, the safe group and the group up for elimination. We watched Gianne as she waltzed through a kitchen door that was nothing more than a working prop. She was dressed in black slacks and a sparkling baby doll top in peach. Her thin, bare arms looked graceful as she clutched the card she'd held the night before. My, she was a skinny little thing.

"Good morning, teams. I've come to bring you news," she said as the show's contestants fidgeted. Once again she paused dramatically. "Our top two teams who made it through last night's vote are. . . ." She pushed back a strand of her golden hair behind her shoulder as her blue eyes flashed. "Team Batter Up and the Wild Cajun Cooks. You may join the teams on the other side of the room."

After much cheering and shuffling, Team Comfort Cooking and the Boston Bean Team stepped closer together in accordance to Kat's off-camera directing.

Again, Gianne paused. "Boston Bean Team . . . I'm sorry to say your time with us is over. Comfort Cooking, you've been voted through to the next round."

After all the hugs and tears, Gianne said, "Remaining teams, it's time to go to your war rooms to meet the subjects of your next catering event. And here's the big news. You'll be hosting a fiftieth anniversary party."

Soon our team stepped through the doorway of our private meeting room, which was just down the hall from the kitchen studio. Our war room glowed white from both the lighting and the color of the walls and furnishings. I couldn't help but notice that the room would have been private if the walls weren't lined with cameramen. My goodness, a person couldn't even sneeze in here without it being on national television.

The room's centerpiece was a large white table and chairs with an arrangement of yellow daisies. There was also a couple of large off-white sofas with a matching recliner, all accented with bright yellow and red throw pillows. Off to the side was a white desk that sported a yellow phone on top. *Very jazzy.* The walls were blank, except for a white erase board or two.

Seated at the table was an adorable couple who were probably in their seventies. He had thick gray hair and was dressed in a light blue polyester suit, right out of the seventies. She wore a gray A-line dress with gray pumps. I could tell she'd been in makeup, or all that gray from her dress and short under-turned hair would have faded her completely away.

Gianne, with cameras rolling, introduced us. "Team Potluck, this is Mr. and Mrs. Marino. They've been one of the lucky six couples to win a fully catered Golden Anniversary Party. And you, Team Potluck, will be their caterer. The invitations have already gone out, and we are expecting a crowd of 120 this Saturday night to celebrate the lives and marriage of this wonderful couple.

"Take this opportunity to visit with the Marinos, then you'll have three days to put your themed event together. You'll have a budget of two thousand dollars, given to you by Spring Forth Energy Water. With that budget, you'll be responsible for the food, entertainment, additional waitstaff, if needed, and a themed décor. Are you up for the challenge?"

We all hooted and clapped while Gianne opened a black leather satchel and pulled out a couple of envelopes with "Team Potluck" handwritten across them. "Here's an American Express Card with two thousand dollars already preprogrammed into it." She handed

Lisa Leann a standard, sealed envelope. "We thought you'd also like to see Mrs. Marino's winning entry."

Lisa Leann mumbled a thanks as Gianne continued, "Good luck, Team Potluck and Mr. and Mrs. Marino."

Gianne left, but the cameras kept rolling while we greeted and congratulated the couple while Lisa Leann pulled a notepad and pen out of her briefcase. Nelson opened the envelope containing the winning entry and read it to our gathered group.

> My Nicky and I, in all our fifty years together, have never had a wedding or anniversary celebration. We were married by a justice of the peace but never had a chance to celebrate even with a honeymoon. You see, Nicky and I got pregnant on our wedding night. Baby Anthony was only the first of nine children. So there never was any money or resources to celebrate "us." It's not that we haven't celebrated our lives together, we have. We celebrated with the births of our children, their birthdays and graduations and their children. But now, we'd like our loved ones, our nine children, their husbands and wives, our twenty-two grandchildren, and five great-grandchildren, a clan that totals over fifty people, plus our dear friends, to join us as we celebrate our fifty years of marriage. Spring Forth, would you please give us the opportunity to share our joy with our friends and family?—Mr. and Mrs. Nicky Marino.

I sniffed, suddenly thinking of my own first husband whom I lost to the Vietnam War and all the memories we never shared. Then I thought of my own sweet Fred, who had later built a life with me. But I wouldn't be selfish and dwell on my own private heartaches and joys. We had a party to help plan. I reached over and touched Mrs. Marino's hand. "That was beautiful," I said. "How did the two of you meet?"

She patted her husband's knee. "I was coming back to New

York by steamer after visiting my grandparents in Italy. Nick was a member of the ship's band, a trumpet player."

He grinned. "She caught my eye on the dance floor. But I had a time of it getting around her chaperone. She was just nineteen, you know."

Mrs. Marino giggled. "You were all of twenty."

He squeezed her hand. "Now, a little over fifty years later, I'm still stealing kisses from you."

"Don't talk so sexy," she scolded.

Lisa Leann, who had been scribing notes, looked up and said, "My, it reminds me of the movie *An Affair to Remember* with Cary Grant and Deborah Kerr."

Mrs. Marino looked surprised. "Nicky took me to see the show when we landed back in New York. It was our first date on dry land."

"Really?" Lisa Leann said as if she'd just discovered oil on her property. "Well, that gives us a lot to work with. I can hardly wait to get started."

19

Stewed Pair

Henry's final words the day before I'd left for New York had rocked our relationship.

Things had been tenser than usual, so when I caught him sitting at the kitchen table, I'd decided to serve up a peace offering. I pulled out one of my chocolaty cheesecakes and cut him a generous slice before dousing it in thick homemade whipped cream. I sat it in front of him, along with a fresh cup of coffee. "You've been quiet today," I said as I joined him with my own piece of cake. "Is there something you want to talk about?"

He shoved his fork through the cake and looked up. "Lisa Leann, I'm only going to say this once. Please don't go to New York."

I'd been afraid he'd ask me to stay, but my hands were tied. "Thank you for telling me how you feel, Henry. But that contract Nelson had the team and I sign is iron clad, at least according to that attorney, Chris Lowe. I don't have a choice."

Henry chewed thoughtfully. "But you can get out of it if you really wanted to. Right?"

"Not possible." I patted his hand. "But why are you so worried?"

He pushed back his plate and leaned back in his chair, leaving his hands on the table. "Lisa Leann, how can I trust you after you betrayed me? How can I trust you in New York? If you really want our marriage to work, you'll find a way to stay home."

"Come with us," I begged. "Then you'll see. Henry, you'll see my heart belongs to you."

His reply stunned me. "I'm not coming."

"But why?"

"I don't think my heart is strong enough to reinvest it in you and all your shenanigans."

It was as if the air had been sucked out of the room. In that instant I, for the first time in my life, couldn't imagine my future.

I was a pretty good actress, and I hoped that the girls didn't suspect what I was going through. Of course, they knew about my past affair, and they also knew how much I regretted it. Though I'd never told them that my marriage might now be over. I was too ashamed.

I could keep my churning emotions together during the day, but at night I soaked my pillow with tears. I only hoped Evie hadn't noticed my midnight sniffling as I prayed myself to sleep.

It was Friday afternoon, and I'd been working in our *Great Party Showdown* kitchen when Henry called me for the first time since I'd left for New York. When I saw his number pop up on my caller ID, I grabbed my cell phone and literally ran for the kitchen door. The trouble was, I wasn't quick enough to escape Mike Romano.

As I jogged down the hall, Mike was at my heels, recording my every word. All I could hope for was that his camera's microphone wasn't sophisticated enough to record Henry's end of the conversation, though I couldn't be sure. "Henry! I'm so glad you called. I miss you so much."

"Do you?"

"Of course. I wish you were here."

"That's why I'm calling. Fred, Samuel, and Vernon have been trying to get me to commit to coming to New York with them next Wednesday."

"That would be wonderful. I would love to see you, and I know Nelson would too."

"What exactly have you told Nelson about us?"

I dodged into the women's restroom, chagrined that the "women" sign didn't stop Mike. He charged right in behind me. I opened a stall door and slammed it shut, giving the lock a twist before I flushed the toilet.

"Nothing."

"You mean he doesn't know about you and Clark?"

I lowered my voice to a whisper while the toilet continued to gurgle. "It's over. Why would I tell?"

"It's being hinted at on *The Great Party Showdown*'s message boards."

My heart gave a thunderclap instead of a beat. "No!"

"I'll read it to you: 'Word is Team Potluck is working on an event themed *An Affair to Remember*. After Lisa Leann Lambert's outburst that the 'truth will set you free' on live TV earlier this week, we're wondering if she has anything to say about other memorable affairs. There is a buzz that she herself may have some truth that needs to be freed in this regard.'"

I gasped and flushed the toilet again to cover my cry of, "Oh, Henry. I'm so sorry."

"You'd better talk to our son."

"I will. I promise," I said, wondering how I could possibly get any alone time with him without Mike or all the hidden cameras that were rumored to exist. Besides, how would Nelson react? Would he hate me? I hung my head. Probably.

I walked out of the stall and washed my hands, giving Mike a glare.

"Just doing my job," he said for the umpteenth time today.

I walked back to the kitchen with Mike trailing behind me and returned to my pastry cookbook. I tried to turn my thoughts back to this contest. If I didn't, I'd go crazy.

I took a deep breath. How glad I was I'd filled one of my suitcases with cookbooks and notebooks on catering ideas. They were all coming in handy for this challenge. Though it was too bad I didn't have any cookbooks to help me figure out what to do about my personal life. All I had was God.

I had to stop and secretly laugh at myself. Wasn't God all I needed? *Sorry, Lord*, I prayed in the depths of my heart. *Please, only you can turn my marriage disaster into a miracle.*

I walked back to the countertop and turned the page of my cookbook before running my finger down a strawberry sheet cake recipe. This would be perfect. I checked my watch. I could hardly believe it was already Friday afternoon, the day before the Marino's anniversary party. I had to hurry to get my order in for strawberries before the market closed.

Vonnie was already opening the boxes of fresh pears I'd ordered earlier for our caramel pear side dish while Lizzie was going over our recipe for chicken tetrazzini. Evie was on her cell phone checking on our order from the prop house for our linens, china, crystal, and silver place settings. I was so proud of her, as she'd even managed to order dark orange fabric chair covers to cover our padded folding chairs. Our set was going to look just like the ship's dining room set from the movie, which had been brightened by captain's chairs in dark orange.

I stopped to look around our work area. All our other team members were busy with assignments. Wade was picking up the tuxes we'd wear as the waitstaff, while Nelson was in our conference room, which we laughingly called our war room, with his computer making a PowerPoint presentation of Marino family photos. He'd spent the morning scanning them onto a disk at Kinkos and then intermingling the photos with famous lines from the movie, like "Winter must be cold for those with no warm memories."

While he'd been at the printers, he'd had time to use his cell phone and connections to follow up on some leads for a band. Not that paying for a band was within our budget. However, Nelson had heard that Denver and the Mile High Orchestra was playing a concert at a church in New Jersey tonight. He had a call in to their agent to see if they would still be in the area tomorrow and if they'd be willing to help us out on national TV. *Wouldn't that be something if they could?*

The hardest part of our theme, besides the unfortunate comparison to my love life, was trying to work with Donna. She wasn't too keen that I'd given her the assignment to act out a little romantic skit with David. "I'm no Terry McKay," she'd said when I'd told her of my idea.

"But you'll play Deborah Kerr's part beautifully," I'd encouraged. "Plus, David is a natural for Cary Grant, or should I say Nickie Ferrante. Besides, he's the only man here with black hair."

"Why can't we hire a couple of real actors?" Donna had challenged.

"Have you seen our budget? We have to wear every hat on the menu: caterer, waiter, and of course, entertainer. That is, if we want to have both food and décor. When the money is gone, we're done."

I realized I was staring into space and frowned. I had to stop contemplating my so-called affairs and get back to work. It was already four in the afternoon. We had exactly twenty-four hours till showtime.

I hadn't had a minute to talk to Nelson since Henry had called the afternoon before. There was too much to do and no privacy. The team and I had worked late into the night. When we'd finally gotten access to the banquet room late last night, Nelson, Wade, and David had been busy setting up chairs, linens, and place settings, along with our array of props and decorations, until the wee hours of the morning.

But the guys weren't the only ones burning the midnight oil. The girls and I had slaved in the kitchen till nearly three a.m. We'd all stayed busy chopping and stirring, that is, all except Donna. She constantly had to ward off one of the lovesick Cajun cooks who was up late peeling shrimp in the kitchenette next to ours.

Mike Romano, of course, got all of Bubba's advances on tape, complete with Donna's cross remarks. She finally stopped grating carrots and put her hand on her hip. "Cajun cooking and cooks just don't agree with me, Bubba."

"Ah, but you have to taste the spice to know that you like it."

"What you call spice, I call trouble."

"Trouble can be a good thing. It's hot-hot in a kiss."

"Trouble can be poison," she countered. "And poison's just not on my diet."

I grinned. *Touché, Donna.*

We'd all gone back to the hotel to catch a couple of hours of sleep and grab a quick shower. But now that we were back at the banquet hall, our hard work was abundantly apparent. The small round and square tables we'd rented were covered in crisp white linen and set with crystal goblets, silverware, and silver cream and sugar bowls. In addition, our beautiful china salad plates rested at each place setting. Each plate was topped with crisp greens with all the trimmings, including grated carrots, slices of purple cabbage, and red cherry tomatoes. Sterling silver dressing boats that were filled with both creamy Italian and raspberry dressing sat ready on every table.

In the back hallway, our chicken tetrazzini, caramel pears, and rolls were warming on large china dinner plates in heated catering trays, ready to serve. But the grand finish was our strawberry sheet cake, which has been sliced, layered, and shaped into a large heart and covered in elegant white icing with pink trimming. It stood on display on a rolling cart near the entrance to our bash. But the cake's crowning glory was the rice paper printed photo of our happy couple looking good enough to eat.

But that wasn't the half of it. Miracle of miracles, Denver and the Mile High Orchestra had said yes to Nelson's invitation! In fact, they were already setting up their brass instruments in front of our extra-long paper backdrop that we'd applied to the back wall. The backdrop was nothing more than a continuous print of a cruise ship railing topped with a blue ocean and a bluer sky. Above the band, dozens of paper seagulls swayed in the drafts of refrigerated air that poured from the vents. These birds had been hung by Wade from threads attached to the crisscrossed metal framework that supported the acoustic ceiling tiles.

I walked over to shake Denver's hand. "I can't tell you how much we appreciate you and the guys helping us out like this. I've been a big fan of yours since I saw you on *The Next Great American Band.*"

Denver smiled that sweet smile of his as his eyes twinkled. "Glad we were in town with the night off," he said. "We wouldn't have missed this opportunity to be in front of thirty million viewers for the world. So, thanks for thinking of us."

After my chat with Denver, I turned my attention to the latest crisis. And with all the work going on, I was pleased to have a handyman on our team. Wade had just put the finishing touches on the entrance to the room. Instead of rolling out the red carpet, Wade had put together a gray gangplank along with life-size photos of our entire team as well as our celebrated couple. Wade had picked up the posters, which had been donated by the Kinkos store nearby. The cool thing about the pictures was that they'd been placed along the entranceway to make it look like Team Potluck and our happy couple were beckoning our guests to join us on board the SS *Constitution*. I walked up the gangplank and into the banquet hall, stopping to pretend I was seeing it for the first time. The tables looked exactly like the tables from the movie, complete with glass vases with two pink carnations, which were happily within our budget.

Before we went down to makeup and before our guests of honor and their guests started to arrive, we met in our war room to pray. David, to my surprise, asked if he could do the honors, and everyone nodded. We held hands as he bowed his head and said, "Lord, thank you for my friends and family who are here with me tonight. Bless our efforts. Bless the show, and Lord, please be with us here on the set. We love you. In Jesus's name, Amen."

I blinked back the moisture that was gathering behind my lids. That was one sweet prayer for a man who'd only come to faith since he'd arrived in Summit View last year. I said, with as much feeling as I could muster, "Amen!"

An hour later, as the cameras rolled, our guests started to arrive. Lizzie, dressed in her white tux with a black bow tie, greeted them. She helped the families sign the guest book and told them their table number so they could find their seat assignments.

While Mr. and Mrs. Marino sat at the head table, they were greeted by a constant stream of well-wishers. All the while, Nelson's rented projector played his PowerPoint slide show to the delight of the crowd. After twenty minutes of continuous slide show rotation, Denver and the Mile High Orchestra were ready to swing. They played their rendition of "You Make It Easy to Be True," a peppy love song from the movie, while Denver sang the lyrics.

Donna and David, the only ones on our team not wearing the white rented tuxes, began to waltz in front of the band. Donna had learned the steps to the dance from David only that afternoon, and I have to say, I was impressed by their performance. David was dressed in his own black tux, while Donna, who'd spent extra time in makeup, made a perfect Deborah Kerr, aka Terry McKay. She wore a short red wig that actually looked pretty good. She also wore a strapless ivory chiffon gown we'd gotten at 75 percent off at Macy's. It was an amazing reproduction of Kerr's gown. So much so that no one would ever guess that Vonnie had entwined, tucked, and tacked those dark orange scarves on that dress all by herself.

After the dance, the orchestra kept playing and Denver kept crooning while we served the plated chicken, rolls, and pears.

I couldn't help but keep an eye on Teresa Juliette. She, along with Mr. and Mrs. Marino, sat at the head table. She was actually pretty quiet and sometimes appeared bored. (Not a good sign for this generally bright-eyed gal.) But the rest of our dinner guests were anything but reserved. With all the crying babies, the children running the aisles, and the mothers trying to make the children behave for the cameras, it was a pretty lively scene.

Later, after the guests finished dining, Donna and David reappeared and performed a little skit from the movie. First, they pretended to pull away from an embrace. As Donna walked away, she looked over her shoulder and said, "Oh, I should ask you, do you want kids?"

To which David said, "Lots."

The banquet hall, full of Marino offspring, tittered in laughter as Donna pulled a microphone from a nearby stand. "Congratulations, Mr. and Mrs. Marino, on your fiftieth wedding anniversary and your many kids, their kids, and their kids and kids to come. But before we serve the cake, your eldest son has a few remarks."

Anthony, who was wearing a chocolate brown suit, looked distinguished at forty-nine. However, he put his lips so close to the mic that his words buzzed. "Mama, Papa, I can't tell you how proud I am of you. To think you've made it fifty years. What an accomplishment! Just like those love birds in *An Affair to Remember*, you met on the SS *Constitution* too. As I recall the story, Mama was a paying passenger, but Papa, you were the trumpet player who got the girl."

The orchestra's trumpet players played an enthusiastic squeal on their horns while everyone laughed.

Anthony held up what appeared to be a glass of pink champagne. "Here's to you, Mama and Papa!"

The band cued up "You Make It Easy to Be True" as Wade and Nelson, looking svelte in their tuxes, brought over the cart with our heart-shaped cake. The rest of the team playing waitstaff scurried to refill the champagne glasses with our pink carbonated punch. (Well, we couldn't afford the real stuff anyway.)

The guests began to clap, and some of them began to tap their glasses with their knives. "Speech, speech!" they called as the guests of honor rose to their feet. Donna handed Mr. Marino the mic, and he said, "First, I want you all to know how much I love you." He turned to his wife. "Especially you, Marian, you've been a good and faithful wife."

She kissed his cheek and leaned in to say, "You've been a good husband to me, Nicky, and a good papa too."

Mr. Marino put his arm around her shoulder and gave her a squeeze. That's when I noticed how much the man was sweating. *Oh, my.*

He reached for his cloth napkin and dabbed his forehead and tried to catch his breath. "I'm not so good at speeches," he said. "I'm better at love."

Mrs. Marino ducked her head bashfully. "Oh, stop being so sexy," she said while the crowd giggled.

"How can a man not be so sexy when he's married to a beautiful woman like you," he said as the family "awwwed" and chuckled again.

"Oh stop, Nicky."

And he did stop. Suddenly, all the color drained from his face. His smile was replaced with a look of surprise as his legs began to buckle. David lunged to grab him by the arm but missed. In an instant, Mr. Marino lay at his wife's feet.

By the time his wife and family had stopped screaming, David and Donna, in all their finery, were working in tandem to save his life. First, Donna unbuttoned Mr. Marino's top button and loosened his tie while David put his ear to his chest. "I don't have a heartbeat," he told Donna. Donna pushed Mr. Marino's forehead back, arching his neck. She opened his mouth to make sure his tongue wasn't blocking his airway while David began to administer CPR. Kneeling next to the downed man, David locked his elbows as he began to push rhythmically on Mr. Marino's chest. David looked up at the stricken Mrs. Marino. "Don't worry. In real life I'm a paramedic."

Donna stopped to take a breath, but before she continued her mouth-to-mouth resuscitation efforts, she gasped, "It's okay. I'm a deputy."

Wade grabbed the microphone. "Everyone stay calm. We have two emergency workers right here. An ambulance has already been called. The only thing we can do now is pray. Do you mind if I pray now?"

Shouts of, "Please do," and "Yes, pray," filled the room.

Wade bowed his head as the cameramen rushed in for a close-up. "Dear Lord, please bring Mr. Marino back to his loving family. We ask this in the name of Jesus. Amen."

Days later, our beautiful banquet complete with our wonderful band, the little romantic intrigues between Donna and the men on the set, plus our life-saving drama, aired as millions of viewers watched Donna and David save this great-grandfather's life. To top it off, even the judges were complimentary. Brant said, "To say the event was completely dead would be a lie. Hear, hear to the heroic efforts of Team Potluck," while the audience cheered.

Not to be morbid, but it didn't hurt that our package included clips of Mr. Marino from his hospital bed, saying, "Those two love-birds saved my life, you know. Not only have I survived a massive heart attack"—he chuckled till he coughed—"I've just survived a heart bypass." His wife leaned in and kissed his cheek as he said, "Marian, you're stuck with me for another fifty years!"

Mrs. Marino smiled. "Thank you, Team Potluck. You've given us hope and a future."

There wasn't a dry eye in Studio 8 H when our segment was over. After it aired, I could barely concentrate on the other teams' anniversary parties. Not that I meant to daydream, but I didn't really need to watch the competition to make my prediction as to tonight's results. After a party like this, Team Potluck would surely be around to face another week, maybe even to go all the way to the top to receive that cool million dollars.

I gave a sigh of relief. Now I was free to concentrate on what I was really concerned about: whether or not Henry would be at the airport tomorrow. I just couldn't guess. I wanted to see him, of course. But then, he would expect me to have confided in Nelson about my shameful past. But how could I?

Lizzie

20

Consuming Couple

One thing I knew for sure: whatever good the next day would bring, it would also bring sadness and sorrow for some. Maybe even us ladies from Team Potluck.

As soon as Goldie and I returned from the set, got undressed, and then redressed—me in a summer's workout set and Goldie in a floral lounging gown, we set the room's alarm clock for 5:00 in the morning. Goldie took the extra measure of dialing the front desk and asking for a wake-up call at 5:15. "Just in case," she said. "As tired as we are, we might just sleep right through the alarm clock."

She was right, there.

We then decided to call our husbands, first to find out if they were still coming to New York the following day, and second, to talk about how the show had been perceived by those watching in Summit View.

"I'll call Samuel from the lobby," I told Goldie, waving my cell phone at her. "You can call Jack from in here."

Goldie looked something akin to horrified, I initially presumed because I felt I needed to go to another floor entirely in order to have privacy. "I'll take my shower if you'd like," she said. "I can wait to call Jack."

I glanced at my watch. "No, no. It's getting later than late here, and even though it's two hours earlier back home, I'm tired, you're tired, and we need to just make our calls and go to bed."

Goldie raised her brows as though to protest, but then said, "Okay."

As I reached the door she said, "But be careful down there."

I laughed lightly. "Oh, Goldie. Surely you're not scared for me to be in the lobby of *this* hotel, are you? I'm perfectly safe in spite of the hour."

She shook her head. "I'm not afraid of the boogeyman, Liz. I'm more concerned about the cameras that might be lurking behind every fichus tree and work of art down there."

She had a point. "Hmm. I see what you mean. Okay, I'll be careful. I promise."

I opened the door, stuck my neck out into the hallway, glanced to the left, then the right, and then looked back at Goldie. With a wink I said, "Coast is clear."

"Don't joke, Sherlock," she said.

I slipped out the door and allowed it to click shut behind me before heading toward the elevators down the hall. Between my Keds and the rich, thickly padded carpets, my footsteps were muffled. Even Donna wouldn't hear my trek toward the lobby, I decided with a smile.

I pushed the elevator's down button, slipped my phone into the back pocket of my pants, and waited. Then I prayed, *Let this thing be empty when it opens, Lord.*

God was good. When it opened I was met with an empty carrier, which brought a sigh of relief. I stepped in, pressed "L," then watched the doors slide shut. The elevator jerked once then began its slow decent.

It stopped. I looked at the floor buttons and saw that "9" was brightly lit. The doors slid open again. I looked at my feet, then stepped back a notch to allow a young man and woman to step in.

I sensed rather than saw some movement between the two of them. Looking up, I realized they were signing to each other. The woman glanced at me once, then continued in her frantic hand movements. Something was most definitely wrong.

"Hi," I signed to them. "Can I help you with something?"

"Are you deaf?" the young man, a handsome lad who appeared to be no more than twenty-one or twenty-two years of age, signed back.

"No," I signed. "I have a deaf daughter. Is something wrong?"

At this point the doors opened and the lobby was mere steps away. I pointed toward the opening and signed, "Let's go out here and talk."

The young man allowed the woman and me to step out first and then followed. I glanced around the room as efficiently as I could to see if anyone from *The Great Party Showdown* might be about, but registered no one familiar. It appeared the theater crowd was returning and a good deal of life was still moving about near the lobby lounge. I turned back to the couple. "Tell me what is wrong," I signed.

"My wife lost her purse," the young man signed. "Her cash . . . her credit cards . . . her passport."

I held up my hands for him to stop. "Let's take this one step at a time." I looked at the young woman. She had a round face, black hair pulled back in a severe ponytail, and deep-set green eyes. Tear streaks made their lines from the red rims of her eyes to below her jaw line. "Where were you the last time you know you had it?"

She pressed her lips together and looked beyond my shoulder as though in thought, then said, "Seppi's."

"Seppi's? What is that?"

"A restaurant," her husband supplied. "Not too far away. Fifty-seventh Street at Le Parker Meridian Hotel."

"My name is Lizzie."

The young man replied, "I'm Robert." He pointed to the woman. "Sharon," he said.

I looked outside. The city was still vibrant and alive. "How close is the restaurant?" I asked.

"A few blocks," Robert said.

"Too many to walk?"

Robert looked out toward the front of the hotel, then nodded. "Let's ask the concierge."

At the concierge's desk I explained the situation. "Hold on," the young man said. Robert, Sharon, and I waited as he dialed the number for Le Parker Meridian. When he spoke, I listened and signed.

"They do have the purse," he said, hanging up. "I can have someone get it for you."

As soon as I signed the good news, Sharon shook her head and signed back to me, "How long will that take?"

I repeated the question to the concierge.

He looked at his watch. "Could be up to an hour, unfortunately. We're not as highly staffed during this shift."

I repeated the answer. Sharon quickly signed to Robert, "Can we go get it? Please? I'll worry."

Robert nodded.

I told the concierge, "They'll take a cab to the hotel."

Robert and Sharon thanked me, and I wished them luck. I was just about to turn toward the lobby when a sudden and unexpected thought came to mind. "Would you like me to go with you?" I asked. "Just in case there's a problem?"

The young couple smiled. The next thing I knew, we were standing outside and then slipping into a cab.

Minutes later we were heading—in a roundabout way—toward

57th, although it seemed to me the cab driver wasn't taking any direct route to the hotel/restaurant. While we were en route, I called Goldie to tell her what was happening. She was, of course, beyond mortified. "You left the hotel without telling me?" she nearly screamed. "Lizzie, my gosh!"

"It's okay, Goldie. Really, it is. This is one of those moments, you know, when you realize God has you in a particular place at a particular time for a particular reason."

I heard her sigh. "Only you, Liz."

"Did you talk with Jack?"

"Yes."

"And?"

"Practically all of Summit View was at the church tonight, cell phones in hand, ready to make those calls."

I laughed lightly. "Well, who knows? Maybe we'll move one more rung up the ladder to the finale."

Goldie didn't reply.

"Is something wrong?" I asked.

"No. Not really. Well, not for you or me."

"For who, then?"

"Donna. Jack says Faye Gage is coming with them tomorrow. She told Jack tonight at the church."

"Faye Gage? Oh, dear."

The taxi slowed and stopped in front of the spiffy entrance of the hotel and quoted the price for the ride. "Goldie, I have to go. I'll call you shortly."

I disconnected. As Robert paid the cab driver, I opened the back door and slid out of the car. Robert and Sharon followed behind me. We zigzagged between the pedestrians then pushed our way through the revolving doors and into the lobby.

I allowed Robert and Sharon to lead the way to the restaurant, which turned out to be a French bistro that—with one look—I knew was way out of my pocketbook's price range.

We were met by a host who said, "Three?" but I quickly shook my head. "No. This young woman left her purse here."

The man frowned. "Ah, yes. Can she describe it for me?"

I turned to Sharon and signed the question, and as she answered me, I translated. "Coach . . . Ergo . . . tote." I turned fully to the host. "She says the color is called brass."

He smiled then, mostly at Sharon, and said, "I have it in the back. The young lady left it in the ladies lounge."

I smiled at Sharon and watched as she beamed. Robert showed nothing short of sheer relief and gratitude. "Thank you," he signed.

I waved away their appreciation. "The host will be back in a minute," I said to them, then turned and gazed around the room, which was filled with small round and square tables, dark chairs, and booth seating in black trimmed in wide white strips of leather. The tables were draped in white linen and accented by red flowers in the centers. Even at just a little past midnight, there seemed to be quite a crowd. Just as at the Hilton, most seemed to have just returned from an evening at the theater and were either having late dinners or spoiling themselves with dessert.

I caught a glimpse of the host returning with a purse in his hands. As I looked toward him my eyes shot past his left shoulder and to a corner booth. My lips parted, and I sucked in my breath. Bubba, the adorable Cajun chief chef of Wild Cajun Cooks, and Amy Snyder, Kat Sebastian's assistant, were leaning toward each other, deep in conversation, with what appeared to be half-eaten crème brulée smothered in raspberry sauce between them. As the restaurant's host neared the three of us, I stepped to one side for a better look. Amy was stroking Bubba's face, kissing him lightly on the lips, then nuzzling his nose with hers. Adept as Michelle at reading lips, I watched to see if she would say anything to him. She did. "I promise . . . I promise . . ." she said, kissing him lightly again. "Believe me, my love. I have it all arranged."

Goldie

21

Fishy Business

I was nearly frantic by the time Lizzie returned to our room.

Frantic, but I'd showered, changed into my pajamas, and was propped up in bed trying to read Lauraine Snelling's latest novel that I'd picked up from the church library before leaving Summit View. I couldn't concentrate, though, and had started reading page 15 for the third time.

Finally, I heard Lizzie slide the key across the lock on the other side of the door. I bolted upright as the door swung open. Slapping the book shut, I said, "Where have you been?"

Lizzie looked wide eyed.

"What?" I asked. I scurried from under the cover and sort of crawled to the far side of the bed closest to the door. "What happened? Were you mugged?"

Lizzie placed her hands on either side of her face and shook her head.

"Did you see a murder or something?"

"Worse," Lizzie finally said, panting.

"Worse than a murder? What could be worse than a . . . Do we need to call Donna?"

I was reaching for the phone now.

"No!"

I dropped the phone.

Lizzie made her way across the room and sat on my bed. "Goldie. Oh, Goldie. I don't know what to do."

"About what?" I scooted close to her, wrapped her hands in mine. "Oh, Lizzie. You're positively pale."

She pulled her hands out from under mine and brought them back to her face again. "Am I?" She looked toward a mirror, then back at me. "You won't believe what I saw tonight."

"Well, I will if you tell me!"

She took a deep breath, exhaled slowly. "Okay. Okay. I'm okay now."

I jutted my chin forward. "So?"

"I told you I was going to this hotel's restaurant—Seppi's, it's called—over on 57th Street."

"Yeah . . ."

"You won't believe who I saw in there. Sitting in the corner. In a booth. Kissing."

"Who?"

"Amy Snyder and Bubba from Wild Cajuns."

I didn't respond at first. I had to take it in. Amy? And Bubba?

"They were kissing?" I asked Lizzie.

Lizzie nodded. "And there's more. Amy was speaking to Bubba—I read her lips—saying she had, and I quote, 'it all arranged.'"

"What all arranged?"

"I don't know."

"What else did she say?"

"That was it." Lizzie raked her hands through her salt and pepper hair. "I decided I'd better get out before I was seen."

"Did she say anything before that?"

196

"Only 'I promise, I promise.' That was it. 'I promise, I promise' and 'I have it all arranged.' I don't know what it means, but it can't be good. Those two surely shouldn't be seeing each other."

"Of course not." I took a moment to allow the news to sink in a little before adding, "We have to tell the girls."

Lizzie glanced at her watch. "Not this late. My gosh, it's nearly 1:30. I should shower and get ready for bed." She stood from her place on my bed, then extended a hand toward me. I took it in mine. "We'll call the girls together in the morning before breakfast. Most definitely before we go to the studio to find out who was eliminated." Lizzie sucked in her breath. "That's it. Amy has it all arranged that the Wild Cajuns will win."

I nodded. She was probably right about that. "Go shower," I said. "Tomorrow is another day, and there's nothing we can do about it today."

Lizzie scoffed lightly. "Tomorrow *is* today," she said, then retreated to the bathroom.

The next morning, as soon as we'd slipped into the clothes we were going to wear to the studio, I dialed Lisa Leann's cell number while Lizzie dialed Vonnie's, summoning the girls to our room.

"Should we call the guys?" I asked.

Lizzie shook her head. "I'm not so sure it's proper to have them in our room."

Propriety, as far as I could see, had taken a flying leap out the window.

Minutes later the girls were all gathered in our room and Lizzie repeated what she'd told me the night before. I thought Vonnie was going to faint. She turned whiter than Summit View in a blizzard. Donna reached for her and guided her to a nearby chair. "Sit, Von," she said. Then to me, "Can you get a glass of water for her?"

That Donna may be still a young thing, but she sure has a mature and commanding presence in a crisis. I complied with her command. I shot a quick look toward Lisa Leann, whose face and hair had managed to accomplish the same in color. "This one is going to stroke out," I said, pointing to her.

Evie motioned for Lisa Leann to take a seat on the rumpled covers of my bed. "Goodness, Lisa Leann," she said.

Once everyone was over the initial shock, Lisa Leann took her usual position of authority. "We've got to do something."

"And just what do you suggest?" Evangeline asked.

"We'll go to Kat," she said. "That's what we'll do."

"And then what?" Lizzie interjected. "I've been thinking about this all night—as the bags under my eyes can attest. Believe me, I've thought of every angle. If we go to Kat . . . what if she already knows? Amy *is* her assistant, after all. If Kat is in on this and they find out that we know, they'll make sure we're done for."

"What if we're already done for?" Vonnie asked.

Dear Vonnie. Of course she'd be the one to think of that possibility.

Lisa Leann grabbed her oversized purse from the floor where she'd dropped it upon arrival. It was gold lamé, decorated with large gold and silver-rimmed rhinestones. I wondered fleetingly if this was one of the bootlegged purses she and Evie had purchased before our arrival.

Oh, dear. What an argument *that* had caused between Donna and Evangeline. Not to mention Donna and Lisa Leann. I thought Donna was going to arrest them both, haul them down to One Police Plaza (which I know about because of watching *Law and Order*), or at the very least force them to take her to the place where they'd made their big purchase so she could bring down the house, so to speak.

But she didn't . . . though she just may yet.

"I'm calling Nelson," Lisa Leann was saying.

I looked at Lizzie, who said, "It's okay. She's his mother, after all."

Lisa Leann looked perplexed, but then again, who didn't at that moment.

Five minutes later, Wade, David, and Nelson strolled through the door and into the room of women all set to pounce with the news.

"Whoa, whoa, whoa," Nelson said while holding his hands over his ears. "One at a time, please." I chuckled at the way he enunciated every word as though it were a sentence unto itself. He dropped his hands and glared at his mother. "Mother? Can you explain this in a simple sentence?"

"No," Lisa Leann said honestly. "But I think Lizzie might be able to do so."

Lizzie repeated what I had now heard three times. The boys took the news differently than we girls had. They paced a moment, exchanged glances, leaned against the wall, then shrugged.

"Okay," Nelson said. "Here's what I think. I think we don't have enough evidence. But, with a little investigating on my part and Wade's and David's . . . well, we just might have something, ladies."

"What about us? What kind of investigating should we do?" Evie asked.

"Uh-uh," Donna said, taking a step toward her. "You stay out of this."

"Excuse me?"

I could practically see the hairs on the back of Evangeline's head standing straight out.

"Leave it to the guys, Evie. We have to continue to do what we're doing. Besides, Dad and the rest of the men will be here later today, right?" She glanced around the room.

"Yes," I said. "I spoke with Jack last night. They should be here around three or four this afternoon. They're catching the same flight time we did last week." *Last week? Had we only been a week?*

"Personally," Donna said, "I think you should let Dad and me handle the investigating."

"She's right," Lizzie said, then added a moan. "Oh goodness,

I never called Samuel last night. With all the excitement, I just forgot."

"There's one other thing," I said, hating to have to add any more distressing news.

"What's that?" Lisa Leann asked.

I gave my best sympathy look to Donna, then glanced over to Wade. "Your mother will be with the men this afternoon on the plane."

"My mother?" Wade exclaimed.

"His mother?" Donna coughed out.

The two looked at each other while we all looked at them. Wade was clearly shocked and Donna was obviously furious.

"Well," she finally said, "isn't that just great? Just wonderful. Just peachy."

She stormed through the crowd of us, jerked the door open, and then stomped out of it. When the door had closed behind her I looked to Wade, but not without catching David's face.

David looked like the cat who'd swallowed the canary.

We had a quick breakfast downstairs in the restaurant called New York Marketplace. I ordered their Belgian waffle with fresh fruit on the side. After a quick run back to our rooms to brush our teeth and then gather for prayer, we jumped in the limo waiting out front and headed for the studio. There, we went through the usual wardrobe and makeup and hair, then silently strolled down the hallways and to the main auditorium, where a few of the other teams had already been seated. I quickly noted that the Wild Cajun Cooks were not among those who'd already made it.

But Comfort Cooking was, so I broke from my group and went over to theirs. "Hello, girls," I said. "I'm Goldie, as you probably already know, and I just wanted to tell you that I'm also from Georgia."

"Oh?" one of the ladies said, sitting up straight like I'm sure her mama taught her to. She lightly touched the hollow of her throat with her fingertips, and I noted the sheen of red painted on manicured nails. "Whereabout?" Her perfectly arched brow rose a hint. There was nothing—and I do mean nothing—out of place about this woman. I remembered all the proper ladies I'd been exposed to as a child and young adult. My mother had been anything but pretentious, but my sister Diane could out-snob the biggest snob of all.

I was more like my mother.

"Alma," I said.

There is a vast difference in Alma, Georgia, and Savannah, Georgia. Alma is primarily an agricultural community with streets named things like Soybean Road. Savannah boasts a population of 150,000 with streets named Victory Drive and Harry Truman Parkway.

"Oh," the woman said, then smiled, showing perfectly white, perfectly straight teeth. I thought she was going to make some snide remark, but instead she said, "My mama's family came from Douglas, not too far away."

"Really?" I felt myself beaming. "Who are your people?"

Before she could answer, I heard Kat Sebastian's voice instructing all six teams to come up to the stage and stand in clusters. "Team members with team members," she said.

I glanced around. "Where is she?" I asked.

My new friend (and, who knows, probable cousin) stood and said, "Mercy me. Who knows. Probably in the sound booth somewhere." She looked to her comrades. "Come on, girls. Let's see if we're in or out." She smiled at me again and winked. "Good luck, now."

"To you too," I said.

"Goldie!" I heard Lisa Leann before I saw her. She and the others were pulling their pink bib aprons over their heads. Lisa Leann was extending mine toward me, all the while heading in my direction faster than a train running way behind schedule.

201

"I'm coming! I'm coming!" I said.

I slipped on my bib apron and ran up the steps and to our place for the filming of the elimination. The cameras slid into place. The cameramen, wearing headsets with microphones, were speaking to each other and to the producers and director. Everyone else scurried into place. I leaned over from my position to check out the others. The Wild Cajun Cooks had just sauntered in, looking cool and collected.

Well, no wonder.

Kat Sebastian's voice boomed from the great beyond. "About time, boys!"

I glanced up to the sound booth. Kat stood behind the glass, hands on her hips. Like Donna, she was young, but she sure was feisty. I decided there and then she had no idea about Amy and Bubba.

Bubba. I wondered what his mother had really named him.

Bubba called back, *"Laisez les bons temps rouler!"* Then he laughed heartily.

"Look here, Bubbs," Kat shot back. "If you think that impresses me, you've got another think coming."

"I merely said—" The smile held on his face, even as Kat interrupted him.

"I know what you said. Let the good times roll. Well, hear this: we can't let the *cameras* roll until you *all* get here. *Capiche?*"

"She's hot when she's hot, no?" Bubba said to one of his team members.

I looked from Lizzie to Lisa Leann, then to Donna, to Evie, to Vonnie, and finally to the boys. It felt like we were in on Watergate, even before Woodward and Bernstein.

Then a shudder went through me when Kat said, "Team Potluck, pay attention now." Now I felt like a fifth grader called to attention by her teacher.

After a few minutes of buzzing around, everyone came to order, and Gianne came floating out, all five-feet-eleven of her. Her thick blonde hair fell in waves down her back, which was exposed due to the lack of material on her sequined dress. "Hello, lovelies," she said to our group, which stood stage right, a term I now knew meant to the left. Specifically we were standing down right, meaning we were near the stage's apron, closest to the wings. Next to us was Team Batter Up followed by Team Tex Mex. We were the six remaining groups from the week before. Moving to stage left was Team Hollywood, Comfort Cooking, and finally, Wild Cajun Cooks.

Gianne then winked at our boys. "Hello, gorgeous," she said in her best Barbra Streisand voice. "And gorgeous and gorgeous."

After a few minutes more, the director said, "In five-four-three-two . . ." and Gianne stopped flirting and got to work. "Hello, America! Our caterers have plotted and planned and performed to perfection. You, America, have voted! And today we have our winners."

I felt my heart beating behind my eardrums, nearly drowning out anything else the leggy woman was saying. Beginning with Wild Cajun Cooks, she discussed what they'd cooked and then said, "Let's see that video tape."

"Okay, cut!" the director yelled. "Gianne, stand next to the ladies from Savannah, please."

Gianne complied and the director said, "In five-four-three-two . . ."

Gianne smiled at my new friend. "Comfort Cooking Team is from Savannah, Georgia. Judy, tell me: how are you ladies feeling today about your chances?"

"Well," Judy said slowly, "we're thinking they're pretty good. We're just thankful to the good Lord that he's brought us this far and hope for more weeks to come."

She beamed toward the camera, and I beamed toward Lisa Leann. "A believer," I mouthed.

Gianne seemed a little taken aback, but she quickly recovered, looked up toward the rafters, and said, "Well, we'll see . . ." Then back to the camera. "Okay, America. Let's see what happened last time with our Ladies of Comfort."

"Cut!"

Gianne moved to Team Hollywood. After the teams had been interviewed, Gianne took center stage and looked into the camera and waited for her cue. The director said, "In five-four-three-two . . ."

"America, the moment you've been waiting for is almost here. Which team will leave us and which teams, Team Tex Mex, Team Batter Up, Team Hollywood, Comfort Cooking, the Wild Cajuns, or Team Potluck, will continue on to compete for the title?" She then moved toward our clustered team. "But before we announce the winner, we'd like to share a heartwarming story with you." She looked directly at Lizzie. "Lizzie Prattle?"

Lizzie bristled beside me. "Me?" she asked.

"Yes, you." She tilted her head and winked. "Can you step forward, please?"

Lizzie did as she was told but not without cutting her eyes and locking them with mine. I read them easily. *Uh-oh.* Maybe they knew what we knew. Maybe they were going to put Lizzie on the spot. Make her tell about Bubba and Amy.

Maybe.

22

Chilling Note

I think we all held our breath, if you want to know the truth of it. Every one of us Potluckers standing on that stage was thinking the same thing: *They're gonna make her talk.*

I watched as Gianne brought Lizzie center stage and then said, "Tell us a little about yourself, Lizzie."

I've known Lizzie for a lot of years, so let me just say right here and now, that woman was very uncomfortable. She has never liked having the spotlight on her.

"My name is Lizzie Prattle," Liz began. "I guess you all know that." She smiled. So nervous, God bless her. "I'm married. I'm a wife, mother, grandmother . . ."

"Tell us about your children, Lizzie," Gianne coaxed. "Tell us specifically about your youngest daughter."

"Michelle?"

Michelle?

"Well, she's married to a nice young man and—"

205

"Michelle is hearing impaired, is she not?"

"Yes."

"And you communicate using sign language, is that not correct?"

I was beginning to see where this was going. And by Lizzie's body language, so was she. "Yes," she said.

Gianne looked at the camera. "America, last evening our cameraman—unbeknownst to Lizzie here—was in the hotel's lobby when *this* occurred."

The director yelled "cut" again, and then Kat called out from the sound booth. "Lizzie?"

Everyone's attention went to Kat, who I noticed now had Amy standing next to her. "What you did last night was quite special. Our viewers will see you helping the young couple by using sign language, then show the three of you getting in a cab and riding over to Le Parker Meridian."

"I didn't see—" Lizzie began, but Kat cut her off.

"Our cameraman? Well, of course you didn't. They're good at their jobs. They didn't follow you inside but were still there when the three of you came out. We've interviewed the young couple with the aid of one of our staff who also signs, and we'll have them as special guests on our next show." Even from where we stood I could see Kat smiling. I could also see the look on Amy's face, and it wasn't a happy one. I nudged Lisa Leann and with my eyes signaled that she should pay attention to what I saw.

That Lisa Leann is sharp. She caught on, said, "Got it," and then returned her attention to Kat.

Gianne motioned for Lizzie to return to our group, then turned back to the camera, and after her cue, said, "Well done, Mrs. Prattle. Now for the elimination. America, prepare yourselves. Unbeknownst to our teams, this will be a double elimination. Two of our teams will not go forward after today. Who will it be? I'll have the results right after this break."

We cut, and large envelopes were brought out to Gianne. And there we stood, awaiting our fate. Five minutes later, and we knew what I could have easily predicted, seeing as the young couple was coming to the filming of the next show. We were "in."

Team Hollywood and Comfort Cooking were out.

That meant Team Tex Mex, Team Batter Up, Wild Cajuns (no shock there), and Team Potluck would be competing in the next show.

After the two losing teams were escorted from the stage—with Comfort Cooking dabbing at their eyes along the way—Gianne announced the next event. "Here is your assignment, teams," she said. "You will cater a fashion show. Again you have two thousand dollars and only a few days to cook up something wonderful. You will be contacted by the designer assigned to your group by no later than five this evening." She grinned, then with a smile said, "But, in addition to preparing the food, you will also be responsible for creating a theme and working alongside the designer." Again she smiled. "Well, don't just stand there, teams! Go!"

"Well, it's no wonder," I said to the girls. We'd gathered in the room I was sharing with Lisa Leann while the men headed to the airport to pick up our fellows . . . and Faye Gage. "Absolutely no wonder at all. We all know that Comfort Cooking should not have been eliminated. If I were to guess according to the show, I would have bet my Aunt Martha's money on Wild Cajuns getting the boot."

Vonnie looked at me from one of the chairs. She looked one part worried and two parts perplexed.

Dear heavens, I'm starting to think like a cook!

"Evie," Vonnie said, "do you even have an Aunt Martha?"

I did not. "That's not the point, Vonnie, and you know it."

Lisa Leann was pacing. She held a pink pen with feathers on the tip in her right hand, which she used to bop herself in the head. "Think, ladies. We have to think."

"You mean about Bubba and Amy?" Goldie asked.

"Goodness, no. We'll deal with them later. We've got until five o'clock to come up with a theme for the fashion show."

"Are you planning to stay within the movie theme thingy?" Donna asked. She was stretched out on the bed, legs crossed at the ankles, shoes kicked off, black socks covering her feet, which she wiggled from time to time.

"Yes." Lisa Leann stopped pacing long enough to answer. "Any ideas? Think of famous movies set in New York that might have a fashion show in it."

"*How to Marry a Millionaire* has a fashion show in it," Vonnie said.

"Good one, Von," I said. Then added, "So does *That Touch of Mink*."

"*Breakfast at Tiffany's* does, doesn't it?" Lizzie said.

"I think so," Goldie answered.

"Well, we can't do them all," Lisa Leann said.

That's when we all just kind of sighed and stared first at each other and then out the window and then around the room and then back to each other. Finally I said, "Why not?"

"Why not what?" Lisa Leann asked.

"Why can't we do them all? Why can't we have the designer make gowns from classic movies?"

Lizzie was sitting in the chair next to Vonnie's. She sat up straight and said, "Like the gown Marilyn Monroe wore in *Gentlemen Prefer Blondes*."

"And Holly Golightly's in *Breakfast at Tiffany's*," I said.

"How many dresses do we have to have?" Vonnie asked.

Lisa Leann had brought the file from the show back from the studio and laid it on the dresser. She flipped through a few pages. "Six."

"Let's each pick one and suggest it to the designer then," I said.

Donna bolted upright and off the bed. "I'll be back," she said.

She darted out the door, and in no more than a second she was back in, carrying her laptop computer. "I knew this thing would come in handy," she said. She already had it open, and from the sound of it, it was booting up.

Booting up. Now there's a word for you.

"I've just about got this baby up and going," she said, plopping back down on the bed. "We might be able to find copies of the gowns online and then maybe . . ." Her fingers flitted over the keys of her laptop, and then she said, "Okay, here we go. Who wants to be first?"

Lisa Leann nearly skipped to where Donna was sitting. "Me."

"So, who do you pick?"

I could see the expression on Lisa Leann's face changing. That girl is totally in her element when it comes to stuff like this, no doubt about it. "Oh, goodness! Let me think . . . it should be someone with a great sense of style and flare. Like me."

"Oh, brother," I said. Humph. It was going to be a long session.

By the time lunch rolled around, our fellows (and Faye) had joined us amid a flurry of hugs and kisses. Well, not so much hugs and kisses between Donna and Faye, but that's another story. Once the initial "so, this is New York" and "how are you girls doing" were over, Lisa Leann said we'd best get downstairs for a quick bite to eat.

Wade excused himself initially because he was busy getting his mother—who, by the way, had her hair colored a soft shade of blonde before coming to New York—settled in her room. *Her* room, mind you. I don't know where that woman gets enough money to stay in one of these rooms alone, but somehow she has managed. I could tell Donna was both fuming and itching to let Wade have a piece of her mind. She didn't tell me so in as many words, but I know my stepdaughter pretty well at this point.

At lunch, we all made an agreement that Henry (who was somewhat attentive to Lisa Leann and somewhat aloof) and Vernon would room together, at least in theory. The same went for Jack and Samuel. I felt badly for Vonnie from the financial end. She was moving out of Donna's room and into Fred's, but the show wasn't going to compensate them for it. We all agreed to chip in a few dollars to make up the difference.

Just as everyone was ordering some coffee to end the meal, Lisa Leann received a call from a Jacques Moreau, a French designer Lisa Leann was obviously familiar with. "Girls, girls! Do you know who he is?"

We admitted we did not.

But in one hour we would. Before we knew it, a cameraman was walking toward us, lugging his camera and saying, "Ready to meet your designer?"

Whether we were or not, it was time to go. I pouted at having to leave Vernon behind so soon but promised him he'd be happy he'd arrived in New York by the end of the evening.

As a proper lady from the Colorado High Country, that's all I will say about that.

Wednesday evening, after a full day of meeting Monsieur Moreau (who was very excited about our show idea), we grabbed a quick bite in a little eatery on 57th and Park (where I pigged out on sweet potato fries), then headed back to the hotel for a last-minute meeting in what was now my room, shared with Vernon, albeit for only a few nights. Faye Gage had joined us in the restaurant but now feigned a headache and went to her room, which I believe was a relief both for her son and for the woman he loves.

But we didn't talk about the love triangle of Summit View. We talked about the situation with Amy and Bubba.

Vernon, being the superb law enforcement officer that he is, came alive with the information. "Let me think on this," he said. "But right away I can tell you something is amuck here."

"What I want to know is this," Donna said to her father from one of the room's chairs. "How is it we can't go to the ladies room without a camera following us, but somehow Amy and Bubba have managed to go undetected?"

"Good point," Vernon said.

"Well," Lizzie said, rubbing her forehead with her fingertips as she sat on one of the beds, "Amy is a production assistant. She may be able to keep the cameras at bay."

Samuel, who sat behind her, said, "Getting a headache?"

Lizzie nodded.

"I'll go get something for you," he said. He squeezed her shoulders lightly then excused himself and left the room.

"So, how do we find out?" David asked Vernon. "How do we infiltrate the system?"

Vernon sighed. "That's what I need to think on." He looked at Donna. "And I could use your help. Evie tells me Bubba is kind of sweet on you."

Wade groaned. I glanced over to where he stood against the wall, hands tucked into his pockets, shoulders slumped. He looked for all the world like a tired-out cowboy. Poor Wade. I actually felt sorry for him, loving Donna like he has for so long. I then looked over to David, who didn't appear too happy either. But at least his mother wasn't Faye Gage not half a hallway down and three floors up.

Donna nodded her head. "You could call it that," she said. She kept her focus on her father, smart girl. "And I'd love a little undercover work."

"You be careful," Wade said, but not before David made a move toward our little princess and lightly touched her arm. She looked from Wade and then up to David then back to Wade. I could see anger in her eyes, almost as if she figured Wade *brought* his mother to New York rather than having been equally as surprised by her arrival. But at the same time, you have to wonder, if she were so sure Wade was not the man for her, why would she be so ticked off? Why not run to David and declare her undying love? That's what I wanted to know.

It was then that Samuel came back in, a folded piece of paper in his hand. "Looks like trouble," he said, handing it to Vernon.

We all gathered around to read what appeared to be a note. The words were brief. To the point. The letters rounded, as though they'd been penned by a fifth-grade girl. It read:

IF YOU KNOW WHAT'S GOOD FOR YOU,
YOU'LL STAY QUIET

Saturday evening was a beautiful affair, if I do say so myself. Our tuxed waitstaff (Nelson, David, and Wade) served ten viewers—who'd entered a contest we were only vaguely aware of—a delicious meal that began with a mixed baby green and smoked salmon salad served with ricotta cheese, pignoli nuts, fresh cubed beets, and tossed in a ginger honey Dijon vinaigrette, followed by bowls of piping hot minestrone. During the main course (grilled rack of lamb served with crème spinach and roasted potatoes) and dessert (raspberry soufflé for one), our models strolled down a prepared runway as Gianne explained each gown and the movie it represented.

We girls stood on the sidelines dressed in red carpet gowns like nothing I'd ever seen much less worn before, each one designed by Monsieur Moreau. Monsieur Moreau had brought with him six waif-like models who were dead ringers for the actresses they were portraying. The first was a Marilyn Monroe copycat sporting a white billowy dress from *The Seven Year Itch*. The next model was "Julia Roberts" in a skintight replica of the red gown worn in *Pretty Woman*. She was followed by a Vivien Leigh look-alike from *Gone with the Wind*. That one made Goldie beam, Southern girl that she is. The fourth model presented herself as Grace Kelly in *Rear Window* (complete with dazzling bracelets like those worn by Miss Kelly for the movie) and the fifth was a sassy Mia Farrow in *The Great Gatsby*.

The sixth and final model was "Audrey Hepburn" in *Breakfast at*

Tiffany's. When she had returned from the end of the catwalk, each of us girls took our places with our "creation" as Monsieur Moreau, standing alongside Gianne, announced to the wildly applauding crowd that each member of Team Potluck would now descend the walk with the model representing our idea for the show. I floated toward the end of the catwalk next to "Holly Golightly." We were the last of the six sets of two, just behind Lizzie and "Grace Kelly." We then returned center stage and waited for the applause to finally settle down.

All in all, I thought it was a success and hopefully enough to get us ahead. The food was excellent, the guests seemed entertained, and even the judges appeared impressed we'd been able to stick to our movie theme, although Brant Richards did mutter something about being careful it didn't become "old hat."

"And," he clipped, "you can no doubt expect to hear me say this when the show airs."

I leaned over to Lizzie and whispered, "I'll show him an old hat . . ." though I have no idea what I meant.

Lizzie giggled. It was good to see her smile. She'd hardly said a word since we'd gotten the note three nights ago. Donna and Vernon were doing what they could with the little bit of information they had. I thought it would be best to tell Kat Sebastian, but Vernon said no. Not until he had a little more evidence to support our theory.

In my way of thinking, Wild Cajun Cooks were a shoe-in to win. Question was: who initiated the romance between Bubba and Amy?

And when.

Whatever Vernon and Donna had figured out so far, they were staying mum about it, even to me. And I'm family.

Lizzie

23

Tasting Trouble

As a team, we had Sunday "off."

A free day to sleep in, explore a little bit of New York with our beloveds, and—for Team Potluck—attend church. On Saturday afternoon I had checked the hotel guest book in our room and found Saint Thomas Episcopal Church to be close by. None of us were or ever had been Episcopalian, but I figured a little diversity wouldn't hurt us.

Luckily everyone agreed with me.

And so, on Sunday morning, the members of Team Potluck and their spouses plus Wade's mother got all dressed up (or, as Goldie put it, "gussied up") and strolled from the hotel to the church, sans cameras or cameramen.

We entered the French high gothic styled church from the sidewalk on 5th Avenue, immediately stepping into the narthex. Our feet paused for a moment on the marble beneath them, and we observed a large mosaic of our earth's globe split by a cross. I leaned over to read the words carved around it: *Peace on earth to men of goodwill*, it read. "Lovely," I whispered to the person standing next to me, who just happened to be David.

He, in turn, patted my shoulder, then craned his neck to look upward and around.

Everywhere . . . every place within our field of vision . . . was pure architectural and artistic delight. Art and detailed design had come together to worship God and to encourage those who entered in to do the same. We moved to walk through the doors leading into the sanctuary with its incredibly high ceilings and medieval atmosphere and, in doing so, collectively inhaled in awe. Before us, stretching almost as though it would never reach its pinnacle, was a great reredos. I learned later that at eighty feet high, it held sixty intricately carved figures. *The faithful*, I thought. Those who had come before us and had persevered.

We sat in the back. During the service I kept my focus on the structure. I thought about each and every one of the figures and who they represented. I wondered what some of them might have done if faced with a decision such as mine. A decision to make right what was most definitely wrong within the show. As the choir sang its last song, my mind wandered to the story of Esther. "For such a time as this," her cousin Mordecai had said to her. *Perhaps*, I thought, *I had met Robert and Sharon and had then gone with them to the restaurant for such a time as this.*

Granted, my plight and that of Queen Esther could not be compared. But still . . .

After the church service we decided to go to Bryant Park Grill because Wade's mother, Faye, had heard some good things about it and I suppose we were trying to appease her as best we could.

I've known Faye Gage for a lot of years. We aren't best friends or even good friends, but I'd never had anything against her. I felt for Donna, though. Faye Gage is not one to let her son "go" to or for just anyone. I'm sure Donna's history of loving him and leaving him didn't help any. I know how I felt when my sons had their hearts broken—as all sons surely will—but I'd learned to allow them to have their own lives. Faye seemed pretty set on keeping her son as her "little boy" as long as she could.

Though I was still not sure why she'd come along with our men to New York, I knew this was no reason not to extended kindness toward her. "Faye, I believe that's near the New York City Public Library," I said after she'd made her suggestion. "And I must admit I'd like to take a look in there, since we have the day to ourselves."

With the ladies in heels, we all agreed to take cabs.

The restaurant was long and narrow but seemed much bigger thanks to the large windows dominating one side. There was also a rooftop with umbrellaed tables and a café. After a delicious meal (I had the best grilled mahimahi I believe I've ever put in my mouth) filled with laughter and even a few requests for autographs (which still stuns me) from the patrons, we strolled over to the library. Samuel had brought our pocket-size digital camera and insisted on taking a photo of me standing next to one of the lion statues crouched out front so he could frame it for my desk back at the high school's media center. "I wonder which lion this one is," I called to him from my mark. "Patience or Fortitude?"

"With you next to it," he called back before he snapped the shot, "it could be either one."

Fortitude, I thought later, was something I definitely needed. *Give me strength, Lord, give me strength*, I prayed later that night. *Because I know what I have to do. I just need the guts to do it.*

The next morning I got up and dressed and left the hotel before the rest of the team knew I was gone. Samuel knew, of course. He'd even said he'd come with me. But I told him no. "This is something I have to do myself," I said.

I walked to the studio at Rockefeller Center. I needed the time to think . . . to pray . . . Along the way I asked God to reveal all things kept hidden. To light the path my feet were traveling. To keep his Holy Spirit over my words and to let Kat Sebastian accept what I had to say, and then, hopefully, take the burden from my shoulders.

Above all, I decided, I would not be threatened by notes that had been cowardly pushed under my door. And I would not let anything happen to the show, either. The last thing it needed was the scandal of being "fixed" by one of its associate producers. It would be the 1950s quiz show debacle all over again.

I arrived at the studio and set my course purposefully toward Kat Sebastian's office. As I walked the narrow hallway, my footsteps silenced by the Berber carpet underneath, I noticed her door slightly opened. A mixture of fluorescent lighting and sunlight spilled out from around its edges. Good, I thought, she was already at work.

Hearing her voice, I slowed my pace. She might be on the phone or already with someone, and I thought it unfitting for me to interrupt her. I paused, waiting for the right moment to tap on the door.

The voice now speaking told me there was a man with her, clear spoken and direct. "And the ratings are down, Kat. And if you want to have your job this time next year, you might want to see what you can do to shoot them back up."

"Now, wait a minute, I've gone over the stats, and they're not that far down, Jay. I think with the teams we have right now, we'll see a landmine of creativity and even some fun and zany shenanigans. Both team against team and between their own members. That should bring the ratings soaring, even above last year's. And last year's were pretty spectacular, especially after we got down to our last four teams."

"Speaking of shenanigans, what's the deal with the female deputy and the two men . . ." I heard a snap, then again, a thumb and index finger clicking against each other. "What are their names?"

"David Harris and Wade Gage."

"And the girl?"

"Donna Vesey."

"Vesey, that's it."

"The two guys are pretty smitten with her. Should we focus a bit more on that angle? I also hear Gage's mother has shown up and, from what we've overheard from Lisa Leann, there's not a lot of love lost there."

"Sounds good . . . sounds good. See what you can drum up." Pause. "Oh, and what's the skinny on the deputy and that Creole guy?"

"I don't think it's anything except a very good-looking guy who knows he's very good-looking trying his hand and a cute little deputy who is just not all that interested."

Pause. Just long enough for me to realize I'd stopped breathing. Unless I wanted to be found lying face down and blue on the carpet, I decided I'd best start up again.

"Tell your lead cameraman—"

"Mike."

"Mike . . . tell him to stay on Deputy Blondie. And tell . . . what's the little assistant's name?"

"My assistant?"

"Yeah."

"Amy."

"Amy. Tell her to see what she can stir up between the two of them . . . between the sexy Creole and the officer I'm sure every single man in Colorado wouldn't mind being pulled over by."

"That's a sexist comment if I ever heard one, Jay."

A deep chuckle followed by a female's. "All right then, Ms. Sebastian . . ."

I heard the sound of human rising from leather, the shuffling of papers, the rolling of casters against a chair mat. I turned quickly and headed back the direction in which I'd come.

I opted for taking the stairs versus waiting for the elevator. When I'd made it to the first floor I shot out of the stairwell door into the lobby and then out of the building before I had a chance to think beyond the moment. Outside, I headed for the sidewalk extending up one side and down the other of 5th Avenue, where I slipped into the morning crowd of Starbucks-sipping New Yorkers on their way to work at the start of the week.

I pulled my cell phone out of my purse, nearly dropping it my hand was shaking so. I dialed a familiar number, then waited. After a few rings a very sleepy-sounding deputy from Summit View, Colorado, answered. "Lizzie?" she asked, no doubt having read her caller ID.

"Donna," I said, nearly breathless and my voice trembling. "Girl-friend, we need to talk."

24

Marriage Melts

Henry had been pretty quiet since last night's meeting. Though "quiet" was not an unusual state for him. In fact, he'd been quiet for most of our marriage. In the past couple of months, since we'd been meeting with the pastor for some much-needed marriage counseling, I no longer saw Henry's silence as him having nothing to say. I saw it as a cloak he hid behind.

So help me, it was a cloak I hoped to rip open.

Last night, with the lights off and Henry scootched to the edge of our bed, I'd said, "Henry, do you remember that old sitcom *Get Smart*, from the sixties?"

"Sure."

"Despite our red hair, my sisters and I were always pretending we were the glamorous 'Agent 99.'"

Henry actually chuckled. "Why am I not surprised?"

"Do you know what image keeps replaying in my mind?" I'd

waited for him to answer, and when he didn't, I plowed ahead. "Whenever Maxwell Smart and the Chief needed to talk secretly, the Cone of Silence would drop over them."

When Henry still didn't respond, I said, "It was a large plastic bubble that came down like an old-fashioned hairdryer, remember?"

"What about it?" Henry asked.

"Well, since the girls and I have been in New York, we really haven't had much privacy. I mean, you never know when Mike or one of his crew might be in our faces. For all we know, the show's execs are listening in on our conversation right now."

"Something tells me you'd welcome that."

I dropped my voice to a whispered reproach. "No, I wouldn't, Henry."

Henry turned to face me. "Then why are you even here in New York?"

I sighed, knowing we were about to rehash our old argument, which I decided to abbreviate. "You know . . . the contracts . . . Nelson. What could I do?"

Henry turned back to his edge of the bed without a reply.

"You know what I wish?" I said. "I wish the Cone of Silence would lift off our marriage. I wish you would talk to me, like you used to."

"Did we ever really talk?"

"Of course," I whispered. "We'd sit late into the night, talking about your job, our children, and the funny things that happened to me as I tried to organize my favorite projects at church. Remember how we'd laugh together?"

Henry softened his tone. "I do remember."

I moved closer. "Remember how we used to make love?"

Henry turned to face me then. "That was when there was only the two of us."

"There's only the two of us now," I said.

221

Henry's voice dropped almost to a whisper. "And Clark makes three."

I shuddered at the mention of his name. "Clark was the biggest mistake of my life."

"If you really feel that way, why are you flaunting your affair for the world to see?"

"I am doing no such thing."

"Really? Didn't you do a segment for your beloved *The Great Party Showdown* program called *An Affair to Remember*?"

My breath caught. "The theme choice of our party had nothing to do with my *mistake* with Clark."

"After that segment aired, the blogs painted a pretty ugly picture of you. You know that, right?"

"It was only idle gossip."

"No, it was the worst kind of gossip; what they insinuated was true. Which reminds me, Lisa Leann, have you spoken to our son to explain that gossip, like I requested?"

"Well, no . . ."

"Why not?"

"Well, Nelson's seen it, but he doesn't believe it. There's so much trash talk about different members of our team, he thinks it's nothing but lies."

"Trash talk?"

"You know, they're saying that Donna's pregnant by Bubba from Wild Cajun Cooks, that Evie had a sex change, and that our son and Gianne are having an affair."

His tone dry, Henry said, "How do you know Gianne and Nelson aren't having an affair?"

I sat up in bed. "Henry, what kind of son do you think we raised?"

"It's just that the apple never falls far from the tree."

His verbal slap startled me. "That was unkind."

"I guess. Sorry." Henry climbed out of bed and snapped on

the floor lamp by the lounge chair in the corner. He reached for a copy of the latest Grisham book, which he'd left on the writing desk. "Do you mind if I read for a while? I'm finding it hard to relax."

"Don't let me stop you," I said as I rolled over to hug my edge of the bed. "I guess there's nothing else to do anyhow."

With the dawn, I found Henry standing at the window of our room, holding aside one of the heavy cream drapes as he stared into the New York skyline.

I climbed out of bed and walked up behind him and gave him a hug. "Sorry about last night."

He glanced down at me then back at the high-rises blushing in the early morning sun. "Me too."

I patted his arm. "Ready for me to make a pot of coffee?"

He nodded.

"Good. The Spanish omelets I ordered from room service should arrive soon. I hope you're hungry."

He nodded again. "I am."

"Henry, for what it's worth, I know I can never make you forgive me, but I really am sorry."

Henry looked down at me. "I know."

I felt faint hope stir my heart. "Does that mean you've decided to forgive me?"

"I would, if your betrayal didn't hurt so much."

I wrapped my arms around my husband and rested my head on his chest, my voice barely audible. "It hurt me too. I'm so sorry."

He slowly accepted me into his arms as he breathed into my hair. "It's just that I don't think it's within my power to forgive you."

I buried myself deeper into his embrace and whispered, "But it's within God's power. Have you asked him to help you forgive me? To forgive me through his power?"

I could feel our hearts longing for reconciliation as he said, "If only that were possible."

My tears soaked into his terry robe. "Maybe if we could pray together and ask God for help."

He looked skeptical. "Maybe."

I blinked my lashes free of my tears. "How about we pray right now?"

He slowly shook his head, then stared out the window. "I'm not ready."

"Do you mean you're not ready *now* or do you mean you're not ready *ever?*"

His grip loosened, though he continued to hold me. "I dunno."

We stood in our pitiful embrace, each wondering if our marriage could ever be restored, unsure if we were clinging to one another because we were trying to say good-bye or if we were trying to hold on. It was only when room service knocked at our door did we pull ourselves away, the moment as broken as my heart.

25

Cajun Cooking

When Lizzie called to tell me about what she'd overheard at Kat's studio office, I was stunned. "Let me get this straight," I said as I stared out my hotel window to look down on the streets teeming with yellow cabs, some thirty stories below. "You're telling me that Kat and company are about to turn the heat up? On me?"

"That's exactly what I'm saying."

I turned and stomped a few paces toward the middle of my room, wishing I still had Vonnie to talk to, though glad she was enjoying her visit with Fred. "Then how do I investigate Bubba without being caught on tape?"

"If anyone can do it, Donna, you—"

"Hold up. You also believe, as you explained last night, this contest is more than likely rigged?"

"Right."

"Maybe my next move should be to take the next plane to Denver."

Lizzie sounded shaken. "You can't!"

"You know me well enough to know that once I make up my mind, nothing can—"

"But we need you here, Donna. As your friend, I'm asking you not to abandon ship, at least not yet. Think of the church, think of the legal entanglements, for everyone."

I sighed and flopped into the overstuffed chair. "Okay. I'm willing to stick around another week. Besides, maybe we'll be voted off the show on Wednesday and we can all escape this circus."

Lizzie muttered, as if under her breath, "We can pray for that."

I allowed a smile to twitch my lips. "If two agree on anything in my name . . ." I said, referencing Matthew 18:19.

Lizzie giggled. "I'm so with you. But Donna, what are you going to do?"

"Do?" I leaned back and crossed my ankles. "Well, I'm hoping to make a date with Bubba to see if he's willing to, as they say down on the Gulf, spill his red beans and rice."

After I hung up, I thought about the possibilities of how to pull off a rendezvous with Bubba. Being it was Monday, the day before our show aired, the teams who weren't taping their parties had the day off, including Team Potluck and the Wild Cajun Cooks. So, even with the bus tours that Lisa Leann had set up for us, there was plenty of time to see if I could get Bubba alone. It wouldn't be all that hard to reach him, especially as he'd slipped me his cell number only a few days ago. "Call me," he'd pleaded.

Instead, I decided to text him.

4 your eyes only. Meet me 2nite at Café Camelot @ 9? Potluck Donna

Two minutes later, my phone chimed a texted reply.

Bebe, I b there 4 u.

I texted back. *Keep this secret.*

Yes. This is hot hot!

I sat my phone down on the desk and grimaced. Bubba sounded

a little too eager. Surely he wouldn't try to pursue me romantically. He had his hands full with Amy. Right?

Later that evening, I applied a bit of makeup and slipped into my one nice pantsuit, a black number I wore on special occasions. I grabbed my pocketbook—the one Lisa Leann and Evie had sort-of-illegally bought for me in some back room—then headed down to the lobby. Without stopping I slammed through the double doors to the curb, where a doorman signaled a cab for me. Twenty minutes later, I got out of the cab in front of Café Camelot.

The café was nothing more than an all-night diner, a little on the seedy side. But even so, it appeared inviting as warm light spilled through its windows and onto the sidewalk. Before I pushed open the glass door, I scanned the area, hoping no one from the studio had actually taken the time to follow me. I mean, we still hadn't figured out how they'd followed and taped Lizzie's off-site adventure last week. So I was on red alert.

When I was satisfied I was alone, I stepped inside the restaurant as the bells over the door gave a jingle. I momentarily froze as all eyes turned my way.

If I'd had any sense, I would have taken that as the cue to abandon my mission, but instead, I squared my shoulders and walked inside.

Bubba, who looked fine in a red golf shirt and jeans, waved from a far booth in the corner.

When I arrived at his table, he reached for my hand then kissed it before saying, "Bebe, what took you so long?"

"I'm not late," I said, pulling my hand away and glancing at my watch.

"Ah, but I have been waiting for you my whole life."

"Lay off the charm, Bubba," I groused as I slid across the tan cushions that padded my wooden bench.

Bubba's eyebrows arched over a pair of intense brown eyes

feathered with long black lashes. He leaned toward me, his elbows resting on the tan Formica tabletop as he cradled his chin on top of his hands. "Ah, but this is a date, no?"

The gray-haired waitress wearing a maroon bibbed apron approached with a couple of menus, which she handed to each of us. "Can I get you anything to start?"

Bubba looked up at her. "Coffee for me." His eyes caught mine. "For you too?"

I nodded. "Make that two. Oh and . . ." I reached into my pocketbook and pulled out a photo and one of my personal business cards, which listed my name and cell number. "I'm looking for an old friend." I handed her the photo and then my card. "Thelma Horn? I heard she might be working here."

Cheryl, at least according to her name tag, took the picture and studied it more than casually. "Your friend, huh?"

"Yeah, from back home in Colorado. She told me that I should look her up if I came through, that she'd be here."

Cheryl thrust the picture back to me, though I noted she kept my card. "Sorry, I can't help you."

"If you see my friend, have her give me a call, okay?"

"Don't know her," Cheryl said as she turned on her heels and headed for the coffeepot. Bubba reached for the photo, then studied it before asking, "Who's the bebe?"

"A missing woman from Summit View. She's got a couple of kids who really miss her."

"Does she want to be found?"

I shrugged. "I'd respect that if that's the case. But I want to be sure she's safe. Otherwise, I may have to start digging up the woods behind her trailer."

"*Galee!*" Bubba looked in the direction the waitress had disappeared. "I think da waitress know your friend."

I nodded. "You've got good instincts, Bubba. Are you in law enforcement too?"

Bubba laughed heartily. "No! My friends and I are full time in our Baton Rouge catering business. You could say I live to party."

"I see."

His eyes twinkled. "Speaking of parties, I would love to show you a good time, bebe. May I?"

I tried to play coy. "Let's see how it goes."

The waitress came back to pour our coffee. "Can I get you anything else?"

I stared at the menu then looked up. "I think I'd like to try one of your apple cider donuts."

"Make that two," Bubba agreed as he snapped his menu shut.

Within moments, Cheryl had plopped two large apple donuts, filled with chunky applesauce and smothered in whipped cream, in front of us.

I took a bite and said to Bubba, "This is good! Can you taste the maple in the whipped cream?"

Bubba nodded then blotted his lips with his napkin. "Not as good as my *beignets*, but then we're not back home," Bubba teased.

"Are bengays like donuts?"

"*Ben-yays*," he said, stressing the pronunciation. "They're better than donuts, fried till they puff. Then there's nothing left but to sprinkle them with powdered sugar so they can melt in your mouth. *Oh la la*. Perfect served warm with chicory coffee."

"I see you love your work too," I teased. "Is that how you met Amy? You catered a party she attended?"

I couldn't tell if Bubba looked surprised or confused. "Amy? Amy who?"

"Snyder. The word on the set is that you two are an item."

"No, no, no. Who says this?"

"Everyone. They say you were seen kissing in a restaurant."

"I have not been kissing the little assistant." He chuckled and wiggled his eyebrows. "I would remember that." Suddenly his eyes sparked. "But maybe my cousin . . . Boudreaux knows something. We look much alike, you know. He'd be easy to mistake."

"You have family here?"

"Oh yes, like you." He hesitated. "Are there other rumors I should know?" he asked as he took a large sip of coffee.

"Yes, I hear I'm pregnant with your child."

Bubba spewed coffee over his donut before he tilted his head back in booming laughter. "And to think I missed the fun!"

I felt my face burn. "Ah, well, yeah."

Still chuckling, he asked, "Is that it for the rumors?"

I took another sip of my coffee before I replied. "You mean besides the fact that the show is rigged?"

Bubba looked shocked. "No! You heard that too?"

I shrugged. "I did. That's why I'm asking around to see if it could be true. I mean, why waste my time in New York City when I could be back in the High Country earning a paycheck?"

Bubba took my hand in his. "Be careful, bebe. I would hate if there was more than one person missing from Summit View."

I pulled my hand away. "Is that a threat?"

"No, it's just that I am afraid you are right. Team Batter Up may be on the inside track, I myself have suspected this is so. You must be very careful. In fact, I should tell you—"

Suddenly, the café door jingled as a mob seemed to burst inside.

Bubba and I turned and stared as a wild Faye Gage marched to our table, bringing with her Mike and his camera and what appeared to be a couple of reporters with flashing bulbs.

"There you are!" she shouted, her face red with too much rouge and fury. "I knew the rumors were true."

Bubba did nothing to protest our innocence. He blurted, "How did you find us?"

Faye crossed her arms over her "I Love NY" T-shirt, which she wore over jeans. "I've had a detective trailing Donna. When he called and told me what was going on here tonight, I thought it was only fair to expose you both."

"What are you doing?" I asked.

"I'm trying to prove to my son what kind of girl you really are."

"But Wade already knows—"

"Is it true you're carrying Bubba's child?"

"No! I never . . ." I turned to look to Bubba for help. But somehow, in all the confusion, he'd disappeared, leaving me to face this wild woman and her band of paparazzi alone.

Well, if that wasn't the limit.

I pursed my lips and turned back to my accuser as I slapped a twenty on the table. I stood and pushed through the circus as I headed for the door. Only then did I turn around. "Listen, Faye, you need to get a life and you need to stop messing with mine. And you need to stop calling me and hanging up while you're at it."

"Then just let me hear you say you are through messing with my son."

I turned on my heels, pushed through the door, and hailed a cab. As the cab drove me through the streets of New York, all I can say is Team Potluck was lucky I didn't head for JFK.

26

Knock-Out Punch

The phone rang early Tuesday morning, and Fred answered. After a pause, he asked, "Donna, are you okay?"

I sat up in bed as Fred listened to her response and said, "I see. We'd better have a look."

By the time Fred hung up, I'd kicked off the covers and was already in my blue floppy slippers with my matching housecoat. "What's happened?"

"Apparently Donna ended up front and center on some grocery market tabloid. She's on her way up to our room now to show us a copy."

"Oh, dear!"

By the time Donna tapped on the door, our coffeepot was brewing our first cups of the morning. When Fred let Donna in, she stormed inside, clutching the gossip rag. "Look at this!" she practically squealed as she waved it in my face.

"Let me see," I said as she handed it to me. I laid the crumpled copy on the desk then smoothed out the wrinkles with my hands. We leaned over the paper, and Fred let out a low whistle. There, in living color, were the shocked faces of Donna and Bubba with a headline that read, "Deputy Donna Pregnant with Wild Canjun's Baby?"

"Can you believe it?" Donna said, pacing the floor.

"Why don't you sit down, Donna," I said, beckoning to the desk chair, "and tell us what happened."

Donna folded her arms across her black T-shirt, tennis-shoed feet planted apart as she hissed, "Faye Gage, that's what."

"Faye? I don't understand."

"She hired a detective to trail me so she could prove to her little Wade that I was nothing more than the tramp she always thought I was."

I ran to Donna and wrapped her in my arms. "Oh, dear! What does Wade have to say about all this?"

She accepted my embrace then pulled away so she could pace. "He probably hasn't seen this yet, but if I know him, he'll put his tail between his legs and pretend this never happened."

She sat down on the edge of the bed and put her face in her hands.

I sat down next to her. "You still care about Wade, don't you?"

Donna shrugged. "I didn't come here to talk about my love life."

"Then there's something else?"

She dug her elbows into her jeans, then peeked above her spread fingers. "The tabloids weren't the only ones to get this shot. So did Mike."

"Oh no!"

"This is going out into thirty-five million households tonight, all for the sake of ratings. The commercials featuring Bubba and me 'caught in the act' have already started to play."

"You're kidding!"

"There doesn't appear to be anything we can do to stop this."

Fred, who had been standing by the window with his arms folded over his blue-striped robe, said, "This is outrageous."

Donna looked up. "The way I see it, Team Potluck has been put into an impossible situation. It's like we're all being held hostage here in New York while the producers play games for ratings, all at our expense."

"Speaking of games, do you still think the show might be rigged?"

Donna held up her hands in an exaggerated shrug. "Who knows? I did mention 'the rumor' to Bubba, and he didn't really deny it, though he tried to shift suspicion to Team Batter Up. He was about to tell me something important when Faye interrupted our meeting."

Donna's cell phone rang, and she looked at the caller ID.

"Who is it?" I asked.

"Wade. He must have just heard the news."

"Aren't you going to pick up the call?"

Donna put the phone back in her pocket. "Nope."

Fred said, "I'll go have a talk with Faye and Wade after breakfast. I'll strongly suggest it's time Faye went home."

Donna looked relieved. "Would you? That would be great. I'd ask Dad to try his hand, but he seems to have his head in the clouds, likes he's on some sort of second honeymoon with Evie." She turned to the window and looked out. "If I could just get through this show without any more of Faye's shenanigans, then, well . . . maybe we won't win a million dollars, but at least I won't lose my mind."

A few hours later, Fred met with Wade and Faye, but according to him, the meeting had gone nowhere. "That woman is impossible. The way she carried on, then cussed me out . . . well, no wonder Wade ended up with a drinking problem."

"Didn't Wade try to stop her tirade?" I asked.

"Well, he repeatedly asked her to calm down, but that had no effect. It appears to me that woman's going to ruin that boy's life."

"Fred, Wade's thirty-two, he's hardly a boy."

"Then it may already be too late."

Later that afternoon, there was no joy in the limo that drove our team, dressed in our "Go Team Potluck" tees, to the studio for a stint in hair and makeup. Fortunately the rest of our family members were to arrive by taxi later, so they could join the studio audience, though the report was Faye would stay at the hotel, as she had another one of her headaches.

On the way over, Wade cleared his throat and leaned toward Donna. "Hey, will you forgive me for what my mother put you through?"

Donna wouldn't look at him. "Wade, until you stand up to your mom, don't expect any forgiveness from me."

David put a protective arm around her, then addressed Wade. "Just lay off, Gage."

Once the live show started, we sat with the other contestants in the audience as the clip of Faye's angry attack on Donna and Bubba ran on the JumboTron. I have to admit, even though I knew what to expect, I was shocked. Faye's outburst as well as the clip of Bubba, who said, "*Cho! Co!* That lady was half crazy. Here's what really happen. The deputy bebe and I were only swapping recipes. That Donna say she wants to know how to make my gumbo, so I tell her. But trust me, my gumbo is hot hot, but it never make anyone pregnant. So, if the deputy is playing madame, it's not with me."

The crowd laughed, and the screen showed a prerecorded message from Donna saying, "This ugly rumor is not only false, it's hurtful. That's all I have to say."

I caught myself stealing a glance at Wade, who slouched in his chair. He was the perfect picture of misery. I only hoped this episode didn't turn him to trade his sobriety for a drink at the hotel bar later tonight.

The rest of the show seemed like a blur as clips showed our team shimmering down the runway in movie-styled gowns before hosting a sit-down dinner for our guests. Next, Team Tex Mex twirled their way into a live fashion show with plates of stuffed jalapeños and tamale balls that they served as they walked off the runway and into the audience. Then the Wild Cajun Cooks served oysters Rockefeller, barbecued shrimp, and homemade pralines while dressed in short T-shirts that said "Vote Wild! Vote Often!" while showing off their hairy bellies, much to their designer's chagrin. Team Batter Up, dressed like the New York Yankees, personally escorted each model and guest to a pasta buffet with large vats and varieties of pastas, meatballs, and an assortment of sauces and salads.

When the voting opened, we got word that we were dismissed with an order by Kat to return to the studio at nine a.m. sharp for the reveal.

But it was a pretty sad bunch that climbed back into our limo to return to our hotel.

"How do you think we did?" I asked whoever would answer.

Wade said, "What does it matter? We were humiliated. I don't know how much more of this I can take."

Even Nelson agreed. "If this show is rigged, I need to get back to school. My fall semester is about to start."

"I've enjoyed my time here with Vernon," Evie said, "but I hate what this is doing to us as a team."

By George, she's right. "There's only one thing to do," I said. "We've got to pray . . . together."

Everyone nodded, and we bowed our heads. I kicked off our prayer time with a prayer based on one of my favorite psalms, Psalm 143. "Dear Lord, let the morning bring us word of your unfailing love, for we have put our trust in you. Show us the way we should go—"

"Home," Donna interrupted.

With a raised brow I continued, "For to you we lift up our souls.

Rescue us from our enemies, O Lord, for we hide ourselves in you. Teach us to do your will—"

"Even if we stay in New York," Lisa Leann said.

"For you are our God; may your good Spirit lead us on level ground."

Everyone else prayed too, for protection, blessing, favor, that the truth be revealed, and so forth, until it was Wade's turn. He simply said, "Lord, my family and I have wronged my team. I'm so sorry for what's happened. Help us all come back together in the spirit of love. Give me the strength to face my mother and to send her home. I need you now more than ever."

I could hear Donna sniffing. She prayed next, "Help me to forgive and give me compassion."

David said, "Protect us from hurts and betrayals."

Evie added her "amen" just as we arrived at the hotel. We all exited the van, a bit teary eyed but with hearts that had been renewed and strengthened. As we entered the elevator together, Lisa Leann said, "Courage, everyone. If we get through this round tomorrow like I think we will, I have an idea about our next challenge."

"But you don't even know what that challenge will be," Lizzie said.

"Don't I? If the past shows are any indication, I'd say it was time for the celebrity cocktail party."

"With alcohol?" I asked.

"We're changing the rules," Lisa Leann said. "From now on, the game belongs to us. We'll serve whatever we feel like serving."

The next morning back at the studio, it was exactly as Lisa Leann had predicted. After Gianne completed her elimination theatrics, Team Tex Mex said *adios*. That left Team Potluck, the Wild Cajun Cooks, and Team Batter Up to face off in the semifinals.

Gianne stood before us, looking gorgeous. She was wearing a yellow chiffon halter dress dotted with an occasional large rose. Her ropes of blonde curls swept over her bare, tanned shoulders.

"Now, for the challenge you've all been waiting for. You will each be hosting your own celebrity cocktail party. Each team will have four thousand dollars and a room full of celebrity guests to pamper with a special theme, food, and entertainment. It's time to put your best spoon forward, caterers. When the parties are over, we'll see which two teams will be left to compete for our million dollar prize."

Gianne then dismissed us to gather in our war rooms. But even with our entourage filming our every move, I noticed there was a new excitement in the air. I leaned over to Wade. "Did you have a talk with your mother?"

"She's promised to leave for Denver."

Donna touched his arm. "Really? When?"

Wade glanced at David, who was listening. "I'd like to tell you more, but not now. Let's try to find a quiet place to talk later, okay?"

Donna nodded, relief relaxing her pretty face.

We sat down at our table and listened as Lisa Leann announced, "I have an idea that will make you go bananas."

"Then we're doing a luau theme?" Evie guessed.

Lisa Leann giggled. "Nope, we're taking direction from yet another movie based in New York."

We all leaned forward in anticipation as I asked, "Which one?"

Lisa Leann giggled. "The 1933 version of *King Kong*." She winked as we collectively gasped. "We're going to use props to simulate the top of the Empire State Building, we're renting gorilla suits, and we're serving everything 'banana style.'"

"You mean like banana daiquiris?" I asked.

"Absolutely not, well, unless they're 'virgin.' We're not wasting our money on alcohol; we're going to show our celebrities they can have a good time without it, like us church folk do at our own potlucks back home."

David cleared his throat. "Hmm. I know a lot of celebrity types. They may not, let's say, get the *punch* line."

Lisa Leann laughed and wrote "banana punch" on the white board.

"Are you sure about this?" Lizzie asked. "I mean, I support you, we all do, but are you sure?"

Lisa Leann turned and faced us, her hands on her thin little hips, which sported the lace edge of her red top over a denim skirt. Her brown cowboy boots completed the package. "Let's just go out there and have some fun. Besides, what do we have to lose?"

Goldie

27

Going Bananas

Before we left the war room, Kat came with clipboard in hand and Amy at her side to announce our event would be held on Sunday.

"Sunday?" Lizzie said. "That's God's day. Considering we've made a stand as to our faith, I think it would be wrong of us to work on Sunday."

Amy cast a wry grin as Kat looked down at her clipboard, flipped a few pages, and said, "Some people would argue that with you, you know."

"What does that mean?" I asked.

Kat looked directly at me. "It means, Goldie, that there is a theological debate as to when the 'Lord's Day' is." She managed to use the index finger of her right hand to place quote marks in the air.

"I realize that," I said. "But the point is, Sunday is when we celebrate the Lord's Day and—"

Before I could finish, Amy cut in. She glared at Lisa Leann and

Evie, who just happened to be standing shoulder to shoulder. "If I remember correctly, weren't the two of you here on a Sunday before the rest of the crew arrived?"

Lisa Leann pinked, and Evangeline muttered, "I told you we should have been in church." Then to Amy, "That was a slight error in judgment."

I cocked my head. "Wait a minute. How did you know what Lisa Leann and Evangeline were doing before the rest of us got here?" Working for an attorney was paying off in my "think ahead" tactics.

This time Amy pinked, but only for the briefest of moments. "That's my job," she said.

Kat, I noticed, looked perplexed. She cleared her throat. "Okay, Team Potluck. Here's what we'll do. I had you down for a cocktail party/political fund-raiser hosted by George Clooney, but I'll trade Team Batter Up's event, which is scheduled on Saturday, and give you theirs."

She pulled a mechanical pencil from behind her ear and began jotting notes.

Personally, Sunday or not, I was relieved not to be involved with anything political. Daddy always said, "Never argue religion or politics, Goldie." So, make that one for Team Potluck.

Though, to be honest, the win was bittersweet. I wouldn't have minded mingling with George Clooney.

I thought of my husband and sighed. I love Jack, but George Clooney he's not.

Not catering the political event, of course, led to the next question . . .

"So, what will we be catering?" Lisa Leann asked.

Kat looked up from her note-jotting and said, "An event to raise funds for the Prevent Cancer Foundation."

We all smiled. "That speaks to all of us," Vonnie said. "We lost our pastor's wife last year to cancer."

241

"Who are we working with?" David asked. Mr. Hollywood would think of such a question.

Kat smiled. "Probably some folks you know, Mr. Harris. David Zayas and Katie Couric, to name a couple."

"Anyone else?" Lisa Leann probed.

"Oh yes. Lance Armstrong, Eva Longoria, and Scarlett Johansson."

"Scarlett Johansson?" Vonnie exclaimed. "I loved her in *The Horse Whisperer*."

"Love her or not," Kat said, "you now have one less day to get your act together and cater this event. You'll be contacted by a man named London Goodman, who is the overseer of the event, probably first thing in the morning." She looked around the room. "Okay. Any questions?"

We all shook our heads no.

"Oh, one more thing," Kat said. "This is a dessert-only affair."

"Of course," David said with a nod.

Kat and Amy turned on their heels and left the room, leaving us to gape at one another. Finally Lisa Leann said, "Well, girls and boys, back to work."

We—all of us but Faye Gage, who Wade had ordered to stay in her room—went out for a late dinner that evening. It was there our men announced they'd be leaving the next afternoon for Summit View.

I'm not sure who looked more shocked of the five of us with spouses, but I have to admit Lisa Leann looked the most despairing.

"I've got to get back to the sheriff's office," Vernon was saying. "With both Donna and me out of the county, who knows what might be going on."

Donna nodded in her father's direction. "We've got some good deputies—I mean, other than me—but Dad's right. He can't stay gone forever. It's kinda like leaving Barney alone in Mayberry for too long and expecting anything less than pandemonium."

There were a few giggles, but I slipped my arm into Jack's and whispered in his ear, "I don't want you to go."

He turned to me and kissed my cheek. "I'd love to stay forever in this city with you, Goldie. But school starts soon, and I've got football camp coming up."

I broached a subject I'd left unsaid in the privacy of our hotel room. "Is that what's wrong? Is the team on your mind?"

"What do you mean?"

I was grateful for all the conversation going on around us as I whispered close enough for just him to hear, "Jack, not once since you've been here have we . . . you know . . ."

Jack blushed fully then turned pale. "We'll talk later."

I pressed my lips together. Something was wrong. A wife has a way of knowing these things. Was there now another woman— again—in Summit View? Or Denver or Breckenridge? Or any of the other number of small ski towns dotting the map around our town? Had I been gone too long from our bed? At our age, one would think a wife and husband could be apart for a few weeks and be okay, but Jack's libido had always been that of an eighteen-year-old boy's. Maybe our couple's therapy hadn't been enough. Maybe nothing I ever did would be enough. Maybe . . .

"It's not what you think." Jack's words were spoken low but with certainty, but I wasn't so sure.

"What do I think?" I kept my eyes locked with his.

He looked pained. "Goldie," he whispered. "After all these years, I know you better than you know yourself."

This time I pinked, then turned from his gaze and focused on the chatter at the table. I took a deep breath and sighed. I had one more night with my husband here in New York. I'd best make it a night to remember.

Well, at least I tried. I took a long, hot soak in scented water, slipped into a pretty nightgown, and stepped out of our bath with all the sultriness of Rita Hayworth I could muster. Jack was sitting up in bed, several pillows at his back and head, with an open book before him. Though he appeared to be reading, I could tell he wasn't paying attention to the words on the page.

"Jack," I said, keeping my voice low.

He glanced up from the book and smiled. Then—just as quickly—frowned. I felt my brow furrow. He patted the bed beside him and said, "Come here, Goldie. Come sit down."

I did.

Jack took a deep breath and then released it as he closed the book and placed it on the bedside table. Then, turning to me, he took my hand and said, "Goldie, I'm not going to lie to you."

"It's someone else," I said, jerking my hand from him.

"Don't go there," he said. "Because that's not it. That's not even close."

In the past, Jack's affairs had all been a matter of the physical. He'd felt little to no affection for the women he'd bedded. Our therapist and pastor had confirmed the reality of this claim. "Men who have sexual compulsions," Pastor Kevin had explained to me during one of our sessions, "are rarely in another woman's bed because of love, Goldie. They turn to others out of . . . well . . . compulsion. Which is why Jack came to me, to find help."

The help—I thought—had worked. Now I had to wonder. What was Jack getting at? Was he actually in love this time? With someone else? He hadn't shown me a lack of attention since he'd been here, but he hadn't shown me any physical interest either.

"Does your heart belong to someone else now?" I blurted my thoughts.

Jack appeared genuinely shocked, then chuckled. "You could say that."

My mouth fell open. "How can you laugh?"

My husband shook his head. "I'm not laughing, Goldie. I'm . . . I'm trying to tell you that I've not been well lately and . . . my heart . . . well, it belongs to Dr. Kelleher."

I grabbed my husband's hand. "The team doctor? What do you mean, you haven't been well? Jack?"

"Remember when you asked me to see him about my chest pains?"

"Yes."

"Well, I did. And then I went to see another doctor in Denver, a Dr. Luma."

"Why didn't you tell me?"

"And interrupt what you have going on here? No way. Dr. Luma assured me the surgery could wait."

"Surgery?" my voice squealed.

"Right after you left I saw Dr. Kelleher. The next day I saw Dr. Luma—"

"I cannot believe you didn't tell me."

"Just listen."

"I'm listening. What did this Dr. Luma say?"

"He did an EKG while I was in his office, then ordered a stress echocardiogram, which I had about two days later."

"Is that like a stress test?" My shoulders ached from sitting so straight.

"Something like it."

"What did that show?"

"It showed a few problems, so the doctor ordered an angiogram, which showed some blockage."

"Blockage? Oh, Jack!" I felt tears burning my eyes, then spill down my cheeks.

Jack wrapped me in his arms. "Shhh . . . Goldie," he said. "Don't cry. If the doctor had thought I was in any real danger, he wouldn't have let me come all the way to the East Coast. He put me on some meds, told me to watch my diet, and when I go back we'll talk about bypass surgery. I told him I didn't want your opportunity out here thwarted, and he said I should be fine." He drew back. "But I tire

245

out easily, as you can tell, and quite frankly, with this medication, sex is the last thing on my mind."

I slipped off the bed and walked toward the closet.

"Where are you going?" he asked.

"I'm going to start packing. I'm going home with you tomorrow."

Before I could pull the closet door open, Jack was scrambling out of the bed and heading toward me. "Oh no, you don't. If you get on that plane, I won't. I will not be responsible for you not seeing this contest through."

I felt my shoulders sag. I stomped a foot and balled my fists. "Jack!"

Again he wrapped me in his arms. "No, Goldie. I'm fine. I am. The doctor said so."

I slipped my arms around his broad shoulders and squeezed. "Jack, don't you dare leave me. Not now. Not after all we've been through and all we've done to get it right."

He chuckled again. "I'm not going anywhere. Well, I'm going back to Summit View." He leaned back, kissed my pouting lips while holding my face between his hands. "And I promise I'll take care of myself."

I nodded.

"Are you okay?"

I nodded again.

"Okay. Let's go to bed." He took a few steps, pulling me with him. "And sleep."

That night we lay like spoons, his arms tight around me, my hands gripping his, his heart beating steadily against my back.

And we slept.

The next day our men—and fortunately for Donna, Faye Gage—left New York City amid tear-filled "I love you's" and "good-byes." I held on to Jack for as long as I could, then said to him, "You'd better call me the minute you land in Summit View."

"We have a layover in Chicago," he said. "And we'll be home sometime around seven or eight your time tonight. I'll call you around nine."

When we'd returned to the hotel—with not a minute to spare for any dillydallying—we quickly moved our things back into our original rooms then went to our *Great Party Showdown* kitchen to discuss our plans for the fund-raising event. A cameraman followed us in, appearing almost magically. Truth be told, I was getting used to the little buggers. They were like a third arm or a second thumb.

I admit, I was only half listening as Lisa Leann quoted prices and places for purchasing what we needed. At one point Lizzie leaned over and said, "Are you okay?"

I merely nodded. Jack had made me promise not to say anything to anyone, and I'd complied.

"Are you sure?"

"I'm fine. I just miss Jack already."

She patted my hand.

Lisa Leann gave us our assignments, and I was grateful for her take-charge attitude. If I'd been the one to organize this soiree, we'd be in sad shape for sure.

"Goldie," Lisa Leann was saying to me. "Are you with us?"

I jerked a bit then said, "Yes. I'm just missing Jack."

Lisa Leann sighed. "I know how you feel." She handed me a piece of paper with typing stretched from top to bottom. "Here's a recipe I want you to look over. I don't want to take any chances, so let's all go out and get what we need for our prospective dishes, then come back, prepare the dish, and we'll have a taste-off. I'm not serving anything that's not absolutely fabulous. Fortunately, this event is a dessert-only affair."

I looked at my recipe for banana pineapple delight. "So what do we do? Go out, buy what we need, and come back here?"

Lisa Leann looked at me as if I had three heads. "Isn't that what

I just said?" she asked. "I talked to Mr. Goodman—London Goodman—this morning before we went to the airport, and he said the event will be held at the Sofitel on 44th near 5th. I'm heading there now to check out the banquet room we'll be using and all that."

"What do you know about this place?" Nelson asked.

Lisa Leann smiled at her son. "Nothing, so why don't you come with me?" she asked. "I understand we'll be in the Grand Ballroom. Mr. Goodman said it has stunning windows that stretch two and a half stories high." She practically beamed as she added, "This is going to go well with our *King Kong* theme." She turned toward Wade and David, then whipped out a card and handed it to Wade, who was standing closest to her. "Here's the address of a costume rental place. You'll want three gorilla costumes."

Wade shook his head. "Look, Lisa Leann, I've been thinking about this thing. I mean . . . I have a reputation to uphold and . . ." He cut his eyes to the cameraman, who had the lens of his camera pointed directly at Wade.

"Come on, cowboy," David said with a laugh, no doubt realizing the hilarity of the moment caught on tape. "Surely you aren't afraid of a little monkey business."

Wade glared at the camera. "I am nobody's monkey."

Donna moved over to him then, locked her arm with his, and batted her eyelashes like an overdramatic actress. "Oh, come on, Wade. For me?"

Wade narrowed his eyes. "I'll make you a deal. You dress like Fay Wray and I'll dress like Kong."

Donna blushed, David shifted uneasily, and Lisa Leann practically cheered. "Yes! What a fabulous idea!"

It was then Lizzie's cell phone rang. She pulled it out of the front pocket of the beige capris she was wearing, looked at the face, then said to everyone, "It's Samuel. They must have landed in Chicago." She flipped the phone open. "Hello?"

We stood and watched as her smile faded and her face grew

pale. "When?" she asked, followed by, "Okay . . . okay . . . I'll take care of it . . . okay." She swallowed hard. "Is he . . . okay. Okay . . . I love you too." She closed the phone and looked at me.

I felt myself grow weak. It was Jack. I knew it. I just knew it. "Jack?" I said.

"What's going on?" Evangeline asked. "Lizzie Prattle?"

Lizzie took a deep breath, glanced at the group, then brought her attention back to me. "It's Jack," she said. "He had a heart attack on the flight and—"

I screamed and felt myself go limp. David, who was a couple of people away, darted toward me. I was vaguely aware of his arms catching me, of him saying, "Get some water," and of the sudden movement around me as he eased me to the floor. I squeezed my eyes shut, then reopened them. "Is he . . ." I couldn't bring myself to say the word. I focused solely on Lizzie. "Is he?" I screamed at her.

Donna appeared with a glass of water, which she handed to David. Vaguely I saw the cameraman directly over her shoulder. *Jack . . . the whole world will know . . .*

"Here, Goldie," David said. "Sip on this." He eased the rim to my lips, and I took a swallow as Lizzie leaned over me.

"He's alive, Goldie. He's alive." She straightened, looked at Lisa Leann. "We have to get Goldie to the airport," she said. "Call Kat and see what we can do to get her to Chicago tonight."

"I'm on it," Lisa Leann said. I heard rather than saw her scurry to another side of the room to make the call.

"Gather round," Lizzie said. "Let's pray."

28

Heart Beats

After we'd prayed I helped Goldie from the floor and wrapped an arm around her shoulders. Lisa Leann approached us and touched my arm to gain my attention. "Kat said she'll handle everything. All you have to do is get Goldie to the hotel and then someone will contact you in your room as to the details of her flight."

I nodded. "Got it. Did she say anything else?"

Lisa Leann shook her head. "No. Only that she's very sorry to hear this and can the rest of us go on without Goldie." The words brought a grimace to Lisa Leann's face, as though saying them in front of Goldie was more than she wanted to do.

"Of course we can," I said, giving Goldie's shoulders a squeeze. I looked at our friend. "It won't be the same, but don't you worry about a thing, you hear me? Think about nothing but getting to Jack for right now. God is in control."

The rest of our team, still gathered around, acknowledged my words.

Minutes later, Goldie and I were piling into a yellow cab and heading toward the hotel. We took the ride holding hands but saying nothing. Goldie cried silently while I mostly stared straight ahead, not knowing fully what to say. A dozen questions were going through my mind, none of them with any answers better than "God is in control."

We arrived at the hotel and went to our room. I checked the phone to see if the red message light was blinking, but it wasn't. Goldie began packing while I called Samuel on his cell phone. As it rang I broke the silence by saying, "They've taken Jack to a hospital in Chicago."

Goldie only nodded as she folded clothes and placed them in the luggage spread wide on her bed.

Samuel's voice mail message came on. I pushed a key to bypass it and then spoke into the phone. "Samuel, call us and let us know what's going on. Goldie is packing, and I'll get her to the airport. We're waiting to hear from Kat now—"

The room phone rang. Goldie jerked as she looked over at it, then turned to me. "You get it," she said.

I hung up on the message to Samuel and then answered our room phone. It was Kat. She gave her blessings to Goldie. "I've got Goldie flying out of here around seven this evening," she said, then gave me the particulars. I wrote the information on the small pad of paper near the phone, then thanked her.

Just as I hung up, my cell phone rang. I ran to it, glanced at the face, and saw it was Evangeline. "Hey, Evie," I said.

"How is she?"

"She's packing." I glanced toward Goldie and smiled. She didn't smile back.

"I didn't ask what she's doing, Liz. I asked how she is doing."

"It's hard to say," I admitted. "I just got off the phone with Kat. They've got her flying out at seven this evening. She won't get into Chicago until nearly midnight."

251

I heard Evie sigh just as Goldie said, "Midnight?"

"I'll have Sam pick you up, Goldie. He's staying with Jack."

Evie continued, "I'm in charge of Goldie's banana dessert and Vonnie is taking over yours," she said. "I just didn't want you to worry about anything extra."

Worry about it? I'd actually forgotten about my recipe for banana nut cheesecake, which—upon my first and only glance—looked pretty yummy. I was grateful for Vonnie and Evie being willing to step in, and I said so.

"Keep us posted," Evangeline said, and I told her I would.

An hour later, Goldie sat on the edge of her bed. Her luggage was neatly arranged at the door. We had the television turned on to Animal Planet, and though we pretended to watch, we weren't. Goldie had hardly spoken two words since the news had come about Jack's heart attack, and I wasn't sure how to broach any questions I had. I finally decided to just ask.

"Goldie, did you have any idea Jack might be heading for this?" I was sitting in one of the room's chairs that sat catty-corner near the window. Beside me, outside, the weather had turned gray and rainy. Splatters of raindrops hit the glass and then made rivulets to the sill.

"He didn't want me to say," she answered. "But yes. He's not been feeling well, he's had some tests, but the doctor in Denver said he'd be okay to travel."

I sighed and nodded. "Goldie, if the doctor said he'd be okay to travel, then I'm sure this is just a mild attack."

Goldie began to weep again. I walked over and sat next to her, wrapped her in my arms, and allowed her to cry to her heart's content. We stayed like this for several minutes until Samuel called to say that Jack was resting comfortably at Cook County Hospital. "The doctor here says he had a mild heart attack. He should be released within a couple of days for transfer to the hospital in Denver, where they're going to do bypass surgery."

"Bypass?" I spoke out loud before I could catch myself.

"Bypass? Already?" Goldie jumped from the bed. I looked at her; she was clutching her chest.

"Hold on, Samuel," I said. Then to Goldie, "Are you okay?"

"He said the doctor would *talk* about a bypass. Is it for sure now?"

"I don't know," I told her. "But we'll know something soon enough." I turned my attention back to Samuel. "Can Jack talk? I think it would do Goldie good to talk to him."

Goldie was approaching me now. "Hand me the phone," she said.

I held up a finger as Samuel said, "He's asleep. I'm just down the hall in the waiting area. Tell Goldie I'll pick her up from the airport and bring her straight here. I won't leave Chicago until Jack's ready to leave too. I'll be right here with the two of them the whole way."

I conveyed the message, then disconnected the call. "Goldie," I said, "do you want to take a nap or call room service before we go?"

Goldie shook her head to both suggestions. "No," she said. "I'll just watch TV until it's time to leave."

The studio sent a limo to the hotel, and we left for LaGuardia a little after 4:00 that afternoon, arrived at the airport, got Goldie checked in at curbside, said our good-byes, and then I returned to the hotel. I called Evangeline to see how things were going. She told me everyone—including the film crew—was at the studio kitchen with Team Potluck preparing their banana specialties and getting ready for the taste test.

"Do you want to come here?" she asked. "Do some taste-testing?"

"No," I said. "Being with Goldie was exhausting. She's so distraught, poor thing. Oh, Evie . . . all I can think about is that those two have finally got their marriage issues worked out and surely God isn't going to call Jack home now."

"What was it you said earlier?" she asked. "God is in control?"

I nodded but said nothing.

"We'll come by your room later if that's okay," she said. "To update you on everything."

"Sounds good."

I disconnected the call, then called Samuel to tell him Goldie should be at the gate by then and to call me when she got to Chicago. Also, to call me if there were any changes in Jack's condition. He said he would.

Then I napped until the limo stopped in front of the hotel. I thanked the driver and slipped out of the cool leather interior and onto the heat of the sidewalk. Seconds later I was in the lobby, the elevator, and finally down the hallway toward the room I'd now be sleeping in alone. I felt heartsick and homesick. I wanted things to go back to the way they'd been before we'd ever heard of *The Great Party Showdown*. I wanted, more than ever, to be able to call my mother and talk with her about my concerns and have her speak to me lucidly and with wisdom. But those days were pretty much gone. The thought, however, reminded me to call my daughter-in-law, who I'd left in charge of Mom. I would wait, I decided, until after my nap. Any more bad news and I wouldn't be able to sleep.

Lord, I prayed silently, *help me to find your place of rest.*

I arrived at my door, pulled the key out of my purse, and slipped it into the keypad and back out. The green light flickered. I turned the doorknob and pushed the door open. As I did, my eye caught on a lavender card-sized envelope that had obviously been slipped under the door. Perhaps, I thought, a note from Kat and the other producers for Goldie, passed on by one of the hotel staff. I bent to pick it up just as the door clicked shut behind me. I walked to the wide window—setting the envelope and my purse on the desk in the process—and closed the thick draperies. The room was bathed in warm shadows. I switched on the desk lamp and sat in the executive-style chair, allowing my shoulders to rest against its tufted back. I reached for the card, which was not addressed, and tore the seal. Inside was an unlined index card with words printed neatly across the middle.

DO NOT THINK WE ARE DONE.
B

"Bubba," I gasped with a shudder. I dropped the card onto the desk and then quickly went to the door. After double-securing the lock I returned to the desk and fished my phone from my purse. I dialed Donna's number and waited for her to answer. When she didn't, I hung up without leaving a message, redialed, and waited. Finally, on the fifth ring she answered. "Donna," I said. "You'd best come quick."

29

Locked in a Low Boil

When I heard the alarm in Lizzie's voice, I left my duties in the catering kitchen, grabbed a cab, and went straight to Lizzie's hotel room. She opened her door before I could knock. "What is it? You're pale as a ghost," I said as she ushered me inside.

Without speaking, she handed me an opened lavender envelope. I pulled out the card and studied the handwritten words.

"Done? Done with what?" Lizzie asked, her voice almost a whisper.

I walked over to the window and turned over the card in the stream of dust-speckled light that flowed in between the closed drapes.

I looked up as Lizzie joined me. "If this had been slipped under my door, I would have assumed it was from Faye Gage."

"At least she's safely tucked away in Summit View," Lizzie said. "But it's signed 'B'—for Bubba?"

"Or Boudreaux."

Lizzie ran a hand through her hair. "Is that Bubba's last name?"

"Boudreaux is Bubba's cousin, who's supposedly here in New York with the Wild Cajun Cooks, though I haven't seen him. Bubba claims he's the one you saw with Amy." I peered into the envelope for a closer look. "Hang on, what's this?"

With Lizzie's head almost touching mine, I pulled out a dark hair that was stuck to the glue on the envelope's inside flap.

Lizzie almost squealed. "Can we run a DNA test?"

I laughed. "Not possible. No crime's been committed, and who's to say this note card actually poses a threat? The language is a bit ambiguous."

"It reads like a threat in my book," Lizzie answered. "Don't you agree?"

"Sure I do, but trust me, the authorities wouldn't see it that way."

"So what do we do now?"

"I guess we put every person with dark hair who's involved with the show on our suspect list."

Lizzie began to pace. "Goodness, that would cover everyone on both Team Batter Up, the Wild Cajun Cooks, the camera crew, and—"

"You," I teased.

Lizzie plopped down on the edge of her bed, her shoulders slumped. "For what it's worth, I'm innocent."

I sat down next to her and patted her leg. "Don't worry, my friend. You couldn't hurt a fly."

Lizzie lifted one brow. "Unless my friends were threatened. Then I'd be a force to be reckoned with."

I actually giggled, imagining Lizzie in full angry librarian mode, giving our phantom note writer a good "Shhh!"

"This isn't funny," Lizzie snapped. "Besides, who can even concentrate with poor Goldie dealing with Jack's heart attack?"

I sighed, put my arm around Lizzie, and gave her a squeeze. "Goldie's been on my mind all afternoon."

Lizzie stood up. "And here we are playing games. How did we ever get into this mess?"

I nodded, suddenly feeling weary. Lizzie looked back, then stopped her tirade. She sat down next to me again. "Donna, here I am ranting about my woes when the powers behind this show have continued to harass you."

"And on national TV."

"How are you holding up?"

I returned to the window and parted the curtains with my hand to peer down at the busy streets. "I'm hanging in there."

Lizzie joined me. "But how are you really doing?"

I shrugged. "I feel confused, kinda angry."

"Angry at Faye, you mean?"

The depth of my emotion surprised me as it exploded. "Why won't Wade protect me from her?"

Lizzie raised her brows and folded her arms across her pink Team Potluck shirt. She cocked her head. "Tell me. I know you're dating David; so what is it with you and Wade? Do you still care about him?"

"No . . . yes." I raised my hands in surrender. "I don't know. I mean, we were in love once, back in high school. But after so much loss and time, you'd think I'd be able to move on, but . . ."

"But you can't, can you?"

"When I stop by Wade's trailer and see him with little Pete . . ."

"Are you attracted to Wade or to Wade *with* Pete?"

I blinked hard. "Pete's close to the age of the baby we lost when Wade and I were in high school, and, well, when we're all together, it seems . . ."

"Like the family you missed."

"Exactly."

258

"How would you feel about Wade if Pete's mother showed up and took Pete home with her?"

My voice dropped. "I'm not sure. But I have to find Thelma. I have to know Pete's future. Plus, no offense, Lizzie, but we all know that recovered alcoholics sometimes relapse. How do I know Wade will stay sober?"

"No offense taken, friend. And believe me, I understand your concern. It's been a struggle to stop my little drinking habit. In a way, I'm really grateful that you pulled me over after I'd had one too many."

"That was hard on me, Lizzie," I admitted.

She gave me a hug. "That makes me appreciate it all the more."

The next couple of days were a blur of activity, though we were all greatly relieved to get regular reports from Goldie about Jack's steady progress. But the good news didn't undo the trauma of me getting fitted for the Fay Wray dress, which was nothing more than a yellow satin nightgown.

Lisa Leann held it up at the costume store. "Isn't it adorable?"

"What there is of it."

"Don't worry, you'll wear a slip."

"What it really needs is an army jacket."

Lisa Leann giggled then touched my short curls. "We'll get Sasha to give you a few hair extensions, and you'll look just like Wray in the bedroom scene."

"Excuse me?"

"You know, where Kong reaches in through the window and pulls her out of bed before carrying her to the top of the Empire State Building."

I rolled my eyes. "Lovely."

Lisa Leann patted my arm, "Trust me, you'll be one drop-dead gorgeous emcee."

"Speaking of, how's the entertainment coming along?"

Lisa Leann seemed to quiver with excitement. "During the

reception, we've got the green light to show rotating clips from the original *King Kong* movie, avoiding, of course, the scene where Kong gets shot and falls off the tower. Then, to open the show, we've got a couple of jugglers who volunteered to perform in exchange for national exposure, and they're pretty entertaining, plus we've got a choreographer who's directing his troupe of costumed dancers, so that should be kinda fun."

"Costumed?"

"Imagine this: there will be ten Fay Wrays and ten King Kongs dancing in front of the windows overlooking the New York City skyscape next to our twelve-foot-tall model of the Empire State Building. Isn't that a riot?"

"I guess."

"But that's not the half of it. Nelson discovered that both Cher and Dolly Parton are in town this weekend, and they both volunteered to sing a duet or two."

"Wow! That ought to be worth the price of admission. Do you know what they're singing?"

She lowered her voice. "They've been secretly practicing arrangements of 'Jolene' and 'If I Could Turn Back Time.'"

"That's unbelievable! Good job, Lisa Leann."

The day of the event was crazy, there were so many last-minute details. In the midst of it all, the boys kept jockeying for my attention. Wade would say, "I can't wait to see you dressed like Fay Wray." To which David would say, "Why? Don't you think she looks fine now?"

But just before I was to head to the makeup chair, David stopped me. "Do you have a minute?"

"What's up?"

"I found something, a clue to the puzzle you've been working on."

I laughed. "Which puzzle?"

"This 'B' thing. Look."

David pulled a napkin out of his pocket with a handwritten note penned with the now familiar handwriting.

I'LL BE WATCHING.
B

I stared into David's chocolate brown eyes. "Where did you find this?"

David pointed to a side door that led to a back hallway, which was usually used by the hotel's staff but was now temporarily under our domain. "It was on top of a crate of bananas, back in the prep room. What do you make of it?"

I looked at the card and shook my head. "My reaction? As of Tuesday night, the whole world will 'be watching.'"

"But don't you take this as a threat?"

I nodded. "Unfortunately, yes. Though it's not clear how."

"I have some thoughts. Where can we talk? In private, I mean."

I looked at my watch. "That's not possible right now. I've gotta run to hair and makeup."

"I'd go with you, but I'm needed to start making several gallons of virgin banana daiquiris."

I laughed. "Better you than me."

David took my hand for a moment. "You be careful, okay?"

"No need to worry about me. I'm on the job."

David's forehead wrinkled, and he leaned over and brushed the top of my head with his lips, then pulled back. "That's exactly why I am worried."

The party got off to a great start. The celebrity guests had arrived, posing on the red carpet for the paparazzi. Our guests seemed happy to be served by our troop of gorillas and Fays with an occasional Team Potluck gal in a hot pink apron. When someone complained about the lack of alcohol, we used the answer David had suggested. One of the non-gorilla-masked members of our team would explain that our drinks were the latest trend in frozen organic party drinks.

Happily, that explanation seemed to do the trick.

But things weren't going so smooth in prep. Somehow, an entire gallon of our daiquiris had been toppled, creating a sticky mess, plus a whole tray of one of our banana desserts was upside down and smashed into the carpet. As I, along with Mike the cameraman, surveyed the damage, Wade walked in and pulled off his gorilla head. "What happened?"

"Who knows? We've had a lot of people in and out of here."

"I guess you just can't get good help these days," he quipped.

I nodded. "Quite an admission from a guy who makes his living as a hired hand."

Wade laughed. "There's a difference. I'm the kind of help who can be trusted. But you know that."

I smiled, then continued to blot the mess with a large sponge before someone could slip in the sticky goo. "Good thing we still have plenty of food."

Vonnie, who was next on the scene, saved the day. "You two run along and keep serving our guests. I'll stay back and clean up."

"Are you sure you'll be okay?" I asked.

"You kids go. I'll be fine"

But moments later, when I returned to the kitchen area, I noticed that not much of the spill had been cleaned and Vonnie and Mike were nowhere to be found.

When I went back on the floor with another tray of desserts, I began to canvas my pals and the waitstaff. I even asked Judge Isabelle, "Have you seen Vonnie or Mike?"

Without exception, everyone shook their heads, including all the gorillas.

But a few minutes later, one of our furry beasts handed me a napkin, which appeared to be written in David's neat penmanship.

MEET ME IN CONF. ROOM B, 16TH FLOOR,
5 MINUTES. RE: VONNIE. DAVID.

I looked hard at the gorilla. "David, is that you?" I whispered.

The black hairy beast before me nodded, then disappeared into the crowd.

I checked my watch. I was supposed to start the entertainment portion of our event as the night's emcee in just ten minutes, but with Vonnie gone missing, the show could wait.

Somehow, I managed to slip away from the cameras and crowd and rode the elevator to the floor David had specified. When the doors opened, I was surprised to see the lights were dim and the hallway decorated with a couple of ladders and paint-splattered drop cloths as well as a large white sign that read, "Please pardon our mess."

Ah, this floor was being renovated, which made it isolated. It was the perfect rendezvous point away from the cameras and noise of the party to meet quietly with David.

When I found the conference room, I tried the knob of the heavy door. It was unlocked. Quietly I pushed it open and entered the dark room, groping for the light switch. "David?"

Instead of an answer, the door slammed behind me. I rushed back and tried the door again. This time it was locked. I rattled the handle and pounded on the door with my fists. "David, this isn't funny," I said into the darkness. "Not funny at all."

30

Half-Baked Accusations

We had synchronized our watches before our event started, pledging to keep things on time, and so far we had. While the JumboTron on the far wall showed clips from the original flick with Fay Wray and King Kong, we served our virgin daiquiris and myriad treats like my personal favorite, our creamy banana split cake. So far the food was a hit. Plus, Judge Isabelle was having such a good time, I couldn't help but wonder if she'd somehow managed to spike her own drink. But then, who wouldn't have a good time at a party that included our guest celebrities? I especially enjoyed meeting Eric Roberts. He even winked and lifted his banana drink into the air to toast me. "Here's to Team Potluck taking the whole banana."

"Thanks," I said as I looked over my shoulder to see if the camera guy, who had been dogging me all evening, had gotten Eric's comment on tape.

While I continued to greet and serve our guests, I felt anxious for the entertainment to start, entertainment we couldn't have purchased even if we'd had a budget of fifty thousand.

But as it turned out, Cher and Dolly had been happy to help our cause. The other guest entertainers had also offered their work pro bono, bless their hearts.

"This will open so many doors for us," choreographer Vince Giordano had told me. "Troupe Dance Delight will be happy to help."

When the hour hit eight, Nelson dimmed the house lights, and a revolving disco ball sent a spray of rainbows throughout the ballroom. At the same moment, a recording of the song "The Theme from the Monkees" blasted through the house speakers. On cue, our dancing gorillas and Fay Wrays from Troupe Dance Delight bolted out of the crowd to leap onto the stage. The costumed gorillas swung from our Empire State Building and grabbed their Fay Wrays before twirling them high over their heads.

The crowd laughed and applauded until the music ground to a sudden halt midsong.

I ran to where Nelson was working the sound system. "What happened?" I cried.

Nelson, minus his gorilla head, was crawling on his hands and knees beneath the table. He held up a disconnected cord before plugging it back in. "Looks like someone pulled our plug."

But the music had already ground to a halt. "Where's Donna?" Nelson said. "She can introduce the jugglers while we reset the music."

When Donna didn't materialize, I found myself jogging up to the stage. With the sound back on, I grabbed the mic. "Sorry for the technical difficulties, y'all. We'll bring Dance Delight back in a moment, but now, let me introduce our next act, the Armstrong Brothers Jugglers."

With that announcement, two red-headed young men clamored up the platform steps. They were dressed in jeans and lime green tees and began to toss bananas, oranges, plates, and anything else that would fly through the air.

Grateful for the time their act allowed my team to recover, I ran back into the audience looking for Donna, but I found Vonnie instead. "Have you seen Donna anywhere?"

Vonnie's blue eyes narrowed into worried slits. "Not since the big spill in the prep room. That's when I found the other note."

"What note?" Lizzie, who'd emerged from the crowd, asked.

Vonnie pulled it out of the pocket of the apron as she quoted, "I'm watching you. B."

David pulled off his gorilla head. "Mom, Donna was looking for you not too long ago. Where were you?"

Vonnie looked surprised. "Didn't you get my message? I've been in the lobby outside the room with Mike Romano, doing an interview."

I put my hand on my hip. "You're joking!" I glared at one of the cameramen who was zeroing in on our conversation. "Now's not the time for such nonsense. The party's in full swing."

"Has anyone seen Wade?" David asked. "He disappeared about the same time as Donna."

"How can you tell?" Nelson asked. "All us monkeys look alike in these hot, itchy costumes."

David frowned and wiped his forehead with the back of a furry paw. "I make it my business to know these things."

"Speaking of missing," Vonnie added, "I haven't seen cameraman Mike since the lobby."

"Do you think Mike could be interviewing Donna and Wade in the lobby now?" I asked.

"Let's look," David said. The team slipped out of the banquet hall, minus Nelson, who stayed to work the sound desk. We'd only just stepped outside when the elevator door chimed, and Donna and Wade stepped out.

I crossed my arms. "The show's already started. Where have

the two of you been?" I demanded as Mike Romano miraculously materialized to film our banter.

Donna looked more than a little cross. "I got locked in a room downstairs. Wade came along and helped."

I was incredulous. "Most of these rooms open from the inside out, don't they?"

"Not when they're chained and padlocked," Wade replied.

I gasped, and David crossed his arms. "So Wade, how did you even know to look for Donna?"

"When I saw Donna hurry off to the elevator, I wondered if something might be wrong. I couldn't catch up with her, so I waited for the elevator to get back. I could tell from the elevator's overhead indicator that she'd gotten off at the sixteenth floor. So, when the car came back empty, I took a ride down to look around. When I found her, she hardly needed my help. She was already taking the door off its hinges."

"Heavens!" I said. "Are you okay, Donna?"

She nodded. "Yeah, but I'm fighting mad and—"

I peeked through the doorway to see the juggling act was concluding. "Donna, you'll have to fill us in on the details later. It's time to introduce Dolly and Cher."

With little more ado, Wade, who'd popped his gorilla head back on, swept Donna into his arms and bounded toward the stage, just as they'd rehearsed.

Donna landed on her feet, grabbed the mic, and while the audience cheered, announced, "Ladies and gentlemen, Team Potluck is proud to present Dolly Parton and Cher singing 'Jolene'!"

The audience went wild as our two musical guests, looking fabulous in shimmering silver gowns, belted out the song, playing off each other's performance, as if each accusing the other of being the "other woman" in the song.

As they sang, I bumped against Lizzie's shoulder to get her attention. "Lizzie, would you stand guard over the plug and cords? We want no more monkey business tonight."

"I'm on it."

Later, during mop up, Donna told us her whole story, and I have to admit, I was puzzled.

"Who do you think did this to you?" I asked as I bagged up another bunch of banana peels. Donna paused from wiping down our workstation. "Bubba, maybe."

"What about Amy, Boudreaux, or even one of the show's judges? I mean, Brant hates us, you know," Lizzie offered.

"He hates everyone," David said. "But maybe we're caught in a plot executed by the entire *Great Party Showdown* crew designed to bump up their ratings."

"Exactly," Lizzie said. "At least that goes along with what I heard in Kat's office during her meeting with Jay."

"But who's B?" Vonnie asked.

"That, my friend," Lizzie replied, "is the million dollar question."

I added with a low chuckle, "You mean, the answer to the question as to whether we'll win a million dollars."

By the time Tuesday night arrived, I was a nervous wreck. Here I was, surrounded by my friends and sitting in an auditorium full of people, yet all alone. Not only was my marriage in question, but with a saboteur at work and Goldie gone, I felt more than a little disconcerted. Though I was glad for the latest news about Jack, glad to hear he and Goldie finally made it out of Chicago and back to St. Luke's Presbyterian in Denver for yet another round of tests, still, I was worried. Goldie promised us more news as soon as the Denver doctors made their assessments. But soon hadn't arrived soon enough to stop my ever-growing fear of the future.

Despite my gloom, I was anxious for the show to start. I was curious to see how my team and our wacky *King Kong* event would be portrayed.

But I had to wait to almost the end of the show to find out. First up was the Wild Cajun Cooks. Their event included a reception sponsored by Google Earth's Brazilian Indian Tribe Project, aimed to counter deforestation in the Amazon. A topic, I must admit, I knew nothing about. But it was fun to see their special guests Leonardo DiCaprio, Harrison Ford, and Charlize Theron drinking coffees while eating pralines and beignets with the Wild Cajuns.

But the Wild Cajuns' entertainment was nothing new. Once again, they fired up a Cajun band while the celebrities drank long-necks and danced to the fiddling of "Jambalaya" and other toe-tapping melodies.

But the funniest moment came when Bubba gave a toothy grin as he explained, "Back where I'm from, deforestation would stop if da hurricanes would quit blowing the tops off da pines."

Next was Team Batter Up.

I enjoyed seeing the celebrity guests, including Michael Douglas and Barbra Streisand, though I was shocked that Team Batter Up hadn't asked Barbra to sing. It would have been nice to have heard "The Way We Were" or one of her other hits. Instead, Team Batter Up invited some of the cast from the Broadway hit *Spamalot* to whistle and sing a couple of rounds of "Always Look on the Bright Side of Life." But even with the cute musical number, I wasn't im-pressed with the team's menu of cheesecake balls, cheeses, and wines.

The only team that was left was us. I got a bit weepy when they showed Goldie's heartache over Jack's heart attack. But by the end of our package, I was furious.

With clever editing, they'd made it appear as if Donna had aban-doned her duties to sneak off with Wade. The cameramen had somehow followed the drama from the gorilla passing Donna the note, to a close-up of what appeared to be the note.

DONNA, MEET ME IN CONF. ROOM B FOR KISS—
WADE

Our entire row gasped simultaneously. *Poor Donna.* I gave her a sideways glance and could see her face burning bright even in the darkness.

But despite the lie, the big smash of the night was Dolly and Cher singing "Jolene." The audience of Studio 8 H broke out in wild applause at their rendition. The only other negative came when Judge Isabelle accused us of skimping on the alcohol.

"How can you have team spirit without spirits?" she'd asked us. "And why did you say that no alcohol is the new trend? No way, José!"

The camera focused on me, so I replied, "We are the trendsetters. So, after tonight, America will fall in love with our banana drink, with the recipe posted on our blog! Show these judges we're right, America, vote Team Potluck!"

The audience affirmed us with their laughter and applause.

Later, when we met in my room for our prayer time, Donna was still burning mad. "Gang, what do you say we call it quits?" she asked as soon as we were all seated around the room.

Vonnie, who was stretched in the lounge chair, leaned forward and shook her head. "Donna, I'm so sorry for what they did to you tonight, switching the notes an' all, but . . ."

I sat on the edge of the bed and finished what Vonnie couldn't. "We have too much time invested to walk off now."

Lizzie shook her head. "But if this thing is rigged, then why . . ."

"But we don't know that for sure," I said. "Let's see if we make it out of this round tomorrow. If we're in the final party-off, I think we should stay. Agreed?"

Everyone nodded but Donna, who said, "I'm not a quitter, but the next time anyone messes with me I'll, I'll . . ."

"What will you do, dear?" Vonnie asked, lines of worry creasing her pleasant face.

"Walk off the set, pack my bags, and head home, million dollars or not."

I shuddered at the thought.

The next day, when we arrived at the studio, our team surrounded Kat Sebastian before Gianne could start the elimination process.

Hands on my hips, I demanded, "What was the meaning of embarrassing our Donna?"

Kat, dressed in a black, short-sleeve mock turtleneck and matching pants, look confused. "I know we played up the rendezvous angle a bit, but . . ."

"But it never happened," Donna challenged, her arms folded across her Team Potluck tee. "I was tricked down to that conference room, and not by Wade."

"Are you sure? I saw Wade's note, the whole world did and—"

Wade stepped forward. "I didn't write that note."

Kat looked puzzled. "Maybe my team took a few liberties. If so, I apologize. We're under a lot of pressure from the network to get the ratings up. So, I'll look into your accusations. In the meantime, no hard feelings, okay?"

She dismissed us by clapping her hands. "Gather round, everyone. Great news! Going into our final competition, I'm happy to announce our show hit an all-time high in the ratings last night with over forty million viewers."

Everyone but Team Potluck applauded. Kat continued, "Places, everyone, it's time for Gianne to announce the eliminations. Good luck."

Donna muttered under her breath, "In this case, good luck would mean good riddance."

Gianne, dressed in a rose-colored silk frock with a screaming-short hemline, bid Team Batter Up a mournful farewell. Then she brightened as she looked from first the Wild Cajun Cooks to Team Potluck as we stood on our markers. "Before me I have two deserving teams, each so close to winning a cool million dollars. But who will it be?" She paused dramatically. "Will it be the Wild Cajun Cooks, who have brought us fiddles and gumbo with just the right amount of spice? Or . . ." Gianne turned to face our team. "Will it be a team who has brought us laughter, great food, and red-hot romance? Only time will tell. Stay tuned, America, it's up to you."

31

Soup Kitchen

Team Batter Up had struck out.

Team Potluck and the Wild Cajun Cooks were scheduled for the final cook-off, which—according to Gianne—was for our team to cater a fund-raiser for the New York City Rescue Mission at the American Museum of Natural History, while the Wild Cajun Cooks were scheduled to host an event at the New York Public Library for the oncology department of the Morgan Stanley Children's Hospital of New York–Presbyterian. Our event would be held on Saturday evening, which meant we had three days to design the theme, determine the food served, purchase the necessary items, prepare the food, and then serve the food to the one hundred prestigious guests along with themed entertainment.

Three days.

When the filming was over and we were sent to our war rooms, Lisa Leann went into action as she always does. "Donna, what are the chances you have your laptop with you?" she asked.

"None. It's in my room back at the hotel. Why?"

"Rats. I have an idea . . ."

"Of course you do," Evie piped in.

Lisa Leann turned to look at her. "What does that mean?"

"It means you always have an idea."

"And have I steered us wrong thus far, Evangeline Vesey?"

"Girls!" I said. I rubbed my head. "Where is all *this* coming from?"

Evie placed her hands on her hips, splaying her fingers and drumming them along her hipbones. "I just think that for once we might like to hear someone else's idea."

Lisa Leann crossed her arms. "All right, missy. What idea do you have? I'm listening."

Evie blanched, then said, "I don't have an idea this minute. But if you give me a second or two, I might come up with something."

I pressed my lips together. "Evie, while you are thinking and Lisa Leann, while you are calming down, I want to mention that we are minus one caterer and we might need to find out if she can make it back for the next event."

"Good thought, Lizzie," Vonnie said. "Why don't you call her?"

I pulled my cell phone from my purse, walked over to a chair in the corner of the room, and dialed Goldie's cell number. It was still a bit early in Colorado, and I hoped not to wake her. Unfortunately, she answered, groggy.

"Oh, Goldie. I'm so sorry. I didn't mean to wake you."

"It's okay," she half whispered into the phone. "We had a long night last night and I was sleeping in." She paused. "What time is it . . . oh . . . you're at the studio by now."

"Yes."

"And? Are we in or out?"

"We're in, Goldie. We made it to the finals." I didn't know whether to laugh or cry.

"That's wonderful," she said, her voice still in a whisper. "Tell everyone I said congrats."

"I will. We're trying to decide on a theme now. We have three days to put together an event to raise money for the New York City Rescue Mission at the American Museum of Natural History."

"That's nice."

I waited to see if Goldie would volunteer her return. When she didn't, I said, "Goldie, how's Jack?"

"We had a rough night last night. The doctor is expected in soon, and then we'll know more."

"I thought he was getting better."

"He was. But yesterday he began having mild episodes. Last night they had to give him nitroglycerine several times. The doctor is going to talk to us about doing the bypass surgery within the next day or two. I guess they wanted to see if other treatment would work first."

"Apparently not, huh."

"Apparently."

"Oh, Goldie. You sound so tired."

"I am tired. And concerned. I know the Bible tells us not to worry about anything but instead to pray about everything, so I'm trying not to worry. But I've got the market cornered on concern."

I smiled at her words, then looked up at the team, who were looking back at me, and shook my head. Goldie would not be coming back.

"Goldie," I said. "Listen, you give Jack our love and remind him he is in our prayers."

"I'll do that."

"And call me later to let me know what the doctor says . . . about the surgery." I glanced up again and frowned at my comrades.

"I will. Thank you, Liz. Give everyone my love."

I disconnected the line, then sighed. "Well, I suppose you've guessed. Goldie won't be coming back."

David cleared his throat. "What was that about surgery?"

"They have to do a bypass. Probably within the next day or two. They'd hoped meds would help, but . . . no."

About that time the door opened and Donna stepped in with a laptop clutched in her hands. "When did you leave the room?" I asked.

"While you were talking. I went and borrowed one of the office laptops." She placed the laptop on a nearby table, opened it, and then turned it on, all in one flourishing move. "What did Goldie say?"

I shook my head. "Jack has to have a bypass within the next day or two."

Donna grimaced. "Man."

"While that thing is turning itself on," Vonnie said, "I vote we pray for Jack."

"I second that," Wade said.

"Hear, hear," Nelson added.

We prayed earnestly and for quite a few minutes before the last "amen" was echoed. Then I turned to Evie. "Well, what did you come up with?"

Evie frowned. "Nothing. But David had a great idea."

"Oh?" I turned to David.

"*Guys and Dolls*. We've got a fund-raiser for the New York City Rescue Mission, which reminded me of the Save-a-Soul Mission from the play and the movie."

"Here we go," Donna said. She was bent over the laptop, her fingers lightly tapping the keys. "The New York City Rescue Mission . . . founded in 1872 . . . the objective is to provide spiritual hope, food, clothing, and shelter to people in crisis."

"I like the spiritual part," Vonnie said.

"Hey," Donna said, "did you know it's the oldest mission in the United States?"

"Give us some of the history," Lisa Leann said. By now we'd all gathered around Donna and were trying to peer over her shoulder.

Donna tapped on the computer and said, "Look at this. It was founded by Jerry and Maria McAuley after Jerry had a God-encounter while serving time in Sing Sing." She drew back. "In my line of work, we hear about jailhouse conversions all the time, but apparently this one was for real." She returned her attention to the screen. "Wow, look at the services they provide. This is pretty impressive. The bottom line for them is that everyone deserves a fair chance in life. That's cool."

Lisa Leann clapped her hands. "Okay, everyone. We've got to plan. We've got to think. Evie and Wade, why don't the two of you head down to the mission and find out a little more about them, then meet back up with the rest of us . . ." She looked at her watch. "Let's say in three hours. Vonnie, Nelson, and I will go to the Museum of Natural History. Kat told me before we came in here that we'll be serving in a place called the Powerhouse." She waved a finger at Donna, twirling it about. "Look up the museum on the computer and see what you can find out about the Powerhouse, if you don't mind."

"Sure," Donna said.

"That leaves Donna, David, and me," I said. "What should we do?"

Lisa Leann clapped her hands together. "There's a revival of *Guys and Dolls* on Broadway right now at the Richard Rodgers Theater. I noted it when Evie and I first came in. In fact, I was torn between seeing it and *Les Misérables*. Your assignment will be to see what it will take to get a few of the performers to come to the event and do a few numbers."

"Our high school drama club performed *Guys and Dolls* last year. I can think of four or five numbers off the top of my head I'd like to see done by the pros."

"Donna, what do you know about the Powerhouse?" Lisa Leann asked.

"I've got it pulled up now. It's newly renovated, it overlooks the Arthur Ross Terrace and the Rose Center for Earth and Space. It accommodates up to six hundred guests."

"Thank goodness we don't have six hundred guests," Evie said.

Lisa Leann nodded in agreement. "Okay, everyone. On your mark, get set . . . go!"

David and I waited in the war room while Donna returned the laptop. I fidgeted for a while with my purse, returning my cell phone to its little compartment within, reapplying some lipstick, then placing my compact and the tube in the little makeup bag I keep with me at all times. I took a deep breath and then sighed. Finally David said, "Lizzie, if you don't mind me asking . . . what's on your mind?"

I was sitting in the same chair where I'd called Goldie. I looked up at the handsome young man and smiled. "You are very wise."

"I know when someone has a lot on their mind. You definitely appear to be somewhere other than here."

I shook my head. "Actually, my mind is exactly here. I'm concerned about this show."

"In what way?" He stepped over to where I sat and joined me in a nearby chair.

"Well, I think we have a stab at winning, which will be wonderful for the church . . . the money and all . . . but I can't help but be concerned about these notes I've received."

"How many have you received exactly?"

"Just two, but . . ."

"That's really two too many."

I nodded. "Yes. Then there's the one Vonnie found, the one that sent Donna to that room . . ."

About that time, Donna returned to the war room, said, "Okay, you ready?" then stopped short. "What's going on?" She crossed the room and stood before David and me.

"Lizzie is worried about the notes."

"And about the fairness of the show. I want us to win. I really do. I think we can do so much good with that money, and I'm not sure what Wild Cajun Cooks will do with it."

Donna shook her head. "I haven't heard."

"The point is, I want to win, but I want it to be fair. If Amy or Kat or Bubba or whoever is in on some plan that will make all our efforts for naught, then what's the point?"

"Okay," Donna said, grabbing a chair and pushing it toward us so that we were in a grouping. She sat, slapped her hands on her knees and said, "Let's go over what we know exactly."

"Okay," I said. "I saw Amy and Bubba—at least I think it was Bubba—at the restaurant that night."

"And she was saying?" David asked.

"She said 'I promise, I promise. Believe me, my love, I have it all arranged.'"

"You said you think it was Bubba?" David asked.

"According to Bubba," Donna answered, "his cousin Boudreaux, who is here as familial support, looks a lot like him."

David nodded. "Have you seen this Boudreaux?"

"No," Donna said. She looked at me and raised her brow.

"No. I've seen not one person in the audience when they show the family members that looks even remotely like Bubba."

"Bubba," David said, "is no doubt lying."

"You're probably right," Donna said. "In fact, I'd be willing to bet on it." She paused. "What else do we know?"

"We know they know I saw them," I answered. "We know I've received two notes. They definitely want me to keep my mouth shut."

"Have you received any other threats?" David asked. "Have you at any time felt uncomfortable . . . like someone was following you?"

"No, not at all."

We sat and stared at each other until I said, "I also know that when I came to talk to Kat, I overheard her and Jay talking about needing a jump in the ratings."

"Which means," Donna said, "that any of these antics that have been going on could be from her office. Maybe she knows exactly what Amy is up to. Maybe she put Amy up to it."

"How would Amy and Bubba have known each other before we all got here?" David asked.

"What do you mean?" I asked.

"Amy called Bubba 'my love.' Obviously they have a relationship. But surely they couldn't have developed much of one so soon."

"You don't know Bubba," Donna muttered. "He thinks he's God's gift to the female race. Maybe Amy gets turned on by that kind of thing."

"Maybe," I said. "Or maybe Bubba came in to town early, like Lisa Leann and Evie. Maybe he came in for the purpose of getting to know Amy."

"Men like Bubba," David said, "and I say this because men understand men a lot better than they will ever understand women—are capable of scoping out the lay of the land, figuring which woman would be the easiest prey, and then swooping in for the kill. As soon as the Wild Cajuns win the title—if they do—he'll drop her like a hot potato."

"You bet he will," Donna said.

"Maybe it was Amy behind having you locked in that room, Donna," I said. "Maybe it was Amy who was behind the sound system going out. She'll be doubly devious now . . . now that the competition is down to the two groups."

"Then we need a plan," Donna added. "We've got to make everyone in our group aware of what Amy and Bubba are capable of doing."

"But we can't go to the powers that be," David said.

"Why not?" I asked.

"Because if there is enough of a scandal, they could cancel the finale. We want to win, but we want to win fair and square."

"Absolutely."

Again we stared at each other until Donna said, "Well, are we ready to go to the theater district?"

I nodded. "Let's do it."

Hours later we met back with the rest of the group, this time meeting around a table at a trendy restaurant called Whym—pronounced "whim"—on 9th Avenue near Columbus Circle. I ordered a grilled ham panini sandwich, no fries, and a large glass of water. All this eating out had added a couple of pounds to my usually thin frame, and my clothes were beginning to show the telltale signs.

Lisa Leann went first in her report. The Powerhouse, she said, was absolutely breathtaking. "It holds six hundred for a reception, three hundred for a sit-down dinner. We're doing a sit-down dinner." She pulled brochures from her oversized purse and began passing them out. "The Powerhouse used to be the power plant for the museum. It's five thousand square feet. It has ceilings over twelve feet high, maple floors with such shine you can put your makeup on in the reflection." She took a quick breath. "Oh, and these gor-ge-ous French doors that take you to an outdoor terrace. Oh! And the views of the Rose Center for Earth and Space." She flipped open her copy of the brochure and pointed to a photograph of the Center, taken at night, from the viewpoint of the Powerhouse. "Look. Is this breathtaking or what?"

I had to admit it was quite spectacular.

Lisa Leann concluded with the menu preparations and other fine details we'd need to know.

"Our turn," Evie said. She looked over to Wade. "You tell them."

Wade smiled. "We met with the director of the rescue mission, and I have to tell you, I'm just as impressed with it as Lisa Leann is with her fancy-schmancy reception hall." He looked over at Lisa Leann. "No offense."

"None taken."

"Here's the scoop. They've been operating for 136 years. They have beds for 96 men, 20 of which are reserved for the men who are in the long-term recovery program. They have 4 beds for program graduates, which leaves 72 for overnighters. They have a meal program, the residential recovery program—that I've already mentioned—and spiritual counseling programs, an eye-care and dental program. The success stories are inspiring and—as an ex-addict—I can tell you my heart is ready to burst that we're doing something to help these people." He looked over to Evangeline. "And we've brought goodies."

Evie reached under the table and brought out a medium-sized gift bag from which she began pulling out white bib aprons with the mission's logo in the center. "One for each of us," she said.

I took mine and examined it. The New York City skyline was etched in white on black with a white dove at the top right center. "Thank you," I said.

"The money," Evie said, "will help with their food program. The director will be at the event, of course, as well as several of their success stories, who will share their testimonies. And what testimonies they are! Full of God's power and grace."

"Okay," Lisa Leann said. "What about you three? Donna, David, Lizzie . . ."

"We did it," David said. "We got part of the *Guys and Dolls* actor lineup and their orchestra. They'll perform 'A Bushel and a Peck,' 'Sue Me' "—David held up one finger for each song—" 'Luck Be a Lady,' 'Adelaide's Lament,' and 'Sit Down You're Rocking the Boat.' "

"Which will be the finale," I said.

"Because it has the Save-a-Soul prayer meeting theme," Donna chimed in.

Lisa Leann clapped her hands again. "Perfect, perfect, perfect," she said. "Okay, team. Let's talk menu!"

32

Bubbling Betrayal

Before heading to dreamland Wednesday evening, I propped up on my bed and called Vernon to update him on the issues of the day. He knew we had moved ahead to the final competition, so I filled him in on what we would be doing and that I was in charge of the first course.

"You?"

"Very funny."

"What are you serving? Cheese and crackers?"

I frowned. "I'll have you know I've learned a thing or two from the little redhead. I'm in charge of the chilled tomato soup."

"Yum," he said. His voice held absolutely no enthusiasm.

"Well, it's more than just tomatoes, you know. There's roasted garlic and basil for seasoning. It's quite nice, actually. Lisa Leann gave me the recipe today; I went out and got the ingredients, went back to the kitchen, and prepared it. Very tasty."

"Where is Lisa Leann now?"

"In the shower. She's going to get up first tomorrow so she's going to bed while I shower." I stretched my legs and pointed my toes, then flexed them. "She's heading to the market down in Chinatown early. The camera crew is set up to follow her, to watch and video her as she deals with the fresh food vendors. She's getting to be quite the New Yorker."

Vernon chuckled. "Rooming with Lisa Leann has done you a world of good."

I humphed, then said, "Have you spoken with Goldie?"

"I called her about an hour ago. Jack is scheduled for surgery first thing in the morning."

"What? She hasn't called us!"

"I told her I'd tell you and that could be one less thing on her list. Jack's got a long road ahead of him, Evie-girl. Makes a man like me think."

"What do you mean by that? A man like you?"

"Jack is younger than me. In better shape, at least on the outside."

"There is nothing wrong with your shape."

"I'm not saying there is," he said with a chuckle. "But what I'm saying is this: if a man like Jack, whose livelihood has depended on being physically fit, can have a heart attack and then need bypass surgery, then a man like me needs to start eating better, exercising more, that kind of thing."

"A little more exercise and sensible eating would do us all some good."

"Maybe you and I should talk about what we can do when you get back . . . to become healthier."

I paused. "Vernon, are you and the guys coming back for next week's grand finale?"

"Sure we are. Of course."

"Good. Win or lose, I don't want it to be without you here."

"What do you mean, 'win or lose'? You're the winners here, Evie-girl. You should see all the support around here. It's a major deal, every Tuesday night down at the church, watching the show. And Pastor Kevin told me yesterday that if you win and the money does come to the church, it will have all happened at just the right time. Our sour economy has hit even God's house, I'm afraid."

"Don't I know it." I heard the water from the shower in the bathroom turn off. "Vernon, Lisa Leann is out of the shower now and it's my turn, so I'll say good night."

"Good night," he said, his voice low and sexy.

I felt a tingling in my toes, and I curled them. "Good night to you too."

My bedside phone rang at 6:30 the next morning. I jumped, flipped over to look at the other side of the room. A small shaft of dusty light had slipped between the curtains and allowed me to see Lisa Leann's bed already empty and the room still. I turned over again and grabbed the handset of the phone. "Hello?" My voice was thick with sleep, my tongue sticking to the roof of my mouth.

"Evie?" the voice on the other end said.

"Lizzie?"

"I need to come to your room. May I?"

I blinked several times, grabbed the clock with my free hand, and shifted it to see it better. It was 6:31. "Now?"

"Please, Evie. I need to talk to you."

"Okay. Give me a minute to wash my face and . . . whatever."

"See you in five," she said.

Sure enough, five minutes later, a light tap came to the door. I'd washed my face and made a pot of coffee by then. When she entered, I offered her a cup, then saw she already had one in her hand. "From my room," she stated. "I've been up for hours."

I prepared a cup for myself. "Have a seat, Liz. What's on your mind?"

"These notes," she said. "I talked with David and Donna yesterday, and we tried to come up with some logical explanation as to whether this is Bubba threatening or who exactly."

"We've done okay so far, Liz. Even with the threats."

"But now the stakes are raised, and I feel like I have to do something. I spoke with Samuel last night and told him I think I should go to Kat, but now I'm thinking I should go to Amy."

"Amy? Why Amy?"

Lizzie crossed her legs, took a sip of her coffee. "You know that old saying about going to the horse's mouth? I think, maybe, if I go to Amy to find out exactly who she was with and what she's up to, it would be a good place to start. After all, Amy is not that much older than the kids I teach at school. Why should I be afraid to go and talk to her? But then I thought maybe it would be better to talk to Kat as I'd planned originally."

"Why haven't you already?"

"Because they're looking for a ratings booster, and somehow they've gotten that with us. We're the team with the adorable blonde who everyone wants to marry. We've had these great movie ideas and have had some kind of catastrophe around each event. America seems to love us. And what if Wild Cajuns have moved on only because of Amy? If there is something underhanded in the voting process, then we can bet she's behind it."

"Is that possible? Do you really think?"

"I do. And I think that it's time to do something about it. If we're going to win, it should be fair. And if we're going to lose, it should be because the Wild Cajuns presented an affair better than ours. Not because of any affair between Bubba and Amy."

"Bubba," I said. "What kind of mother names her son Bubba?"

Lizzie smiled. "So, are you with me?"

"What do you mean, Lizzie Prattle? With you?"

"I'm going to see Kat, but I don't want to go alone. Goldie isn't here to go with me, Donna is somewhat involved—what with the tabloids catching her and Bubba together at that restaurant—Vonnie is too skittish, and Lisa Leann is already out and about with the camera crew."

I took in a deep breath, blew it out. "You are right there. All right. Give me a minute to change my clothes and we'll go."

I stood and walked halfway to the dresser, then looked back at Lizzie. "But be careful Lisa Leann doesn't find out. She'll think we're goofing off from doing what we're supposed to be doing."

Lizzie shook her head. "She'll understand. Especially if this puts us on even footing with the Wild Cajuns."

We arrived at the studio around eight and were waved in by the guards who'd come to know us by face and by name. Lizzie led the way to the offices and then specifically to Kat's office where, as God would have it, the door was opened revealing Kat and—what do you know?—Amy going over notes on clipboards. Hot drinks from Starbucks were on the desk before them. They looked up, apparently hearing us stop at the door. Kat smiled. Amy did not.

"Lizzie. Evangeline," Kat said. "What are you doing here?"

"We need to talk," Lizzie said. "May we come in?"

"Uh . . ." Kat looked around nervously. "I'm not sure how kosher that is. What's this about?"

Lizzie stepped in, and I followed. She looked at Amy. "Actually, it's about Amy."

"Me?" Amy blushed and straightened her shoulders. "What about me?"

Lizzie crossed her arms. "Amy, we all know that I saw you and Bubba at Seppi's that night, and we both know what you said."

Amy coughed out a giggle. "What I said? What did I say?" She looked from Lizzie to Kat and then back to Lizzie.

"You said, and I quote, 'Believe me, my love, I have it all arranged.'"

"Have what all arranged, Amy?" Kat asked.

"I don't know what she's talking about." Amy glared at Lizzie and me. "And neither do you. You might have seen me there, but you and I certainly were never close enough for you to hear me."

Lizzie smiled just so. "That's where having a deaf daughter comes in, Amy. I can read lips, just as my daughter does. And I read yours plainly. You were kissing Bubba, you called him 'my love,' and you indicated you had something arranged." She looked back at Kat. "I'm here to make sure that whatever it is she has arranged is not the final outcome of the show. I'm here"—she turned slightly to me—"we're here to make sure that *should* the Wild Cajuns win, it is because they deserve to win, not because of any relationship between Amy and Bubba."

Kat crossed her arms and cocked a hip. "Amy? What about you and Bubba?"

"Then you didn't know?" I asked. "This isn't part of the ratings booster?"

Kat gave me a harsh look. "Of course not. We need a ratings booster, yes, but we've gotten that by playing the Donna-Wade-David card."

"What role have you played," Lizzie asked Amy, "in some of the shenanigans that have taken place at our events?"

Again Amy pinked. "I don't know what you're talking about."

"Then obviously you haven't watched the show. Because all of America knows some of the problems we've had. Especially at our last event."

"What I want to know," Kat interjected, "is what the relationship between you and Bubba is."

"Kat!" Amy all but squealed as though she were a schoolgirl standing before a parent, pretending she hadn't been caught slipping out her window on a school night.

"Amy!" Kat parroted, looking none too happy.

Amy blew air from her lungs. "Oh, all right. Bubba and I have been seeing each other. So what? I have nothing to hide. Nothing to be ashamed of. It's not a crime, you know."

"But it is against the rules, Amy. You know that." Kat paused. "How long?"

"How long what?"

"Don't play games, Amy. How long have you been seeing Bubba?"

Amy didn't answer right away. If my suspicions were correct, the love affair and the show's season beginnings probably ran hand in hand. "Not long," she finally said. Then quickly added, "But you don't understand, Kat. We met just before the season started. We just happened to meet at a restaurant. He didn't know who I was, and I certainly didn't know who he was and . . . well . . . you've seen him. He's gorgeous! I'm single, he's single, and . . ."

"Oh, Amy," Lizzie said. I suppose as the mother of two daughters she has had to deal with this kind of thing in the past. As a woman who stayed single nearly all her life, I wanted to walk over and bop her in the head. How dumb can you be? But Lizzie has that sweet way of talking to the young people. Sweet but firm. Amy, I knew, was about to get a taste of it. "Amy, surely you don't believe his meeting you was accidental."

"Yes, I do."

Kat shook her head. "Oh, Amy," she said, repeating Lizzie's words but giving them more of a "what an idiot you are" tone. Then her shoulders dropped, and she said, "Let's all sit down, shall we?"

There were just enough chairs in the room for each of us. We sat. Lizzie crossed her legs and leaned over in a non-intimidating way. "Amy, listen to me. I've raised daughters. I've been a high school teacher for a lot of years. Maybe even more than you've been alive. I have also raised sons. If there is one thing I know— besides books—it's the way young men—some of them—try to work their way around young ladies such as yourself. You are a pretty girl, Amy . . ."

Amy began to cry. Actually began to cry. She shook her head as though to say no, she was not a pretty girl. But Lizzie didn't hesitate. "Yes, you are, Amy. But something tells me you don't see it. That's why you let men like Bubba walk into your life when you know better. When you know the rules forbid it."

Kat reached for a tissue box on her desk and handed it to Amy. Her actions were kind, but her demeanor showed a different attitude. Kat was ticked. The message was written all over her face. If this got out, it could kill her show, not raise the ratings.

Amy sniffled as she took a tissue, then blew her nose. "You don't understand," she said again. "We saw each other for a week before he even asked me what I did for a living. When he found out, he was shocked. He was hurt. He told me we'd have to break off our relationship. *I'm* the one who insisted we keep it going. *I'm* the one who said I'd help them get to the top."

"Then you're the one who is going to be in the unemployment line," Kat said.

Lizzie raised her hand as Amy gasped. "Wait a minute, Kat. Hold on." She looked at Amy again. "Amy, there is no doubt in my mind that Bubba knew who you were, what you did for a living, everything. What do you really think are the chances he met you in a city of millions by happenstance?"

Amy took a moment to process the question. "Probably very slim."

"Right." Lizzie looked at Kat. "You do what you have to do when it comes to firing or keeping Amy. Personally, I hope you don't fire her. She's young and naïve and this is all in the process of learning. Evangeline and I both could fill this room with stories of past mistakes under the category of love."

I shifted in my chair. Maybe Lizzie could "fill the room." I had but one story. My whole life had been spent loving and pining away and sitting at home bitter because of Vernon Vesey until he finally saw the light and asked me to marry him. So what did I know?

"But I would suggest, Amy," Lizzie continued, "that you stop the affair now and leave Bubba's team to win or lose the show on their own merits."

"Have you altered the results in any way, Amy?" Kat answered.

Amy didn't answer, which was, of course, an answer.

Kat nodded. "I see. Amy, I've given you a list of things to do for the day. Go do them. You and I will discuss your job later. In the meantime, contact your friend Bubba and tell him the affair is off. Do you hear me?"

Again Amy pinked. "I hear you."

Lizzie softened the blow by adding, "When you do end it, Amy, you will see by the way Bubba reacts whether or not his love for you is real. I'd be willing to bet you'll be hurt by it. Allow me, please, to encourage you now. Stay strong. Know you are not the first woman to be duped by a man. You won't be the last. But from now on, you'll be a lot wiser in your choices."

Amy nodded, reached for her coffee cup as she stood, and said, "Well, if you will excuse me." She left the room, leaving the door open behind her.

Kat asked me to close the door, and I did. As I returned to my seat she said to Lizzie, "I have to fire her, Lizzie."

"Do that," Lizzie said, "and you can bet she'll go to the tabloids with anything and everything. True or not."

"She signed a contract," Kat said. "It prohibits her from talking about the show."

"Never underestimate a woman scorned. Especially a young woman."

"Amen to that," I said.

Kat nodded. "I'll have to talk to Jay. See what he says. Maybe he'll insist she keep her job until this season is over. After that her contract is up for renewal, anyway."

Lizzie stood. "Thank you, Kat. We'll leave you now. I'm sure you have a lot to do, and I know we do." Lizzie smiled.

I stood too. "Thank you," I said to Kat.

"Thank you, ladies. Have a good day."

We left by the same path we'd entered, neither of us saying anything until we reached the sidewalk outside. "Let's walk," I said.

"Maybe stop and get something to eat," I added. "I'm a little hungry now."

"Sounds good."

Lizzie and I turned to the left and strolled up the avenue, both of us silent. Finally she said, "A penny for your thoughts."

"Well," I said, "since you asked. I was thinking about what you said about a young woman scorned."

"Okay."

"And I was wondering what would happen if Amy called Bubba and told him they had to stop seeing each other. Bubba will, no doubt, work his charm on her, talk her into continuing with things the way they are. Amy is not stupid. She'll realize she's going to lose her job eventually. So what does she have to lose? Staying with Bubba at least guarantees her his love, or so she'll think. You and I both know he'll drop her like yesterday's newspaper as soon as all this is over. He's a player, not a true man at all."

"I know."

"So, she tells us she has ended it with Bubba but in fact she has not. That's what I suspect will happen."

Lizzie walked quietly beside me for a half block before she said, "In other words, we've got to watch our backs even more now than before."

"Exactly," I said.

Lizzie sighed. "Great." Then she nodded. "We'd better alert the girls and the guys to this."

"All's fair in love and war, Liz," I said.

"Greater is he who is in me than he who is in the world," she countered.

"Amen," I said. "Amen."

33

Team Brunch

Saturday morning found Team Potluck dining on an early breakfast we'd prepared in our catering kitchen in the GE building. We'd chosen to eat together so we could discuss the last-minute details for that night's event. As I slathered melting butter and peach preserves onto my steaming buttermilk biscuit, Lisa Leann continued her briefing in our war room. "Since the entertainment and door prizes fell into our laps, we're blowing our entire five thousand dollar stipend on food and décor," she said.

"We have door prizes?" Donna asked.

"We have some nice things from Tiffany's, Macy's, as well as some restaurant gift certificates," Lisa Leann said as she grinned at her son. "All thanks to Nelson's hard work and phone calls."

"Great job, Nelson," I said as the young man crunched into a slice of thick bacon.

Nelson wiped his mouth with his napkin. "It was easy, really. Everybody wanted to help."

"That's terrific," Evie said. "But what I want to know is the really important thing: what are we wearing tonight?"

Our team laughed. Mike, the ever-present cameraman, zeroed in on our smiling faces.

"Along with the Rescue Mission's aprons and our new giant buttons that say 'Vote Team Potluck,' we're wearing black eveningwear. Tuxes are being sent over for our guys, and Macy's is sending over a complimentary selection of gowns for us girls."

"Gowns?" Donna asked, wrinkling her nose. She poured herself another cup of coffee.

"The gowns are a must," Lisa Leann said with a giggle. "Especially for you, Donna. Because you're as cute as a bug's ear, you're playing our Vanna when I do the door prize drawing at the end of the evening. Didn't I tell you?"

Donna shook her head and grimaced. Lisa Leann, oblivious to Donna's angst at dressing up, began to rattle off our menu. "Most of you already know what we're serving, but for those of you who don't, we're dishing up a chilled tomato soup, then triple A prime rib with sides of new potatoes, fresh lemon-zinger asparagus, and hot, homemade rolls."

"And for dessert?" David asked, licking his lips in anticipation.

Lisa Leann actually glowed as she announced, "Peppermint patty stuffed brownies."

I hadn't heard this news, so I gasped. "Brownies? For such an elegant event?"

Lisa Leann nodded solemnly. "Peppermint patty brownies with real York Peppermint Patties have always been my ultimate secret weapon." She lowered her voice. "These treats have even won me a couple of best dessert blue ribbons at a few prestigious contests back in Houston. So, I'm thinking they may be the very thing that unlocks the vault to the grand prize."

"It's not unlocked yet, Lisa Leann. We do have a competition to win first, you know," Lizzie said under her breath.

"As you know, the event we're serving tonight airs on next Tuesday night's regular show. That's also when the final voting occurs. Then, the following night, Wednesday, *The Great Party Showdown* airs a special grand finale where the winner will be announced."

"That means two shows next week. That's a lot of pressure," Wade commented.

Lisa Leann grinned. "Try not to think about it like that. With the results show two hoots and a holler away, all we can do today is our best. In fact, I got a call from Pastor Kevin last night, and he told me there's a church prayer team praying for us around the clock today."

"Really?" Donna asked.

"Pastor Kevin said he didn't want to put any extra pressure on us, but winning the prize will keep the church from losing our building, since we'll be able to pay off our mortgage."

"Plus, we'll be able to start building that youth wing," I added, beaming.

Nelson practically laughed. "From where I sit, I can't imagine why God would want us to lose."

I smiled. Nelson was only a young man, so how could he possibly know what lesson God really wanted to teach us. For all we knew, God was looking for us to respond to this event by simply trusting him with or without the bonus of a reward.

The day was an absolute blur as we carted our food and equipment back and forth to the museum in the van we'd rented. Then, once we finally got moved in to the Powerhouse event room, we still had to oversee setting up the tables and chairs, make sure everything was in place for our guest entertainers, work with the florist to display their gorgeous sunflower bouquets on the tables, and carve our roast beef.

As the afternoon drew to a close, I surveyed our chocolate-colored linen-draped tables topped with our sunflower arrangements.

I have to say the effect was stunning, especially combined with the table candles and the golden, blue, and lime green lights that backlit the room's many columns.

With the doors scheduled to open at four, we were already in makeup and dressed in our finery, topped with our Rescue Mission aprons. We scurried to finish presetting our strawberry salads at each place setting. We were almost done when Lisa Leann called us to the terrace.

As soon as I saw her, I knew something was wrong. "What happened?" I cried.

Her face pale, Lisa Leann announced, "I just got word from Goldie that Jack is about to go into surgery for his bypass."

Our huddled group gasped as one. "Now?" Donna asked.

Lisa Leann nodded solemnly. "The poor dear didn't call me to tell me because she didn't want to worry us. But Pastor Kevin called me, and I just got off the phone with Goldie."

"How's she doing?" Lizzie asked.

"She's scared. I mean, she knows very well sometimes things go wrong in surgeries. She knows this could be it for Jack. But at the same time, she's leaning as hard as she can on God, thanking him for the turnaround their marriage has seen this past year and for whatever time they have left."

I spoke up. "Lisa Leann, do you mind if I lead off in prayer now? I don't think I can face tonight if we don't stop and pray."

Donna, who was standing next to me, reached for my hand and gave it a squeeze. "Vonnie, go for it," she said.

I bowed my head. "Lord, somehow this news puts everything into perspective, for we see that life is not always about living for the future, but living in the now as we trust in you. So first and foremost, we come to you on behalf of the Dippels. Please comfort Goldie as we can't. Please protect Jack as he faces this hour. Please bring him safely through the procedure."

One by one, the other team members prayed prayers much the

same as mine before Lisa Leann concluded, "Amen, and Lord, bless us tonight, win or lose, help us to shine for you."

As the team parted to rush back to their tasks, Donna wiped a tear from her eye. "Donna, are you okay, dear?" I asked.

She nodded. "Kinda."

Noticing we were miraculously alone as the camera crew had followed the other members back into the Powerhouse room, I pointed to a nearby cluster of chairs that overlooked the Rose Center and motioned for Donna to sit with me. "You wanna tell me what you're feeling?"

Donna hesitated. "We don't have time, do we?"

I sat down and patted the chair next to mine. "Let's make time, especially now that the camera crew is following our friends."

Donna's laughter was strained as she sat down next to me. She took a deep breath and said, "Vonnie, this time in New York hasn't been easy for me. But what's happening to Goldie and Jack makes me realize I'm living my whole life on the bypass."

I felt my forehead knit together. "Meaning?"

Donna stared at the back of her hands, which perched over the lap of her satin evening gown. She looked up through damp lashes. "My whole adult life, I've skirted my feelings. I've missed out on love because I didn't want to risk getting hurt again. But if I continue to live like this, I'll never experience real life. I'll bypass it altogether."

"So, what are you going to do?"

"I've got some decisions to make."

"About Wade and David?" I ventured.

She nodded and dropped her voice. "Yeah."

"Is there one you love?"

"I've locked my heart so tight, I'm afraid to look inside for the answer. But I'm praying for courage and the wisdom to know."

Out of the corner of my eye, I saw Mike spy our private moment and bolt in our direction. "Here comes trouble," I whispered, indicating Mike's approach. "But we'd better get back to work. I'll be praying for you, Donna."

"Thank you, Vonnie."

As I pushed through the terrace door to return to my duties presetting the salads, I noticed Donna reach into her apron pocket and glance at her vibrating cell phone. She stared at the display a moment, then snapped it open.

"Hello?" I heard her gasp. "Is it really you?"

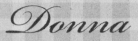
34

Taste of Deception

I felt as if I was speaking to a ghost. I lowered my voice. "Thelma Horn? Did you know you're classified as a missing person back in Summit View?"

"I ain't missing; I'm in New York City. Though, I hope I haven't caused too much trouble being gone from home so long."

"Where are you?"

"At the diner, Café Camelot, where you came looking a couple of weeks back. Cheryl gave me your card, and I finally worked up the nerve to call."

"I'm relieved to know you're okay."

"Sorry for all the fuss, but I just had to get away, to clear my head, you know?"

"But how could you leave your kids? Especially since your husband broke Pete's arm."

She gasped in surprise. "I . . . I didn't know. The night I left, Mike slapped me around for the last time, and, well, when I picked myself off the floor, I grabbed my purse, then hitched a ride to the bus station in Denver. That night I caught a bus to the fartherest place I could think of."

"Yeah, New York is a far cry from the Colorado high country."

"Well, I'm only passing through. In fact, I've got an opportunity to get a better job over in Milwaukee."

I felt stunned that she wasn't ready to go back to her kids, but since I'd never walked through the abuse she'd suffered, I decided to save my judgments. "Listen, Thelma, I'm still in town, and I'd love to tell you about how your kids are doing."

"How fast can you get here?"

"How about midnight?"

"That's too late. I'm leaving for the bus station in an hour."

I shot a look at my watch. The gang could get along without me for half an hour or so, I figured. They wouldn't like it, but under the circumstances, I knew they'd understand. "Okay, here's the deal, I'm going to drop what I'm doing here, and I'll be there in about fifteen minutes. But I can't stay long."

I looked up to see Mike zooming in on my conversation. I turned my back on him. "Now stay put, okay?"

"Yes, ma'am, Donna. I knew I could count on you."

Within moments I'd pulled my apron up over my head, wadded it on top of the gift bags filled in the prep room, grabbed my wallet and cell phone, and headed out the door. I ran toward the taxis that were just arriving with our distinguished (as well as homeless) guests, a few who even applauded me. Like a beauty queen in a sparkling dress, I merely gave them a wave as I dove inside the cab. "Do you know Café Camelot?" I asked the driver, a dark-skinned man wearing a turban.

He nodded as I slammed the door shut. "Then step on it, this is an emergency."

I flipped open my cell phone and tried to text David so he would know I would be right back. When he didn't respond, I figured he'd turned his phone off. My only hope now was that he would check it if he noticed I was missing.

In the meantime, I could only stare out the window as New York zipped by in a blur. I must have miscalculated the distance from the museum to the café, though, because it was a good twenty-five minutes before my cab arrived. I hurried inside, but not before throwing the cabbie a twenty and asking him to wait. "I'll only be a minute," I said. "Promise you'll be here when I come back."

"Sure, sure," he answered with a laugh. "For pretty lady, sure."

When I barged through the door, Cheryl looked up from wiping down a booth near the door. "You look like you're late for the ball."

"I am," I said. "Have you seen Thelma?"

"Poor girl, she's in the back crying her eyes out."

I pushed through the kitchen's double doors, then rushed through the back hallway to the small break room. I stopped in the doorway, stunned.

I hadn't expected to see such a crumpled mess of a woman. Her dark hair streaked with mousy gray was pulled back into a severe ponytail. She was only thirty or so but looked near forty, at least according to the lines etched into her once pretty face. She glanced my direction and sniffed. "You came."

I collapsed into a chair across from her and watched as she dabbed her eyes with her soggy tissue. "Girl, you don't know how glad I am to have found you."

"Are my kids okay?" she asked, her eyes meeting mine for the first time since I'd entered the room. When I saw how frail and tired she looked, I could only answer with a nod till I reconnected with my voice. "Yeah, the little ones are with Wade's sister, Kathy."

Thelma looked relieved. "That's good. And Pete?"

I glanced at my watch, feeling a bit overwhelmed with the knowledge that the banquet was now in full swing without me. The stress of the moment caused my head to nod like a Scooby Doo bobble doll in the rear window of a taxi. "Yeah, he's good. He's been living with Wade."

"Your old Wade?"

I nodded again, then started the speech I'd rehearsed in the taxi. "I thought maybe you could take a cab ride with me, so I can get back to the event I'm helping to host. I wanted to tell you, Thelma, that your kids need you and—"

"They didn't need what I'd become," she responded, blowing her nose. "I was so beat down, I couldn't even protect them from their own father. That's why I've decided to leave. I wasn't doing anybody any good."

"I wish you'd consider postponing your trip to Milwaukee tonight. I mean, maybe it would be a better idea to take a quick trip back to Colorado, you know, before you continue with your plans. If travel money's a problem, I think I could help with that."

Her pale face pinked. "Actually, Donna, it's more than a job I'm going after. I met someone, someone I think I could have a future with."

As if on cue, the back door of the restaurant creaked open and Thelma rose to her feet. "Here he is now. Donna, meet my new boyfriend, Boudreaux."

I stood, my hand poised on my satined hip as if I were reaching for my gun. I turned and looked at the man whose familiar frame had filled the doorway. "Believe we've met," I said to Bubba. "I didn't realize your name was actually Boudreaux."

"Bubba's just my nickname," Boudreaux explained.

"Did you get the bus tickets?" Thelma asked.

"Well, there's been a change in plans," Boudreaux explained. "I've got some business I need to take care of in the next few days, here in New York."

I all but snorted a laugh. "I'd say you do."

Thelma looked confused. "How do you two know each other?"

"We've been in New York, attending the same . . . ah, conference," I explained.

Thelma stood up and really looked at me then. "Is that why you're so dressed up?"

I glanced at my watch again. "Well, Thelma, now that you're not leaving for Milwaukee tonight, I've got to be going. I have some friends who are counting on me. Let's say you and I meet back here about midnight, okay?"

Thelma nodded as Boudreaux reached for my hand. "Eh? Not so fast, deputy. I'm fixin' to ask you a few questions myself."

I tried to pull my hand from his, but Boudreaux held it tight.

Thelma came to my defense. "Boud, Donna needs to scoot."

Boudreaux's grip tightened.

"Thelma, let me guess." I looked at Boudreaux as I narrowed my eyes. "You met this joker right after I came in looking for you, right?"

Thelma nodded and turned from me to Boudreaux. "I thought it was only a meeting of chance . . . and . . ."

"Didn't you recognize this man's face in the tabloids?"

"I really haven't been following the news lately," Thelma said.

With a jerk, I pulled my hand free, then rubbed it. "Listen, Thelma. I don't believe this man has your best interest at heart. He's trying to win a contest, a contest I'm competing in tonight. He's trying to keep me here so I'll be out of the game. He actually came with me the night I was looking for you. That's how he knew how to set the both of us up."

Thelma looked stricken. "Is that true, Boudreaux?"

He shrugged and looked at his watch. "Bête cher, as they say in the bayou, *pee-yoo!*"

"Meaning?"

"Foolish girl, that sure stinks, don't it."

Thelma looked stunned, and I put my hands on my hips. "Okay, that's enough from you, Bubba or Boudreaux or whoever you are. I've gotta run. Can you come with me, Thelma?"

She shook her head. "No, I need to speak to Boudreaux. He's got some explaining to do."

Boudreaux continued to stand in my way. "I don't see your hurry," he said to me.

"Meaning?"

"I sent your cab away."

"You what!" I pushed past him then ran back to the dining room.

Boudreaux, who followed me, laughed. "You know, it's really murder to catch a cab on Saturday night in this part of town. Even if you call for one now, you might not make it back to the museum until your event is over."

I pulled my cell phone out of my bag and pushed open the café door as Boudreaux's laughter rang in my ears. Ignoring him, I turned back to Thelma, who had just stepped into the dining room. "I'll call you later, Thelma, okay?"

"I'll be here at Camelot's, waiting," she said.

I ran to the street corner to see if any cabs were in sight. But Boudreaux was right, the place was deserted. When I called a cab company on my cell, I was informed the wait could be at least another hour. If I'd had a clue as to the nearest subway station, much less which line to pick, I might've had a chance. As it was, all I could do was start walking to search for a cab. I pulled off my heels and began to pad in my bare feet down the still-warm summer evening sidewalks. Somehow, feeling the pavement beneath my toes put me in touch with the beauty of the evening. As I started to jog, I noted the blue of the late afternoon sky had settled into a deep evening turquoise that danced between the skyscrapers. It would have all struck me as a lot nicer if my heart wasn't hammering so hard.

After zigzagging across several blocks, I found myself on Broadway, a street almost yellow with cabs. I smiled and waved, but not one would stop for me, probably because I looked like a hooker in this getup.

I finally resorted to tapping on cab windows at a stoplight, but even then, the cabbies would explain they either had a fare or were en route to pick one up.

Another half hour later, when I'd finally climbed out of a cab in front of the museum, I checked my watch. I'd been missing for a full two hours.

It took some talking to get past security at the museum's entrance, but I was able to push my way through the doors of the Powerhouse room, just in time to greet the eye of Mike's camera. Vonnie saw me and rushed over. "Where have you been?"

"Long story," I said. "Did I miss much?"

"Only the entire banquet," Vonnie answered, her hands on her hips. "They've even finished dessert."

I tried to brighten the situation with a weak smile. "Were the peppermint patty brownies a hit?"

Vonnie nodded but looked puzzled. "Donna, you're absolutely covered in sweat. Is everything okay?"

"I . . . I don't know. I . . ."

Vonnie's face softened. "What happened?"

"It's kinda hard to explain."

"Well, your absence has caused quite the stir. The boys are sure you were kidnapped, and Lisa Leann is just about ready to call in the police."

"I am the police," I teased.

"Not in New York."

I turned and watched the Broadway chorus girls dressed in neckline-plunging yellow suits with peacock-like tail feathers bouncing on their bottoms as they kicked their legs high into the air. They were singing a rendition of the famous *Guys and Dolls* song "A Bushel and a Peck" as the actress playing Adelaide squealed out her comedic solo.

"Looks like the entertainment is going strong," I said. "What's up next?"

"There's one more number, then I think it's time for the door prizes," Vonnie explained.

I looked around, expecting to see the prizes up front. When I realized they weren't there, I asked, "Are the prizes still in the prep room?"

"That's where I saw them last. They were on a big rolling cart, where we found your apron. Why don't you go ahead and wheel them in so you'll be ready to play Vanna. In the meantime, I'll let Lisa Leann and the boys know you're back."

As I slipped out of the room, the Broadway troupe began to sing "Sit Down You're Rocking the Boat" in honor of our Save a Soul theme. From the program Lisa Leann had showed me earlier, I knew this was the last song of the night, as the performers had a line of limos waiting to whisk them back to Broadway for their evening show.

With Mike filming my every move since I returned, I rushed to the back hallway and pushed open the doors to the prep room and switched on the light. I gasped. The cart was empty. Our door prizes were gone.

35

Instant Prayer

After our last guest had left, our group huddled at one of the cleared tables to discuss the evening, before I handed out cleanup assignments.

With the table candles flickering a dance of lights onto our faces, I said, "That had to have been one of my most awkward moments ever," referring to Donna's announcement that our door prizes were missing. "Your timing couldn't have been worse, Donna. Why did you wait till I pulled the first name from our drawing before you rushed the stage to share your news?"

Donna looked miserable. "I'm sorry, Lisa Leann, I . . ."

Evie, looking cross, gave a sharp sniff. "What I want to know, Donna, is where've you been all evening?"

Vonnie's voice squeaked in an octave higher than usual. "Is it true you left in a cab?"

Donna rubbed her temples with her fingertips, then slid her cheeks into the palms of her hands and held them there. "It's true.

307

Thelma Horn called. She said she had an hour before she was going to hop a bus to Milwaukee without any forwarding address or number. I had to see her."

Wade leaned forward. "Why didn't you come and get me?"

Donna shrugged. "We couldn't all go."

David, who was sitting next to her, reached for her hand. "You look upset. Did something happen?"

She lightly shrugged a shoulder. "Yes, and the something was Boudreaux. In fact, he's why I was so late getting back."

Lizzie's jaw dropped. "But Boudreaux isn't real . . . we all decided, remember?"

Donna smirked. "He's real. We all know him by his nickname, Bubba."

Wade's eyebrows shot up his forehead. "Wait. What are you saying? Thelma's with Bubba? But how?"

Before Donna could answer, my cell phone vibrated in my apron pocket. I pulled it out to check the caller ID. "Hang on, everyone, it's Goldie." I put the phone on speaker and sat it in the middle of our table. "Goldie, dear, we're all here, listening in. How's Jack?"

Goldie's voice sounded tired but good. "I only have a minute, but I wanted you to know that Jack's made it through surgery. There are some concerns, minor, we hope, but concerns nonetheless."

The ever-ready nurse, Vonnie asked, "What kind of concerns?"

"Oh! The doctor just came in. Gotta run."

"We'll be praying for you and Jack," I responded as the line went dead.

I looked up at Mike and his crew, each busy filming close-ups of our reactions. I cleared my throat. "Gang, let's take a moment to pray for Goldie and Jack, then we've got to clean up. But first, are there any other needs we need to pray about? Donna?"

"Pray for Thelma. She's still in town, and I'm going back to the café at midnight to meet with her."

"Not without me," Wade said.

"Or me," David added.

After our prayer, we each tackled our cleanup assignments, all the while hoping we'd come across the missing gifts. But after about an hour of hauling things back to our rental van, I approached Donna. "About our gift bags—do you think we ought to call the cops? A lot of those gift cards and other items were pretty valuable. See, here's the list Nelson gave me."

Donna scanned it, then gave a low whistle. "This is a lot of stuff. Let's go back to the scene of the crime and look around."

"Have you noticed that the camera crew is still here?" I said as we pushed the door open into the back hallway. "It makes me think they're hanging around because they know something we don't."

"You're probably right," Donna said. "I asked them what they knew about the theft, but as usual, they kept their mouths shut. Still, it feels to me like they're waiting for us to make some sort of discovery."

As if to confirm my suspicions, I saw Mike motion for some of the other cameramen to follow us. I turned to Donna as I raised my brows and stopped in front of a large door. "Maybe we've arrived at the moment the crew's been waiting for."

We looked at the door, marked with a black plastic sign that read "Storage."

"Got the key?" she asked as she jiggled the knob.

I shook my head. "No, and I tried it earlier. This door's been locked all evening."

Donna reached for the latch and gave it a twist. "It's not locked now," she said as she pushed it open.

I let out a gasp. There on the floor before us stood a heap of rainbow-colored foil gift bags. I stepped inside and bent over to retrieve a lavender envelope that had been carefully placed on top of Donna's missing apron.

"What does it say?" Donna asked as I pulled out a note card with handwritten words.

I looked up at her. "It simply says, 'You lose. Love, B.'"

"Of all the nerve," Donna said. "Of all the nerve."

The next morning, the team met in my room for a continental breakfast that room service delivered only moments before they arrived. We munched bacon, ate apple cranberry muffins, and drank about a gallon of coffee while Donna filled us in on all her adventures of yesterday, including the meeting with Thelma at midnight.

Wade seemed excited. "Thelma's coming home, maybe not to stay, but she's going to let the family buy her a plane ticket so she can see her kids."

I glanced at Donna, whose brows were knit above her troubled eyes. "What's your view on this development?" I asked her.

"I'm only worried about Wade and Pete," Donna said, frowning as she sat on the floor. "They seem to belong together and—"

Wade, who was plopping a sugar cube into his cup of coffee, interrupted, "Now don't get me wrong. Pete's a great kid, but he cries himself to sleep at night. In my opinion, the boy needs his mom in his life any way he can get her."

"But do you really think she's ready to be a mom again?" Donna asked.

"I don't know," Wade said. "That's something my family will have to work through."

"Not to change the subject," Lizzie said as she perched on the bed next to the nightstand. "But has anyone heard from Goldie this morning?"

I stood up and walked to the window, next to David. "It's still early back in Colorado. She's probably not even up yet."

Vonnie leaned back in her padded chair. "I had a hard time sleeping last night on account of her and Jack."

I nodded. "The same goes for me. I was up most of the night."

David smiled down at Donna. "Makes you think about what's really important."

Nelson walked over to the tray on the edge of the bed and reached for another muffin. "Until now I'd thought the point of this venture was to win the million."

Lizzie leaned over and pulled the Gideon Bible out of the drawer and thumbed through it. "It's not the money that's the issue," she said. "It's our relationship with God. Listen to this, from Hebrews chapter 13: 'Keep your lives free from the love of money and be content with what you have, because God has said, "Never will I leave you; never will I forsake you." So we say with confidence, "The Lord is my helper; I will not be afraid. What can man do to me?"' "

"That's a good word, Lizzie," Vonnie said, "and trusting God is exactly what we need to do here. We don't know how the show's going to portray the events of last night, or how America will vote. But win or lose, I know we can trust in the Lord."

"Even if losing means I can't pay my rent?" Donna asked. "I hadn't planned to be gone from work this long, and paying my bills was how I planned to use the stipend we agreed we'd each receive if we win."

Wade muttered under his breath, "You're not alone in that, Donna."

Nelson asked, "But can we trust God when it comes to Goldie and Jack?"

I nodded. "What other choice do we have?"

Donna

36

Final Feast

As we slid into our places in the limo, Lizzie grabbed my hand. "Donna, I just got a call from Kat before I left my room."

"What did she say?" I asked.

"Amy hid our packages and wrote the note. They have it on tape. In fact, Kat just called to tell me Amy was just escorted out of the GE building between a couple of security guards."

"But why did she do it?" Nelson asked. "She knew she'd be caught."

Lizzie replied, "According to Kat, Amy felt she was going to be fired anyway, so hiding our door prizes and leaving that note was her parting gift to us."

"Nice," I said. "But why did she sign her name 'B'?"

"That stood for 'bebe,' meaning 'baby' in English. I guess that's what Bubba called her."

I blinked. "Oh, brother. That's what he calls everyone."

As the show aired live from New York and we watched the clips about Bubba and his team, we were treated to details about their lives. But most shocking to me was the footage of Bubba with his wife and their darling two-year-old son.

I leaned over to David. "Who would have guessed Bubba to be a family man?"

David shrugged. "I'm not surprised."

Still, I was impressed with the job the Wild Cajuns did, hosting their event at the New York Public Library Sunday night for the oncology department of the Morgan Stanley Children's Hospital of New York–Presbyterian. It was a nice affair. I was especially captured by the sweet children, their parents, the hardworking doctors, plus the testimonies of children whose lives had been saved by the hospital's team of specialists. But even with such a great client, the Wild Cajun's event was not without complications.

Astor Hall, the grand entrance hall of the New York Public Library, which served as the event's location, had no air-conditioning, which was always a problem at summer events. The Wild Cajuns' chocolate cake was half melted before the night was over, plus the children absolutely refused to eat the crawfish etouffee, though the fried okra seemed to fare better. But despite the problems, Judge Brant Richards gave the Cajuns his highest recommendation directly into the camera. "America, I'm dining here with the winners tonight. All you have to do is vote so we can award Bubba and the boys the million dollar check they deserve."

A few minutes later, when our half of the program finally started, I felt David lean against me. "Hang on," he said. "How bad can it be?"

"We're about to find out," I whispered back.

It was bad. The camera team had done a great job showing me running away from my duties and leaving the team short of waitstaff. One gentleman from the mission even cracked a toothless grin as he told the camera, "Tomata soup's cold, but it's still good."

313

Evie whispered loudly, "It's supposed to be cold, it's *chilled.*"

Judge Teresa Juliette smiled for the camera. "I don't know what's going on here tonight. The stage was set for this team to knock home a winner, but the beef was dry and one of their main players, Deputy Donna Vesey, left the party without so much as a word."

I slid down into my seat but perked up when the next clip showed Thelma back at Camelot Café.

"The deputy had a good reason for leaving tonight. She did it to help me get back with my kids." The camera panned back, showing Thelma with her arm around Pete and his little brothers and sisters, whom the studio must have flown into New York earlier today. Thelma continued, "Thank you, Donna. You saved me from making the biggest mistake of my life, walking out on my kids forever."

The next clip showed Lisa Leann. "We're a team," she said. "We were down two members, Goldie, who had to fly home to Colorado when her husband had a heart attack, and Donna, who was on a life-saving mission of her own. But we survived it."

Vonnie's face appeared next. "If one of our team members fall, we're here to stand in their place. Things might not have gone as smoothly as we'd have liked, but tonight, we were here with the fine people of the New York City Rescue Mission. Tonight, win or lose, Team Potluck made a difference."

The next clip showed Wade and David handing out the door prizes to the patrons and staff at the mission itself, a duty they had performed Monday afternoon. The director's face came onto the screen. "We thank Team Potluck for all they did for us this week. You're not only great cooks, you're our heroes. And thanks for the wonderful gifts you collected for us."

The last clip was actually a live feed from back home, showing our entire town wearing hot pink "Go Team Potluck" T-shirts as they shouted, "Good luck, Team Potluck, we love you!"

"How do you think the voting will go?" Nelson asked his mother for the umpteenth time Wednesday afternoon.

"I don't know," she replied as we'd gathered back in hair and makeup for the last time.

"Forget the vote," Lizzie said as Sasha combed her hair. "It's been two days since we've heard from Goldie. I'm worried sick."

Lisa Leann put down the magazine she'd been staring at for the last ten minutes without turning a page. "I haven't been able to reach Henry, either, and I'm really worried."

From my chair across the room, I shot a look at Nelson. I wanted to ask Lisa Leann more questions, but I wasn't sure just how much Nelson knew about his mother's past affair or the state of his parents' marriage, so I kept my mouth shut.

"Well, the waiting will be over soon," David said as he rubbed his cleanly shaven chin. "Then we can get on with our lives."

"Any word from Kat about what's planned on the program tonight, besides announcing the winner?" I asked Lisa Leann.

"She told me to prepare everyone for some special surprises."

"Like?"

"Like we'll have to wait, like the rest of America, to find out."

When the show finally started, both Team Potluck and the Wild Cajun Cooks were perched on stools on either side of the stage in Studio 8 H while Dolly Parton returned to sing "Here I Come Again." As she sang, different family members walked onto the center of the stage and joined their individual team members. First it was a reunion between Bubba and his wife, then other family members of the Wild Cajun team. Next, Dad walked in and gave Evie and me a hug. Fred came along beside David and Vonnie, and Pete ran to Wade. It seemed everyone had someone from home, that is, except Nelson and Lisa Leann.

When I saw Lisa Leann's face when she realized Henry hadn't flown in with the rest of our family members, my heart nearly lurched out of my chest.

But a sparkling Gianne was soon at the microphone, announcing, "We have one more surprise to introduce tonight. A certain someone wants to give the woman he loves—a proposal."

My heart lurched again. Surely David and Wade knew not to try a proposal on me on live television!

I gave the boys a sideways glance, then followed the studio audience's gaze to the monitor. Henry appeared on the screen. He said, "There's been a lot of speculation about my marriage to Lisa Leann, and I have to admit, we certainly hit a rough spot in the road these past few months. Until recently, I was ready to throw it all away. But tonight, I'm announcing to the world my undying love for the bride of my youth."

Henry stepped out from behind a curtain and walked directly to Lisa Leann, who was already wiping the tears from her eyes. Henry dropped to one knee and held a ring consisting of a circle of diamonds that sent prisms of rainbows in every direction. "Lisa Leann, would you marry me all over again?"

Lisa dropped to her knees too as she tossed her arms around Henry's neck and smothered him with kisses. "Oh yes, yes! Yes!"

I turned to see Gianne wipe a tear from her eye. "Team Potluck, we have one more surprise. This clip was recorded earlier this afternoon at Saint Luke Presbyterian Hospital in Denver."

Suddenly Goldie's smiling face appeared on the screen. "Friends, I'm happy to report Jack is officially on the mend." The camera swept back to show she was indeed sitting next to her husband, who had his arm around his wife. Jack said, "Thanks for praying for us, America. We wish we could be in New York with all the festivities, but we're still thrilled because I get to go home today."

The next clips and packages the producers came up with were in honor of the Wild Cajun Cooks. It was good to see them in their real lives. In fact, seeing them with grandmothers, spouses, and children made them seem less like villains. Even Bubba seemed less threatening when hugging his grandmother.

But the clincher of the evening was the final dramatic moment of the show, as the producers had arranged live feeds from both Summit View, Colorado, and Baton Rouge, Louisiana. As our hometowns cheered, Gianne finally opened the envelope after the final commercial break.

"Your winner, America," Gianne announced as a hush fell across the land, "is . . . Team Potluck!"

The stark silence exploded into cheers.

We jumped, we hooted, we hugged, we fell to our knees. When the microphone came to Lisa Leann, she grabbed it, though she was still holding onto Henry. In a voice almost overcome with tears, she said, "All I can say, America, is thank you."

Lizzie leaned into the final shot. "We faced so many challenges in this competition, and God's carried us through each one. God bless you all!"

The Potluck Catering Club Recipes

Leek Quiche

1	frozen pie crust
2 tablespoons	butter
1 tablespoon	water
2 cups	chopped leeks
2 cups	sliced mushrooms
1	diced red pepper
3 cups	chopped spinach
1 cup	cubed ham
1 cup	grated cheddar cheese
3	eggs
1 cup	half and half
1 teaspoon	dried parsley
½ teaspoon	salt
½ teaspoon	pepper

Defrost frozen pie crust for 15 minutes while oven heats at 425 degrees. Bake pie crust for 10 minutes, remove, and allow to cool. Next, in pan on stove top, melt butter, add water and leeks, then cover and cook for 5 minutes, stirring occasionally. Add mushrooms and peppers and stir until liquid evaporates. Add spinach and stir for 2 more minutes. Remove cooked vegetables to mixing bowl. Add ham and cheese and mix gently. Pour mixture into pie shell.

In medium bowl, whisk eggs, half and half, dried parsley, salt, and pepper. Pour egg mixture over vegetables. Bake for 15 minutes, then reduce heat to 350 degrees for 20 to 25 minutes.

Yield: 8 slices.

Lisa Leann's Cook's Notes

Double this recipe and cook two pies. Put one in the freezer for a quick fix when you're in a pinch.

Mississippi Mud Cake

2 cups	sugar
1 cup	shortening
4	eggs
1½ cups	flour
⅓ cup	cocoa
¼ teaspoon	salt
2 teaspoons	vanilla
1 cup	chopped pecans
1 bag	miniature marshmallows

Frosting

⅓ cup	cocoa
1 box	powdered sugar or 3⅔ cups, sifted
1 stick	margarine
½ cup	evaporated milk
1 teaspoon	vanilla
1 cup	chopped pecans

Cream sugar and shortening. Add eggs, one at a time, and beat well after each. Sift flour, cocoa, and salt. Add to mixture, mixing well. Stir in vanilla and pecans. Bake in a greased and floured 9-by-13 pan for about 35 minutes at 300 degrees. Remove from oven and spread a large bag of miniature marshmallows on top while cake is hot.

To make frosting, sift cocoa and sugar. Add melted margarine, milk, vanilla, and nuts. Mix well and spread over marshmallows while cake and frosting are both still warm.

Vonnie's Cook's Notes

This is the best chocolate dessert in the world. It's really like a giant brownie with marshmallow fudge icing. I gained 5 pounds just thinking about making it.

Vanilla Latte Mix

⅓ cup   instant coffee
1 cup   instant dry milk powder
½ cup   powdered coffee creamer
⅓ cup   sugar
¼ cup   instant vanilla pudding mix

Add ingredients into a mixing bowl. Stir with fork until well blended. Pour mix into a resealable container or jar.

To Prepare

Add ¼ cup of mix into a mug. Add hot water, stir, and serve.

Yield: 8–9 servings.

Donna's Cook's Notes

Because of the addition of the pudding mix, this stuff dissolves beautifully. It's just my cup of joe.

Scalloped Potatoes

1 (10.5 ounce) can	cream of chicken soup
¾ cup	milk
2 tablespoons	finely chopped onion
¼ teaspoon	pepper
4 ounces	shredded cheddar cheese
4	medium potatoes, thinly sliced
1 tablespoon	margarine

Heat oven to 350 degrees. Combine soup, milk, onions, pepper, ½ cup of the cheese, and potatoes. (Suggestion: put potatoes in the mixture right away so they don't turn brown.) Mix everything together and pour into a 9-by-13 baking dish. Dot the top with the margarine and sprinkle with remaining cheese. Bake 1 hour and 15 minutes or until tender when you pierce them with a fork.

Serves four.

Evangeline's Cook's Notes

This recipe was given to me when I was in my thirties. I like it because it's easy to prepare and is perfect for potluck suppers—or any supper, for that matter.

Honey- and Soy- Glazed Salmon

2	salmon fillets
2 teaspoons	olive oil

Glaze

2 tablespoons	honey
2 tablespoons	soy sauce
1½ tablespoons	fresh lime juice
2 teaspoons	Dijon mustard
1 tablespoon	water

Mix the glaze ingredients together in a small bowl and set aside. Heat olive oil in a small skillet over moderate heat. Place fillets in skillet and cook for 2 to 3 minutes on each side, or until golden and just cooked through. Transfer salmon to 2 plates. Add honey glaze to skillet and simmer, stirring, 1 minute. Pour the honey-soy glaze over salmon. Serve, eat, enjoy!

Serves 2.

Lizzie's Cook's Notes

A perfect fish dish when you are cooking for two, whether at the beginning of your marriage or after you've settled in to the empty nest.

Easy Banana Cream Pie

2 bananas
1 cup water with 1 tablespoon lemon juice
1½ cups milk
8 ounces sour cream
1 small package instant vanilla pudding mix
1 store-bought graham cracker crust
3 ounces cream cheese
1 small package of Cool Whip

Slice bananas and coat with lemon water, then drain well. Mix together milk, sour cream, and pudding mix. Gently fold bananas into pudding mixture. Put bananas and pudding in crust. Next, beat cream cheese until smooth. Fold Cool Whip into cream cheese and spread over pudding. Chill.

Vonnie's Cook's Notes

Talk about easy. I could make this pie in my sleep. The nice thing is it tastes so rich and creamy you'll wonder why you made only one.

Captain's Stew

½	medium onion
1 pound	ground beef
1 (24 ounce) can	V8 juice
1 can	cream of mushroom soup
1 can	cream of celery soup
1 package	mixed frozen vegetables
1	bay leaf

Sauté onions and meat in a Dutch oven. Cook until meat is done. Add soups and juice and cook until boiling. Add frozen vegetables and bay leaf. Simmer till the vegetables are warmed through. This stew is best when simmered all day. Transfer from Dutch oven to a Crock-Pot if desired. Keep setting on low.

Goldie's Cook's Notes

My mother-in-law gave me this recipe just after I married Jack. It's always been a favorite in cold weather as well as hot.

Twice Baked Potatoes

10	(8 ounce) baking potatoes
½ cup	melted butter
½ cup	heavy cream, hot
½ cup	sour cream
½ cup	onions, diced fine and sautéed
3 ounces	cheddar cheese, grated
3 ounces	bacon, fried and crumbled

Bake potatoes at 350 degrees for about an hour. Cut top off and scoop out potatoes. In mixer, cream together butter, cream, and sour cream. Spoon back into potato skins and top with onions, cheese, and bacon. Bake 15 minutes at 400 degrees.

Yield: 10 potatoes.

Donna's Cook's Notes

If I were to plan a dinner party without the team, I think I would serve these and nothing else.

Happy Trail Mix

2 cups   sunflower seeds (without shells)
1 cup   dried fruit
½ cup   shredded coconut
1 cup   nuts (I like cashews or unsalted peanuts)
1 cup   dried cranberries or raisins
optional: 1 cup   chocolate or caramel chips

Mix all of the ingredients together and pack ½ cup to 1 cup in resealable plastic baggies.

Evangeline's Cook's Notes

Actually, this is Lisa Leann's recipe. That girl sure is handy when you're hungry and on a trip. Apparently, this is so easy, even I could make it!

Cappuccino Mix

⅔ cup	instant coffee
1 cup	powdered non–dairy creamer
1 cup	powdered chocolate drink mix
½ cup	granulated sugar
¾ teaspoon	ground cinnamon
⅜ teaspoon	ground nutmeg

Put the instant coffee into blender or food processor and process into a fine powder. In a large bowl, combine creamer, chocolate mix, sugar, cinnamon, nutmeg, and instant coffee. Stir well and store in covered containers or jars.

To Prepare

Mix 3 tablespoons of powder with 6 fluid ounces hot water.
Yield: 16 servings.

Lisa Leann's Cook's Notes

Ever since I went to New York, I've searched high and low for a good cappuccino. Finally, I experimented with how I could make one myself. I hope you like the results.

Tex-Ranch Dip

16 ounces	sour cream
1 package	ranch dip mix
½ cup	salsa
½ teaspoon	chili powder

Stir sour cream and ranch dip mix in medium bowl until well blended. Stir salsa and chili powder into prepared dip. Cover and refrigerate an hour. Stir and serve with tortilla chips.

Donna's Cook's Notes

This dip recipe has all the ingredients I look for in a recipe: (1) easy; (2) good; (3) party pleasing!

Homemade Protein Bars

3½ cups	quick oats
1½ cups	powdered nonfat milk
4 scoops	chocolate or vanilla protein powder
2	egg whites, beaten
¼ cup	orange juice
1 teaspoon	vanilla
1 cup	pancake syrup (you can use sugar free)
¼ cup	natural applesauce

Preheat oven to 325 degrees. Mix all dry ingredients in bowl (blend well). In a separate bowl, combine egg whites, juice, vanilla, syrup, and applesauce. Blend well. Stir liquids into dry ingredients until blended. The consistency will be thick and similar to cookie dough. Spread batter on baking sheet coated with nonstick spray. Use a 9-by-13 baking dish if you want a thicker bar. Bake until edges are crisp and browned. Cut into 10 bars and store in airtight container. Can be frozen. If you want a moister bar, add a little more applesauce to the recipe for softness.

Evangeline's Cook's Notes

This is one potlucker who was pretty grateful having Lisa Leann's culinary abilities take the lead on snacks when it came to our NYC trip!

Homemade Danish

1 (8 ounce) package	cream cheese, softened
½ cup	sugar
1 tablespoon	lemon juice
2 (8 ounce) cans	Pillsbury refrigerated crescent dinner rolls
4 teaspoons	preserves or jam

Glaze

½ cup	powdered sugar
1 teaspoon	vanilla extract
2 teaspoons	milk (can add up to 3 teaspoons)

Preheat oven to 350 degrees. Blend first 3 ingredients until smooth. Separate crescent dough into 8 rectangles; firmly press perforations together to seal (2 triangles are pressed together to make the 1 rectangle). Spread about 2 tablespoons of cream cheese mixture on each rectangle. Starting at longer side, roll up; press edges to seal. Gently stretch each roll to about 10 inches. Coil loosely into spirals with seam on inside. Seal ends. Make a deep indentation in center of each coiled roll. Fill with ½ teaspoon of preserves/jam. Bake on an ungreased cookie sheet for 20 to 25 minutes or until deep golden brown. While baking, prepare glaze by mixing ingredients together. Drizzle over warm rolls.

Goldie's Cook's Notes

Take it from me, you are going to adore this recipe!

_____

_____

_____

_____

Sweet Roasted Almonds

3 cups	almonds
½ cup	honey
2 tablespoons	butter
½ teaspoon	cinnamon

Mix ingredients and microwave 3 minutes on high. Stir, then heat for another 3 minutes.

Yield: 3 cups.

Lisa Leann's Cook's Notes

Ever since I got back from New York, I've been experimenting with how to get the great taste of hot New York nuts right from my microwave.

Moroccan Lentil Soup

¾ cup	red lentils
4¾ cups	water
1 package	Knorr minestrone soup mix
1	garlic clove, minced
2 teaspoons	cumin, ground
1 (19 ounce) can	chickpeas, drained
¼ cup	parsley or cilantro, chopped

Rinse lentils, then drain. In a large saucepan, combine lentils, water, soup mix, garlic, and cumin. Bring to a boil, stirring occasionally. Reduce heat and simmer 15 minutes, stirring occasionally. Add chickpeas; simmer another 5–10 minutes or until lentils are tender. Garnish with chopped cilantro or parsley.

Serves 4.

Evangeline's Cook's Notes

I'm not sure what recipe the restaurant used, but when I returned from New York, I looked in several recipe books until I found this.

Chicken Potpie

2 (10¾ ounce) cans	cream of potato soup
1 (16 ounce) can	or package drained mixed vegetables
2 cups	cooked, diced chicken
½ cup	milk
½ teaspoon	thyme
½ teaspoon	black pepper

2 (9 inch) frozen pie crusts, thawed

Combine all potpie ingredients and then spoon into one prepared pie crust. Cover with other crust; crimp edges to seal. Slit top crust. Bake at 375 degrees for 40 minutes. Cool 10 minutes before serving.

Lizzie's Cook's Notes

You will love this potpie. It is simply delicious. If it got any easier, it'd be the frozen kind you find at the supermarket.

Red Hot Tea Mix

1 cup	nonfat dry milk powder
1 cup	powdered non–dairy creamer
1 cup	French vanilla flavored powdered non–dairy creamer
2½ cups	white sugar
1½ cups	unsweetened instant tea
2 teaspoons	ground ginger
2 teaspoons	ground cinnamon
¼ cup	red hots
1 teaspoon	ground cloves
1 teaspoon	ground cardamom

In a large bowl, combine milk powder, non-dairy creamer, vanilla flavored creamer, sugar, and instant tea. Stir in ginger, cinnamon, red hots, cloves, and cardamom. Pour into sealable jars or containers.

To Prepare

Stir 2 heaping tablespoons tea mixture into a mug of hot water.

Yield: 36 servings.

Donna's Cook's Notes

This has a chai-like flavor, but to me, it tastes like love. Every time I have a cup, I think of Sasha and her kindness to me.

Bubba's Jambalaya

1 dozen	medium shrimp, peeled, deveined, and chopped
4 ounces	chicken, diced
5 ounces	andouille sausage, sliced
½ teaspoon	paprika
½ teaspoon	salt
½ teaspoon	garlic powder
¼ teaspoon	black pepper
¼ teaspoon	cayenne pepper
¼ teaspoon	oregano
½ teaspoon	thyme
½ teaspoon	onion powder
2 tablespoons	olive oil
¼ cup	chopped onion
¼ cup	chopped green bell pepper
¼ cup	chopped celery
2 tablespoons	chopped garlic
½ cup	chopped tomatoes
3	bay leaves
1 teaspoon	Worcestershire sauce
¼ teaspoon	Tabasco
¾ cup	instant rice
3 cups	chicken broth
	salt and pepper

In a bowl, combine shrimp, chicken, sausage, paprika, salt, garlic powder, black pepper, cayenne, oregano, thyme, and onion powder. Next, heat oil in a large saucepan over high heat, then add onion, pepper, and celery and cook for 3 minutes. Add garlic, tomatoes, bay leaves, Worcestershire sauce, and Tabasco. Stir in rice, then add broth. Reduce heat to medium and cook until rice absorbs liquid, about five to ten minutes. Next add shrimp, chicken, and sausage mixture. Cook about 10 minutes more or until meat is done. Season to taste with salt and pepper.

Vonnie's Cook's Notes

There's a lot of chopping that goes along with this recipe, but trust me, it's all worth it. If you like Cajun food, this is the dish to try.

Caramel Pears

⅓ cup	orange juice
3 tablespoons	brown sugar
⅛ teaspoon	ground cinnamon
dash	of ground cloves
2	peeled pears, cored and cut into 1-inch-thick wedges
	cinnamon sticks

Combine juice, brown sugar, cinnamon, and cloves in a medium saucepan and bring to a boil. Reduce heat and simmer for 5 minutes. Add pears and cook until tender (about 10 minutes). Divide pears and sauce between 2 dishes. Garnish pears with cinnamon sticks, if desired.

Yield: 2 servings.

Lisa Leann's Cook's Notes

Sometimes simple things are the best. I love to add a little spice to a plate of food with these beautiful pears.

Crème Brûlée

2 cups	heavy cream
5	egg yolks
½ cup	sugar
1 tablespoon	vanilla extract
½ cup	or so of light brown sugar

Preheat oven to 275 degrees. Whisk the cream, egg yolks, sugar, and vanilla extract together in a bowl, mixing until creamy. Pour into 4 7-ounce ramekins. Place ramekins in a baking pan. Fill baking pan with hot water, about halfway up the sides of the ramekins. Place the pan with the ramekins in the oven for 45 minutes then begin to check them every 10 minutes. The custards are done when inserted knife comes out clean. Remove ramekins from baking pan and set on counter. Allow them to cool for at least 15 minutes. Place in the refrigerator and chill overnight. Sprinkle a *thin* but *complete* layer of light brown sugar on the top of each custard. You can either torch (with a kitchen torch) or put custards under the broiler for approximately 1 minute.

Lizzie's Cook's Notes

In honor of my time in New York City, I learned to make this dessert recipe. I wouldn't serve this every night of the week, but it gets rave reviews when I serve it at family dinners and dinner parties.

Belgian Waffles

2	egg yolks
5 tablespoons	white sugar
1½ teaspoons	vanilla extract
½ cup	butter, melted
1 teaspoon	salt
2¾ cups	self-rising flour
2 cups	warm milk
2	egg whites

In a large bowl, beat egg yolks and sugar together. Beat in vanilla extract, butter, and salt. Alternately mix in flour and milk until blended well. In a separate bowl, beat egg whites until they have formed soft peaks. Fold egg whites into batter and let stand for 40 minutes. Spray preheated waffle iron with nonstick cooking spray. Pour mix onto hot waffle iron. Cook until golden brown and fluffy.

Serves 6.

Goldie's Cook's Notes

Belgian waffles have always been a Sunday favorite in my home and also a favorite when we have breakfast out.

Sweet Potato Fries

½ teaspoon ground cumin
½ teaspoon salt
¼ teaspoon ground red pepper
1½ pounds sweet potatoes
1 tablespoon vegetable oil

Preheat oven to 400 degrees. In a small bowl, combine cumin, salt, and pepper. Set aside. Peel potatoes, cut each in half lengthwise, and cut each half into 6 wedges. In a large bowl, combine the cut potatoes, oil, and spice mixture. Toss until potatoes are evenly coated. On a baking sheet, arrange potatoes in a single layer and place on the middle shelf of the oven. Bake until edges are crisp and potatoes are cooked through—about 30 minutes. Serve immediately.

Serves 4.

Evangeline's Cook's Notes

When we returned home, I looked up a recipe for sweet potato fries and found this one in the stack of cookbooks I've recently purchased. If you like fries and love sweet potatoes, this is the way to go! Note: sweet potato fries are delicious with apple butter.

Grilled Mahimahi

¾ cup	olive oil
¼ cup	soy sauce
1	orange, cut in half
1	lemon, cut in half
1	lime, cut in half
2	bay leaves
12	black peppercorns, toasted and crushed
½	bulb fennel, thinly sliced
½	red onion, thinly sliced
6	cloves garlic, thinly sliced
1 (1-inch)	length of ginger, peeled and thinly sliced
4	boneless mahimahi fillets, about 8 ounces each

Pour olive oil and soy into large mixing bowl. Squeeze in the juice of the orange, lemon, and lime, and toss in the squeezed rinds. Add the remaining ingredients and mix well. Prepare the grill. About 20 minutes away from dinnertime, put fish in the marinade and let sit for 10 minutes, turning once or twice. Remove the fish and grill for 4 minutes on the first side and 2 minutes on the other side.

Serves 4.

Lizzie's Cook's Notes

You don't have to go out to dinner in order to have delicious mahimahi. You can prepare this at home for a truly delicious fish dish. It doesn't take much time and it's well worth it.

Spanish Omelets

1 pound	russet potatoes, peeled
⅓ cup	olive oil
1 medium	yellow onion, thinly sliced
1½ teaspoons	salt
¼ teaspoon	black pepper
6	eggs
1 tablespoon	finely chopped fresh rosemary (optional)

Heat oven to 350 degrees. Halve the potatoes lengthwise and cut each half into ¼-inch-thick slices. Heat the oil in (oven proof) skillet over medium heat. Add the potatoes and cook until almost tender, about 10 minutes. Add the onion and cook about 5 minutes until softened. Pour off all but 1 tablespoon of the oil then season with 1 teaspoon of the salt and the pepper. In a medium bowl, combine the eggs, rosemary, and remaining salt. Pour the eggs over the potatoes and reduce heat to low. Cook, without stirring, for 1 minute. Stir once and cook until the eggs begin to set (about 3 minutes). Transfer to oven and bake until set (about 8 minutes). Loosen the omelet from the side of the skillet with a knife then slide or invert it onto a plate. Slice into wedges. Serve hot or at room temperature.

Yield: 4 servings.

Lisa Leann's Cook's Notes

This is a great dish to make for your family on a lazy Saturday morning. I love to make it when my family gathers at the house in Summit View. It's always a big hit.

Apple Cider Doughnuts

Special equipment: mini Bundt pan(s). Use one repeatedly or use several at a time.

3 tablespoons	granulated sugar
2 cups	all-purpose flour
1½ teaspoons	baking powder
1½ teaspoons	baking soda
½ teaspoon	salt
2 teaspoons	ground cinnamon
1 large	egg, lightly beaten
⅔ cup	packed brown sugar
½ cup	apple butter
⅓ cup	pure maple syrup
⅓ cup	apple cider
⅓ cup	nonfat plain yogurt
3 tablespoons	canola oil

Maple Glaze

1¼ cups	confectioners' sugar, sifted
1 teaspoon	vanilla extract
¼–⅓ cup	pure maple syrup

Preheat oven to 400 degrees. Spray mini Bundt pans with cooking spray, then sprinkle the inside of the pan with granulated sugar, then shake out the excess. Mix flour, baking powder, baking soda, salt, and cinnamon in a mixing bowl; set aside. Whisk together egg, brown sugar, apple butter, maple syrup, cider, yogurt, and oil in another bowl. Add dry ingredients and stir until just moist. Spoon 2 tablespoonfuls of batter into each Bundt pan. Bake until springy, about 10 to 12 minutes. Loosen edges and turn the cakes out onto a rack to cool. Clean the mini Bundt pan, then recoat it with cooking spray and sugar. Repeat with the remaining batter.

Maple Glaze

Combine confectioners' sugar and vanilla in a bowl. Gradually whisk in enough maple syrup to make a coating consistency. Dip the "top" of the doughnuts in the glaze to coat. Then set them glazed-side up on a rack over wax paper until the glaze has set. Serve warm with (optional) scoop of vanilla ice cream.

Donna's Cook's Notes

I researched this recipe after trying it in New York, and if I get ambitious, I might even make it myself. In the meantime, I'm going to slip it to Lisa Leann to see if she'd be willing to make it for one of our own Potluck prayer times.

Wild Cajun Spicy Chicken Sausage Gumbo

⅓ cup	flour
⅓ cup	cooking oil
1 large	onion, chopped
½ cup	green pepper, chopped
2	garlic cloves, finely chopped
½ teaspoon	pepper
¼ teaspoon	red pepper
4 cups	hot water (or Swanson's chicken broth)
1 pound	chicken thighs, skinned and boned (cut in bite–size pieces)
1 pound	boned and skinned chicken breasts (cut in bite–size pieces)
1 box	frozen okra (some people don't use okra)
1 can	tomatoes (chopped) (some people don't put in tomatoes)
12 ounces	smoked sausage (½–inch slices)
	hot cooked rice

In Dutch oven (4-inch) stir flour and oil until smooth. Cook over medium-high heat 5 minutes; stirring often. Reduce heat to medium; cook and stir the roux about 15 minutes or until a reddish dark brown roux is formed. Stir in the onion, green pepper, garlic, black pepper, and red pepper. Cook and stir over medium heat 3 to 5 minutes until vegetables are tender. Gradually stir the hot water (or chicken broth) into vegetable mixture. Stir in chicken. (If used, add okra and tomatoes.) Bring mix to boil; reduce heat, cover, and simmer 40 minutes. Stir in sausage, cover, and simmer about 20 minutes more until chicken is tender. Remove from heat; skim off fat. Spoon over rice, garnish with okra.

Vonnie's Cook's Notes

It's no surprise to me why the Wild Cajun Cooks did so well in The Great Party Showdown. Those boys can cook. I'm glad I was able to snag this recipe before they headed back to Baton Rouge.

Banana Pineapple Delight

2 cups	crushed graham crackers
½ cup	margarine, melted
½ cup	margarine
2 cups	confectioners' sugar
2	eggs
4 tablespoons	cornstarch
1 tablespoon	vanilla extract
3	bananas
¼ cup	lemon juice
1 (20 ounce) can	crushed pineapple in heavy syrup, drained
1 (8 ounce) container	frozen whipped topping, thawed

Combine graham cracker crumbs and melted margarine and pat into bottom of a 9-by-13 pan. In a medium, nonstick saucepan over medium heat, combine remaining margarine, confectioners' sugar, eggs, cornstarch, and vanilla. Bring to a boil, stirring frequently. Continue stirring, reduce heat, and simmer 8 to 10 minutes. Let cool, then spread over crust. Peel and slice bananas, dipping each piece in lemon juice to prevent browning, and layer over custard mixture. Layer pineapple on top of bananas. Cover all with whipped topping. Keep refrigerated until serving.

Serves 24.

Goldie's Cook's Notes

I had never heard of this until our King Kong themed event. But I fell in love with it and have made it several times since.

_____

_____

_____

Banana Nut Cheesecake

1 cup	chocolate wafer crumbs
¼ cup	margarine, melted
16 ounces	cream cheese, softened
½ cup	sugar
½ cup	mashed ripe bananas
2 large	eggs
¼ cup	chopped walnuts
⅓ cup	milk chocolate chips
1 tablespoon	margarine
2 tablespoons	water

Preheat oven to 350 degrees. Combine crumbs and margarine; press onto the bottom of a 9-inch springform pan. Bake 10 minutes. Combine cream cheese, sugar, and banana, mixing at medium speed of electric mixer until well blended. Add eggs, one at a time, mixing well after each addition. Stir in walnuts, pour over crust. Bake for 40 minutes. Loosen cake from rim; cool before removing rim of pan. Melt chocolate pieces and margarine with water over low heat, stirring until smooth. Drizzle over cheesecake. Chill.

Lizzie's Cook's Notes

I've heard of banana nut bread, of course, and New York style cheesecake, but this recipe takes the best of both worlds and brings them together!

Virgin Banana Daiquiris

2 cups	ice
½	banana
6 ounces	lemonade
4 ounces	lime juice
	pineapple wedge

Fill a blender with two cups of ice, then add half a banana, lemonade, and lime juice. Replace the lid tightly and blend. Next, pour the concoction into a tall, 16-ounce glass and garnish with a pineapple wedge. If the concoction is too thick, add a splash of water when blending.

Serves 1.

Donna's Cook's Notes

All I need is a trip to the Bahamas to get the full flavor of this delicious drink.

Banana Split Cake

1 (16 ounce) package	vanilla wafers, crushed
1 cup	margarine, melted
1 (8 ounce) package	cream cheese
2 cups	confectioners' sugar
1 (20 ounce) can	crushed pineapple, drained
6	bananas
1 (12 ounce) container	frozen whipped topping, thawed
¼ cup	chopped walnuts
8	maraschino cherries
	chocolate syrup

Combine the crushed vanilla wafers and melted margarine, then pat mixture into bottom of a 9-by-13 pan. Beat the cream cheese and confectioners' sugar together until light and fluffy. Spread over the top of the vanilla wafer crust. Spoon crushed pineapple over the cream cheese layer. Then layer sliced bananas over the pineapple. Cover with the whipped topping and sprinkle top with chopped walnuts and maraschino cherries and drizzle with chocolate syrup.

Lisa Leann's Cook's Notes

This is not the most beautiful dessert in the world, but it sure tastes good. And you gotta love it because it's really pretty easy to make.

Grilled Ham Panini Sandwich

2 slices	sourdough bread (multigrain bread works nicely too)
1 tablespoon	mayonnaise
4 slices	shaved smoked ham or brown sugar ham
2 slices	tomato
1 slice	cheese

Spread bread slices with mayo. Top 1 of the bread slices with ham, tomatoes, cheese, and remaining bread slice. Cook, over medium heat, in skillet or on griddle that has been sprayed with nonstick cooking spray, for 5 minutes on each side or until lightly browned.

Lizzie's Cook's Notes

Okay, so this is an easy one. And you'd be surprised what a restaurant will charge you for such a simple idea. But it's great for a quick lunch designed to make you feel special or if you are having a girlfriend over. Serve with fresh fruit on the side.

Chilled Tomato, Roasted Garlic, and Basil Soup

4	garlic cloves, unpeeled
2¾ pounds	vine-ripened tomatoes, quartered
1½ teaspoons	balsamic vinegar
	Tabasco, to taste
	salt and pepper, to taste
⅓ cup	fresh basil leaves, washed well, dried, and chopped

In a small heavy skillet, dry roast garlic over moderately low heat, turning occasionally, until skin is browned and garlic is tender (about twenty minutes), and then peel. In a blender, puree garlic and tomatoes in batches and force through a fine sieve into a bowl. Stir in vinegar, Tabasco, and salt to taste. Chill soup, covered, until cold (about six hours and up to one day). Before serving, stir in basil and season with salt and pepper if necessary.

Serves 4 as a first course.

Evageline's Cook's Notes

I had not heard of this until our last event in New York, but I quickly grew to love it. I've made it for Vernon a few times since then.

Fancy Strawberry Salad

3 cups	of salad greens
¼ cup	pecans, chopped
2 tablespoons	canola oil
1½ tablespoons	raspberry vinegar
1 tablespoon	sugar
½ teaspoon	cinnamon
¼ teaspoon	ground cumin
⅛ teaspoon	salt
¼ teaspoon	black pepper
½ cup	sliced strawberries
1½ ounces	goat cheese (chèvre), crumbled

Place salad greens in a large serving bowl. Next, heat pecans in small nonstick skillet on medium-high heat and stir 2 minutes or until lightly browned. Set aside to cool. In separate bowl, whisk oil, vinegar, sugar, cinnamon, cumin, salt, and pepper and pour over salad, tossing gently to coat. Add strawberries and pecans; toss again. Top with goat cheese.

Yield: 4 (1½ cup) servings.

Vonnie's Cook's Notes

I love fresh, healthy dishes that actually taste delicious. This strawberry salad is exactly that and more.

Peppermint Patty Brownies

1½ cups	butter or margarine
3 cups	sugar
1 teaspoon	vanilla
5	eggs
2 cups	all–purpose flour
1 cup	unsweetened cocoa
1 teaspoon	baking powder
1 teaspoon	salt
24	small York Peppermint Patties

First, mix butter, sugar, and vanilla. Then beat in eggs till well blended. Stir in flour, cocoa, baking powder, and salt. Blend well. Set 2 cups of batter aside. Grease 9-by-13 pan before spreading remaining batter into the pan. Arrange peppermint patties in a single layer over batter ½-inch apart. Spread reserved 2 cups batter over patties. Bake at 350 degrees for 50–55 minutes till brownies begin to pull away from sides of pan. Cool completely in pan on wire rack.

Yield: 2 dozen.

Donna's Cook's Notes

Yum! I used a brownie mix to make this, and it came out great.

_____

_____

_____

_____

_____

_____

_____

Apple Cranberry Muffins

2 cups	all-purpose flour
¾ cup	sugar
2½ teaspoons	baking powder
1 teaspoon	ground cinnamon
½ teaspoon	salt
½ teaspoon	ground nutmeg
¼ teaspoon	baking soda
⅛ teaspoon	ground allspice
⅛ teaspoon	ground cloves
2	eggs
1½ cups	(12 ounces) sour cream
¼ cup	butter, melted
1 teaspoon	vanilla extract
1 cup	chopped apple
1 cup	dried cranberries

Topping

¼ cup	packed brown sugar
3 tablespoons	all-purpose flour
2 tablespoons	cold butter

In a large bowl, combine the first nine ingredients. In second bowl, whisk the eggs, sour cream, butter, and vanilla. Stir into dry ingredients just until moistened. Fold in apple and cranberries. Spray muffin tin with cooking spray then fill each cup two-thirds full with batter.

Topping Directions

Combine brown sugar and flour. Cut in butter until mixture resembles coarse crumbs. Sprinkle over batter. Bake at 375 degrees for 20–25 minutes or until a toothpick comes out clean. Cool for 5 minutes before removing from pans to wire racks.

Yield: 18.

Lisa Leann's Cook's Notes

This is one of those fussy recipes that's worth all the work.

_____

_____

_____

_____

_____

_____

_____

_____

_____

_____

_____

_____

_____

_____

_____

_____

Fried Okra

2 pounds	okra pods
1 teaspoon	salt in pan of water
2	eggs, slightly beaten
2 tablespoons	milk
½ teaspoon	salt
½ cup	cornmeal
½ cup	vegetable oil

Wash okra and cut off stem ends. Slice into ½- to 1-inch lengths. In a medium saucepan bring salted water to a boil. Add okra and cook about 8 to 10 minutes until almost tender. Drain. In separate bowl, whisk together eggs, milk, and salt. Put cornmeal in a shallow dish. Dip okra pods into the cornmeal, and then into beaten egg mixture, then back into the cornmeal again. Fry okra in hot vegetable oil in skillet until browned on all sides.

Serves 6.

Donna's Cook's Notes

The only place I'd ever had fried okra was a cafeteria in Denver, but Vonnie made this for me one night after we got home from New York. Delicious!

Metric Conversion Guide

VOLUME

U.S. Units	Metric
teaspoon ½	ml 2
teaspoon 1	ml 5
tablespoon 1	ml 20
cup ¼	ml 60
cup ⅓	ml 80
cup ½	ml 125
cup ⅔	ml 170
cup ¾	ml 190
cup 1	ml 250
quart 1	liter 1

LENGTH

Inches	Centimeters
1	2.5
2	5.0
3	7.5
4	10.0
5	12.5
6	15.0
7	17.5
8	20.5
9	23.0
10	25.5
11	28.0
12	30.5
13	33.0
14	35.5
15	38.0

TEMPERATURE

Fahrenheit	Celsius
250°	120°
275°	140°
300°	150°
325°	160°
350°	180°
375°	190°
400°	200°
425°	220°
450°	230°
475°	240°
500°	260°

WEIGHT

U.S. Units	Metric
1 ounce	30 grams
2 ounces	60 grams
3 ounces	90 grams
4 ounces (¼ pound)	125 grams
8 ounces (½ pound)	225 grams
16 ounces (1 pound)	500 grams

Note: The recipes in this cookbook have not been developed or tested using metric measures. When converting recipes to metric, some variations in quality may be noted.

For more information about the Potluck Club,
go to www.PotluckClub.com

Meet the Women of the Potluck Catering Club

Evie Vesey—The new wife of Sheriff Vernon Vesey and founder of the Potluck Club. Will Evie win back the right to rule the club?

Lisa Leann Lambert—Owner of the town's new wedding boutique, High Country Weddings, and president of the Potluck Catering business. Will *The Great Party Showdown* eliminate her ability to pull her marriage off the rocks?

Goldie Dippel—Legal secretary married to Coach Dippel, a man with a roving eye. Will Goldie continue to try to save what's left of her marriage or will fate have the last say?

Donna Vesey—Deputy sheriff who fights for justice and seeks out the truth, as she tries to unlock her conflicted heart.

Lizzie Prattle—Sober high school librarian who's on the lookout for her team.

Vonnie Westbrook—Retired nurse who embraced her secret past when her birth son knocked on her door.

Linda Evans Shepherd has been married thirty years to Paul and has two young adult children. Linda also serves as the CEO of Right to the Heart Ministries and is an international speaker and media personality. Currently, she's a popular guest host appearing on *Denver Celebration* (Daystar Television); channel host for *Web TV 4 Women*; host of *Web TV 4 Women's* programs, *Be a Miracle*, and *Cooking Up Wonders*; co-host of *Miracle Quest*, a popular internet radio program; publisher of *Right to the Heart of Women* electronic magazine; founder and CEO of AWSA (Advanced Writers and Speakers Association); and host of the webinar platform *Miracle Lane*, where she conducts live online classes.

Linda is also a bestselling author and has written 30 books, including co-authoring the The Potuck Club and The Potluck Catering Club series. Linda's nonfiction book *Share Jesus Without Fear*, co-written with Bill Fay, will soon be in over 100 languages. Look for Linda's book *When You Don't Know What to Pray* from Revell in the spring of 2010.

To find out the latest on Linda or to book Linda to speak at your event, go to www.VisitLinda.com.

Award-winning author and speaker **Eva Marie Everson** is a Southern gal who's not that crazy about being in the kitchen, unless it's to eat! She has been married to a wonderful man, Dennis, for three decades and is a mother and grandmother to the most amazing children in the world.

Eva's writing career and ministry began in 1999 when a friend asked her what she'd want to do for the Lord, if she could do anything at all. "Write and speak," she said. And so it began.

Since that time, she has written, co-written, contributed to, and edited and compiled a number of works, including the award-winning *Reflections of God's Holy Land; a Personal Journey Through Israel* (which includes her photography among the spectacular photographic works), The Potluck Club/Potluck Catering Club series (with Linda Evans Shepherd), *Sex, Lies, and the Media*, and *Sex, Lies, and High School* (co-written with her amazing daughter Jessica). Eva Marie has a new series of Southern fiction novels, the first being *Things Left Unspoken*, with *This Fine Life* releasing in 2010.

Eva Marie is both a graduate of Andersonville Theological Seminary and a mentor with the Jerry B. Jenkins Christian Writers Guild. Eva Marie speaks nationally and internationally about her passion: drawing believers to the heartbeat of God. In 2002 she was named AWSA's first Member of the Year. Also that year she was one of six journalists chosen to visit Israel for a special ten-day press tour. She was forever changed.